DEATH AT THE MANOR

ALSO AVAILABLE BY KATHARINE SCHELLMAN

LILY ADLER MYSTERIES

The Body in the Garden

Silence in the Library

Last Call at the Nightingale

DEATH AT THE MANOR

A LILY ADLER MYSTERY

Katharine Schellman

CROOKED
LANE

NEW YORK

Copyright © 2022 by Katharine Schellman Paljug

Published in the United States by Crooked Lane Books, an imprint of The Quick Brown Fox & Company LLC.

Crooked Lane Books and its logo are trademarks of The Quick Brown Fox & Company LLC.

Library of Congress Catalog-in-Publication data available upon request.

ISBN (hardcover): 978-1-63910-078-1
ISBN (ebook): 978-1-63910-079-8

Cover design by Nicole Lecht

Printed in the United States.

www.crookedlanebooks.com

Crooked Lane Books
34 West 27th St., 10th Floor
New York, NY 10001

First Edition: August 2022

10 9 8 7 6 5 4 3 2 1

*For Reagan, because it takes a village, and she created a wonderful one.
And for Brian, because we're in this together.*

CHAPTER 1

"Admit it, Captain, you are delighted to be heading to sea once more." Lily Adler gave a pointed look to the man seated across the table from her, the light that straggled through the inn's dirty window catching on the gold buttons of his coat. "You'll not spend a moment thinking of us once you are aboard ship."

The inn was respectable, and the meal served in the private dining room had been surprisingly good fare. But everything this close to the docks in Portsmouth seemed to be dingy, and the autumn light that clung to the afternoon was cold and meager. Lily had arrived that morning in the carriage of Sir Edward and Lady Carroway, who had offered to accompany her to bid Captain Jack Hartley farewell. Lily had been glad they would only be there for a few hours when she had first looked around the port city. But now that it was nearly time for their departure, she wished she could start the day over again. She was not ready to say goodbye to her friend, for who knew how long.

But she hid her sadness behind a light and teasing tone, not wanting to put a damper on the day. Jack had been so eager to get back to sea, she didn't want him to know how much she would miss him when he was gone.

Now, he ran a hand through his black hair, shaking his head and smiling. "I've been on land so long this year, I do not know what I will feel. I had begun to think the ship's repairs would never be done."

"Be honest, Captain Hartley." The young woman seated at one end of the table leaned forward. "Do you think you have lost your sea legs after all this time? Shall you become seasick and shame yourself in front of your crew?"

Jack laughed. "If I do, Lady Carroway, I shall confess it only to you, and I will expect you to keep such an admission in the strictest confidence."

"Oh, I could never do that!" she protested, laughing with him. "I would have to tell Neddy." She smiled at her husband as she stood and reached across the small table to steal the mug of ale from in front of him, quaffing it with a cheerful enjoyment that stood in sharp contrast to her expensive, modish gown and otherwise elegant manner.

"Ofelia," her husband said mildly, not really objecting. She giggled at him and took another drink before sliding it back across the table. He caught it just before it slid right off the edge.

"But not Mrs. Adler?" Jack asked, looking from Ofelia to Lily and raising an eyebrow.

"I would not need to. Mrs. Adler would know the moment she next saw you," Ofelia said impishly.

Lily smiled. "No one can hide a guilty conscience from me, sir."

"As several unfortunate souls have found out," Ned Carroway added, raising his mug in a toast. "The murderers of London quail before you."

"Hardly," Lily protested, feeling her cheeks heat as the other two raised their drinks toward her as well—Ofelia this time lifting one of the glasses of wine that the innkeeper had brought for the ladies.

Her friends were not wrong. After stumbling across a dead body the very first night she'd returned to London, Lily had found herself swept into a frightening puzzle that had only been solved when she unmasked the killer behind what had become known as the Harper murders. And then, when the furor from that had finally died down, the death of one of her father's oldest friends had caught her up in another scandal and intrigue, that one a tangled mess of love and desperation.

Ofelia and Ned had been there for both. And so had Jack. Lily met his eyes as he drank the toast, grinning at her. Jack had been her companion and co-conspirator for months, helping her find her feet in the world after the death of her husband—his friend—and keeping her safe when she insisted on putting herself in danger. She didn't know what she was going to do without him.

Glancing at his pocket watch, Ned Carroway groaned and hauled himself to his feet. "I must see about having horses put to our carriage," he said. "We shall need to leave within the half hour if we're to arrive at your aunt's home before dark."

"I shall come with you," Ofelia said, jumping up. "Mrs. Adler, Captain, we will see you outside?" Her gaze lingered pointedly on Jack for a moment before she took her husband's arm and allowed him to escort her from the room.

"What did that mean?" Lily asked.

"What?" Jack, who had been eyeing the Carroways' departure with his mouth twisted into a wry smile, turned back toward her, his brows rising.

"That odd look she gave you." Lily frowned. There was nothing really wrong in their being left alone together—only the strictest of moralists would raise an eyebrow at it, as Lily was nearly three years widowed and Jack had been the childhood friend of her late husband. But there had been something almost guilty in the way Ofelia had looked at him.

"If you don't know, then I am sure I do not," Jack said, his voice unconcerned as he turned his mug of ale in fidgety circles.

It was almost as if he didn't want to meet her eyes, Lily thought, and she was debating whether to press the matter, when he looked up and grinned at her.

"Shall you get into trouble with me away? It does seem to follow you."

Lily laughed. "I doubt it. I cannot imagine anything odd happening at the home of my aunt and Miss Clarke, and I have been visiting them for enough years by this point."

"Against the will of your father?" Jack suggested.

Lily shrugged. "Most things I do are against the will of my father, as he made so clear when he was last in London. That has not stopped me before, and it will not stop me now." She smiled, leaning her elbows on the table and resting her chin on her clasped hands. "I wish you could come with me. You would like my aunt very much."

"I remember her from your wedding," Jack said, clearing his throat and leaning back abruptly in his chair. "Miss Pierce seemed like exactly the sort of woman you shall grow up to be."

"Why, am I not grown now?" Lily teased as she stood up. Jack, always a model of politeness, did the same. "Will you write me?"

"Of course. I shall tell you how revered I am aboard ship and how no one ever dares tell me I am wrong about anything. Perhaps it will influence you and Lady Carroway to treat me with more respect when I return."

Lily smiled, holding out her hands to him. It was easier to be honest, now they were in private. "I shall miss your teasing, Jack, but I am glad you will be back with your ship. I know how you have missed it."

"And I shall miss you, of course. Though being back at sea may seem dull in comparison to being in London when Mrs. Adler is in town." His own hands were large and warm as they closed around hers, his expression growing more serious as he met her eyes. "Is that all you will miss while we are both away?"

"I dread to think what that might mean." Lily swatted him on the shoulder, pretending to be offended. "If you mean to imply that I have been seeking out trouble in London—"

For a moment Jack's serious expression lingered, but before she had a chance to wonder at it, his teasing grin returned once more. He captured her hand and looped it through his arm, leading her from the dining room. "I think you would have been very bored in London if trouble had not managed to find you. I hope you will be able to bear the monotony in Hampshire."

There were two vehicles waiting in front of the inn for them: the Carroways' elegant traveling chaise as well as a smaller coach for their personal servants and the luggage. Lily's maid, Anna, was just climbing into the second coach when they stepped outside, Lily tugging her hat forward so she wouldn't have to squint against the bright cloudiness of the sky.

"I am looking forward to some monotony," Lily admitted as they entered the coaching yard. "Two whole months of it, in fact, if you include my visit to Surrey. Monotony sounds lovely."

Jack shook his head, smiling as he held out a hand to help her into the chaise. "I shall believe that when I see it."

★　★　★

The rolling hills and water meadows of Hampshire were beautiful in spite of the dreary autumn day, but after more than two hours in the carriage, even Ofelia's cheerful appreciation was wearing thin. From exclaiming over the picturesque scenery, she turned to quizzing Lily about her aunt and aunt's companion, whom she and Ned would meet for the first time during their short visit before they left for their own property.

"And how long have Miss Pierce and Miss Clarke lived at the cottage?" Ofelia asked, her eyes bright with curiosity.

"It was the year after my grandmother's death, so that would be . . ." Lily frowned in thought, swaying back and forth with the motion of the carriage. "Twelve years ago, I think? My aunt and Miss Clarke were at school together as girls. When neither of them had married after a few years, they began to talk of setting up their own household together, rather than remaining with their families in their spinsterhood." Lily's eyebrows rose. "You can imagine my aunt did not relish the thought of remaining my father's dependent after the death of my grandfather."

"And Miss Clarke?"

"She was one of seven children in her home, and the younger boys had already been packed off to various occupations to make their own way in the world. I think perhaps one of her brothers became a banker and another a curate? In any case, she had a small sum settled on her, either to serve as her dowry or for her maintenance should she remain unwed. But it was not until my aunt Eliza inherited Longwood Cottage from her own great-aunt that they were able to combine their resources and set up their household."

Lily smiled, her gaze wandering back to the window as she contemplated the independent existence that her aunt and Susan Clarke had created for themselves. Their housekeeping was modest by worldly standards, though sufficient for them to keep a manservant and a one-horse gig for excursions around the parish. And they were happy—something she might not have aspired to herself, growing up under her father's critical, cheerless care had she not had their example to strive for.

"And are you your aunt's heir, or is Miss Clarke?" Ofelia asked with cheerful bluntness. Raised as the only child of a practical, wealthy, doting father in the West Indies, she had been nearly a partner to him in his export business since she was a child. As a result, she had a better head for business and finance than nearly anyone Lily had met, as well as a sunny disregard for the polite bounds of such conversations, at least among her intimates.

Lily laughed. "Both. The cottage comes to me, with the provision in her will that Miss Clarke is to be allowed to reside there as long as she wishes. But her income passes to Miss Clarke before coming to me—I believe they have both arranged things similarly so that the other might continue to live independently."

"An equitable arrangement," Ofelia said, satisfied, as she dropped back against the seat cushions and covered a yawn. "I am eager to meet them. Is your aunt much like you?"

"A great deal in looks," said Lily, growing a little thoughtful as she added wryly, "but I think she has an easier manner. You will like her very much. And I have been writing to her of you all year, so she and Miss Clarke are both glad of the chance to meet you. And you, of course, Sir Edward," she added, nodding to the young baronet, who had been reading contentedly while the two friends talked.

At the sound of his name, he glanced up, the sly smile on his face making Lily think that he had not been quite as absorbed in his book as he seemed. "Looking forward to meeting your aunt, of course, Mrs. Adler. But I've not heard you mention the other charm Hampshire has this year."

Lily, caught off guard by this sudden attack, felt herself growing hot with embarrassment and hoped that the sensation wouldn't translate to a blush. "I . . . what could you mean?"

Ned Carroway's smile grew to a grin, which lit up his still boyish face. "Oh come now, ma'am. Surely you aren't going to pretend to be unaware that Mr. Matthew Spencer lives not far from your aunt? He must have mentioned it, as much time as the two of you have spent in each other's company these past months."

Lily bit the inside of her cheek, pretending to be unflustered by his teasing. "He lives nearly three miles on the *other* side of the village from Longwood Cottage," she said firmly. "That is hardly in the same neighborhood."

"So you do not expect to see him?" Ofelia asked. There was no telling from her expression what she thought of the matter one way or another.

Lily glanced down at her hands, unable to keep a small smile from rising to her lips. "I expect he will be much occupied with his children, now he has returned home," she said quietly. "But yes, I am hopeful of seeing him. He said he did not think the distance so great an obstacle."

"For a fellow who loves to ride as he does?" Ned grinned. "Should expect him to think nothing of the distance. Not even an hour on a good horse." He turned to his wife, nudging her shoulder with his own. "Splendid idea, isn't it, my love, that Mr. Spencer should visit Longwood Cottage while Mrs. Adler is there?"

Ofelia hesitated, regarding her friend more seriously than Lily had expected such a teasing question to occasion. "He seems a genuinely nice man, which is not something one can say of every person so handsome and charming," Ofelia said at last. "I shall be happy to see him again if Mrs. Adler is." Apparently deciding to change the subject, she asked, her voice light and easy once more, "Why is it that your father so disapproves of your aunt?"

Lily was grateful for the diversion; she enjoyed Matthew Spencer's company, and he seemed to enjoy hers. But she did not like knowing that her friends were so openly speculating about the two of them. It was hardly surprising—for a well-off widow and a handsome widower to be seen in each other's company was to invite gossip, even if their interaction had been purely friendly. But she did not know Matthew Spencer's thoughts on the matter, and she still could not bring herself to think of remarrying.

Lily held back a sigh. Visits to her aunt were supposed to be quiet and restful. But while she had no intention of seeking out trouble—not that she ever had in London either, no matter how Jack might tease—she had a feeling that this visit would be a little more fraught than usual, at least as long as the Carroways and their watchful eyes were there as well.

Lily was distracted from answering as the carriage rounded a bend, and a familiar, cheerful stone building came into view, perched on the top of a gently sloping hill. "There," she said, leaning forward, unable to keep the smile from her face. "That is Longwood Cottage at the top of the rise."

CHAPTER 2

"I hope your friends will not feel too cramped in the second spare room."

Lily smiled at Susan Clarke's anxious hovering. "Not at all. It really is so kind of you to invite them to stay for a few days."

Eliza, standing with Susan just inside the doorway of Lily's room, made a dismissive noise. "It is no short distance to Somerset from here. We should have been embarrassed to send them on their way too quickly."

"Oh, of course," Susan agreed. But she frowned as she glanced around the room once more. "It is only that I don't expect our rooms are of the size and comfort to which they are accustomed."

Longwood Cottage was cheerful and pretty, well furnished, decorated with taste, and enhanced by beautiful views of the surrounding countryside. It was Lily's favorite place to visit in the world. But it was not large, with two adjoining bedrooms and a third separate room upstairs, a fourth bedroom on the first floor, and only one downstairs parlor.

After Lily's husband had died, she and her aunt had briefly discussed whether she ought to come live at the Cottage. But the smallness of the house had made all three women decide against the plan, worried that such close living, and during such a difficult time, would spoil the pleasure they normally felt in each other's company.

Even now, the smallness of the house was hard to ignore. Lily normally stayed in the larger upstairs spare room, but she was currently installed in the smaller downstairs one, to give Ofelia and Ned more space. Still, there was no reason the arrangement could not be comfortable for the three or four days that the Carroways planned to break their journey.

"Truly, you have nothing to worry about," Lily said, taking off her hat and handing it to her maid, Anna, who was busy unpacking a fresh gown and checking the temperature of the wash water that had been brought up. "Sir Edward and Lady Carroway are eager to be pleased, no matter where they find themselves. And especially here." Lily was rarely openly affectionate, but she crossed the room to wrap an arm each around Susan and her aunt. She smiled down into Susan's plump, pretty face, then had to look up to meet her aunt's eyes; Lily was tall, but Eliza was even taller, a beautiful, sturdy woman, rather than willowy or delicate. "They have heard me speak about you a good deal."

"And we were eager to meet them after all your letters this last half year," Eliza replied, giving Lily a quick peck on the cheek before stepping away. Susan, more naturally affectionate than anyone brought up in the Pierce family could be, kept her arm around Lily's waist and beamed while Eliza surveyed the room with a critical eye. "Do you have everything you need, dearest?"

"Is there anything else we need, Anna?" Lily asked.

"No, Mrs. Adler," Anna said, straightening from where she had just finished laying out Lily's things on the dressing table and bobbing a quick curtsey to the ladies of the house. "And the water is hot, if you are ready to wash."

"Then we shall leave you to freshen yourself from your journey," Eliza said, holding out her hand to her companion. Susan gave Lily one more quick squeeze before dropping her arm, then took Eliza's outstretched hand as she followed her out the door. "Will you join us in the parlor when you are ready?"

★   ★   ★

Ten minutes later, Lily's cheeks were red and warm from washing, and she was clad in a fresh gown that had most of the wrinkles pressed out of it. Wrapping a fringed shawl around her arms and shoulders—the days were growing shorter and the afternoons cooler, though the autumn sun still streamed through the windows—Lily gave her maid a stern look. "You're not to worry about unpacking everything right away, mind. Take some time to rest. No doubt John and Addie will be glad to hear the news from London, and the Carroways' servants will want to have you there to introduce them."

Most of Ofelia and Ned's servants had remained in London, and those who were needed at the house in Somerset had traveled directly there. But Ofelia's personal maid and Ned's valet had come to Hampshire to look after them while they traveled. The servants' rooms belowstairs, which normally only housed a maid and manservant, would be crowded with five occupants. Luckily Ned's coachman would not be there as well; the carriage and horses had to be stabled in the village, and he would stay there as well, to keep an eye on them and care for the animals, stopping by each morning to see if his services would be needed that day.

"Yes, ma'am." Anna smiled. "I'll be glad to see John and Addie both, and they always lay a good tea in the kitchen when we arrive. But I'll see that your bronze silk is ready for tonight before I take myself downstairs."

Lily paused in the doorway, surprised. "I doubt we will be so formal here, especially when we have only just arrived."

Anna shook her head, already kneeling by Lily's trunk to pull out the gown in question. "Miss Clarke mentioned to me when we first came in that you would be dining out tonight and that you would want to be smartly turned out for the invitation."

Lily frowned. But if Anna knew more, she would have shared already, so the best route to answers was to join the others.

She found them gathered in the parlor, which was situated to take advantage of the afternoon light. A cheerful fire crackled in the hearth, and Susan presided over the tea service that had been spread in the center of the room, pouring for everyone and serving up thick slices of cake. She and Ned were already chatting like old friends while Eliza stood to one side with Ofelia, gesturing to a watercolor painting that hung over one of the chairs. As Lily entered, Ofelia turned, her eyes lit with mischievous delight.

"Mrs. Adler! Your aunt tells me that this was one of yours from school. I had no idea you painted," she said. "What other talents have you been concealing from us?"

Lily grimaced in embarrassment at the painting, which was a faithfully executed and very dull landscape that she had made a decade before. "I doubt anyone could call that the result of any particular talent. I had much more skill at embroidery," she said, taking a seat by the window and accepting a cup of tea from Susan. "Though skill and taste are not the same thing. I must admit to being responsible for every embroidered pillow that decorates this house. I went through an unfortunate phase of showing off how elaborate my stitchery could be, so they are uniformly gaudy. But my aunt keeps them anyway for inexplicable reasons."

"They are very well done, even if none of them match," Eliza said. "And someone needed to be proud of your accomplishments, since my brother never would be."

"I like them," Susan added with a cozy smile, adding another slice of cake to Ned's plate while he beamed at her. "The colors are very cheerful in winter."

"I shall have to request some for our own house then," Ofelia said. "I adore gaudy things. They always inspire the most entertaining conversation."

"Wait until you actually see them," Lily cautioned as she took a sip of tea. "You might change your mind. Now, Aunt, what is this my maid tells me about us dining from home this evening?"

"Well, as to that"—Eliza set down her own cup, giving her niece a curious look—"we had a surprising visitor yesterday, a pleasant man who lives only about four miles away but whom we had not yet met. He begged our pardon for calling without a proper introduction but said he hoped his name might be known to us." Her expression grew a little sly. "Can you guess, dear niece, who it might have been?"

"That depends, Aunt," Lily said, ignoring the sharp looks suddenly fixed on her from the Carroways, "on whether his name was actually known to you or not."

Eliza laughed. "Ice blooded, as always, Lily. Shall I never be able to fluster you? His name was indeed known to us, as he had appeared in several of your own letters."

"And if you need further hint, I may add that he was absurdly handsome and accompanied by two very pretty-behaved children," Susan put in. "It was shocking."

That made Ofelia laugh. "Why shocking?" she asked. She abandoned her study of the watercolor and went to sit next to Lily, where her own refreshments were already waiting.

"Because parents who insist on bringing their children for afternoon calls usually have unpleasant children," Susan said as she handed Ned a second slice of cake, apparently well aware that young men needed a great deal of feeding. "For some reason, the ones with pleasant offspring always leave them at home. It is too bad, really. But these two were charming."

"Very well, then," Lily said, trying to keep her expression calm in the face of her aunt's scrutiny. "Mr. Spencer and his two charming children called yesterday."

Eliza smiled, looking far more pleased than Lily was comfortable with. "He did, and he invited us all to join him for dinner tonight, to welcome you to the neighborhood."

"Splendid idea!" Ned put in, glancing at Lily. His wide smile lit up his whole face, his beaming pleasure turning his cheeks nearly as red as his hair. "Happy to volunteer our carriage, if you will permit, Miss Pierce, to convey us all there."

"How kind of you, Sir Edward," Susan said, patting his hand in a motherly fashion. "It is exactly what we hoped for."

"Might be a little cozy with five," Ned admitted, frowning before his face lit up once more. "But what's that among friends? At what o'clock . . ."

Lily kept her eyes on her own teacup as they continued to chat, not wanting to meet her aunt's eyes. But a moment later, Ofelia's hand crept into her line of sight, laid gently over her own.

"Do you wish to see him, Mrs. Adler?" she asked in a low voice.

Lily glanced up, surprised at the tone in her friend's voice. It was not quite unhappy, nor concerned, but it was . . . hesitant. That was the best description Lily could put to it. And that same hesitancy was there in Ofelia's eyes as she waited for Lily's answer, the edge of her lip caught between her teeth.

"Of course," Lily said. "I told him I should look forward to meeting in Hampshire, and I do. Why?" she asked, suddenly confused. "Do you not wish to? Is there something—"

"No, no, of course not." Ofelia smiled. "Mr. Spencer is a dear man, and he has been a good friend to you. I merely wanted to be sure . . ." She shook her head. "It is nothing. Thank goodness my dresser insisted on packing at least one evening gown for me for this leg of the journey." She raised her voice, turning back to the group. "I am so sorry, I was not attending. At what time shall we need to depart?"

★　★　★

Ned's carriage was ready for them two hours later; it would take them just under an hour to arrive at Matthew Spencer's property, known locally as Morestead Park. Lily was worried she would have to undergo a barrage of personal questions on the way there, but to her relief, her companions were too tactful for that. After a short discussion of Mr. Spencer's visit, manners, looks, children, property, military service, and work with Parliament, Eliza and Susan were content to change the subject to gossip from London—and in particular, to hear the Carroways' perspective on the two murder investigations that they had been swept up in, along with Lily.

"And where is the dear boy now?" Susan asked after hearing how Ofelia and Ned had sheltered the sixteen-year-old son of a murder victim, a child whose unusual mind had not only caused his family to keep him secluded from the notice of the world for his whole life, but which had also left him unknowingly possessing the clue that would unmask his father's killer.

"In Devon, at the moment, I believe," Ofelia said. "I hear his guardian plans to buy property in Hampstead Heath, though. Close enough to London for the occasional carouse, but enough in the country for Arthur to have a little more freedom in his life."

"I still cannot believe it," Eliza said, shaking her head. "Lily, how is it you became mixed up in such morbid goings-on?"

"Bad timing?" Lily suggested.

"Or good timing." Ned laughed. "Considering the outcome, I mean. Still." He looked out the window as the carriage slowed to a stop in front of the torchlit facade of Morestead Park. "Nothing like a visit to the country for a little peace and quiet. Do you not agree, my love?"

Ofelia smiled fondly at him. "We can only hope, Neddy." She glanced out the window. "And there is the charming Mr. Spencer, ready to greet us all. Goodness, he is even more handsome than I remembered."

"I say," Ned protested mildly as Mr. Spencer stepped forward to swing open the carriage door and hand them out one by one.

He welcomed them as they descended, offering compliments to Miss Pierce and Miss Clarke and greeting the Carroways as old friends. Lily was the last one out of the carriage, and she could not help smiling as he turned to greet her. Matthew Spencer was tall and broad-shouldered, with skin tanned brown from his love of riding. His left arm was missing below the elbow, where a battlefield injury years before had required an amputation rather than risk an infection taking the entire arm or his life. And the smile that stretched across his almost too handsome face was a force of nature, even in the flickering torchlight.

"Mrs. Adler," he said, holding out his hand to her. "What a pleasure to see you again."

"And you, sir," she said. Since he had helped her investigation into the Wyatt murders, they had spent more than a little time together in London, and she had been surprised to discover how much she enjoyed his company—even though he was far fonder of riding than she could ever be.

But she was worried she would blush when he took a moment too long to release her hand, and she took a quick step back, looping her arm through Susan's. "How kind of you to invite us."

His eyes lingered on her for a moment, and she could not tell whether her retreat had surprised or dismayed him. Then his mouth lifted in a gentle smile, and he turned to offer his arm to Eliza—a charming gesture, if not an entirely proper one, since Ofelia was the highest-ranking lady present. Beside her, Lily heard Susan sigh softly, clearly impressed by his gallantry.

He favored the entire company with that smile. "Shall we go inside? There is someone waiting who is eager to meet our newcomers."

CHAPTER 3

The "someone" turned out to be his daughter, who had been promised dinner with the guests and was clearly over the moon to be classed with the adults for the evening. If Lily had been skeptical of a formal dinner after a day of so much travel, her doubts were instantly laid to rest by the girl's presence.

Eloisa was a sweet girl of only twelve years old, a little shy at first in company, but eager to tell of her studies, her playmates, and the horrors of having a ten-year-old younger brother, when drawn out by Susan and Eliza's friendly questions. The dinner itself was an informal affair during which they contentedly chatted across the table and Eloisa twice contradicted her father.

Lily was a few places removed from where Mr. Spencer sat; Ofelia was seated to his right and Eliza to his left. But that gave Lily an easy view of his face, and she could see the fond looks he turned toward his daughter, even when she told him that the cows had got into the horse pasture in June and not July, as well as the subtle, silent instructions he managed to convey without embarrassing her when she became too eager in her conversation or forgot some point of etiquette. For Lily, who had not spent much time with children since she herself had been one, and whose own father's manner had been far more domineering than encouraging, watching them interact was as heartwarming as the good food and friendly conversation.

She was also pleased to see that he was as attentive to her aunt and Susan as he was to his younger guests, drawing them into talk of local acquaintances they had in common until Susan wondered aloud that their paths had never yet crossed.

Mr. Spencer smiled sadly. "Alas, my business takes me so often from home that when I return, I spend almost all my time in my own house or on my own property."

"And with us, Papa," Eloisa put in.

"And with you and Matthew, pet," he agreed fondly. "You two keep me busy enough to consume all my hours."

"I seem to remember you saying that your children's aunt resided with them while you were away," Lily said, nodding an assent to the servant who had stepped forward to refill her wine-glass. "Does she depart when you return?"

"Not usually. My late wife's sister," he explained, turning to where Eliza and Susan were making no secret of their curiosity, "came to care for the children after their mother's death, as I was still in the army and stationed on the Continent at that time. She is quite part of the family now. But she has gone to visit her own mother this month, so I am afraid she will not have the pleasure of meeting your houseguests." He smiled at Lily across the table as he spoke. "Another time, perhaps."

Given the informality of the meal, Lily expected that the whole party would remove together to the drawing room. But she—and, judging by the indulgent smiles around the table, the others as well—was entertained when, at a nod from her father, Eloisa rose and asked, "Shall we go through to the drawing room and leave the gentlemen to their port?"

After a moment of being startled, the ladies all rose in agreement. Lily caught their host's eye as she rose, and he surprised her with a wink—so quick that there was no risk that Eloisa would see.

The girl led the ladies to the drawing room, where the housekeeper had just brought in the tea cart. Eloisa—with a frown of worried concentration on her face and an occasional helpful suggestion from the housekeeper—did the honors of pouring tea and coffee for her guests. Lily felt more than a little awkward accepting her cup from a child's hand, and Ofelia twice disappeared behind her handkerchief in an attempt to hide her smiles. But Susan and Eliza rose to the occasion beautifully, matching Eloisa's childish gravity with questions about the instruments and art in the room and eventually encouraging Ofelia to go to the pianoforte and play for the group. Lily watched them fondly, remembering how she had always felt like an adult in their company and enjoying the chance to see their encouragement and kindness directed at another motherless child.

But she also had very little idea what to say to a girl of twelve, so she eventually drifted across the room to stand by the pianoforte. "What is that song called?" she asked, watching her friend's fingers move nimbly across the keys. "I do not recognize it."

"It has no name because I never gave it one," Ofelia said, glancing up and smiling pertly. "I wrote it when I was Eloisa's age, and it is always the first thing my fingers remember when I sit down to play. My father used to call it the ghost song, however, because of this part."

The air slid into a minor key, its formerly cheerful sound mirrored in slow, haunting chords that grew quieter and lighter, higher and higher, before tumbling back down to the middle register and resolving once more into a bright, major sound.

"Ghost song, indeed," Lily laughed. "I did not know you wrote music."

"You are not the only one with hidden talents," Ofelia said as she flourished through the finale, smiling at the applause of her small audience.

"That is exactly what I think the ghost here must sound like," Eloisa said, sounding eager and nervous at the same time.

Lily turned to her, surprised. "You have a ghost in your house?"

"Not our house, no." Judging by her disappointed sigh, Eloisa would have enjoyed something as exciting as a ghost haunting her home. "And Papa says it probably isn't a real one, in any case. But Mr. Wright says—"

She was interrupted, however, by the arrival of the men, each still carrying a glass of port. Lily was glad they had not lingered; being hosted by a child was not a prospect that promised to bear up well over time. But though she was sorry not to hear what Eloisa might have said next, that did not stop her from enjoying the graceful view of Mr. Spencer surveying the room with pleasure before crossing to his daughter and motioning to the housekeeper as he bent down to whisper in Eloisa's ear.

She instantly rose. "Papa says it's my bedtime," she said, blushing a little.

"Well, we mustn't gainsay your papa," Susan said, smiling. "But we shall look forward to another visit soon, my dear."

"And we thank you for hosting us so beautifully this evening," Eliza put in, giving a pointed look at Lily and Ofelia, who quickly added their own thanks and praise.

Blushing a brighter pink with pleasure, Eloisa said her goodnights, kissing her father on the cheek before allowing the housekeeper to herd her from the room.

Matthew Spencer smiled at his guests after she was gone, and he took a seat near Susan. "I thank each of you for your indulgence. We do not often have dinner parties, and she was so excited to play hostess."

"She was delightful," Ofelia protested, leaving the pianoforte to join her husband and retrieve her tea. "And you ought not to have sent her away so quickly—she was just about to tell us something fascinating."

Mr. Spencer raised his brows with good humor. "I dread to think what secrets she was about to reveal."

"Not yours, fortunately," Lily said, trying not to wonder if Mr. Spencer had chosen his spot to be near the fire or because it placed him directly across the room from her. "She was about to tell us something of a ghost."

"She has been listening to gossip about the Wrights, I believe," Eliza put in, rising to refill her coffee cup and fetching a fresh cup of tea for Susan at the same time. "Though perhaps you know more about it than we do. All we have heard is that one of the servants claims to have seen a ghost in their house."

"Apparently it is more than that," Mr. Spencer said, leaning back and crossing one ankle over his knee. "It seems the whole family has seen whatever the apparition is, at one point or another. Apparently, it wanders the halls of Belleford at night. Half their servants have quit in fear, but it doesn't seem to have intimidated the Wrights. I even hear that Thomas Wright—the son of the house," he added, with a nod at his guests who were not local, "has talked of giving tours as they do at the great houses."

Lily frowned. "But surely no one believes such nonsense," she said, holding her teacup out for Eliza to refill. "Do they?"

"Enough do—or at least are intrigued enough by the story to want to learn more." Mr. Spencer shrugged, setting his glass of port down on a side table as he leaned forward. "I am unsurprised to find you a skeptic, Mrs. Adler."

She met his eyes, her own expression teasing. "And you, sir? What are your thoughts on ghosts?"

He smiled as he admitted, "Skeptical, but undecided. There are certainly enough things in the world that appear inexplicable to make me open to the possibility in my mind." His brows rose a little. "I hope that does not lower me in your estimation."

"Are there not many stories of ghosts in the West Indies, Lady Carroway?" Susan asked, looking eager as she turned toward Ofelia. "Surely you are intrigued by our local haunting?"

Ofelia looked a little irritated. "Many, indeed, but I think no more than in England. And perhaps fewer than in Scotland, from what I have been told. While I may have had a West Indian mother, my father was a pragmatic British businessman. As he was the one who raised me, I have to agree with Mrs. Adler in this instance—I will remain highly doubtful of any ghost unless offered firm proof."

Susan looked embarrassed, and Eliza reached out to pat her friend's hand. "Do not hold Miss Clarke's question against her, Lady Carroway. She was hoping for company. Susan is convinced this spirit is real, and she finds my own skepticism very disappointing."

That made Ofelia smile. "In that case, you shall find a sympathetic ear in my husband. Neddy is sure to be convinced by any tales of local haunting, are you not, my love?"

Ned Carroway scowled as everyone turned toward him. "Nothing amusing about ghosts. My father's uncle died two days after seeing one when I was a boy. You'll not convince me to laugh at these Wrights and their apparition."

"Especially not when so many people have seen it," Susan put in earnestly. "If half their staff has departed because of the ghost, does that not provide some proof of its existence?"

"It provides proof that they believe in its existence," Eliza said. "Which is not quite the same thing, my dear."

"Well, one girl apparently believed in its existence so much that she became injured when fleeing from it," Mr. Spencer put in. "One of their maids, it seems, not only saw the ghost, but it actually chased her down the hall. I hear she fell down the stairs and broke her arm. After that, the servants started leaving."

In the silence that followed his statement, a log popped suddenly in the fireplace. All of them jumped at the sharp sound. Once they realized what it was, Ofelia and Eliza looked entertained that they had been so startled, though Ned and Susan still looked worried. Mr. Spencer smiled, clearly enjoying the company, as he rose to tend to the fire himself rather than calling a servant.

"Is the ghost always seen only at night?" Lily asked curiously, sitting forward.

Mr. Spencer turned toward her, the poker still in his hand. The firelight cast a warm glow over his features, the dim light making his deep blue eyes look mysteriously black. "I have heard it has recently been seen twice during the daytime. Though as both times were in the early morning, perhaps it simply had not returned to its bed after a night of haunting." When Lily and the others laughed, his smile grew. "Are you hoping to solve the mystery, Mrs. Adler?"

Lily rolled her eyes. "Indeed not. Merely curious as to what sort of ghost makes its home in a small village in Hampshire."

"They can make their homes anywhere," Ned said seriously, his hands tapping on his knees. "Anywhere there is death. Which is everywhere."

"Goodness," said Susan faintly, fanning herself. Ned, apparently embarrassed by his earnestness, blushed nearly as red as his hair.

"Oh, but what a splendid idea!" Ofelia exclaimed. "Of course we should attempt to prove whether the spirit is real or not. And Mrs. Adler, you are just the person to do so. What good entertainment that would be while we are here."

Ned looked horrified. "Get mixed up with a haunting? No, thank you, I'll not go anywhere near it."

"Oh, don't be so silly, Neddy," Ofelia teased. "Mrs. Adler, you are not scared to see what you can discover, are you?"

Lily shook her head at her friend's eagerness. "I rather doubt the Wrights would like us poking about their home."

"Well, if that is your only concern, I can set your mind at ease," Mr. Spencer said, settling into his chair once more. "Mr. Wright, I understand, loves any interest in their ghost. He seems to take it as interest and attention to them, and Mrs. Wright and her son dearly love to be the center of attention."

"There, you see? Why not pay a visit and see what we can discover?" Ofelia said, her voice dropping into a cajoling tone. "If nothing else, hearing the story from the family themselves would be amusing, would it not?" She turned to Eliza. "And did you not say, Miss Pierce, that you and Miss Clarke had yet to do so? Surely you should be kept abreast of such important local news."

"Local gossip, you mean," Eliza said, laying aside her coffee cup and looking thoughtful at the idea. "Though I suppose in a village like this, they are often the same thing. But I am afraid Miss Clarke and I do not know them well enough to pay such a visit with guests."

"If you wish, I would be happy to be of service in that regard." Mr. Spencer's chuckle was as rich as his voice, and he seemed more than happy to enter into Ofelia's spirit of playfulness. He slanted a teasing look in Lily's direction. "I confess myself eager to see what Mrs. Adler would do with such a mystery, as I have not had the opportunity to see her solve one yet."

Lily shook her head. "I have yet to tackle the mysteries of the supernatural and offer no promises to do so in this instance. But as long as no one is expecting me to actually make any pronouncements or discoveries, I am happy in the scheme." She turned to Susan. "If you would not find it too distressing, of course, dear Miss Clarke?"

Susan smiled, though she looked embarrassed and her cheeks were a little pale. "I think it an excellent way for you young people to pass the day, and I am sure it would be well for Eliza to further our acquaintance with the Wrights. But I believe I shall absent myself from the visit."

"Perhaps you will permit me to remain with you, Miss Clarke?" Ned said quickly. "Shouldn't want you to spend the day alone."

Lily hid her amusement behind her teacup, and Ofelia gave her husband's hand a fond pat, though she looked like she wanted to laugh instead.

"That is very thoughtful of you, Sir Edward," Susan said warmly. "I would be delighted with the company." She cast a sideways look at Eliza. "I imagine my dear Miss Pierce will want to join the party, however?"

"Of course," Eliza said with unruffled calm. "As I am the most proper person to introduce our guests."

"And as you do not believe in a word of ghosts and want to go be entertained by our neighbors," Susan said, eyebrows raised.

"There is no point in neighbors if they are not amusing in one way or another," Eliza said, shrugging. "I am sure we shall give them plenty to talk of over their own tea and supper, so it will be a mutual exchange of amusement, at least."

"Are we really going to see whether there is a ghost in their hall?" Lily said in disbelief.

"Of course we are," Ofelia exclaimed. "Mr. Spencer, you were not joking, were you? You will accompany us to—what was their home called? Belleford?"

"With great pleasure, Lady Carroway."

"There, you see?" Ofelia beamed. "It is all settled. What splendid fun it will be."

CHAPTER 4

Matthew Spencer was as good as his word, arriving soon after breakfast the following morning in an open landau with a beautiful set of matched bays. After Ned spent several minutes exclaiming over the horses while Mr. Spencer answered every question regarding their paces and bloodlines, the ladies were ready to depart.

The autumn day was brisk but sunny enough to make driving in an open carriage a pleasure. The rolling Hampshire fields were beginning to brown, and though it was not a forested part of the county, there were enough trees to make a border of orange and gold against the blue of the sky.

Matthew Spencer was friendly and attentive to all three of them, but he seemed to be glancing Lily's way and directing his comments to her more than the others. At first, she wondered if it was her imagination. But when she saw both her aunt and Ofelia casting sideways looks between the two of them, she thought she might not be mistaken after all. Lily, both pleased by his attention and unsure whether she should be pleased or not, was glad when they finally clattered into the drive of Belleford.

The manor was a stately old building of the kind that looked beautiful in the autumn light and was likely unbearably drafty in the winter. It was large for a country house, bigger than Mr. Spencer's home had been, and clearly meant to be the oldest and grandest home in the neighborhood. It was built to evoke many of the country's great houses, though it was smaller in size and lacked imposing grounds. But it was elegant and well situated, with just enough of both aged stone and gnarled trees to give it an air of picturesque beauty. Lily, looking it over, could certainly see how a visitor might picture a ghost or two wandering the grounds and halls at night. The thought made her smile as she took the groom's hand, allowing him to assist her down the landau's step.

They were not the only ones in the drive. As Eliza was being handed down, a smart curricle drew up a short distance away, stones tossing up from the hooves of the horse as the vehicle pulled to a quick stop.

The driver, a man of perhaps thirty-five years, looked confused to see another party in the drive, but recovered quickly, tossing the reins to his groom and swinging down. "Spencer! What a surprise." The stranger walked toward them, stopping a few feet away and looking them over with curiosity. Lily thought there was a touch of uneasiness in his expression as well, but a moment later he was smiling so broadly that she wondered if she had imagined it. There was certainly no hesitation in the hearty way he reached out to clasp Matthew Spencer's hand. "What brings you to Belleford this morning?"

"Mr. Wright, a pleasure, as always." Mr. Spencer's greeting was a little less warm to Lily's ear. Though he returned the handshake with goodwill and smiled, there was a distance to his manner that she had rarely seen in him. It made her wonder if there was something he disapproved of in his neighbor. "Were you out for a morning drive?"

The query was accompanied by the slightest raise of his eyebrow, a gesture that Lily might not have noticed if she hadn't been watching the two men closely. It gave his words an ironic edge; when it was answered by a slight flush around Mr. Wright's collar, Lily suspected that both men knew the question was a polite fiction. She wondered where Mr. Wright might actually have been.

But he answered easily. "Bright and early. You know me—always up with the dawn. Have you come to pay a visit?" He turned to the ladies, his eyes landing on Eliza. He bowed. "Madam. Your face is familiar to me. I think you live in this neighborhood, but I shamefully cannot recall if we have ever formally met."

Eliza smiled regally. "You are forgiven because we have not, though I know your mother. I am Miss Pierce."

"Oh, of Longwood Cottage! Of course." Thomas Wright took the hand she offered and bowed over it politely.

He was built on stocky lines, with ruddy cheeks, dark hair that was in need of a good combing, and a round face that many would think attractive, though Lily was put off by the way he was eyeing them all with such open speculation. He was dressed in the height of town fashion, a surprising thing to find out in the country. There was something rumpled about him, as though he had put on the same clothes he had worn the day before, though his cravat was impeccably tied, and he moved with the flair of a man who was used to finding himself the center of attention.

"A delight to officially make your acquaintance, Miss Pierce. Will you introduce me to your lovely companions?" He looked at both Lily and Ofelia with a gleam in his eye that Lily did not like, his eyes traveling over them with a leisurely appreciation that put her on edge.

She cast a sideways glance at Ofelia, who met her eye with a look of pursed-lip displeasure that was quickly transformed into a polite smile as Eliza gave their names, explaining that her niece and niece's friends were making a short visit in the country.

"This is Mr. Thomas Wright," Mr. Spencer supplied, unnecessarily and somewhat stiffly. Lily's impression that he did not care overly much for the younger man grew, though there was nothing impolite in Mr. Spencer's manner that anyone could have pointed to as a sign of dislike. "Mr. Wright, Lady Carroway and Mrs. Adler were most intrigued when they heard of your ghostly resident."

At that, Thomas Wright stepped a little closer to Lily and Ofelia and offered them a dazzling smile, clearly with no doubt in his mind of their finding him very charming indeed. Lily resisted the urge to take a step back. "We are quite the talk of the neighborhood, it seems. I should be happy to show such beautiful visitors over the house. You will not believe the many encounters our family and staff have had with the spectral creature. I hope neither of you are prone to nerves or fainting?" he added, looking momentarily serious.

"Rarely," Lily replied, a little more dryly than was perhaps necessary. Mr. Wright looked taken aback for a moment, but he recovered his easy manner and bowed, holding his arm in Ofelia's direction. "Shall we go in?"

Eliza was still standing closest to him, and there was a devilish gleam in her eye as she took his arm without hesitation. "Thank you, young man," she said, turning him toward the house and away from the two younger women. "My eyes are not what they used to be, and you are kind to offer your assistance."

Lily smothered a snort of laughter at the surprise on Thomas Wright's face. But politeness prevented him from protesting that his offer had been for another lady entirely, and he managed to respond with creditable smoothness as he led her up the steps toward the front door. Eliza cast a quick wink over her shoulder at the others before launching into a loud commentary on the weather in perfect imitation of the aging spinster aunt that she was not.

Ofelia held out her arm to Lily. "Shall we go in?" she asked gravely, raising her eyebrows in imitation of Mr. Wright as she did so before dissolving in a fit of silent laughter.

Lily struggled to hold back her own amusement as she glanced at Mr. Spencer. "Not Mr. Wright's most ardent admirer, I see?" she murmured. The other two were nearly at the top of the broad steps, and Eliza's overly loud conversation made it unlikely that Mr. Wright would hear anything she said. But that was no reason to be indiscreet.

Mr. Spencer flushed a little. "I never said so," he protested.

Lily smiled, patting his arm. "You did not have to, sir. He makes quite an impression." Still smiling, she took Ofelia's arm, and they followed Mr. Wright's lead up the steps, with Mr. Spencer close behind.

Thomas Wright had just led Eliza inside, and the other three joined them in the entrance hall. It was a gloomier and less imposing space than Lily had imagined based on the impressive sweep of stairs outside. Belleford was built on narrower and darker lines than many modern buildings, with thin windows, an expanse of ceiling that was lost in shadows, and a staircase leading from there to the upper floors.

Three or four rooms opened off the front hall, which was mostly occupied by an unlit fireplace and towered over by several large, dark paintings. They, along with the rest of the furnishings, looked in need of a good cleaning—or perhaps of being replaced entirely. The hall was decorated in the height of fashion forty years prior, and everything Lily could see was growing worn and threadbare. The whole space had a musty, almost unlived-in feel, and the chill that hung over the room made her shiver.

"Odd that Isaiah was not here to open the door," Mr. Wright was saying as the others joined them, a frown creasing his forehead. But a moment later, he shrugged and turned to Ofelia and Lily. "One of the hazards of life in a haunted manor is that it is difficult to keep a full staff on the premises. More than one servant has, unfortunately, been scared away by our ghost," he said, his eyes lingering on them once more. "You find us embarrassingly underserved at the moment, dear ladies, but never fear." His smile returned as he gestured for them to follow him upstairs. "I shall be conducting your tour personally, so you shall not need to worry about being well attended. I myself have seen the ghost on several occasions, usually at night, but recently once in the very early morning when I was rising to take myself out on a drive. We shall begin in the upper hall, where the spirit was first encountered by our head housemaid more than four months ago . . ."

He continued speaking as he climbed the steps, his voice growing warmer as he made his way through what sounded like a well-practiced recitation. The carpeting on the stairs muffled their footfalls as they climbed upward. For a few steps, Lily could still hear the creaking and rattling of the carriages being led away outside, but by the time they were halfway up, the sounds had faded. Nothing replaced them, not the morning bustle of servants, not the echo of distant conversation, not even the sounds of birds or wind from outside. A heavy silence descended, broken only by their own steps and the sound of Thomas Wright's voice.

He paused at the top of the stairs, where the upper hall was illuminated by large windows on one side, and for a moment the silence was almost overpowering. "Where the devil is everyone?" he muttered, frowning as he glanced around. There was genuine confusion on his face, and a touch of unease, as he looked up and down the silent, empty halls. But a moment later, he was all smiles again, though he looked less confident than before, as he gestured for everyone to join him by the windows.

As they walked, he fell in step next to Ofelia. "Have you ever seen a ghost before, Lady Carroway?"

"I have not," she replied, as polite as ever in spite of the hint of skepticism in her voice. "Pray, what does it look like?"

"Like a lady in white and gray," he said, and Lily was surprised to see how serious his expression was. His frivolous, unctuous manner had dropped away, and he shivered a little as he gestured toward the windows. "No one has seen her face. The first time I saw her she was standing right there, bathed in moonlight, when I was returning from a late night in the village. And my sister saw her in the early morning only two days ago. Some nights, we have heard her wails echoing through the halls, even when she is nowhere to be seen."

Lily exchanged a look with her aunt, who seemed surprised by the detail in Thomas Wright's story and the quaver in his voice. Either he believed wholeheartedly in his ghost, or he was putting on a very convincing performance for his audience.

"And what does she do?" Ofelia asked, sounding a little more somber now, as they drew to a halt in front of the windows. The small party looked around the corner of the hall. It was unremarkable enough, with several large paintings, and a tall, handsome curio cabinet standing in an alcove. An old-fashioned tapestry hung across one wall, though it was worn and faded enough that it was hard to tell exactly what picture it had originally presented.

"Nothing, so far," Mr. Wright said, a sort of forced theatricality in his voice that left Lily puzzled.

She had expected, based on what Mr. Spencer had said the night before, to find an eager showman in Thomas Wright, ready to bask in the attention of curious neighbors, not a true believer in the supernatural. Glancing at Mr. Spencer out of the corner of her eye, she thought he looked equally puzzled.

"She stands and weeps, or floats around the hall and wails. Usually, if someone tries to draw close, she vanishes. But last month—" Mr. Wright's voice dropped a little. He still glanced uneasily toward the other end of the hall, as if momentarily distracted or looking for someone, before quickly returning his attention to his audience. "Last month she became angry when one of our housemaids came upon her unexpectedly. The lady in gray pursued her down the hall, wailing. Poor Etta was so scared that she fell down the stairs in her haste to get away. That was when our servants started leaving."

"I trust the housemaid has recovered?" Mr. Spencer asked, sounding genuinely concerned.

"She has," Mr. Wright replied. "But no one has tried to approach the lady in gray again. We think she wishes to be left alone."

"Well," Lily said, attempting a return to lightness, "as far as ghosts go, that sounds reasonable enough. I confess I feel that way often enough myself, especially after too many busy nights in a row."

Ofelia, who had been looking a little wide-eyed, giggled, and Mr. Spencer quickly covered a cough that might have been a chuckle. Mr. Wright scowled, his expression halfway between unease and displeasure. "I take it you are not a woman who believes in ghosts, Mrs. Adler?"

"I have never had the opportunity to find out whether or not I am," Lily replied. "The homes I have lived in have all been stubbornly unhaunted."

"For your sake, madam, I hope they remain that way," Mr. Wright said. There was an unexpected note of resignation in his voice as he added, "It is not a comfortable thing to live with."

"I would have thought you to be fond of yours, sir," Lily said. "If you dislike her so, why go to the trouble of showing visitors around and telling them the story?"

Mr. Wright smiled, some of the showman creeping back into his manner. "Because you are here, dear ladies. And how could I resist such a beautiful audience?"

"Tell me, has your family any idea who this lady in gray might be?" Eliza asked politely.

He nodded, his voice dropping even further, and they all reflexively drew closer to hear what he was saying. "We each have our own theory, of course," he said. "I believe it is my father's great-aunt, Tabitha, whose bedroom was just this way. If you would care to see the spot?" He held out his arm to Eliza, who took it. Mr. Wright, engrossed in his story once more, turned to lead them down the closest passage. "Tabitha died there some fifty years ago, of a broken heart, they say, after news arrived of the death of her betrothed in the colonies—"

His story was suddenly cut off by screaming. Not a single shriek of surprise or dismay, but a cry that seemed to go on without ceasing. Thomas Wright froze, the genial smile dropping from his face in shock. "Selina?" he called.

The screaming continued, growing more hysterical. Dropping Eliza's arm, he ran toward the sound, which was coming from the far hallway, past the stairs.

The others, stunned into stillness, stared at each other, unsure what to do.

"I think it's Miss Wright," Mr. Spencer said, all traces of merriment gone from his face. "Wait here—I shall see if they need any assistance." He made to go after, but Thomas Wright was already returning, rushing down the hall next to another man, who was carrying the screaming woman.

"The parlor, just next to you, Spencer!" Mr. Wright called. "Open the door!"

Mr. Spencer, the closest to the door, flung it open, and the hysterical woman was carried in.

She was laid on a chaise longue in the middle of the dim little room, Mr. Spencer stepping forward to help settle her as the man who had carried her stepped back. Lily, glancing around as she and the other ladies crowded through the door, thought it looked like a space reserved for the family's private use, which made sense on an upper floor. Thomas Wright knelt next to the hysterical woman for a moment, clasping her hands.

"Selina?" he said loudly. But she kept screaming, her eyes wide and darting about the room without seeing anything.

Judging by the round cheeks and dark hair they both shared, Lily thought she must be his sister. Whether they had other features in common was hard to tell when Selina Wright was in the middle of hysterics.

"Miss Wright?" Matthew Spencer tried giving her shoulders a little shake. "You must stop this at once!"

But she clearly could not hear either of them. Thomas Wright took a deep breath and looked grim as, with a surprising degree of practicality, he slapped her across the face.

The screams stopped abruptly, her blank expression resolving into one of terror before her eyes latched on her brother. Her face crumpled in misery. "Oh, Thomas!" she sobbed, gasping for breath.

He gave her shoulders a little shake. "Selina, stop this—you must tell me what happened."

But she only shook her head, clutching at his coat with desperate fists and dropping her head against his shoulder, her weeping shaking them both.

Mr. Wright turned to the servant who had carried his sister. "Isaiah, what happened to her?"

Isaiah was a young Black man with very short, curly hair and broad shoulders. His plain, dark clothing marked him clearly as a servant, though it was nothing so formal as the livery that would have been worn in a great house. His wide stance spoke of confidence, and the easy way that Thomas Wright addressed him indicated long service and familiarity.

But there was no confidence on the manservant's face as he hesitated, gulping visibly and shaking his head. His eyes were wide, and he stumbled over his words as he tried to answer, either unsure how to respond or not wanting to. "It's . . . it's Mrs. Wright, sir. She didn't open her door when we knocked, and Miss Wright . . . she asked me to open it, since no one has the key . . . and she was there, sir—Mrs. Wright. She was there but she wasn't moving. There was nothing we could do, but there was no one else there what could have done it. She's dead, sir," he finished in a rush. "Mrs. Wright is dead. She was killed in the night."

Beside her, Lily heard Ofelia gasp, though she didn't turn to look at her friend, and Eliza clutched her arm with viselike strength. Mr. Spencer looked up, his dark eyes wide as he met Lily's from across the room. She stared back at him, frozen in shock, unable to believe what she had just heard.

"Killed?" Thomas Wright demanded, his voice rising with his own disbelief and his arms tightening around his sister.

"It killed her, Thomas," Selina Wright said, raising her head at last. Now that her hysterics had faded, her cheeks had gone ashen with fear. "There was no one else who could have entered that room. The lady in gray killed our mother."

She burst into sobs once more, burying her face against her brother's jacket.

CHAPTER 5

The silence in the room was painfully loud, broken only by Selina's crying.

Mr. Spencer was the first to speak. "Miss Wright," he said gently, "surely you must be mistaken. If your mother has indeed died in the night, then I am unspeakably sorry for your loss. But that does not mean anyone killed her, least of all a ghost."

"Tell them." Miss Wright lifted her head just enough to glance at the manservant, then pressed it once more against her brother's chest, as though she could not bear to look at the world. Her voice was muffled, but her words were insistent. "Tell them!"

"Begging your pardon, sir, but Miss Wright isn't mistaken," Isaiah said quietly, his own voice shaking. "We found Mrs. Wright dead as a post, her face all frozen-like, looking scared out of her wits. No one who dies in her sleep looks like that, sir. She was frightened to death. There was no one else in that room. And the door was locked from the inside—you know how she insists, sir," he added, a pleading look on his face. "It took us an age to get it open. No one else could have got in. She's dead. And something unnatural killed her. It's the only thing as makes sense."

There was a clatter of hurrying feet in the hall, and they turned to see the other servants approaching. The oldest one, a rail-thin, ancient butler with a fringe of gray hair around his head, stepped into the room first. He cast a frowning look at Isaiah and a surprised one at the number of visitors gathered there, before bowing.

"I beg your pardon, Mr. Wright, for our unseemly arrival. We heard screaming from downstairs. Is Miss Wright well? Do we need to send for the doctor?"

"A doctor . . ." Thomas Wright looked dazed. "Yes, Mr. Mears. Someone should immediately—my mother—"

"Mrs. Wright is dead," Mr. Spencer said, stepping forward authoritatively. "Dr. Mills will need to examine her immediately and tend to Miss Wright."

Both the butler and the maids behind him gasped, and Miss Wright moaned, her sobs renewing in fervor at the blunt words, gently though they were spoken.

Mr. Mears was already nodding, his face grim. "Certainly, sir. Isaiah, will you—"

"Of course, Mr. Mears."

"My sister will need something—"

"Etta, bring up tea and brandy, Miss Wright's had a shock—"

"Right away, Mr. Mears."

"And the local magistrate," Lily said loudly. The others fell silent, gaping at her. A moment later Eliza was nodding in firm agreement, though she looked a little green.

"I beg your pardon?" Mr. Wright said at last.

"Whoever your local magistrate is, you will need to summon him immediately. No one should touch anything in your mother's room until he and the doctor arrive. And they should be shown in together, not separately."

Even Miss Wright had raised her head now, and she and her brother were staring at Lily while the servants looked between them, hesitant to take instruction from a woman they didn't know at all.

Mr. Wright fixed his gaze on her. "Just what do you think a magistrate can do against a ghost?"

"It is a wise idea, Wright," Mr. Spencer agreed, giving Lily a quick look and an even quicker nod. "There will be questions. Best to get them all answered right away."

For a moment, there was silence in the room. Then Mr. Wright nodded. "Etta and Isaiah, you can each take one of the horses. Dr. Mills and Mr. Powell. Be quick."

"Yes, sir," said the maid who was presumably Etta, her dark eyes wide with shock as she peered over Mr. Mears's shoulder. Isaiah echoed her, both of them hurrying out of the room, the sound of their footsteps disappearing a moment later as they rushed down the stairs.

"Miss Wright will still need something," said Mr. Mears. "Mr. Wright, perhaps the entire company will? It will take me a moment with Etta gone—"

"I can help, Mr. Mears," said the other maid quickly, looking eager to be away from the crowded room.

The butler glanced behind him as if surprised, then nodded. "Ah, Alice, of course. Good girl. Hurry downstairs—"

"Mr. Spencer, do you think everyone ought to stay here until the magistrate arrives?" Lily asked. Her gaze latched on him as she spoke, and she knew that he would understand it was not really a question.

"Indeed," he agreed swiftly. "Wright, I think Mr. Powell would want to be sure that no one has been wandering around Belleford. The ladies should stay here with Mr. Mears and"—he glanced at the maid—"Alice, was it?" She nodded, ducking her head nervously. "They can stay here while you and I do a quick search of the house, to be sure there is no one else on the grounds."

"Are there no other servants?" Eliza asked, surprised out of her silence. "I thought Mrs. Musgrave's girl was working here?"

Thomas Wright grimaced. "As I mentioned before, most of our staff have been frightened away by the—" He broke off, glancing at his sister and swallowing visibly. "Well, perhaps they were wise. Mr. Mears, Isaiah, Etta, and Alice are the extent of our staff at the moment. It is a good idea, Spencer, for us to look around." He was easing his sister away from him as he spoke, until she was sitting back on the chaise longue, her eyes closed and her shoulders still shaking, though she seemed to be regaining control of herself at last. "But I don't like to leave the ladies alone, even if we are still on the grounds. What if . . ." He trailed off, glancing around the room uneasily. "No, it is long past dawn. I doubt it will return before the night."

It took Lily a moment to realize he was talking about the ghost, and she glanced at Ofelia, relieved to see her friend looking as surprised as she herself felt. The Wright siblings, it seemed, were fervent in their belief that the spirit was real. Had there truly been something wandering the halls of Belleford? There must have been, to leave them so convinced.

"We shall attend to Miss Wright while you are gone," Ofelia said, stepping forward into the uncomfortable silence. "If you are to search the grounds, I am sure you ought to move quickly."

Selina Wright opened her eyes, sitting forward so suddenly that it made the rest of them jump. "What is the point?" she asked, her voice quavering. "It was the lady in gray, I tell you. Nothing natural could have done it."

"The magistrate will want us to be sure," Mr. Spencer said gently, as Selina's brother headed toward the door. "It would be wise for all of you to stay here, and the others when they return. If the doctor or magistrate arrive, they should wait for Mr. Wright before proceeding."

"We shall make sure of it," Eliza said, drawing herself up and nodding firmly.

As the gentlemen left, Mr. Spencer paused a moment next to Lily, lowering his head slightly. "Try to be gentle with your questions," he murmured. "Remember, she has had a shock."

"What questions?" Lily asked, her eyes wide with attempted innocence.

His expression might have been a smile if his eyes hadn't been so serious. "We will return soon" was all he said in reply.

Eliza, efficient and soothing, took over as soon as the gentlemen were gone. "Miss Wright?" She chose a chair just next to the chaise longue, reaching out to take the younger woman's hand in a maternal fashion. "I believe we have crossed paths a time or two at the church in the village, though I do not blame you at all if you fail to recognize me at the moment. I am Miss Pierce. My companions are my niece, Mrs. Adler, and her friend, Lady Carroway."

Lily and Ofelia each bowed as their name was given and murmured a greeting, the polite introductions feeling both reassuring and farcical.

"You are very understanding, Miss Pierce—I thank you. I would welcome all three of you to Belleford, but . . ." Miss Wright's words faded away as she glanced around the room. She was younger than her brother and not nearly as handsome or stylish, even when she was not in hysterics. "I suppose we should all sit down and wait for whatever happens next. Mr. Mears, do take a seat as well. I know it is odd, but everything is so . . . well, we are all stuck here until the magistrate arrives, so we may as well be comfortable."

Mr. Mears looked decidedly *un*comfortable as he took one of the chairs closest to the wall—it was not often that a servant, even a member of the upper staff such as a butler, was invited to sit in the presence of his employer, never mind his employer's guests. The little maid Alice, who had not been invited to take a seat, hovered by his shoulder, her eyes darting around the room and toward the door anxiously until the butler sighed with impatience and instructed her to sit down and stop fidgeting. Lily and Ofelia took seats on the settee across from where Eliza and Miss Wright were seated.

Silence descended, heavy and smothering, broken only by the sound of the wind outside. All of them exchanged glances, no one quite sure what to say in a situation that was so far outside what any of them were prepared to handle. The room itself only added to their discomfort. There was no fire laid in the fireplace, and the walls held in the autumn chill as though determined to chase away visitors. Glancing around, Lily could see the same signs of neglect that she had noticed downstairs in the once fashionable, now outdated furnishings and the worn spots on the rug, where too many feet had trod the same paths over and over. The room did not seem unlived in—there were signs of yesterday's fire in the fireplace—but it was cheerless and grim.

Ofelia, at last, cleared her throat. "We must apologize for intruding on you in such a manner," she said gently. "In light of what has happened, our visit feels so poorly timed."

Miss Wright's eyes filled with tears. "You came to hear of our ghost, I imagine."

Eliza nodded. "We were dining with Mr. Spencer last evening when the story came up, and it seemed a harmless amusement for the young people. I am so very sorry."

"It has been quite the local sensation. Thomas does enjoy showing guests around and . . ." Miss Wright swallowed, her voice faltering as she glanced toward the door. "Well, things can be quiet here," she added, sounding a little defensive on her brother's behalf. "I do not mind, myself. But for a man like Thomas—he says he would be more suited to a life in one of the cities or popular watering holes, and he is always looking for some kind of entertainment."

"We all must make our own amusements in a village like this one," Eliza said soothingly, patting the younger woman's hand, "though your brother seemed to believe most earnestly in the specter's existence."

"We all do," Miss Wright said, pulling her hand away as she sat up, the defensive note growing in her voice. "It has been impossible to live here these last months and not be convinced. And now . . ." She sank back again, shivering, her gaze locked on the door once more.

Lily glanced at the two servants in the room, wondering if they agreed with their employer. The butler was nodding along as Selina Wright spoke, rigidly upright, though from his expression it was impossible to tell whether he agreed with her assessment or was supporting her out of principle. The maid, by contrast, nodded fervently, her eyes wide in her peaked face, and her gaze darted nervously toward the door every few moments.

"Mr. Mears, would you check in the sideboard and see whether my brother has anything there? If we cannot have tea, I think we must have something to support our spirits."

Mr. Mears did as he was bid, reporting that there was half a bottle of sherry tucked in with the glasses. These were filled and passed around, though Ofelia demurred. As Selina Wright sipped hers, a little color returned to her cheeks, but her eyes still looked as haunted as her house seemed to be, and her hands trembled.

She gestured with her glass at the two servants. "If you need something yourself in the face of such tragedy . . ."

"No, thank you, Miss Wright," said the butler firmly, answering for both of them. The pale little maid, who had sat forward eagerly, slumped back into her chair until the butler poked her sharply in the side to make her sit up straight once more. "A most generous offer, indeed, but we've no wish impose. And we'll need our wits about us if—" Mr. Mears broke off, clearing his throat uneasily. "That is to say, we'll need to be ready when the gentlemen say we can get back to our duties."

A sudden gust of wind rattled the windowpane, causing everyone in the room to jump, and the feeling of cold air seeping in made Lily rise and cross to the window to check that it was fully closed. She had to pull aside the heavy curtains with some effort; they draped and pooled with a luxurious amount of fabric, but the edges were frayed and the folds dusty. Shoving them out of the way and trying not to cough, she pushed against the casement, closing it more securely.

"Is there a sign of anyone returning?" Miss Wright asked anxiously.

The window looked out over the front drive. The crisp autumn sunshine had been dimmed by fretful clouds that left much of the ground shadowed. Lily shivered and quickly turned back to the room. "No one yet. But I am sure we'll not need to wait long."

But she didn't return to her seat immediately. She wanted, as Mr. Spencer had guessed, to find out more. As she was debating the merits of open questions versus delicate probing, the decision was taken out of her hands by her aunt, who leaned forward and took Selina Wright's free hand in her own.

"Do you wish to tell us what happened, dear Miss Wright?" Eliza asked. Lily thought her aunt might have cast a quick look in her own direction, but the glance was so fleeting she could not be sure. "It might help you to gather your thoughts before the magistrate arrives."

"Yes, I suppose . . ." Miss Wright hesitated.

Lily held her breath, now with no intention of moving. The spot by the window afforded her a view of both Miss Wright and the servants, and she was curious to observe all their expressions.

"I think you said you went to wake your mother, did you not?" Eliza prompted gently.

Miss Wright nodded, her face drawn and tight with misery, though she did not begin crying again. "She had not yet rung for her chocolate, which was odd for her. Always up at the break of dawn, always with instructions for everyone in the house. She had more energy than anyone I have ever met, for all that her health was not good in recent years. And with the ghost . . ." She shivered. "Mother was afraid of it," she added, almost in a whisper. "How could one not be? Especially after Etta was injured. Thomas tried to convince her that we should sell the house and leave. Mother refused of course—she said she would not be chased from her own home. But for all she put on a brave face, she was afraid."

Lily checked the servants' faces to see how they reacted to that statement. Both had been sitting, impassive and unreadable, with the careful expression so many servants cultivated. The butler's hands rested in his lap, his eyes moving slowly from one lady to the next, wide and unblinking, though Lily thought they narrowed when they came to Ofelia. But at the mention of Mrs. Wright's fear of the ghost, there was a shift in his expression, the tense lines around his eyes and mouth growing more pronounced, and his posture becoming even more rigidly upright.

The maid shrank further into her chair, her eyes darting around the room fearfully before her gaze settled on her own hands, which were clasped so tightly in her lap that the knuckles were white.

Outside, the wind whistled under the eaves, low and faint.

"She insisted on us sitting with her every night, before the fire in her room," Miss Wright continued. "We would play cards or read or some such until she was ready for bed. And she would lock the door behind us when we left."

Lily drew in a sharp breath, which was echoed by both her aunt and friend, and turned from her study of the servants to fix her attention on Miss Wright. "The door of her room was locked last night? You are sure?"

The look the other woman gave Lily was so sharp and resentful that it made her want to take a step back. "Why do you think I have been so certain nothing natural could have killed her?" Selina Wright demanded. "There was one key to that room, and Mother used it every night to lock her door. From the inside, mind you. And the door was still locked this morning. She did not . . . she did not kill herself. So it had to have been . . ." She shuddered, then drained the rest of her sherry in one sharp swallow that made her cough and wipe her eyes. "She wanted to be sure nothing could go in or out of her room while she slept. And nothing could have. Nothing *alive*."

"But neither you nor your brother had any inkling anything was amiss?" Ofelia asked, leaning forward. "Nothing that you heard in the night?"

"Nothing. That is, I heard nothing. And Thomas was gone all night."

Lily could not stop her eyebrows from climbing. "All night?"

Miss Wright gave her another baleful glance. "I assume he was out at the tavern with his friends. Hardly an uncommon thing for young men." She shivered, her expression falling once more. "I'd not seen him since he left last night until . . . until . . ." Her eyes filled with tears again, and Eliza quickly produced a handkerchief for her, murmuring something soothing.

"But then how did you get in the door?" Ofelia asked. "If your mother locked it from the inside, and there was only one key? Did you break it down?"

"No, George did it," Miss Wright said, her voice muffled by the handkerchief.

Ofelia frowned in confusion, glancing at Lily, who shook her head, equally puzzled. They had not met a George, and Thomas Wright had said there were no other servants in the house.

"Begging your pardons," Mr. Mears said, speaking up when it became clear that Miss Wright was too occupied with wiping her eyes and catching her breath to say anymore. "She means Isaiah, who you saw. Mrs. Wright always called manservants George, as she found it easier than trying to remember different names. Isaiah's father was a locksmith. He knows how to open doors, though it takes him some time."

"And he don't like to do it much," the maid, Alice, spoke up, looking a little terrified at her own daring. When all the eyes in the room turned on her, she looked down at her hands. Her voice was barely above a whisper, and she had to clear her throat before continuing. "He says he don't want to give people the wrong idea or seem mistrustworthy."

Lily nodded slowly, turning that over in her mind. It was a reasonable worry on his part, not to want to demonstrate a skill that could be associated with criminal behavior. But it was also, under the circumstances, more than a little curious.

If the servant had picked the lock that morning, who was to say it had not been done in the night?

"And then we found her . . . we found her . . ." Miss Wright swallowed, one hand going to her mouth as if to hold in a sob. "The room was empty, but we could see her on the bed, all wound in the bedclothes as if she had been thrashing around. Isaiah shook her, but it was too late, and I . . ." She shuddered, her words growing faster. "She looked so awful, lying there, her face all frozen like that, looking terrified beyond anything I have ever seen. I think I screamed. I cannot remember anything past that until we came in here." She glanced around the room, looking very much like a scared and confused child. "What do you think the magistrate will do?" she asked, her voice rising and her breath starting to come in quick and shallow bursts once more.

Eliza, clearly fearing another bout of hysterics, pressed her own untouched glass of sherry into Miss Wright's hand, urging her to drink it all and then lie back once more. "Deep breaths, my dear. You cannot afford to go to pieces again. Not yet."

Ofelia frowned in thought. "I imagine the magistrate will want to see your mother's—" She broke off as Miss Wright's face grew even paler. "Your mother's room," she finished gently. "And he will want to talk to you. All you need do is tell him what you have just told us."

"And speaking of the magistrate, he may have just arrived," Lily said, glancing out the window at the sound of hoofbeats. The two servants on horseback had returned just ahead of a carriage that rattled to a stop in front of the broad sweep of stairs. Two men—one tall and broad, the other short and wiry—emerged, clearly in the middle of an intense discussion. "Or perhaps both he and the doctor?"

Two more figures came down the front steps to greet them; after Thomas Wright had spoken briefly to Etta and Isaiah and sent them around the back of the house with the horses, he gestured for the two new arrivals to follow him inside. Lily couldn't hear any of the words exchanged, but there was no mistaking the grim expressions on the faces of all four men as they climbed the stairs.

"I believe your brother and Mr. Spencer are leading them here even now."

A moment later, her guess was confirmed by the sound of masculine voices and the thump of brisk feet on the stairs. The ladies in the room sat up straighter. Mr. Mears stood, pulling the maid to her feet as well when she did not move quickly enough.

There was an awkward silence when the men entered, all of them staring at each other and unsure how or where to begin. Selina Wright at last broke it. "Thomas," she said, her voice quavering as she sat up, "did you tell them what happened?"

"As best I could," he said, crossing to her and taking her hand. "Gentlemen . . ." He studied the two newcomers who both stood in the doorway, looking ill at ease. "What happens now?"

Mr. Spencer stepped in, taking charge of introductions, and Lily was impressed that he had noted the servants' names as well and included them so the magistrate did not have to ask. Both men were known to Eliza also; she enquired gravely about the tall magistrate's family, and the short doctor, who Lily gathered was also the local coroner, asked after Miss Clarke. All of them took refuge in polite greetings before they turned their attention to the matter that had brought them together.

At last, polite conversation could no longer put off what needed to be done. Dr. Mills went to attend Miss Wright, who was ashen and shaking once more. Eliza drew back, and Lily and Ofelia found themselves taking seats closer to the door. When Etta and Isaiah returned from stabling the horses, the magistrate Mr. Powell gestured them into the room, his expression turning sorrowful.

"Mr. Wright, Miss Wright, let me begin by saying how sorry I am for your loss. We shall try to prevent our being here from adding too much to your distress. But I am afraid I need to ask some questions."

"Of course, sir," Thomas Wright said stoutly, looking ill.

"I understand your sister found the—" Mr. Powell cleared his throat. "I understand you entered your mother's room this morning, Miss Wright?"

But she was weeping once more, silently this time. Dr. Mills, busy checking her pulse, met the magistrate's eye and shook his head, gesturing toward the others in the room. Mr. Powell, after a moment's hesitation, turned to Eliza.

"Perhaps, Miss Pierce, you could begin? What brought you and your guests here this morning, what you recollect, that sort of thing?"

"Certainly, sir," Eliza agreed, casting a worried look at Miss Wright as she began to recount their plan for the morning. The magistrate, who after all was local, seemed unsurprised by their scheme of entertainment, and after a few interjections to ask

Lily and Ofelia what they could add—which was not much more than what Eliza had already said—he turned to Dr. Mills. The physician nodded, and Miss Wright, who was sitting up again, her tears quieted, lifted her head.

"And now, your recollections, if you would be so good," said the magistrate gently.

She nodded and took a deep breath, but Lily was distracted by a gentle tug on her arm. Frowning, she allowed Ofelia to pull her into the hall, unobserved by the others in the room, who were all watching Miss Wright intently.

"What is it?" she whispered once they were out of sight of the door.

"We already heard what she had to say," Ofelia murmured back, tilting her head toward the hall from which Isaiah had carried the hysterical Miss Wright. "Now is our best chance." She raised her eyebrows. "You *do* want to see what we can find in the old woman's room, do you not?"

Lily did want to, her curiosity about the ghost and the locked room close to getting the better of her. But she could only imagine what the magistrate and the coroner might say, never mind the Wrights. When Lily hesitated, glancing back toward the door, her friend shrugged.

"Well, *I* do," Ofelia whispered, her eyes gleaming with curiosity. "And I think you ought to come with me. Unless you believe a ghost did it after all?"

Lily frowned. "Don't be ridiculous," she whispered back, knowing she was being goaded but not caring. "Come on. Let us see what we can discover."

CHAPTER 6

With every living resident of the house in the parlor, there was no one to spot them as they hurried down the hall.

Ofelia Carroway did not believe in ghosts, and she didn't for a moment think it possible that some sort of specter was responsible for the death that had taken place. But there was something about Belleford that made her uneasy, and it was not just knowing that a woman had died—had perhaps been killed—not far from where they walked.

The sounds of their footfalls seemed far more muffled than the threadbare carpet could account for. Ofelia half felt that even if she were to shout that sound, too, would be swallowed up by the silence.

They passed several open doorways, peering inside each cold and empty room before continuing their search, and she found herself glancing around as though she expected to see someone else. Once or twice, she caught Mrs. Adler looking over her shoulder, though whether that was because her friend also felt the same oppressiveness or simply because she was checking for pursuit, Ofelia could not say.

They smelled the room before they reached it, and both of them drew to a halt at the same time. There was the scent of a fussy woman's boudoir, which Ofelia had come to know well in the months before her marriage when she had suffered through living with her Aunt Haverweight: camphor and cedar, hartshorn and rose water, all mixed together with a certain mustiness, like a linen press that had not been properly aired in several months. But under that hovered the smell of death, the undignified leavings of a body in its final moments when all physical restraints were loosed.

Ofelia swallowed. It had seemed a fine adventure, back in that crowded parlor, to sneak away and try their hands at detection once more. And as she often did, she had followed her impulse, eager to see what she could discover. In that moment, though, the cold hallway and the smell of death made her hesitate.

It was a relief, then, to see her uncertainty reflected on Mrs. Adler's face as well. "I have a feeling this will not be pretty," her friend said in a quiet voice that was almost lost in the heavy stillness of the hall.

"No," Ofelia agreed. "Do you think we should turn back?"

The look the other woman gave her was wry. "As soon as we returned to that parlor, we would be kicking ourselves for losing the opportunity. I am no good at leaving anything undiscovered if I might know more about it, and you rarely like to keep to your own business."

Ofelia would have laughed at the very accurate assessment of their respective characters if she hadn't wanted to keep quiet. But the moment of levity still provided the boost she needed. "Then shall we press on?"

"A moment." Mrs. Adler approached the room, but instead of going inside, she bent to examine the door, running a single finger over the lock. "There are very few scratches. And they look quite fresh."

Ofelia drew next to her, squinting at the metal plate. When her father had once gently suggested that she consider wearing spectacles, she had told him airily that she was too young and too vain to consider such a thing. But the difficulty making out such close details made her regret her previously dismissive attitude. She drew back a little, angling her head until the scratches that Mrs. Adler was pointing to came into focus. "They said the manservant Isaiah had to pick the lock because the old woman kept the only key inside with her."

"So either these scratches are from him, or someone else did the same thing last night." They both kept their voices low as they spoke, and Mrs. Adler glanced back over her shoulder as though worried someone would overhear them.

"In that case, he would either have had to not recognize them or to have chosen not to say anything," Ofelia said thoughtfully as she straightened, rubbing the spot between her eyes.

"And if they are from him this morning, that would indicate that either the lock was not picked before or that someone did it very carefully."

"A difficult feat at night, when someone might have noticed a bright light being carried through the hall."

"Indeed." Mrs. Adler straightened as well, her shoulders drawing back as though she were gathering her strength as she finally looked at the room. "But the door is rarely the only way into a room for someone wishing to remain unseen. Shall we continue?"

The room was chilled; with no chance for a maid to come tend to it, the fire had died, not even the banked embers still smoldering. But the curtains were half drawn, and the clouds had parted enough that there was light coming in. Ofelia took deep breaths through her mouth, trying to ignore the smell of death, and glanced at Mrs. Adler. "Where do you want to begin?"

"Well . . ." The older woman frowned thoughtfully, glancing around. "As I said, the door is not the only way in. And the others are much more difficult to lock from the outside once you have departed."

While she strode across the room, brisk and determined, to check the windows, Ofelia took a survey of the room. She couldn't quite bring herself to look at the bed and its lonely occupant—not yet. Instead, she walked slowly around the other three walls, looking for anything to catch her attention.

On the wall next to the door was a small wardrobe, built of heavy, dark wood that looked as though it hadn't been moved in over a generation. Glancing down, Ofelia could see the wood of the floor had bowed under its weight, but the door swung open noiselessly when she peered inside. Almost no clothing hung there—only one long coat and three dresses that were fussy with lace and nearly a decade out of fashion. Pegs held a lace cap and two limp purses that hung lifelessly from their strings. It could have been the clothing of any genteel but impoverished lady in her declining years. The door was inset with a beautiful mirror, though, but Ofelia caught a glimpse of the bed reflected there and quickly closed it.

Opposite the door was the sitting area in front of the cold fireplace, where presumably Mr. and Miss Wright had sat with their mother before they all retired for the night—though as Miss Wright had let slip, retire was not quite what Mr. Wright had proceeded to do.

On the wall between the main door and the fireplace were two things. The first was a door to a small chamber off the main room. Peeking in, Ofelia saw that it was a privy closet with a fireplace—cold and clean, indicating it hadn't been used in a few days—a hip bath, and a chamber pot discreetly tucked in the corner. The room was otherwise empty.

The second thing was a writing desk with a chair tucked underneath, and the desk was the only spot in the room that looked crowded. Ofelia stepped over to it eagerly. A crowded desk was often one that had something to reveal about its owner.

In spite of its fullness, though, the desk was surprisingly tidy. There were stacks of unused writing paper on one side of the blotter, a dish full of pens in need of mending, and a single, usable one set out on a tray with the ink bottle. Letters slotted neatly into cubbies, and Ofelia could see as she sifted through them that each cubby was dedicated to a single correspondent. Several of them looked to be lawyers or accountants, one local and one in Winchester. There were no letters from either of her children.

Ofelia frowned. Neither of the Wright children had married or moved away from the family home, a circumstance that spoke of a degree of attachment in the family. But devoted children would have been likely to write to their mother whenever they traveled or visited friends. The absence of any correspondence was . . . strange.

Ofelia was still puzzling over that when she opened the single drawer in the desk and discovered it held one of her favorite things: a ledger of the household accounts. She seized it eagerly. There were very few things, in her opinion, that could shed more light on a family's secrets and idiosyncrasies than their daily finances.

It only took her a few minutes of scanning the pages to realize there was indeed something odd about the Wright family's accounts: they were unexpectedly wealthy.

Ofelia frowned and, flipping back several pages, read through the columns more carefully, doing the sums in her head as she went. There was a great deal of money coming in, noted in a neat, tiny, feminine hand: a mixture of investment income that arrived every month and rents on several buildings in two nearby villages. But there were very few expenditures beyond basic household expenses. The servants, she was glad to note, were not being underpaid—but it seemed as if Mrs. Wright's children were, with almost no notations for personal expenses or an allowance. Even Thomas Wright, whom Ofelia would have expected to be the actual owner of the house and main recipient of any income from the family's invested or real holdings, received only an occasional moderate sum to cover his bills. And these, she could see, were paid directly where they were owed, rather than to the son of the house.

It didn't make sense, not when the house contained such worn furniture and threadbare carpets, so many cold fireplaces and so few servants. Even the old woman's wardrobe spoke of entrenched penny-pinching and shabby gentility. Ofelia even went further back, expecting to find a large expense for repairing the house or notes about long-standing debts. There was nothing of the sort. As far as she could tell, the Wright family had enough money to live in far more comfort and style than they currently did.

So why did they look as though they were teetering on the edge of poverty?

"They're all locked from the inside."

Mrs. Adler's sudden statement made Ofelia jump, and she slammed the ledger shut without thinking, which in turn made Mrs. Adler jump. They stared at each other for a moment, wide-eyed and alarmed, before each laughed a little nervously.

"My apologies," Mrs. Adler said. "I had no intention of startling you. What were you looking at?"

"Household accounts." Ofelia slid the ledger back into its drawer. "Nothing wrong with them, but plenty that is peculiar. What did you find?"

"The windows." Mrs. Adler gestured at the bank of windows, their glass spotlessly clean but wavy with age, showing the grounds outside as though through a puddle of water. "There is nothing wrong with them, and *that* is plenty odd. They are all locked from the inside and show no signs of being tampered with."

Ofelia came to stand next to her friend, both of them frowning at the unmistakably locked windows. "So no one could have come through there," she said.

"I suppose someone might have come in," Mrs. Adler said slowly, "but not gone out—not without leaving one of them unlocked."

"And anyone who did come in that way would have needed to scale the wall straight up," Ofelia said, craning her neck to peer out through the wavy glass. "There is no roof, or even a trellis, below."

"So that likely rules out the windows." Mrs. Adler let out a frustrated huff of breath. "Did you discover anything?"

"Their finances are beyond comfortable. I would even call them rich," Ofelia said, straightening. "According to the old woman's household accounts, they have plenty of income. And it seems she allowed almost no expenses."

"This is getting stranger by the minute. Did you discover anything in the privy closet?"

"Deeply ordinary. And uncomfortable looking." Ofelia glanced around the room, an exciting idea occurring to her. "Do you think there is a secret entrance somewhere? Old houses are full of such things, are they not?"

"Perhaps in novels," Mrs. Adler said, a hint of laughter in her voice. "Though, if they were once owned by Catholics . . . perhaps a priest hole would not be out of the question. But I do not think this is that sort of house."

"One can never be sure," Ofelia pointed out, stepping eagerly toward the fireplace. Everything was scrupulously clean, with no convenient layer of dust to indicate where someone might have pulled or pressed a secret lever. Ofelia methodically moved each object on the mantelpiece. When those all proved entirely ordinary, she bent to examine the few decorative carvings that surrounded the fireplace itself. These were a little grimier, but they also failed to produce a single secret passage or bolt hole.

"Did you try the wainscotting?" Mrs. Adler suggested. "Perhaps there is a false panel there."

Ofelia looked over her shoulder, narrowing her eyes. "Are you laughing at me?"

"Only a little," Mrs. Adler said, coming forward to follow her own advice and beginning to nudge each panel of the wainscotting with her toe. Ofelia joined in the examination, though it also proved fruitless as they made their way around the room. "As you say, it is not entirely out of the realm of possibility that old houses might contain such things."

"And I still do not believe that a ghost murdered someone." Ofelia shivered a little, though she tried to hide it. "Someone had to come into this room. Somehow."

"On that we are agreed." Mrs. Adler fell still as her search brought her toward the bed. Ofelia, on the opposite side, stopped as well. "And I do not think we can put off the inevitable any longer. We do not know how much more time we have to poke about."

"It is a miracle no one has yet come after us," Ofelia agreed, steeling herself as she met her friend's eyes. "Shall we?"

They turned as one, and Mrs. Adler, after a deep breath through her mouth, began to walk toward the bed. Ofelia wanted to hang back, but she could hear her father's voice in her head even as she had the thought. *"Once you have made up your mind, never let anyone see you hesitate or be afraid to do what must be done,"* he had always said. *"Do not be brash or assertive, but you must be confident. It is one of the first lessons you must learn if you wish to help me in my business. And it will be doubly true for you in all parts of life, dear one. There will always be someone looking for weakness in you. Do not show it, no matter how you truly feel."*

He had never come out and said why it would be doubly true for her. He had not needed to. Ofelia hadn't needed anyone to explain what she had felt in unkind stares and whispers nearly every day of her young life.

She walked toward the bed only a moment after Mrs. Adler.

The curtains around the bed had been drawn back on one side, presumably by Miss Wright, as Isaiah would have hesitated to approach the old woman's bed. Ofelia had thought she was growing accustomed to the smell, but it grew worse as they drew next to the bed and Mrs. Adler pulled the curtain farther back so there was room for both of them.

Ofelia had never seen a dead body before, not in close quarters, though she knew Mrs. Adler had. Once she looked, it was impossible to tear her eyes away.

The old woman was twisted in the bedclothes, her bulging eyes bloodshot and the skin of her face mottled blue and red.

Her jaw had fallen open, and there was something in her frozen expression that spoke of terror and fury in her final moments.

Ofelia shuddered. Mrs. Wright looked frail, alone in that large bed. But there was a wiriness to her body that made Ofelia think she would have been a forceful personality in life.

"I can see why they thought she was frightened to death," Ofelia whispered, swallowing rapidly against the sick feeling that was rising from her stomach. "It was not a peaceful end."

"No," Mrs. Adler calmly agreed, "and she fought against it." She shivered a little, then shifted her shoulders, as though steeling herself for hard work. "But that does not mean there was anything supernatural involved. Does anything strike you as strange or out of place??"

The two took opposite sides of the bed. Neither of them wanted to get too close to the body, but they searched through the linens as best they could and on the floor around the bed.

"This is odd," Ofelia said after a moment. "Look at her right hand."

Both Mrs. Wright's hands were locked into rigid claws, but while one of them was empty, the other was flung out from her body, the fingers still clutching at the edge of one of the pillows.

"Do you think she reached out and grabbed it in her final moments?" Mrs. Adler asked, coming over and leaning far closer to the corpse than Ofelia had any desire to get, to peer at the hand in question.

"If she did, someone flipped her arm over afterward," Ofelia said. "Look at the way she's positioned. Her hand is upside down but still holding on tightly. No one reaches out and grabs at something like that. Not thoughtlessly. It is too awkward."

"Unless both things happened," Mrs. Adler mused softly. When Ofelia gave her a puzzled look, she held her hands up on either side of her face, as though pretending to hold something. "If the pillow was on top of her, she could have grabbed at it in that position. And then whoever else was in the room moved both her hands and the pillow."

"You mean you think someone smothered her," said Ofelia, feeling cold all over. She took a quick step back from the bed, feeling suddenly even more disturbed, though nothing had truly changed.

"It is a possibility," Mrs. Adler agreed. "And I never yet heard of a ghost who could do that."

"But why not move the pillow farther away, then? Why leave it in one hand for someone to notice and wonder at?"

Mrs. Adler raised her brows. "Would you wish to touch the body of the woman you had just killed any more than you had to?"

Ofelia swallowed. "No, likely not."

"Nor would I." Mrs. Adler's voice did not sound quite as calm as her serene expression might indicate, and Ofelia was glad to know she was not the only one feeling unsettled. "Especially not if she was someone I had seen every day. Perhaps even my own mother."

"Do you mean—" Ofelia's question was cut off by a sudden, angry voice from the hallway.

"Just what in God's name do you think you are doing?"

Both women turned quickly, and Ofelia tried to look as innocent as possible as they found themselves confronted by the four men coming through the door. Of the four, only Mr. Spencer didn't appear surprised to see them there. Ofelia saw the wry look he cast at Mrs. Adler, his brows raised and a slight shrug to his shoulders as if to say that he was sorry for the interruption.

Ofelia wanted to glance at Mrs. Adler, to see how she responded, but she kept her attention on the other men eyeing them with varying degrees of displeasure.

Mr. Wright mostly looked tired and confused to find them there. But his concern was clearly about his mother, whom, Ofelia remembered with a sudden jolt of discomfort, he had not yet seen since learning of her death. He made as if to step toward the bed, and Ofelia would have moved respectfully out of his way, but the doctor's arm shot out, hand up, blocking Mr. Wright's way.

"Not yet, if you please," he said, his voice as gruff as the look on his face. It was he who had asked what they were doing, and he now turned a ferocious gaze on the two women, his bushy eyebrows drawing into a single disapproving line. "I ask again, what are you two doing here?"

"Should we not be here?" Ofelia asked, her eyes wide and guileless.

Dr. Mills opened his mouth, then closed it again, frowning even further. "Of course not," he said. "No one should interfere until we are done with our work."

"We would not dream of it," Mrs. Adler said politely, stepping away from the bed. "I assure you, we had no intention of any interference."

"Then what are you doing here?"

"We came to keep watch with poor Mrs. Wright," Ofelia said earnestly, looping her arm through her friend's and trying to look as young and innocent as possible. "So that she was not alone."

"Did you know her well?" Mr. Powell asked, eyebrows rising. "I do not believe I have seen either of you in the neighborhood before."

"We did not know her at all," Mrs. Adler admitted. "But as she had not been attended to yet this morning, because of the tragic circumstances, we thought it best that we ensure her poor body was decently covered before you entered the room, sir." She dropped her voice, sounding a little embarrassed. "It did not seem appropriate to have a passel of men—even gentlemen such as yourselves—traipsing into her room before we had assured ourselves that she was respectable."

The magistrate looked as though he would bluster at them more—not unreasonably, Ofelia had to admit to herself—but Thomas Wright spoke up.

"I thank you for your care of my mother, ladies," he said earnestly. "Even after her death, even without knowing her. Of course such womanly delicacy must be expected. My sister would thank you equally were she here. I am sure the magistrate and the doctor can have no objection."

Dr. Mills clearly did have objections, but after such a speech, he could not bring himself to say so. Mr. Powell cleared his throat several times. "Yes, well," he said meaninglessly, stepping forward. "Seeing as Mrs. Wright is decently covered, I must ask you to step aside while Dr. Mills and I look around. In fact, I imagine you will wish to return to the parlor with the other ladies? We have spoken with your aunt, Mrs. Adler, who has given her recollections of your morning. I believe the good Mr. Mears has gone to prepare tea for everyone. And once we have had a chance to speak to the servants as well, you all will be free to take your leave."

It was a dismissal, though a polite one. Ofelia wanted to protest. She had no confidence that the blustering Mr. Powell would be an astute observer, and she wanted more than anything to call his attention to the pillow clutched in the dead woman's hand and the oddness of the family's finances.

But putting the man's back up, and calling his work into question when he had barely begun, would not earn them any goodwill. When Mrs. Adler caught her eye and gave a slight shake of her head, warning her against speaking, Ofelia subsided with only a slight grumble under her breath.

"Do you require my escort to find your way back to the parlor?" Mr. Spencer asked, stepping into the room and gesturing toward the doorway.

"I thank you, no—we shall have no trouble finding our way," Mrs. Adler said. "I am sure you will wish to stay with Mr. Wright and the magistrate in case you can be of any use."

And so that he might hear and be able to report anything they said, Ofelia suspected, wondering if Mr. Spencer would be willing to carry such news to her friend. Mr. Spencer nodded gravely, his expression giving nothing away.

"Then when Mr. Powell and Dr. Mills have finished, I shall be at your service to convey you home."

They had to leave the room then, but as soon as they were out of sight from inside the room, Mrs. Adler held up her hand, silently drawing Ofelia to a halt and placing her finger on her lips.

"And where did your mother keep the key to her room?" They heard Mr. Powell ask.

A long, sad sigh. "I am afraid that she had taken to hiding it in a different place in her room every night," Mr. Wright said. He spoke in such a muted tone that Ofelia could not tell whether there was any embarrassment in his voice at the admission. There was certainly weariness and sorrow. "She was that terrified of the gray lady, though what a ghost might want with a key, I could not tell you. She traveled easily enough through the rest of the house with no need to worry about doors or windows. But we shall find the key tucked in here somewhere, eventually, I am sure."

Mrs. Adler nodded, as though what they had just heard had confirmed her suspicions, before setting off down the hall once more.

Ofelia, frowning in thought and wondering what they might learn when the magistrate was done, followed.

CHAPTER 7

Selina Wright still lay where they had left her, with Eliza still sitting at her side.

Two of the four servants hovered around the edges of the room. Isaiah, the manservant, was nervously nibbling on a thumbnail, glancing between Miss Wright and the door, though whether he was hoping he would be permitted to leave or that someone else would arrive, Lily couldn't have said. Etta had placed herself near him, one hand resting on his broad shoulder and rubbing it comfortingly.

Lily tapped gently on the frame of the open door to announce their arrival, and everyone in the room jumped. Etta gasped, her hand clutching at Isaiah's arm, and Selina Wright let out a little scream. Even Eliza tensed for a moment before her shoulders relaxed and she nodded at her niece.

"Mr. Mears has gone to fetch tea for us all," she said, filling the silence in what Lily suspected was an attempt to make sure no one had the chance to ask where she and Ofelia had been. "Won't you both come sit down and tell Miss Wright news from town while we wait for the gentlemen to return?"

Ofelia immediately took a seat on the other side of Miss Wright's chaise and began to talk of London, quick to follow

Eliza's lead and avoid any troublesome questions. Lily joined in more slowly, mostly content to watch the faces around the room.

It didn't take long for Mr. Mears to return with the tea tray for the ladies, trailed by the younger housemaid, Alice, who bore tea for the servants. After setting the tray down, Alice retreated a few steps away from the others, shrinking against one wall and glancing around the room at no one in particular, still looking peaked and fearful. Ofelia, after a glance from Eliza, poured out the tea when Selina Wright didn't seem inclined to move from her fainting couch, and they were all grateful to have something to do with their hands as they waited for news from the magistrate and doctor.

Lily sipped her tea, staying silent unless Eliza directed a specific query her way, and turning over what she had seen in Mrs. Wright's bedchamber. There was no saying exactly how the old woman had died after such a short inspection, but Ofelia's discovery about the family's finances was curious. Lily glanced at Miss Wright, wondering what she had thought of her mother's miserly ways or whether she'd been oblivious to it all. She seemed overwhelmed by Mrs. Wright's death, but Lily knew only too well how a pretense of extreme grief could be used to mask other, more suspect feelings, especially when a woman presented herself as hysterical or weak.

Lily still believed that a living being was responsible, rather than anything supernatural, but the house seemed determined to persuade her otherwise. The wind had picked up, and the sound of it gusting underneath the eaves sent a chill skating down her back, especially when it was accompanied by the occasional scrape of a tree branch against the windowpane. The musty heaviness of the parlor felt like a physical weight, and for a moment Lily thought she heard the creaking sound of slow footsteps out in the hall.

"What was that?" Etta exclaimed, clutching at Isaiah's arm as she looked toward the door.

The awkward attempt at conversation stumbled to a halt as everyone turned to stare, first at the door, then at Etta. Isaiah gave her hand a quick pat, shaking his head.

Lily frowned. Had the sound of footsteps not been in her imagination after all?

Mr. Mears began scolding Etta for interrupting, but Miss Wright cut him off. "I am sure none of our guests will take offense. We are all more than a little on edge right now. And the gray lady . . ." She trailed off, shivering, as she pulled a shawl someone had found for her more closely around her shoulders. "When do you think my brother will return?" she asked the room at large, her voice faint.

No one had an answer, but luckily, they did not have to wait long. The gentlemen returned far more quickly than Lily had expected. Each wore a different expression.

Thomas Wright looked stunned, as if he hadn't been able to believe his mother was truly dead before being confronted with her body. Dr. Mills looked sorrowful, shaking his head as he nodded to the ladies and settled into a chair with a heavy sigh. Mr. Spencer was the most impassive of the group; his expression was solemn but otherwise unreadable as he stepped politely out of the way, pulling out a chair next to Miss Wright for her brother, which the other man dropped into before reaching out blindly to take his sister's hand. And Mr. Powell, the magistrate, looked thoroughly perplexed—and, to Lily's eye, attempting to hide it behind an air of confidence.

"A sad business, to be sure," he said, pulling out a handker-chief to wipe his brow before he accepted a cup of tea from Ofelia. "Thank you, my dear. Mr. Wright, Miss Wright, once again, my deepest sympathies. We shall require only a little more of your time this morning, and then I am sure you shall wish to be left alone while you make the necessary arrangements. I've only a few more questions."

"Certainly, sir," Mr. Wright said while his sister nodded tremulously.

"At what o'clock did you leave your mother's side yesterday evening?"

"I left at perhaps . . . nine o'clock, would you say, Selina?" Mr. Wright asked, rising and pacing in front of the fireplace as he thought. "Yes, I think it was nine o'clock. We had our tea while we played a hand of cards, and then I read aloud for a little while. Etta came to clear the tea things at perhaps . . . eight thirty? After we were done with reading, and the fire was banked for the night, I said good night and took my leave of Mother. Selina stayed a few minutes more."

"She was already prepared for bed before we had tea," Miss Wright explained. "She said she was planning to read in bed for a short while, so I made sure her candles were lit, then said my own good night around quarter past." Her hands fluttered. "I'd no idea it would be goodbye, not good night."

"And that was the last anyone heard or spoke to her?" the magistrate asked.

"No, sir," Etta spoke up, looking a little overwhelmed at needing to address the whole company. When Mr. Powell nodded encouragingly, she continued. "I always check on Mrs. Wright—at least, I *did*, I mean to say—a little while after Mr. and Miss Wright take their leave for the night."

"How do you get in if the door is locked?" Mr. Powell asked, frowning.

"I don't sir. I just tap on the door and ask if there is anything I can do for her before she goes to sleep. Mrs. Wright lets me in if she needs—needed—something. Otherwise, she sends me away with the door still locked."

"And which happened last night?"

"She didn't need anything, so I wished her a good night and left."

"What time was that, Etta?" Mr. Wright demanded, stopping his pacing to look fixedly at her.

The housemaid hesitated, and Lily thought she looked a little nervous as she met his eyes. "I couldn't say exactly, sir. Around ten o'clock, perhaps? I didn't look closely at the clock as I went through the hall. It hadn't rung the half hour, I don't think. Where's Alice?" she asked, frowning. "She might know."

"I'm still here," the younger housemaid said from her spot in the corner. Mr. Wright jumped a little, as if he hadn't really noticed her either. There was an edge of irritation in Alice's quiet voice, though none on her face, as she pointed to the slightly chipped teacup that Etta was clutching. "I brought in our tea, remember?"

"Of course, yes," Etta said kindly. "I'm sorry—my head is all topsy-turvy. I can't seem to keep anything straight. You were already in bed, weren't you, when I got back to our room? What time was that?"

"I don't know, Etta. I was asleep," Alice said, and this time Lily caught the flicker of irritation in the tightening of her mouth. "I think I heard the hall clock chime ten when I was lying down, so it would have been after that."

"Oh yes, of course," Etta said, nodding quickly. "I think I must have come in just after that, because you weren't snoring yet."

"I don't snore," Alice snapped, blushing, as she glanced around the room.

"Etta," Mr. Mears said, a note of warning in his voice. "Answer the gentlemen's questions, if you please, with no elaboration." Both housemaids blushed at his correction, and Alice scowled down at her feet, not meeting anyone's eyes.

"And where is your room, girls?" Mr. Powell asked, clearing his throat.

"Upstairs, sir," Etta said. "Female servants upstairs, the men downstairs near the kitchens. Although Cook used to sleep down there, too, before she left."

"Etta," Miss Wright said sharply.

"It's all right, Selina," Mr. Wright said, shaking his head. "It isn't as if our difficulties with servants just now are unknown. Or unaccounted for. Our cook left just last week," he explained, looking at the magistrate. "We have recently begun to advertise for a new one."

"I see." Mr. Powell nodded. "And when did everyone else turn in for the night?"

"Isaiah's room is just next to mine," Mr. Mears volunteered in his quiet, slightly raspy voice. He looked as though he found it distasteful to discuss sleeping arrangements but still answered with a good deal of dignity. "He had finished up his work and turned in before nine. I was up a little later, but not by much."

"And you, Miss Wright?"

"I was in bed all night, of course," she said, her voice trembling. "As I always am."

"And none of you heard anything?" The magistrate looked around the room slowly, fixing each person with a beady stare. Lily watched the servants closely; they all were able to meet his gaze, though both housemaids looked wide-eyed and unsettled as they did so. "Nothing from Mrs. Wright? Or this ghost of yours? Nothing that might have made you think there was anyone at Belleford who ought not to have been?"

There was silence as the manor's residents shook their heads, glancing at each other to see if anyone would say differently. Lily noticed the magistrate had not asked Mr. Wright to account for his whereabouts during the night.

"The gray lady never comes belowstairs, sir," Mr. Mears said. "Of the four of us, only Etta and Isaiah have had the bad luck to run into her. But I at least didn't hear anything last night, and it seems no one else did either."

Dr. Hill spoke up, frowning. "You truly believe, then, that this ghost was responsible for what happened last night?"

"What else could it have been, Doctor?" Miss Wright said, sitting up ramrod straight to fix him with a baleful look, her voice more forceful than Lily had yet heard. "You saw my mother's face—that was no peaceful death in the night. Something did that to her. But there was no one else in the house last night, and even if there had been, you saw the room for yourself. With the door locked, no one could get in or out. What else could have happened to my mother?"

"Is there no one you can think of who might have wished to harm Mrs. Wright?" Mr. Powell asked, less gently than he might have.

Mr. Wright stiffened, moving to stand next to his sister. He took her hand, and the two of them glared at the magistrate. "No one at all," he said firmly. "I cannot think of a single soul who would have wished our dear mother any harm."

"No indeed," Miss Wright agreed, a sob in her voice. "Ask any of the servants—they will all say the same."

The young people all murmured their assent, of course—there was no chance they would have said anything else with their employer right there. But Lily noticed that Mr. Mears said nothing, his face polite and blank, giving away none of his feelings.

The room crackled with tension as Mr. Powell stared at the Wrights, and Lily leaned forward in her seat, almost holding her breath to see who among the three of them would back down first. But to her annoyance, Eliza was the one who broke the standoff.

"If there is nothing more you need of us, Mr. Powell, I think we have intruded on the grief of our neighbors long enough. Do we have your leave to depart?"

He turned to her, brows rising in surprise, as though he had forgotten the odd guests in the home completely. But after a moment, he nodded. "Indeed, I think it may be for the best if all of us depart. I am sure Mr. and Miss Wright are in need of solitude on such a difficult day."

The farewells were awkward and their departure rushed. Eliza fairly hustled her guests down the stairs and out to where Mr. Spencer's landau, along with the carriage that had brought Dr. Mills and Mr. Powell, waited in the drive. But the magistrate blocked their way when Eliza would have herded them all into the vehicle.

"Miss Pierce," he said, his voice sharp. "I must insist—*insist*—that neither of your young guests depart the county until I give them leave." He fixed each of them with a pointed look in turn. "I will confess that, at present, I have very little idea what to make of the events of this morning. But that does not mean this business is done."

★ ★ ★

Susan and Ned were waiting for them when they arrived back at the cottage, both of them blissfully unaware of what had happened that morning. They were ensconced in the parlor, chatting about seaside resorts while Susan sketched Ned's profile and he slowly demolished a plate of sandwiches when she gave him permission to move.

"How was your outing, my dears?" Susan asked, laying down her pencil and rising as Addie collected the wraps and coats of the entire party. "Did Mr. Spencer not want to stay for lunch?"

"Miss Clarke has informed me that I will never have a classical profile," Ned said, rising to kiss his wife's cheek. "But I think that makes me so much more interesting to sketch, does it not?"

"Very interesting," Susan agreed. "But Eliza, dearest, why do you look so solemn? Is aught amiss?" She smiled, gently teasing. "Never say you have come to believe in ghosts after all."

"It was not the ghost that was the trouble, I am afraid," Eliza said, sitting down. "At least, I do not believe it was. But you may disagree. The Wrights certainly do."

Both Susan and Ned listened in stunned silence as Eliza related the events of the morning. Susan's eyes and mouth both grew wide. Ned reached to take his wife's hand.

"But if you do not agree with the Wrights that this gray lady is responsible—yes, Eliza, I know your thoughts about such things, but we needn't argue over them now," Susan said, a little impatiently, when Lily's aunt opened her mouth to protest. "If you do not agree with them, what do you think happened?"

"I could not say." Eliza frowned thoughtfully, cutting her eyes sideways to where Lily stood in front of the window, gazing outside. "But my niece and Lady Carroway certainly slipped away carefully enough. I assume, then, that you saw something worthwhile?"

"Perhaps," Lily said, thinking over what they had seen. There was not much there, to be sure, but she had a feeling that it should be shared with Mr. Powell. If, of course, he gave them the opportunity to do so—and if he did not already know. She glanced at Ofelia, whose usual playful expression was drawn into an unhappy frown. "And perhaps not. There was not much time to look around, though Lady Carroway certainly made the most of it. She was far more industrious than I."

"With far less result than I was hoping for," Ofelia grumbled. "Not a broken window lock or secret passage to be found. I cannot for the life of me say how someone could have entered that room."

"Do you have a theory, then, Mrs. Adler?" Ned asked.

All eyes turned once more to Lily. Slowly, she shook her head.

"I am afraid I am as stumped as the rest of you," she admitted. "Aunt, how do you think Mr. Powell will do, looking into such a matter?"

"He is a fair man," Eliza said, reaching out to take one of the sandwiches that Ned had left behind, "but I do not know how insightful I would expect him to be, especially in such a puzzling case. And I've no idea what his opinion of ghosts may be."

"Then perhaps we shall never know what truly happened," Ofelia exclaimed, looking distraught. "How vexing."

"For you or for the Wrights?" her husband asked pointedly.

"Well, more for them certainly. Though they are content, it seems, to believe it a ghost. Whereas I am not."

"Perhaps they do not actually believe it," Lily suggested.

"Dear, what on earth could you mean?" Susan asked, frowning. "From Eliza's description, it seems they were quite adamant on the point."

"Perhaps that was because they did not wish to consider the alternative," Lily said, turning back to the window as she spoke. Rain had begun to fall outside, a drizzling mist that swept over the fields and hedges like a gray curtain. She shivered a little. "No one wishes to admit that they might be living with a murderer. But if a ghost did not kill their mother, then the most likely explanation is that someone in the house did."

CHAPTER 8

"Will you be all right if I am gone for a few hours?" Lily asked, tying the ribbons of her hat under her chin as she met Ofelia's eyes in the mirror.

"Of course," Ofelia replied staunchly, looking up from her embroidery to offer a reassuring smile. "Your aunt is delightful— you are a great deal like her, you know—and I suspect Miss Clarke is already scheming ways to get Neddy to return as soon as possible. They are taking a turn around the gardens as we speak." Her smile did not fade, but her brows rose a little as she continued. "Though, I must say, I am surprised to see you rushing to visit Mr. Spencer again so soon."

They had spent the rest of the previous day, after returning from Belleford, quietly at home. The conversation stayed firmly on other subjects, none of them wanting to dwell too much on Mrs. Wright's death, but it had obviously been on everyone's mind. Even cheerful Ned would fall silent at random moments, gazing out the window or at his dinner plate, with a frown on his face, before recalling himself to the present with a start and a forcefully bright smile.

Lily hadn't pressed either her aunt or Susan, knowing that they were likely far more distressed by the odd death of a near neighbor than she herself could be. But she only intended to hold her silence, and her curiosity, for so long.

"I have a few questions to ask him," she said in reply to her friend's pointed comment.

"Oh." Ofelia let the panel she was working on fall into her lap. "About the Wrights?" At Lily's nod, she sat up straighter. "I ought to have known you would not let the matter lie for long."

"Of course not." Lily left the mirror and came to sit next to her friend, her voice dropping as she glanced toward the open window, where she could just see Eliza joining the other two outside. "Mr. Powell may have instructed us to stay at Longwood Cottage until he gave us permission to depart, but we are going to leave eventually. And when we do, I've no intention of leaving my aunt and Miss Clarke in the same neighborhood as a murderer."

"What can I do to help?" Ofelia asked, casting her embroidery—in which Lily could see she had made all of five stitches—aside. "And do *not* say, 'Nothing.' You know I'm no better at letting things alone than you are."

That made Lily smile. "I wouldn't dream of it. In fact, I was hoping I could prevail on you to speak to Miss Clarke while I am gone. She was too distressed yesterday to say much, but she loves to gossip, the dear, though she would never call it that. She spends so much time in and out of her neighbors' homes that she tends to know everything about them, or about the people they know."

"And you want me to find out what she has to say about the Wrights? Certainly I can. And what will you be doing in the meantime?"

Lily stood. "Going to find out what everyone else in the village has to say about them."

★ ★ ★

Eliza had no objection to Lily borrowing the gig. She was even kind enough not to comment on her niece's proposed destination, though Lily saw her exchange a pointed look with Susan, who couldn't quite hide her smile.

It had been some years since Lily had driven herself anywhere. But the horse her aunt kept was even-tempered, and he didn't give too much trouble as she reacquainted herself with how to handle the ribbons.

It took slightly longer to reach Mr. Spencer's home than it had in Ned Carroway's well-sprung carriage, but the morning was not completely gone when Lily pulled the horse to a halt before the wide front steps. And she had the good fortune to arrive just as Mr. Spencer himself was coming around the side of the house at the end of a brisk walk.

"Mrs. Adler!" He looked taken aback for a moment, which Lily didn't wonder at. Such a visit, unplanned and unaccompanied, was not a liberty she had taken with him before, nor he with her. And even if it was not strictly improper, there were still some who would raise an eyebrow at it. But his surprise didn't stop him from quickly striding across the drive to hand her down from her seat. "To what do I owe this pleasure?"

"I was hoping I could persuade you to join me for a small trip to the village. I've not visited it in more than a year, but my aunt reminded me that today is market day. Though perhaps, if you have already taken your exercise for the morning, you might not have time?"

"I am at your disposal," he said with a bow, his smile broad and genuine. In spite of the circumstances, Lily could not help smiling back. "Did you want to drive us, or shall I have two horses saddled? Your seat has greatly improved this summer, and I'd not want you to fall out of practice."

This last was said with a lifted brow and teasing tone, and Lily could not help laughing in response, though she hoped she was not blushing. The first time they had gone riding together, she had been determined to enlist his connections, and eventually his aid, in solving the suspicious death of her father's friend. To do so, she had pretended to be as fond of riding as Mr. Spencer was. Though she had acquitted herself well enough for someone who had not sat a horse in two years, Matthew Spencer had seen through the ruse before the end of the morning.

In spite of that, he had been impressed enough with her determination—and her eventual success in uncovering the hands behind the murder—that they had become friends. They had gone riding together in London more than once since then, though Lily would never love the exercise as he would.

"Had I worn my habit, I'd not let you get away with such a challenge," Lily replied, giving her aunt's horse a pat on the nose while he snorted at her, hoping for a treat. "But if it is too painful for you to drive behind such a placid, uninteresting creature, I will allow you to have your own horses brought around."

"I'll not only be happy to sit behind him, I shall even insist that you be the one to drive us so you may see I am not such a snob as you suspect." He also reached out to pat the horse's nose, his fingers brushing hers as he did so and lingering for a moment before he turned back toward the house. "Would you like to come in for just a moment while I tell Eloisa and Matthew? They are at their lessons, but they will want to know where I am gone when they are finished."

Speaking with the children took a little longer than Lily expected. Mr. Spencer took the opportunity to introduce Lily to the high-spirited young Matthew, who insisted on showing her the places he had just that morning learned to find on his globe, and wanted to know which of them she had visited. Lily thought she went down in the boy's estimation when she admitted she had never left England, but he was delighted to find out she had a friend who had actually grown up in the West Indies.

In short order, though, Mr. Spencer bid his children farewell—Matthew and Eloisa decided to use his absence to plot their own voyage to the islands of the Caribbean—and Lily marveled all over again at what an attentive father he was.

The village was seated between Mr. Spencer's house and Longwood Cottage, so the drive would not be long. They headed back the way Lily had come, she feeling a little anxious about demonstrating her lack of expertise as a driver. She mentally scolded herself for the feeling—it wasn't as if she had any particular need to impress him, after all—but she couldn't help it. Ever since she'd been a child, she had hated to be less than proficient at anything she did.

But Mr. Spencer quickly distracted her, leaning back comfortably in the little seat and letting his arm trail along the board behind them as Lily sat upright, the ribbons resting firmly between her fingers.

"So you've not been to Hampshire in some time?" he asked. "You must be glad to see your aunt again. I am sorry that such an odd thing should mar your visit."

"Hopefully, it will not be marred too much," she replied. "Miss Clarke seems determined still to show Sir Edward and Lady Carroway the best foot Hampshire has to put forward. And I always enjoy my time with my aunt."

"And yet, you do me the honor of spending your morning with me instead of her." Mr. Spencer's voice was mild and unassuming, but she could feel his gaze fixed on her, though she kept hers planted firmly between the gently trotting horse's ears.

"I believe my aunt is planning to bring the others to the market once they have finished their morning exercise. And Miss Clarke has an errand to run first."

There was a pointed silence from the seat next to her, and Lily could feel the tension in his arm where it rested along the back of the seat. "I can't help suspecting, dear madam, that I will shortly find myself in the position of being used for my connections once more," he said gently. "May I ask whether your intent is to spend time at the market or to find out what you can about the Wrights?"

"Can I not wish to do both?" Lily said, still not looking at him, her voice quiet. Her heart was hammering far more than she wanted it to, and not because she was afraid of whoever had killed Mrs. Wright. "I will admit I have hopes that being approached by a familiar face may loosen a tongue or two in the village. But my aunt would have served just as well for such a purpose." She glanced sideways, meeting his eyes at last and hoping the uncertainty she was feeling did not show on her face.

"And yet you asked for my company?" His eyes were fixed on her, but she couldn't read the thoughts behind them. "Why is that?"

"I've not yet decided," Lily said, her tone as light as she could manage. She had to look away then, though she told herself it was because she needed to attend to the horse once more, and not because she didn't have the fortitude to continue meeting that blue-black gaze.

He laughed, and the tension of the moment was broken. "Well, then I shall at least be assured that this time you have some interest in my company as well as whatever other services I might provide. What more can a gentleman hope for?"

"Every lady enjoys being escorted by a handsome gentleman when she seeks to make a good impression in new company," Lily teased, glad for the return to levity.

"Ah, so this time you are using me for my face and figure?"

"Precisely."

He laughed again, and she could feel him relaxing in the seat once more. The remainder of the drive passed in friendly conversation. Before long the road in front of them was growing wider and smoother, eventually sweeping its way up toward the edge of the village.

The market was indeed in full swing, with shopkeepers out in front of their stores, farmers in from their farms, and men and women from the surrounding country displaying handicrafts and small goods for sale. Children dodged between buildings and around shoppers, earning the occasional scolding or smack from the people they bumped into, and the innkeeper was doing a roaring business where he had set up tables outside to serve ale. The cacophony of village life filled the air: shouted instructions and friendly greetings and the occasional yowl of a cat who objected to the crowd.

Mr. Spencer waited until she had navigated the cart in front of one of the inn's hitching posts, then turned to her with a wide smile. "Well then, Mrs. Adler, shall we see what we can discover?"

"You truly have no objection?" Lily felt suddenly uncertain as he swung down from the seat to tip the stableboy who had sprung up, as if from nowhere, to attend to their horse. She handed down the basket that she had tucked below the seat—it wouldn't do to browse the village market, after all, and not purchase anything.

He set the basket on the ground, then held up his hand to help her down. When she was on the ground, he bent forward to murmur in her ear, "I am intrigued to see not only what you uncover but how you uncover it."

"I hope I'll not disappoint you, then," Lily laughed, feeling a little knot of anxiety in her stomach. What if she couldn't find anything that would help? What if the magistrate and coroner believed the Wrights, that a ghost had killed their mother, and she had to leave her aunt in a village with a murderer?

The look he gave her was warm and encouraging as he retrieved the basket and handed it to her. "You couldn't," he said simply, offering his arm and smiling as she tucked her free hand into his elbow. "Besides, I see that Mrs. Dennings is selling her gingerbread this morning. That alone would be worth the trip, with no room for disappointment. And in fact, if you want gossip, that is the exact place we should start."

Mrs. Dennings turned out to be the innkeeper's wife, a gray-haired woman with plump cheeks, a wide smile, and a shrewd eye to keep on the customers at her husband's tables. But she smiled with pleasure when she saw the two of them approaching.

"Mr. Spencer! How do, sir? Have you come to fetch some gingerbread for the little ones?" She bustled over to the white-clothed table where a girl was keeping watch over the baked goods and shooing away birds and hungry children alike.

"Indeed yes, Mrs. Dennings. Eloisa and Matthew would bar me from the nursery forever if they discovered I had been to market day and failed to bring them any." Mr. Spencer nodded gravely to the girl. "Miss Dennings, you look very fetching in that bonnet."

Miss Dennings, who couldn't have been more than eleven years old, blushed and curtsied. "Thankee, Mr. Spencer. How many cakes o' gingerbread will you be wanting?"

"A package of four, if you please, to take home. And one each for my companion and me. Mrs. Adler, have you met Mrs. Dennings and her granddaughter before?"

"Only in passing, I believe." Lily nodded a greeting to them both. "I am staying with my aunt at Longwood Cottage, but I've not been in the village in some time."

"Miss Pierce's niece, then?" Mrs. Dennings looked Lily over with a gaze that was shrewd but kind, nodding as she selected four rounds of gingerbread and handed them to her granddaughter to tie up in brown paper. "Miss Clarke was speaking of you last time we crossed paths. My sympathies on your husband's death, ma'am, though I understand he's been gone some years now. Still. A hard passing is a hard passing."

Lily found herself struggling to know exactly what to say in response, suddenly too aware of the way her hand rested in the curve of Mr. Spencer's elbow. She was glad that Miss Dennings chose that moment to hand her the packet of gingerbread, and she took her time about settling it in the basket so she did not have to take his arm again.

Luckily, Mrs. Dennings had continued on without waiting for a response. "Miss Clarke said Miss Pierce was mightily looking forward to your visit this autumn. A real gentlewoman, your aunt is, but not so high in the instep that she don't care about folks in the village, if you'll pardon my saying."

"You may always feel free to praise my aunt or Miss Clarke to me, Mrs. Dennings, and I am sure the praise cannot be too high," Lily said, recovering herself enough to look up from the basket at last.

"Indeed, no." Mrs. Dennings was clearly warming to her audience. "Just last month Miss Pierce and I was in the bakery at the same time, and she was so good as to ask after how my husband's rheumatism was doing in the damp we had, and it had to have been half a year since I'd mentioned it to her. I was much obliged, I don't mind telling you."

"I hope you were able to give her a favorable report?" Mr. Spencer put in.

"Not so good that Miss Clarke didn't send over a bottle of her own liniment for him the very next day, bless her. And I hear she sent one to Walter Cox as well, since I'd said I suspected he was also suffering from the rheumatism in his shoulders this fall, though he'd never say as much. Too proud, poor man, to admit he's getting on in years." She laughed. "Though I've still got near a decade on him, so he may rest easy there at least."

"I would never believe it if I did not hear it from your own lips," Mr. Spencer said gallantly.

She laughed again. "You are a flatterer, you are. Watch out for him, Mrs. Adler," she added, turning to fix Lily with an eye that had the glint of a woman on the hunt for gossip. "Men with a silver tongue like his are known to turn a lady's head, they are. I well remember the type."

Lily, caught off guard by the sudden attack, felt a wave of heat creeping over her collarbone and cheeks, and she could see Mr. Spencer biting his lips to keep from laughing at her embarrassment. She wondered for a moment if he had brought her to Mrs. Dennings expecting just such an unsubtle inquiry, and she had to resist the urge to narrow her eyes at him.

Instead, she gave the innkeeper's wife a calm smile. "You need not fear for me on that score, Mrs. Dennings. My aunt has made sure it takes somewhat more than a handsome smile or a charming tongue to turn my head."

"That I can believe!" Mrs. Dennings laughed comfortably. "A wise woman, your aunt. Though I hear tell she led you and your friend into a spot of trouble yesterday morning?" Her gaze sharpened once more; denied gossip on one front, she was clearly determined to winkle it out on another.

It was exactly the opening Lily had been hoping for; in her eagerness, she didn't realize that she had taken Mr. Spencer's arm once more and given his elbow an excited squeeze. "Mrs. Dennings, it was the most shocking thing," she said, opening her eyes wide and leaning forward. The innkeeper's wife leaned forward in response. "Mr. Spencer had told us all about the Wrights' ghost, of course, and what fun it seemed to go to Belleford in person. How could we have known that we would find poor Mrs. Wright dead when we arrived? And then the magistrate would not let us leave." She shuddered, a gesture that was not quite feigned as she remembered Mrs. Wright's bloated, frightened face gazing out of the twisted bedclothes. "Something was not right in that house, but whether it was a ghost or otherwise, I could not say."

Mrs. Dennings frowned thoughtfully. "Beth, go check if the next batch of gingerbread is ready to go in the oven."

"But—" Beth broke off at a sharp look from her grandmother and, looking grumpy, hurried inside to do what she was told.

Mrs. Dennings didn't say anything for a moment, taking her time about rearranging the baking that was set on the table in front of her. Slowly, she pulled out two more pieces of gingerbread. "Mrs. Adler, I'm not one to gossip," she said, her expression completely serious as she raised her eyes at last. Lily, straight-faced, nodded. "But I won't argue with what you just said. I've lived in this village my whole life, and the Wrights have been the family at Belleford for far longer than that. But ever since old Mr. Wright died . . ." She shook her head. "Mrs.

Wright was a cheerful, pleasant woman when she came here as a new bride, and she took as much interest in the village as any of us could expect—more, in some cases. She was good to folks who needed help. Much like your aunt and Miss Clarke," she added, almost as a polite afterthought. "But . . . over time, she changed."

"Changed?" Lily murmured encouragingly.

"She was a devoted mother once the little 'uns came, and if she hovered a bit, who could blame her?" Mrs. Dennings wrapped up the two pieces of gingerbread separately, her expression grim. "Plenty of women in her position have little else to occupy them. But she was too devoted, if you ask me. And now she don't want to let neither of them out of her sight since her husband died, and that's more'n five years ago."

"Dear me," Lily said as she accepted the second parcel and Mr. Spencer handed over payment. "That must have been so frustrating for them. Mr. Wright seems exactly the sort of young man who would have much preferred to go to London."

"Aye, that he would, I'm sure." Mrs. Dennings shook her head. "And he gets up to enough mischief here, I'm sure there's plenty of folks as wouldn't mind if he—ah, good day to you, Mrs. Cartwright! Yes, I have your order ready—won't be but a moment." She turned back to them. "A pleasure to meet you, Mrs. Adler, and always to see you, Mr. Spencer. If you'll be so good, I must be getting on."

"Of course," Mr. Spencer said quickly. "Market day waits for none of us."

They stepped back as more customers approached, and Beth returned to the table to help her grandmother. Lily handed Mr. Spencer his share of the gingerbread, and they enjoyed the rare treat of eating and strolling at the same time for several silent moments while they put some distance between themselves and Mrs. Dennings.

"Well?" Mr. Spencer asked at last. "What did you make of that?"

"That you were right—the gingerbread is excellent," Lily said, already brushing crumbs from her skirt before crumpling the brown paper and tucking it into the basket.

"I meant about what she shared," Mr. Spencer said, sounding a little exasperated.

Lily couldn't help smiling at him, but her expression quickly turned thoughtful. "I know. It certainly was interesting, though on its own, not much use. What would be useful to know is what Mr. and Miss Wright thought of their mother's hovering."

"They're not likely to share that with the wider world, especially not now," Mr. Spencer said, tossing his own paper into the basket and taking it from her. "Especially not Miss Wright. She's a reserved sort of person."

"Would you say the same for Mr. Wright?"

He started to shake his head, then nodded slowly. "Thomas Wright is sociable, certainly, but not open. I do not know him well—" He cast a sideways glance at her. "As you gathered yesterday morning, his is not the sort of company I find pleasant to keep overmuch of. And as a single man with no children and few responsibilities of his own to attend to, his time is spent very differently from mine. But I would say he is not the sort to make his personal feelings known, however outgoing he may appear in company."

"I would dearly like to know what sort of mischief he gets up to that would make the locals happy to see him gone to London," Lily murmured as they stopped in front of the dry goods store. After asking for two yards of cotton ribbon in a yellow and white stripe—it was exactly the sort of thing Susan would like—she cast a sideways glance at her companion. "Have you any idea what she might have meant?"

Mr. Spencer was running a hand over a pretty bolt of printed cotton. "Eloisa will need new frocks soon; she is growing like a weed," he murmured. "I would assume he gets up to the same sort of things all bored young men do—drinking and gambling and generally being a nuisance too late at night."

"So out all night rather than rising early?" Lily asked, remembering Mr. Wright's surprise to find guests arriving at Belleford at the same time he was.

"Almost certainly." Mr. Spencer nodded to the shopkeeper as Lily paid for her ribbon, reclaimed the basket, and took his arm once more. "Do you want me to find out where he was?"

"Can you?"

He laughed. "I make no promises, but I can certainly see what I uncover. If it would help."

"It would." Lily frowned, glancing around the bustling, happy market. Neither of the Wrights were there—no surprise—but she caught sight of Isaiah, the Wrights' footman, accompanied by one of the Wrights' maids. They each carried a large basket as they moved from stall to stall. The girl's back was to her, so she couldn't see which one it was; they had both been slight and short, with dark hair. Judging by the maid's brisk walk and confident posture, she thought it might be Etta, who she suspected was the elder of the two, but it was impossible to tell at a distance. The two servants moved so quickly through the throng that she didn't long have a view of them. "I cannot like the idea of leaving my aunt with such a thing unsolved. Especially when we so unwittingly stumbled into being involved." Lily shivered, remembering a similar stumble when she first returned to London, a mistake that had placed her squarely in the sights of a murderer who thought she knew more than she did. The idea of anyone thinking the same of her aunt left her chilled. "I would be too afraid that I was leaving her in danger."

"And you've no confidence in our magistrate to deal with the matter?"

Lily glanced up at him. "Do you?"

He didn't answer, and for a while they focused on browsing the remaining stalls and tables. It was not a large market, so it didn't take them long to make a full circle. But the death of Mrs. Wright, and whether or not blame for her passing could be laid at the spectral feet of Belleford's ghost, was on more than one tongue. Lily didn't have to ask any more questions, only keep her ears perked for any interesting information the locals let fall.

Once or twice, Mr. Spencer was hailed by the gossiping parties, as word seemed to have gotten round that he had been there the very morning after the old lady's mysterious death. Each time, Lily was happy to hang back and let him take the lead in sharing what he knew, and his friendly, approachable manner served well to get just about anyone talking. But there was little said that she didn't already know until they reached the bookseller, the last stall that they had not yet visited on the village green.

"Well, I'm not one to speak ill of the dead," a brightly hatted matron—a lawyer's wife, Lily thought, or perhaps the mother of a gentleman farmer—was saying to the bookseller as he wrapped up her purchases. "But maybe now she's gone, poor Mr. Samson will be able to get the rectory repaired. Falling down around the back, it is. And the last time they collected funds for it, Mrs. Wright, I don't mind telling you, refused to contribute her share."

"I'd heard tell they were short of what they needed, but I'd no idea that was why," the bookseller said, shaking his head.

Lily picked up an almanac, just to have something to do with her hands, and kept her head toward the pages while she eavesdropped. But she glanced out of the corner of her eye in time to see the matron lean forward.

"When good Mr. Wright was alive, they was always willing to put funds where they was needed in the village. He had a care for their name and credit, them having been here so long. But it's not been the same since. Miserly, she is."

"Maybe good Mr. Wright ran through all the funds and she didn't have any left," another shopper added, joining in the conversation with obvious eagerness. "After all, it isn't as if she gave Miss Selina any kind of real coming out. Not even a summer at one of those lovely seaside places. It's no surprise the poor girl never married."

"Dear me, I'd not thought of that," the matron replied, looking flustered. "Well, if that's the case, there's little wonder she kept such a tight rein on that flighty son of hers. Lord knows he'd be the type to run a family into the ground."

But that wasn't the case, Lily knew from Ofelia's discovery of Mrs. Wright's account books. She kept a tight rein on her children, certainly, but the matron had been correct in her first assessment: the family had plenty of funds, but Mrs. Wright, it seemed, had not cared to spend any of them. Lily frowned. Not even in the cause of repairing the rectory for the local minister, which was a serious breach of responsibility for a well-off family of local landowners.

"Did you wish to purchase that one, ma'am?"

Lily jumped a little as she discovered the bookseller standing just in front of her, a wide, beaming smile on his face as he gestured to the almanac she still held.

Still lost in her thoughts, Lily paid for the book, not wanting to draw attention to her eavesdropping.

Had Mrs. Wright's children been so accustomed to her tight-fisted ways that they took them for granted? Had they even known what she was withholding from them?

Or had one of them finally grown fed up with their mother's miserliness and decided to take control of their lives at last in the only way they could?

CHAPTER 9

After Mrs. Adler left, Ofelia went to join her husband and Miss Clarke in the garden, only to find them heading back toward the cottage.

"Lady Carroway!" Miss Clarke smiled at her. "I apologize for monopolizing dear Sir Edward's time. What a sweet husband you have found yourself." Taking Ofelia's arm in a comfortable, almost motherly manner, she nodded her thanks as Ned held the garden gate open for them. "Was there something you needed, my dear? Or were you simply in search of some fresh air?"

"In search of company," Ofelia said, allowing herself to be led inside as she glanced at the sky. "It looks as though it might come on to rain soon. You were wise, Miss Clarke, to take your exercise early in the morning."

"This time of year, I generally prefer a turn about the garden when the sun is a little higher, but today I cannot linger in my usual manner. Addie is preparing a basket for me to take to the poor Wrights as they have no cook right now, so I am afraid I must leave you to your own devices for a little while." Miss Clarke looked a little embarrassed as she spoke. Ofelia was not tall, but the other woman was short enough that she still had to look up to meet her eyes, her expression earnest. "I hope you will not mind entertaining yourselves for an hour or two?"

"On the contrary, Miss Clarke." Ofelia tried not to sound too eager as she spoke. "Would you care for some company on your excursion?"

★　★　★

"How very good of you, Miss Clarke, Lady Carroway. I do not know what we would do without our neighbors in such a time as this." Selina Wright's hands trembled as she gestured them to sit. "We are all topsy-turvy here, though Mr. Mears tries to keep us in order. And with no cook, we are certainly grateful for your kindness. Let me summon a servant to take it down to the kitchen."

They were in a downstairs parlor this time, its furniture even more ancient than the pieces in the family sitting room upstairs, its carpet just as worn. Ofelia perched a little anxiously on the edge of her chair, the threadbare cushion offering no comfort and the spindly legs quaking a little beneath her. She shifted forward, trying to put more of her weight on her feet and hoping her calves didn't begin cramping. Outside, the clouds had parted during their drive over, and the sunlight pressed against the windowpanes as though begging to come in. But there was a sharp draft in the room, and Ofelia could hear the low whine of the wind as it crept down the fireplace.

Spring in London had already left her wishing for the warmth of her home, and her first English winter was still to come. She tried not to shiver too obviously and was grateful that mourning visits were generally short enough that they hadn't needed to remove their coats and gloves.

On the drive over, she had tried to gently encourage Miss Clarke to talk about the Wrights. But while clearly happy to chat about her neighbors all day long, the sweet woman sadly knew very little about that family.

"We moved to Longwood Cottage some years before dear Mr. Wright—who was so respected in the neighborhood—passed on," she had said as they bounced along the muddy lane in the Carroways' pretty traveling carriage. "We came to know Mrs. Wright well enough, I suppose. As well as anyone could—she was a rather withdrawn, imperious woman. Very civil, of course," she had added hastily, smiling a little. "And with that elegance that so many women who are not me develop as they grow older."

"You are very elegant," Ofelia had protested, not quite honestly.

Miss Clarke had laughed. "You are a dear to say so, but after a decade living with Eliza, I know my strengths. Elegance is not one of them. Eliza says I am comfortable, and that is enough for me." She had frowned then, glancing out the window. "I never felt that was a word that could be applied to the Wrights. We never knew the children well—Miss Wright keeps to herself, quite content at home, it seems, though I talk with her at church, of course."

"And Mr. Wright?" Ofelia had hesitated, before adding with some delicacy, "Miss Pierce may have mentioned, but he made quite the impression on Mrs. Adler and me, and that was even before the sad business with his mother."

Miss Clarke had pursed her lips, the first sign of disapproval Ofelia had yet seen on her sunny face. "Mr. Wright hasn't much time for old ladies, I am afraid. Why he continues to make his life here in the country . . . But perhaps that is ungenerous. Perhaps he felt a great deal of responsibility toward his family after his father's death and stayed to manage the property and finances, as he should."

That, Ofelia thought as she remembered Mrs. Wright's ledger, was unlikely, but she did not press. Miss Clarke, still looking ashamed of her unkind words, had turned the conversation to the Carroways' travel to Somerset. Ofelia, who had never been there, answered a little absently, her mind still turning over the puzzle of the Wright children and their contradictory personalities.

Now, Miss Wright seemed to gather herself together. She looked almost ghostly herself, her cheeks sallow against the dark cloth of her black dress, as she took a deep breath before standing and crossing to the thick, tasseled pull that hung in one corner of the room. She gave it a sharp tug, the long white shawl that trailed from her arms shivering with the movement. Even that little bit of effort seemed to exhaust her, and she pulled the shawl more closely around her shoulders as she drifted into the nearest chair. It was large and upholstered in dark fabric, and it seemed to swallow her so that only her pale face and the white of her shawl stood out against it. When no servants were forthcoming in response to her summons, her expression fell.

"I forgot, they had to go out at the market today. And we've told Mr. Mears he isn't to go trudging up and down the stairs just because he hears a bell—he simply isn't up to it any longer, poor man, though he insists he needn't stop working. You would think we would have learned to manage with only four servants by now, but everything is just so . . ." She trailed off, looking as though she were about to cry.

Ofelia's heart jumped in sympathy for the poor, overwhelmed woman. "I would be happy to take the basket down to the kitchen," she said, standing. "Would you tell me which way to find the stairs?"

Miss Clarke was nodding in approval, but Miss Wright looked shocked. "Lady Carroway, I could not possible ask you to—"

"Nonsense," said Ofelia gently, already hefting the heavy basket. "We came intending to ease your burdens, not add to them. And there is no reason I cannot carry a basket a little distance. Where shall I find the kitchen?"

Miss Wright finally relented, and Ofelia soon found herself walking through the deserted hallways toward the back staircase, the sound of her footsteps disappearing into the cavernous ceilings above her.

The halls grew even more chilled the farther she got from the front rooms, and Ofelia wondered how often the fires were lit. If there were only three people in residence, and Mrs. Wright had been as tightfisted with funds as her account book suggested, it wouldn't be surprising if she didn't feel it necessary to heat much of the house. But Ofelia, shivering a little, had a hard time imagining that the younger Wrights would feel the same. What would they do now that their mother was no longer there to keep everything under her rigid control? And was that a reason one of them might have wanted her dead?

She found the back staircase eventually—narrow, uncarpeted, and dark as it descended toward the kitchens and male servants' sleeping quarters. Ofelia was halfway down, the basket bumping against her knees with each step, when she thought she heard someone behind her.

"Hello?" she called, turning back, only to be confronted with the empty expanse of steps. Frowning, she went back a little way, peering around the last sharp bend, but there was no one there either. For a moment she stood, uncertain, before shaking her head. It was the height of folly to let all the talk of ghosts and hauntings leave her jumping at every creak of the stairs. Old houses made plenty of noise. And Miss Wright had said the younger servants were out at the market. If it had been the creaky old butler, he would certainly have made more noise than the quiet sound of footsteps. There was no logical reason to be worried.

Satisfied, and glad no one had been there to see her jumpiness, Ofelia continued downstairs, arriving in the kitchen just as the door to the outside swung open. The manservant and one of the housemaids blew in with the sharp autumn breeze, talking with quiet animation as they lugged their baskets with both hands.

They didn't see Ofelia right away, and she took the moment to study them. Their faces were tense and anxious, their voices humming with worry as they argued. But they stood near each other with perfect ease, in spite of their disagreement. However long they had been working for the Wrights, it had been enough for them to get to know each other quite well.

"You still oughtn't have said anything to her, Etta," the manservant, Isaiah, was saying as he hefted his basket onto the table and began unwinding his muffler. "We don't need to be spreading any more gossip than is already flying around."

"It wasn't gossip," Etta protested. "She asked me how things were at the house, and I told her truthfully. Was I supposed to not say he'd seen the ghost again?"

"Yes." Isaiah snapped, sounding exasperated as he took her basket for her and placed it on the table as well. "And you shouldn't be carrying something that heavy either—it isn't good for your arm."

"My arm is fine these days, and I can pull my own weight—" Etta caught sight of Ofelia and jumped, gasping so loudly that it was nearly a shriek. Isaiah snatched up a heavy pan off the table and spun around.

Ofelia, started herself, took a step back before she recovered. "My apologies, I'd no intention of frightening you."

"Oh no, miss . . . I mean, Lady Carroway, was it? I'm so sorry." Etta curtsied, while Isaiah, looking embarrassed, quickly set the pan down and bowed. "We just didn't expect you in the kitchen is all. Can we help you?"

Ofelia hefted her own basket. "Miss Clarke and I came with a few things for the household, to ease the work in such a difficult time. I am afraid no one was able to respond to Miss Wright's summons, so I offered to bring them down."

"Oh, that's very good of you, your ladyship," Etta said, stepping forward to take the basket, though Isaiah beat her to it, giving a pointed look at her arm. She rolled her eyes at him briefly. "Just put it on the table, then, and I'll take care of it with the rest of them. Is that a pie I see on top? That's so kind, thank you," she added, turning back to Ofelia, her manner surprisingly forthright and friendly given the circumstances. "Though I am sorry you had to go to all the trouble of bringing it down here. Mr. Mears is a little distracted today—I'm sure he didn't hear the bell—and I never know where Alice has got to. Will you go check on Mr. Mears, Isaiah?"

"Certainly," he said, clearly unbothered by her giving him instructions. He bowed to Ofelia once more before leaving the kitchen, heading down one of the other long halls that led into the depths of the house.

"Was there anything else you needed, Lady Carroway? May I show you back upstairs?" Etta asked, already hovering over the baskets that needed to be unpacked.

"No, no need. I can find my own way, I'm sure." Ofelia hesitated. She wanted to get back upstairs to find out what else Miss Wright might reveal. But the Wrights weren't the only ones who lived in the house. And servants were often far chattier than those they waited on. There was always the chance Etta might look askance at her questions or report them to her employers, but Ofelia decided not to worry about that. The opportunity was too good to pass up.

"Did I hear you say the gray lady had made another appearance? How chilling!" She pretended a shiver, pleased to discover that it was indeed pretend, and whatever momentary nerves had affected her on the stairs had passed. "That must have been terrifying, so soon after . . ." Her words faded away as she watched the maid with wide-eyed, encouraging interest.

"Oh yes, my lady," Etta agreed, shivering a little herself as she swiftly unpacked and sorted the things in the baskets. "Mr. Wright saw her again last night, or early this morning I suppose. I'd have yelled my head off if it had been me, but he's made of sturdier stuff. Just told her to be gone after the sorrow she had caused. It was tremendously brave of him, I think. She didn't say anything, of course—she never does—just drifted away down the hall."

"And he told you about it this morning?"

For the first time, Etta hesitated, looking a little unsure. Her hands hovered over the packages on the table for a moment before she seemed to remember what she was doing. Turning away from the table, she crossed over to the fireplace, where it was clear that most of the cooking in the old house was still done. "He told all of us, my lady," she said at last, laying wood on the smoldering coals and poking at the fire a bit to encourage it to grow once more. "Wanted us all to be on our guard, after . . . after what happened. Poor Mrs. Wright," she added, setting down the poker and turning back to where Ofelia waited. There was something a little unconvincing in her words, and Ofelia wondered whether Etta had much cared for "poor Mrs. Wright" when she was living.

"I am sure that must have been unnerving for you," Ofelia said. "Miss Wright told us you had your own run-in with this specter?"

"Oh yes," Etta agreed, nodding rapidly. "It was bad enough, her chasing me like she did—that's why Isaiah was so worried about my arm, you know. I fell down the stairs and sprained my wrist a bit, though it's much better now. But it gives me a fright every time I think of it. And now to think what she can do, and it might have been me . . ."

Behind her, the wood in the fireplace caught at last, crackling loudly. Both women flinched, startled by the sound, and Etta rushed to the fireplace to adjust the draught.

Ofelia followed. "How did you come face to face with the gray lady?" she asked, warming to her questions. "Did you hear her? What did she do?"

But her eagerness seemed to put Etta on guard. Ofelia could see the head housemaid shoot her a quick, frowning glance before turning to the line of kettles and pots hanging on the wall. Fetching one, she carried it over to the table.

"I heard a noise, I think, and got up to see what it was," she said at last, opening a drawer and pulling out several large, gleaming knives. "By that point, the gray lady had been coming and going for some months, and I wanted to see her. More fool, me," she added, her voice as sharp as the knife she was now wielding to chop through the pile of carrots with fierce precision. The quick, rhythmic sound of the knife hitting the wood made Ofelia take an involuntary step back. "It was a scary night and not something I like to think about." Pausing, she looked up to meet Ofelia's eyes at last, her hand tight around the handle of the knife. "You must excuse me, Lady Carroway, but I still need to prepare supper for those of us belowstairs, though I know Mr.

and Miss Wright will enjoy what your girl has sent. Is there anything else I can help you with?"

There was a finality in her words. For whatever reason, Etta was ready to be done talking. There was no arguing with that, not without provoking questions that she had no desire to answer, so Ofelia simply shook her head. "No, not at all. I'll leave you to your work."

She could feel Etta's eyes on her as she left the kitchen, and the sound of chopping didn't resume until she was well out of sight.

Ofelia was flustered enough by the end of the exchange that she took a wrong turn, heading further into the warren of unused larders and stillrooms rather than back toward the stairs. She was so busy turning over what Etta had said that it took her a moment to realize she was going the wrong way; when she did, she sighed in frustration and turned back. As she did, she heard two voices at the end of one of the branching halls and paused to peer around the corner.

Isaiah stood there, his head tilted down a little bit to speak with the other maid—Ofelia knew Etta had said her name just a few minutes before but couldn't for the life of her remember what it was. As she watched, Isaiah bent his head a little further, and the maid reached up to loop what looked like a muffler around his neck.

Ofelia couldn't see their expressions at this distance, but the maid's movements were fidgety, and her voice as it carried down the hall had a touch of nervousness to it.

"I knitted it myself, you know. Since days are getting so chilly now." The maid stepped back, eyeing her handiwork. "There's a few mistakes, but I needed to practice. The next one has got to be just perfect, you see."

Isaiah smiled and ruffled her hair as though she were a child, and indeed, she was nearly a foot shorter than his tall, broad-shouldered frame. "Of course you do, Mouse," he said. Ofelia thought he might have even winked. "I'm happy to be your practice. And it's lovely and warm. I thank you."

The maid grew even fidgetier, hunching her shoulders and looking away. Her whispered "I'm glad you like it" barely carried down the hall to where Ofelia stood.

"Have you seen Mr. Mears around?" Isaiah continued, giving the muffler a comfortable stroke. "How soft you made it! The next one will be perfect, I'm sure."

Ofelia didn't want them to see her, so she slipped back down the hall toward the stairs, wondering as she did if there was romance blooming belowstairs. It wouldn't be an uncommon thing—though she would bet money that talkative, outgoing Etta was more the sort of match the handsome manservant was looking for, gifts of mufflers aside.

The thought brought her back to Etta's shifty behavior at the end of their conversation. The head housemaid was clearly hiding something about her run-in with the gray lady.

Ofelia frowned, stopping just outside the door of the sitting room. Inside, she could hear the quiet murmur of Miss Clarke's soothing voice, but she wasn't ready to rejoin the polite visit yet.

Etta had told everyone that being chased by the ghost was the reason she hurt her arm. But what if she had been injured doing something else that night, and she had settled on the ghost as a convenient excuse? There were any number of things a servant might get up to and want to hide from their employers. Some of them might be innocuous enough—but others could get a housemaid sacked, arrested, or worse.

What if Mrs. Wright had found out what Etta had really been up to that night, and Etta had decided to take matters into her own hands?

Ofelia had been lost in her thoughts, staring unseeing ahead of her, for some moments before she realized she was not alone. In the doorway across the hall, half hidden in the shadows, stood the wizened butler, his eyes fixed silently on her.

Ofelia jumped, just managing to catch her shriek of surprise so that it only came out as a strangled squeak.

"Can I assist you, Lady Carroway?" he asked, taking a step forward.

Heart racing, she wondered how long he had been there. "No," she said abruptly. She let out a shaky breath, giving him one more wide-eyed look before she pushed opened the door to the sitting room. Miss Clarke was attempting without success to stir up the fire against the chill in the room, and Miss Wright had sunk even further into her chair until it seemed like it was trying to devour her. Their conversation broke off as they greeted her in the hushed voices suited to a condolence visit.

Ofelia suppressed a shiver. When she turned to shut the door, the butler was still across the hall, watching her silently. She met his eyes only for a moment before she pulled the door firmly closed behind her.

CHAPTER 10

The rumor spread through the market before Lily and Mr. Spencer left.

They were just heading toward their cart, having made a full circuit and gathered what Lily thought would be all the gossip for the day, when her ear caught the edge of a conversation.

"And Mrs. Dennings told me that, according to the maid, poor Mr. Wright saw the ghastly being again last night."

"How dreadful. Why won't it leave them in peace now it's done its terrible deed? Do you think it wants something more from them?"

"Perhaps dear Mrs. Wright was just the beginning. After all, there is no saying what a ghost might want or what leads it to stalk the manor at night."

Lily laid a hand on Mr. Spencer's arm, drawing him to a halt in front of a flower seller's cart at the edge of the market. She pretended to eye the blooms while she listened attentively, watching the speakers out of the corner of her eye.

They were two girls who looked just old enough to have been released from the care of their governesses, but not yet old enough to have left their parents' homes. Well dressed, but not what London society would consider wealthy by the look of them, they were being chaperoned by a young man who was perhaps a few years older, and he rolled his eyes at their whispered conversation.

"Mama won't be pleased if she hears you going on like we live in one of Mrs. Radcliffe's novels, Judith," he said with all the superiority of an elder brother.

"Nonsense, Andrew," one of the girls said stoutly. "The gray lady of Belleford is practically a fact of life by now, not something out of a novel. And Mama will be just as eager to hear the news as you are, for all you pretend otherwise."

"And you cannot deny the ghost must be responsible for what has happened," the other girl added with a great deal of spirit. "Even the magistrate and coroner see no other explanation for Mrs. Wright's death."

"They have not said so," the older brother protested, but the two girls jumped on his words before he could say anything else.

"The coroner ruled this morning that it was death by person or persons unknown. If that isn't a ghost, what else is it?"

"When he was testifying at the inquest, Mr. Powell said he saw no means for anyone to enter or exit the room during the night while the door was locked."

"And both Mrs. Dennings and Mr. Shaw agree that nothing living could be responsible, and Mr. Shaw is one of the most well-read men in the village, so I really think you ought to trust his opinion, at least."

The three young people moved off, arguing in voices that were growing more heated. Lily turned back to Mr. Spencer, intending to apologize for the delay, only to find him holding out a small posy of flowers that he had clearly just purchased.

"For me?" she asked, feeling flustered.

"Of course," he replied, a puzzled smile on his face. "Who else would they be for?"

Lily took them a little hesitantly, suddenly distracted from the conversation she had just overheard. He needed to buy something, she reasoned with herself, since she had forced them to a halt right in front of the flower seller. There was no need to read anything significant into the gesture. Still, she took a deep breath of the flowers' sweet scent before laying the bouquet gently in her basket. "Thank you."

"I take it you were listening to what those young people were saying? About the coroner's inquest?" he asked in a low voice as they continued out of the village square.

"Murder by person or persons unknown is hardly an uncommon verdict from an inquest," Lily said, her brows drawing together in thought. "What matters is whether the magistrate leaves it at that or continues to investigate. Do you think Mr. Powell will?"

Mr. Spencer didn't say anything for a moment as they came to where the gig was tied up. He took the basket from her and slid it under the seat, then held out his hand to assist her in climbing over the wheel. "I do not know," he said at last. "Mr. Powell is a diligent man, but not what one might call a creative one. I could easily see him abandoning a problem that perplexes him too much."

"Well, then." Lily settled her skirts around her, then took the reins as Mr. Spencer untied the horse's head from the picket post and climbed up next to her. "As I, for one, do not like the idea of my aunt living in the same neighborhood as a murderer, it seems we must take matters into our own hands."

"But Mrs. Adler, you heard what those gossiping children said. Mr. Powell is of the opinion that there was no way for anyone to go in or out of that room."

Lily shot him an exasperated look as they began to roll away from the village. "Please do not tell me you also believe it was a ghost."

"No indeed, but if the crime itself seems impossible . . ."

"Nothing is impossible, sir." Lily turned back to watch the road. Something in her determination must have been conveyed along the reins, because the placid horse began to trot with more purpose, his ears pricking up and the gig rolling faster over the dusty track. "A woman was murdered, which means someone must have done it. If we can discover who it was, how the deed was accomplished may become clear."

"You make it sound so simple," Mr. Spencer said with a disbelieving laugh.

"It is simple." Lily took a deep breath. "But things which are simple are not always easy. And I have a feeling this puzzle may be quite difficult to untangle."

★ ★ ★

When Lily returned to Longwood Cottage, she found her aunt bustling around the front hall, directing her maid, Addie, to prepare a basket with oils, soaps, herbs, and cloths.

"What is it, aunt?" she asked as she began to untie her bonnet.

"Oh! Lily, I am glad you're back. I need to get to Belleford, and Miss Clarke and Lady Carroway have not yet returned with the carriage." Eliza took her own hat from a peg in the hall. "With the coroner's inquest done—I assume you heard about that during your snooping at the market? Yes, I know you, and it *was* snooping—some women from the village are going to help prepare Mrs. Wright's body for burial." Tying the ribbons under her chin, Eliza raised a curious brow at her niece. "Do you wish to come with me?"

Lily was just handing her market basket over to Addie; the question made her freeze, her fingers locked on the handle for a moment before a puzzled look from Addie recalled her to herself. She let the basket go slowly.

The last body she had prepared for burial had been her husband's. That had been more than two years ago—nearly three, now—but the memory was still strong. And while she knew she should jump at the chance to visit Belleford once more, she wasn't sure she was ready to participate so intimately in the rituals of death, however common they were.

When she looked up, Eliza was watching her closely, a sympathetic look on her face. "You needn't say yes if you don't wish to."

Lily took a deep breath. "Perhaps I might accompany you, even if I do not assist? I think with the other women there, you will hardly need another set of hands."

"Perhaps you might direct the servants in draping the parlor," Eliza suggested. "The funeral is to be tomorrow, so someone will be sitting up with the body tonight." There was a hint of a smile on her face, in spite of her sympathy, as she added, "You never know what might be said while you are there. Mr. Wright, after all, is a chatty sort of fellow."

Lily nodded, firmly resetting her own hat. There was no reason to be maudlin. She had set herself a task, and she was going to complete it. "Indeed, Aunt. I would be happy to accompany you."

Eliza looked a little smug as she turned away. "I thought you might."

★　★　★

They arrived on the heels of two other women from the neighborhood, a Mrs. Banning and the widowed Mrs. Cutter, who Lily had met on a few other visits and didn't much care for. But she didn't need to spend much time with them. They were shown into the parlor, where Selina Wright was drifting aimlessly about the room, almost like a ghost herself. Her white shawl trailed from one arm, and she was touching things on shelves and moving books absently from one spot to another with what seemed like no real purpose or even awareness of what she was doing. She looked pale, listless, and overwhelmed, and she stared at her guests for several blank moments before she understood why they were there. When she did, she looked like she was about to weep with relief and was quick to accept their assistance in preparing her mother's body for burial.

"Is it dreadful that I feel so overcome at the thought of doing so myself?" Miss Wright asked fretfully, glancing from neighbor to neighbor. "Thomas will sit up with her tonight, of course, before the funeral tomorrow. But I just cannot bear—" She broke off, lifting a vinaigrette of smelling salts to her nose and shuddering.

"It seems perfectly understandable to me, my dear, given the circumstances," said Mrs. Banning briskly, ushering the younger woman into a seat when it seemed like she might begin her wandering again. She fussed about a bit, settling Miss Wright's shawl more firmly about her shoulders. "Of course you'd wish to be spared such thoughts and memories."

"My niece, Mrs. Adler, would be happy to bear you company while we see to the preparations," Eliza suggested. "She might even direct the servants in preparing whatever room needs to be arranged for tonight. We will see to the other preparations."

"You are all so kind," Miss Wright said, wiping her eyes with a frothy lace handkerchief. "I truly do not know what we would do without the kindness of our neighbors under such dreadful circumstances."

Mrs. Banning and Mrs. Cutter murmured further condolences, patting Miss Wright's hands and making sure she was comfortably settled before one of the maids appeared to show them upstairs.

"You just missed Miss Clarke and your friend, Mrs. Adler," Miss Wright said, seeming to pull her mind back to her present circumstances with great effort as Lily settled into a chair of her own. "Miss—no, *Lady* Carroway, is that right?"

"Were they here?" Lily asked, only a little surprised. "How very like Miss Clarke. She is forever trying to care for everyone who crosses her path."

"A very generous woman," Miss Wright agreed, her voice trembling. "And your friend seems a very genteel sort of girl. I am afraid I was not the best company—but I hope they will not hold that against me, under the circumstances," she added, her eyes welling with tears again. "I know everyone wishes to be kind, but trying to hold myself together and have anything resembling a normal conversation . . ."

"I understand, Miss Wright," Lily said gently. She wanted to encourage Miss Wright to talk about her mother, to feel out the women's relationship with each other, but clearly that had to be done delicately. Learning what Miss Wright did or did not know about her family's finances, and what she might have thought about how her mother kept her children so close to home, was essential, Lily was sure. But she wasn't sure how best to go about it. The fire spluttered in the hearth, as though the draught were not quite clear, and the smoke made Miss Wright cough.

Before Lily could figure out the right way to start, the door to the sitting room was flung open, and Thomas Wright came in like a small thunderstorm.

"Selina, has the magistrate been by at all today?" he demanded impatiently.

She glanced up into his glowering face, her mouth trembling. "No . . . no, I don't believe so. Not that I have seen, though I don't think he would ask for me. Was he supposed to?"

"That's just the thing." Mr. Wright scowled as he paced toward the fireplace. "Spencer here says he ought to have, given the results of the coroner's inquest. But I've not seen hide nor hair of him. Not since—" He broke off, glancing at his sister, and cleared his throat. "Not since the first time."

Lily, glancing toward the doorway, was surprised to see Mr. Spencer standing there, his handsome face drawn into a concerned frown. Neither man had yet caught sight of her, as her chair was to the side of the room, and both were focused on Miss Wright.

"I apologize for intruding," Mr. Spencer said, crossing the room to take the hand Miss Wright held out to him. "My own inclination is to let you grieve in peace. But I wanted to impress upon both of you how important it is that Mr. Powell act."

"Our mother is not yet in the ground, Spencer," Thomas Wright said as he crossed to his sister and planted himself between them. "I'm sure you mean well, but we have more to think about just now than what Mr. Powell might be doing with his day."

"If you have not the energy to stir him," Mr. Spencer said, "then your neighbors must until you can do so yourself."

Lily spoke up. "It is in your best interest, Mr. Wright—you and your sister—that Mr. Powell do all he can to find out what happened to your mother."

Both the men were startled, and even Miss Wright looked a little surprised, though whether that was because she had forgotten her guest's presence or because she was taken aback by the speech itself, Lily could not say.

"Mrs. Adler!" Mr. Wright bowed, clearly flustered, when he had recovered himself. He was dressed in full mourning, but it did not suit him as it did his sister. Whereas she seemed born to black draperies, his ruddy features and oily energy made an odd contrast with the somber look of his clothing. "My apologies, I did not see—that is, what are you doing here?"

Lily explained her aunt's errand and her own intent to be of service to Miss Wright. "And Mr. Spencer is quite right," she concluded, catching that gentleman's eye as she spoke. One corner of his mouth tilted up in a wry expression that was not quite a smile. Clearly, he was unsurprised to find her there. "I am shocked that the local magistrate should have stayed away so long. Mr. Powell ought to have been here as soon as the inquest concluded."

"To what purpose?" Selina Wright said. She lifted a handkerchief toward her eyes as she spoke, but her listlessness was suddenly replaced by a sharp tone. "I know I've no wish to have him poking around, asking intrusive questions while we grieve."

"It is his duty to find out what happened," Lily said, not sure whether to be surprised or suspicious that the other woman seemed so unbothered by the magistrate's lack of action. "Do you wish him to shirk that duty? When it was your own mother's life that was taken?"

"But, Mrs. Adler"—Miss Wright's voice trembled once more—"we know what happened. We know who did it. What good can anyone do against a ghost?"

It took real effort on Lily's part not to scoff. "He might well conclude that your ghost was responsible," she said, just managing to keep the skepticism out of her voice. "But if he does so without a full examination of the circumstances, how will that appear to the rest of the village? It will be seen as a dereliction of duty on his part. And—forgive me for saying so—it will cast an unfortunate shadow on your family for as long as you remain in this neighborhood."

Miss Wright's puzzled expression said that she did not follow Lily's line of thought, but her brother clearly had no such difficulty. "You mean to say, ma'am, that if the magistrate does not exhaust all possible means of inquiry, there will be those who suspect either me or my sister," he said sharply. "And that those suspicions will take some time to fade."

"A great deal of time," Lily said as delicately as possible. "They might never disappear completely."

"But that is absurd!" Miss Wright protested feebly. "The whole village knows we loved our mother. Why else would we have remained by her side and shown her such devotion?"

Lily bit the inside of her cheek, holding back the list of reasons that was currently crowding her mind. To her relief, Mr. Spencer spoke up.

"I am afraid Mrs. Adler is correct in her assessment," he said gently, sitting down next to Miss Wright and taking her hand once more. She clutched at him, her eyes wide with worry. "Mr. Powell ought to have called here again. If he fails to do so, it could cast your entire household in a most unfortunate light."

"What should we do, then?" Mr. Wright asked, looking and sounding quite young. "There isn't anything Selina or I can do to make him come here, is there?"

Lily resisted the urge to roll her eyes, as unimpressed by his lack of backbone as she was by his sister's fluttering. Clearly, living in the shadow of their mother's control had done neither of the younger Wrights any favors.

"Go to him yourself," she suggested, a little more sharply than she intended. Taking a deep breath, she tried to sound more persuasive, more sympathetic. "He'll not turn you away if you call on him. Ask him what he intends to do. Tell him your own thoughts. If he sees you will not let the matter remain unresolved, he shall have no choice but to follow your lead."

"I don't think . . . that is . . ." Mr. Wright looked tense. "To be honest, I am not sure where I could begin. I saw the gray lady again last night, you know. What happened seems quite clear to me, and I haven't any other ideas to share with him."

"But he does not need to know that," Mr. Spencer said briskly. "I will come with you, and we will both speak with him. If he eventually concludes that you are correct, that will be the end of the matter. But he must be seen to be making the effort."

"You are too good, Mr. Spencer," Selina Wright said, still clinging to his hand even as he tried to stand. "What would we do without the kindness of our neighbors?"

"Then they should be off immediately," Lily suggested, holding down her exasperation once more. "The sooner they can speak with him, the sooner you will be able to put this dreadful business behind you and mourn your mother in peace."

It took several more minutes for them to be off—due in equal parts to Miss Wright's clinging and her brother's indecisiveness. But at last the men were gone, and Lily found that Miss Wright's interest in conversation had suddenly grown along with her trembling.

"Do you really think it is true?" she kept asking. "Do you think so, Mrs. Adler? Will our own neighbors suspect us of murder?"

"Not the best among them," Lily said, trying to sound soothing, though she did not entirely believe her own words. This time, she chose a seat where she could lean in and speak more intimately.

"As you said, they know your family. But even the occasional whisper is, I'm sure, more than you would wish to bear."

"What could we do if such a thing happened?"

"One hopes it would not. Otherwise, you and your brother might be forced to leave the neighborhood."

"Leave?" Miss Wright gaped at her in genuine horror. "Leave Belleford? But where could we go? I've never been further from home than five miles!"

"Never?" Lily could barely contemplate such a thing, especially for a woman from a family such as the Wrights.

"Never." Miss Wright shuddered, pulling her shawl more closely around her. "My father once tried to persuade me, when I was younger, to go away to school. He said I would enjoy being with other young ladies of my own age. But what enjoyment could one find away from the comforts of home? What could one possibly see or do that would be worth the arduousness of travel? I have never wished to leave."

"And does your brother feel the same?"

Miss Wright sighed, sounding like a world-weary old woman. "Thomas used to speak of going away to London. But I persuaded him it should be a dismal experience. Can you imagine living somewhere so dirty and noisy? And always surrounded by so many strangers, such busyness? No." Her expression took on a hint of self-satisfaction. "I soon convinced him that staying at Belleford would be far and away the better idea. And Mother had no wish for him to leave either, so he would have had to fund the endeavor entirely on his own, which Thomas would never manage to do—he has no head for accounting," she added in an undertone. "The dear boy. No, it was much better that he stay here, where Mother and I could look after him. He was much happier that way."

Again, Lily had to bite the inside of her cheek to keep from saying anything, whether to argue with Miss Wright's assessment of her brother's contentment or to point out that she herself usually resided in dirty, noisy, busy London and quite enjoyed it. Instead, she nodded, as if in agreement. "Then let us hope your brother's errand is successful and that you will not have to even think of the discomfort of leaving Belleford again."

"But even if it is not . . ." Miss Wright grew worried again, plucking at the fringe of her shawl. "We loved our mother. What reason could we possibly have to wish her gone?"

"There is always the question of inheritance," Lily said delicately. "It is, I believe, the first thing most people think of in such an instance."

Miss Wright shook her head. "That would be more to the point if there was any inheritance to speak of. As you can see"— she gestured around the room with fluttering fingers, showing a sudden awareness of her home that surprised Lily—"it takes all the family funds to maintain Belleford, and even then it is not enough. When you add Thomas's debts into the account books . . ." She shook her head again. "No one would suspect us for such a reason."

"Perhaps not," Lily said, watching the other woman closely as she spoke.

There was a guilelessness to Miss Wright's manner that made Lily think she was telling the truth, that she truly had no idea what her mother had been keeping from her. Lily had been wondering if Miss Wright could have killed her mother in an attempt to break free from the confines of her life. But if she was telling the truth, not only did she not resent her mother's control, but she had actively sought it out. And she took pains to convince her brother to do the same. Lily had a hard time imagining how a woman such as Miss Wright appeared to be—fretful, timid, small minded, uninterested in anything outside the sphere of her own home—could encounter any circumstances strong enough to drive her to murder.

But such conclusions could be wrong. Lily had known more than one woman who used the rituals of grief to hide her true sentiments. Selina Wright could easily be doing the same.

Lily could tell, though, that the other woman was losing either interest in or energy for conversation, sinking back into her chair and heaving a quiet, trembling sigh. Lily decided not to press the matter, instead rising and suggesting that she might be of use in directing the servants who were preparing the room where Mrs. Wright's body would rest that evening.

"It is supposed to be done in the parlor across the hall," Miss Wright said, gesturing weakly toward the door. "There wasn't much to be arranged, so I think they will have finished by now. But perhaps you would step across and see that it is? And perhaps use your own judgment about whether it has been done well?" She hesitated, then added, "As a widow I must assume you have some experience to draw on in the matter. I would appreciate the assistance."

It was true, but it felt inconsiderate to hear it said out loud. Lily bristled a little, but she *had* offered her help.

"Certainly. Do you need anything in the meantime? Shall I summon a servant?"

"No, I thank you." Miss Wright leaned back, her lashes fluttering down toward her cheeks. "I will see my brother when he returns, but until then I believe I would like to rest. Would you draw the curtains a little more before you go?"

There was, again, that hint of rudeness, of presumption. Lily felt a little like a servant who had been dismissed. But she knew only too well that grief and tact did not always go hand in hand,

and she tamped down her irritation. There was a bare gap between the curtains, a few inches at most, but Lily made herself murmur something sympathetic as she pulled the curtains firmly shut before taking herself across the hall to see how the other parlor had been arranged.

There, too, the curtains had been drawn—they had been closed all over the house, and the doors hung with swags of black fabric. But in here the dim light seemed heavier; the sunlight that managed to straggle through, weak; the corners of the room, left in shadow. There was no breath of crisp autumn air, as there had been in the hall, to lighten the feel of the imminent death watch that would happen that night.

All the furniture had been draped in white sheets, with black laid over top, except for a long table set in front of the fireplace. It was also covered in black, and two straight-backed wooden chairs had been placed in front of it. Lily wondered if someone would sit up with Thomas Wright that night or if he would keep vigil with his mother's body alone until the undertaker came in the morning.

She had thought she wanted to be alone herself with Freddy, the night before the undertaker came. But in the end, she had been glad that his mother and brother had insisted on sitting with her. It was lonely work, keeping watch with the dead.

"Are you looking for something?"

Lily jumped, a breathless cry of surprise torn from her throat and her feet carrying her backward toward the door almost before she realized it and forced herself to stop. Someone was in the room with her.

CHAPTER 11

The butler seemed to emerge from the shadows. Lily could now see that he had been arranging flowers on the top of a pianoforte that was thick with dust. But the soundless way he moved—and the fact that he had kept so quiet, though he must have seen her come in—sent a chill skating down her back.

He bowed, his face showing no emotion at her presence there. "May I be of assistance?"

Lily had to plant her feet firmly against the urge to flee. There was nothing in his words or tone that she could put her finger on, but she had the distinct impression that he did not want her there. Her throat had gone dry, she realized, and she had to swallow several times before she found her voice. "Miss Wright asked me to look in and see that everything is ready for tonight," she managed at last. "I see you have it well in hand, though, Mr. Mears."

He bowed again. "You're kind to say so, Mrs. Adler. But of course, you must make any alterations that you feel are required." He gestured broadly with one arm, and she could see the tremor in his age-spotted hands. His words were deferential, but his manner said clearly that she was the intruder in his space, in spite of the fact that he was a servant and she was there at the request of the lady of the house.

But then, he was an old servant and might have begun his service at Belleford even before she had been born. In many ways, it was as much his domain as it was the Wrights'.

And if he had been with the family for many years, there was likely no one better positioned to tell her about Mrs. Wright and her children.

Lily crossed to the table in front of the fireplace, smoothing her hands over the black silk that covered it as though straightening the fabric, although it needed no such attention. "It must be very hard on you, Mr. Mears, to be faced with the death of your employer, and under such strange circumstances. I am sure she must have held you in high esteem for you to remain with the family so long."

The butler nodded slowly. "You are kind to say so, madam," he repeated. "I like to think my work is satisfactory."

"How many years have you worked for the Wrights?" It was an impertinent question and obviously none of her business. But Lily was hoping that the long habits of deference that a career in service created would work to her advantage.

Mr. Mears took his time answering. "Near to fifty years," he said at last. He didn't show any outward signs of displeasure at her questions, but there was a blankness to his response that made Lily think he was wary. For an old family retainer, as he seemed to be, it was not surprising—he would be in the habit of guarding both the privacy and the reputations of his employers.

But perhaps he would respond to flattery. Lily hesitated, then pressed on. "I understand Mrs. Wright was very well regarded in the neighborhood?"

"The Wrights are an old family," he replied, his pale eyes never leaving her face. "Such history and presence are often respected."

It was neither a yes nor a no, and Lily began to wish she hadn't tried to question him in the first place. There was nothing she could put her finger on as rude or aggressive, but his staring was beginning to make her skin crawl. She had to resist the urge to make up an excuse to flee the room. "I am sure her children must be equally respected and valued in the neighborhood," she said, speaking in more of a rush than she meant to.

"One can only hope they will live up to their father's legacy." Mr. Mears bowed. "If you'll excuse me, Mrs. Adler, I must attend to my other duties. I hope your report to Miss Wright on the preparations we've made will be satisfactory."

It wasn't until after he and his disconcerting eyes were gone from the room that Lily realized he had done more than just step around her questions. *"Their father's legacy,"* he had said, even though she had been specifically talking about their mother. Was that simply out of his loyalty to the Wrights, a family that Mrs. Wright had married into rather than being born a part of? Or did he have some reason to disapprove of her?

Had it, perhaps, been more than disapproval?

Lily wasn't sure how long she had been standing there when she realized she was shivering. A cold draft was winding around her ankles, though the door and windows were all shut. In the silence, she could hear a thin, plaintive sound, like a whisper or a whimper.

"Is someone there?" she asked sharply, disliking the nervous feeling that was creeping down her spine. No one answered, but the sound continued while Lily's gaze darted around the room, as she tried to decide where it was coming from. It might not be a person, she realized. It sounded a little like the whine of a small animal in distress.

Suddenly worried, she looked all around the edges of the room and under the furniture, trying to find the creature making the sound.

It wasn't until her search carried her behind the table set out for Mrs. Wright's body that she realized the mass of shadows next to the cold, empty fireplace was actually a door, set back in its frame and made of the same dark wood that paneled the rest of the room. It was slightly ajar, and what she had heard was the sound of wind creeping through the crack.

Feeling suddenly foolish, and yet still a little nervous, she was about to pull the door firmly shut. But she paused, then gave it a sharp push. Given the dusty, dark little corner that the door was set in, she expected to hear the screeching protest of hinges that weren't accustomed to moving. But it swung open noiselessly, revealing a steep, narrow staircase leading upward.

Lily hesitated only a moment before venturing up, pulling the door almost, but not quite, shut behind her.

The stairs, like the hinges, had been more recently tended than she would have expected. There was no dust for her to leave footprints in, and they creaked no more than any other stairs in the old house seemed to. After climbing a single flight, she found herself at a small landing with a second door and more steps leading up.

Lily opened the door just a crack, not knowing where she might be in the house and loath to come face to face with anyone unexpectedly. But there was no one there, just an open space that she quickly recognized as one end of the upper gallery. She peeked a little farther, examining the outside of the door she had just opened, and discovered that it was rather like the one downstairs: set back in the wall and paneled. It would be unlikely that anyone walking past would notice it unless they already knew it was there.

It was something like a second servants' stair, she realized, on the other side of the house from the first one, though it did not go all the way down to the kitchens. That seemed logical in a house so large and rambling. Likely, then, it merely went up to the third floor, with another door set unobtrusively into a dim corner of that hall. There was no reason to go up and see, but Lily's curiosity was already getting the better of her. She closed the door and continued upward, the cold draft that had first caught her attention downstairs still twining around her ankles and making her shiver.

The staircase twisted a little as it climbed, but luckily there were small windows set in the outside wall to give a little light and some sense of direction. At the top, she was greeted by a single door. Lily tried the handle and, when it turned, opened the door carefully, expecting to find herself looking out into another hall.

Instead, she was peering into what seemed to be a long, narrow storeroom. Lily wondered whether that second set of stairs had been longer than she realized. She might have been as high up as the attics. Or maybe the storeroom ran along the third floor? She had not yet been invited up to that level of the house, so she couldn't say.

But she could, and did, venture forward to look around. The only light in the room was what trickled through the wavy panes of glass in the small windows along one wall, but it was enough to see by. The room was crowded with the sort of things that filled an old house over time and ended up with nowhere else to go: old furniture, locked trunks, portraits not handsome enough to hang in the gallery downstairs. Lily tried not to look at these; in the dim light, she had the uneasy feeling that their eyes were following her, no matter how she tried to tell herself that such flights of fancy were too childish for a grown woman.

Like the stairs, the room was in better condition than she would have expected. More than once, as she walked down the narrow aisles, she brushed up against some piece of furniture. Each time she glanced down, expecting to see a streak of dust or grime on her clothes and anxious that it would give away what she had been up to. But aside from the occasional cobweb or small smudge that she had to pat away, her clothes were unmarred. Someone was clearly charged with keeping the walkway through the storeroom clear and clean.

The same could not be said of the contents of the chests and trunks that lined it. Lily eased one wardrobe door open, curious to see what was inside, and discovered a bar hung with old-fashioned clothing that had clearly once been fine but was now stained and moth-eaten. The wastefulness of it bothered her, and she closed the wardrobe door so abruptly that it shut with a sharp clatter.

"Who's there?" a panicked voice called, and the sound so startled Lily that she yelped before she could stop herself.

Whirling around, she peered through the clutter and found another face staring back at her. The sight was so unexpected that she nearly screamed again before she realized who it was.

"Alice?" she asked, trying to regain some of her dignity. Frantically trying to come up with an excuse for her presence there, she found herself demanding, "What are you doing up here?" in the hope that it would keep the little maid from asking her the same question.

Fortunately, it seemed Alice was too timid to question a lady of quality, even one found inexplicably wandering through an old storeroom. "Candles, miss—I mean, madam," she said with a quick, nervous curtsey. She pointed to a tall armoire, which, when she opened it, was revealed to contain shelves stocked with surplus household necessities, including candles. "Mr. Mears said they'll need extra for tonight, with poor Mr. Wright sitting up." There was a note of real sympathy in her voice that made Lily suspect Alice knew firsthand how hard it was to keep watch the night before a funeral.

The thought softened her nervousness, as did the maid's seeming disinterest in what a guest might be doing there. But Lily was still cautious enough to try to get ahead of any questions or gossip that might follow her. "I am glad to hear it," she said, nodding as regally as she could manage and acting as though she were there for the same reason. "Miss Wright asked me to look in on the arrangements, and as soon as I walked in the room, I thought more candles would be necessary. But Mr. Mears clearly thinks of everything."

That made Alice smile, though the expression flitted across her pale face so quickly that Lily almost missed it. "There isn't much he don't notice, begging your pardon," she said, looking down at her feet, as though uncomfortable meeting Lily's eyes. But then a frown gathered between her brows, and she glanced up. "What—"

"I am impressed with how clean and tidy it is up here," Lily broke in, saying the first thing that popped into her mind in an attempt to head off any questions she didn't wish to answer. "I imagine that is difficult to maintain, but you do very well."

Alice blushed at the praise. "The second door opens out near Miss Wright's room, and she uses these stairs sometimes when she don't want to walk all the way around to the main staircase. I try to keep it tidy for her."

Lily had been about to hurry away, but this was the most she had heard Alice say at one time. It made her pause. If the little maid was in a chatty mood, then she might be able to learn something, as long as she didn't push too hard and risk drawing too much attention to the oddity of her own presence there. "It must be difficult, between you and Etta, to keep such a large house in such good condition." When Alice stared at her, looking dumbfounded, Lily swallowed nervously. "What is it?"

"No one ever talks to me, ma'am." Alice looked embarrassed as soon as the words were out of her mouth. "I mean, not chatty-like. No one even notices if I come into a room or leave it."

"I am sure that is not true," Lily said. "Not when you do such good work."

Alice blushed again. "Thank you," she whispered, ducking her head.

Lily looked around the crowded storeroom. "Though I imagine you are hoping that Mr. and Miss Wright will hire more servants soon?"

Alice shook her head. "I doubt they could, ma'am. Folks don't want to work here, with the ghost and all, and anyone who comes to take a position here will find out quick enough. More like they'll have to leave themselves, now."

"Will they wish to?" Lily asked, frowning a little as she remembered Selina Wright's insistence that she would never leave her home.

"Wouldn't you want to if your house was haunted?" Alice asked, her eyes wide. "I don't know why Mrs. Wright stayed so long, scared as she was of the gray lady. I'd have thought she'd want to get as far away as possible. I know I would. I don't think they have ghosts in places like Bath or London."

"Then why did you stay when the other servants left?" Lily couldn't help asking.

It was the wrong question, she realized. Alice dipped her head again, her jaw clenching. "My family needs my wages," she said, her voice barely above a whisper. "It's dreadful, first with what happened to Etta and now Mrs. Wright . . . but I can't risk leaving and not finding another place."

Lily was suddenly ashamed of herself for asking. A girl like Alice wouldn't always have the option to simply walk away from good employment. Even though Lily was still skeptical that the ghost was real, she found herself hoping for the servants' sake that the Wrights did close up the house and move. No one wanted to live in a home with a ghost—and even less would they want to live in a home where someone had been murdered.

Of course, before that happened, she intended to find out who was responsible.

"Well, I won't keep you any longer from your work," Lily said, still angry at herself for being so thoughtless. Trying to make up for it, she added, "And I am sure the Wrights appreciate those of you who have stayed by them through such a difficult time."

"You're kind to say so," Alice mumbled, still looking down at her toes, though her eyes flicked up a moment to meet Lily's before darting down once more. "Do you know how to find your way back to the parlor, ma'am?"

"Yes, thank you. I believe it is just straight back that way." Glad to escape without being asked why she had even been there in the first place, Lily turned quickly and began winding her way through the crowded storeroom.

If Mr. Mears had sent for more candles, that might mean he had come back to the parlor or would soon. The thought made her steps quicken, Alice already slipping from her mind. She couldn't risk him realizing she had gone poking around.

The light in the staircase seemed even dimmer as she made her way back down, and she was hurrying enough that the stairs crackled and creaked beneath her feet. But there was no one in the parlor when she emerged, closing the door behind her while she quickly brushed away both stray cobwebs and wrinkles from her dress.

As soon as she paused enough to catch her breath, she heard voices in the hall outside the room. For a moment, the low, anxious tones sent a jolt of nervousness through her until she recognized Mr. Spencer's voice.

She had been upstairs long enough that the gentlemen must have returned from their errand. And she had every intention of finding out what its result was.

Mr. Wright was pacing the hall when she poked her head out of the room, his expression conflicted. Mr. Spencer, his usually expressive face impassive for the moment, leaned against the wall, watching him.

"What do you think I ought to do, then?" Mr. Wright asked, stopping in front of his neighbor, his tone pleading. In the dim light of the hall, his eyes looked shadowed and his expression haggard, as though he had not slept in a week. "I haven't the faintest idea. Damn it, man, my mother just died. My mind's a mess, and my sister is a mess, and now . . ." He ran both hands through his hair.

"I take it your meeting with Mr. Powell did not end favorably?" Lily asked gently.

Mr. Wright looked momentarily taken aback to see her there, but he recovered quickly—more quickly, each time, Lily reflected. He must have been growing accustomed to her interference.

"He does not subscribe to the prevailing theory in the village that it was the ghost," Mr. Wright said, scowling. "He says it was human, right enough, but it might as well have been done by a ghost for all the good it does us. He cannot see how anyone could have gotten into that room—and I cannot either."

"And so he does not mean to take any further action?"

"That seems to be the gist of it," Mr. Spencer agreed. They all spoke in low voices, even Mr. Wright, as they were in the hall, where anyone might overhear. "He said he does not know how one would even begin to find out who did it, and so sees no path forward. I was just asking Mr. Wright whether he was satisfied with the magistrate's intention to let the matter rest."

"I don't know. I mean, no." Mr. Wright looked very young and very confused, although he was nearly of an age with Mr. Spencer and several years Lily's senior. "And I must admit, the points he raised have me doubting my own conclusion. And if it was not the gray lady . . . or even if it was, as you said, he cannot just . . . We have our reputation to think of."

Lily hesitated only for a moment. But if Mr. Wright's waffling was purely a defect of his character—one his sister seemed to share—he was in need of any guidance she could offer. And if it was a ploy to hide his or his sister's culpability in their mother's death, she might get closer to discovering that by offering him a path forward and seeing how he reacted.

And in either case, she had already resolved to do what she could in the matter.

"There is another magistrate who will be arriving within a few days, from another county," she said, stepping all the way into the hall. She wasn't sure when Lord Walter, the husband of her friend, would be arriving to fetch her to Surrey. But it would not be very many days more. "He is a man of great integrity, and he may be willing to be more thorough if you can present him with enough facts on the matter."

"Won't Mr. Powell object?" Mr. Wright looked slightly distressed.

"If he does, it will be without reason, as he has already declared himself baffled and unable to proceed," Mr. Spencer pointed out, taking a step closer to Lily. She wasn't sure if he had done it on purpose or not, but he was very obviously taking her side in persuading Mr. Wright, and she appreciated the gesture. "And if he cares for the responsibilities of his position—as I believe he does, even if he lacks imagination from time to time—then he will welcome the assistance."

"And in the meantime, you should consider sending for one of the officers from Bow Street," Lily suggested, the idea suddenly occurring to her.

Mr. Wright, who had started to nod in agreement as Mr. Spencer spoke, looked suddenly shocked. "One of the runners?" He shook his head. "Good God, I wouldn't know the first thing to say to them. Or whom to write to. Or whether they would be of any use at all. Would they even come here?"

"They travel all over the country now, and many are quite skilled in their work," Lily said, her voice growing sharp with impatience. And with defensiveness—she had great respect for Mr. Simon Page, an officer of Bow Street whom she had discovered to be both a skilled investigator and a man of high character.

But she also knew that he did not always agree with his own colleagues. He had, more than once, been frustrated by the morally porous bureaucracy of the new police force that sometimes considered a bribe as good a reason to halt an investigation as lack of evidence, or by the willingness of his fellow officers to accept the easy solution presented to them by a family more interested in avoiding scandal than uncovering the truth.

Mr. Page would be the first to admit that there were men working with Bow Street who deserved every ounce of Thomas Wright's skeptical horror. But she had no intention of asking any of them for assistance.

"I have the good fortune to know a very fine member of the Bow Street force, one who has proven himself more than competent on several occasions," Lily said, glancing out of the corner of her eye at Mr. Spencer to see how he would react to her suggestion. To her relief, he was nodding in approval. "I would be happy to write to him and ask for his assistance."

"Would it not be better to leave everything to a magistrate?" Mr. Wright said, still looking ill at ease. "Spencer, surely you would agree there is no need to involve these police fellows. What can they know of our home and family?"

"It is precisely because they will not be encumbered by such biases that they might be of assistance," Mr. Spencer pointed out. "And it may be some days until the new magistrate arrives. It would be helpful to have Mrs. Adler's Bow Street fellow already at work in the meantime so that the trail, if there is one to find, does not grow cold."

"Well, if you think it best," Mr. Wright said while Lily bit back the impulse to say something impatient. He was agreeing, and that was what mattered—even if it did irritate her that he had needed someone else to say her plan was a good one first.

"I shall write to him as soon as I have returned to Longwood Cottage," Lily said, pleased that none of her frustration was audible in her voice.

"Then let us summon your aunt," Mr. Wright suggested, springing into action in a way that left Lily more than a little stunned. It seemed that setting a course of action was all he had needed to regain his usual energy. Either that or, she thought wryly, he was eager to have her and her interference gone from his home.

But when Eliza was summoned, she came down the stairs looking harried and distracted. "I am afraid I need some time to speak with Miss Wright before I can depart," she said. "There are a few points . . . well, it is a matter for women. Mr. Spencer, perhaps you might convey my niece home, instead, if she is unable to wait for me?"

Less than ten minutes later, Lily found herself seated beside Mr. Spencer in his elegant little sporting curricle as they rattled down the country lanes toward Longwood Cottage. Lily took a deep breath, suddenly realizing how tense her shoulders and back had felt while she was at Belleford. Leaving there was like shedding a weight she had been carrying without knowing when she had picked it up.

"You look very serious," Mr. Spencer commented, shifting the reins lightly in his grip. "Thinking about what you will say in your letter to the runner? Do you think he will actually agree to come?"

Lily, who had been about to ask him more about Belleford, instead found herself frowning at his words. It hadn't occurred to her to wonder if Mr. Page would come to Hampshire.

"I am certain he will treat the request seriously," she said at last. "If he cannot come himself, he will see to it that one of his colleagues is sent."

"And in the meantime, you will continue to discover what you can?"

Lily hesitated. If someone other than Mr. Page did come, there was no guarantee that he would take her—and whatever she had learned—seriously. It had taken Mr. Page some time to come around to trusting her. What if another runner came and refused to listen to whatever she might have to tell him?

Lily straightened her spine. Whoever came, she would make him take her seriously. She had done it once before, and she could do it again.

"You look very grim," Mr. Spencer said. "Have you decided to abandon your task then, and leave it to others?"

Lily shook her head, recalled to where she was. "I would much prefer to leave it to others," she admitted. "But at least until Lord Walter arrives, or an officer from Bow Street . . .

Someone has to put their mind to the problem, and it seems it
will not be Mr. Powell. So it might as well be me." She shivered
a little, wishing she had a shawl to pull around her shoulders, for
comfort if not for warmth. "It is not a comfortable task to take
on. And there is something about that house . . ."

"It is an unhappy place," Mr. Spencer agreed. "And I would
say it has been for a while. What?" he asked, seeing her staring
at him. "Do you not agree?"

"I do," she said. "I just thought it was all in my head. I've
never been one to assign the feelings of a person to inanimate
things, but I cannot seem to help it in this instance."

"No, you are far too logical to make a habit of such fancies,"
he said, smiling sideways at her while still keeping most of his
attention on the road. "Perhaps you will not need to commit
yourself to the task for too long. As you say, there will be others
arriving soon who may relieve you of the burden while still easing your worries about your aunt."

"Perhaps," Lily agreed, though she couldn't quite keep the
skepticism from her voice.

"Come," Mr. Spencer said briskly. "I think you are in need
of distracting. It is your turn to take the ribbons."

Lily looked at him with astonishment, then looked at his
sporty, high-stepping horse with something like horror. "You
cannot be serious."

"You handled your aunt's gig with aplomb. Why not mine?"

"Because a little gig is a far cry from a curricle such as this,
and that old horse might as well be a different species entirely
when compared to the beasts you own."

Mr. Spencer laughed. "Never tell me you are afraid of a
challenge, dear Mrs. Adler. Do you think you are unequal to
it?"

She bristled, scowling at him. She knew he was goading her on purpose—his broad smile said as much—but she couldn't bring herself to back down. "Very well then," she agreed haughtily, holding out her hands. "Hand them over."

"That is more like it. And I shall be here the whole time to make sure he doesn't run away with us," He settled the ribbons across her gloved fingers, his hand lingering on hers as he did so. For a moment, they were both looking at each other instead of at the horse. His smile faded a little, his expression growing more serious and his voice quieter. "I would never allow any harm to come to you."

It took real effort for Lily to look away, and for a moment she did not want to. But at last she wrenched her attention back to the reins in her hands and the pricked ears of the horse she was now responsible for controlling. "I am glad to hear it, sir," she said, forcing a lightness that she did not quite feel. "I am impeccably skilled at many things, but driving is not one of them. I depend on you to ensure we do not overturn in a ditch somewhere."

He laughed and settled back to stretch one arm along the seat behind her shoulders. "Luckily, it is not far to your aunt's home."

★ ★ ★

"I tell you, Neddy, there was something decidedly unnerving about him," Ofelia said as she stepped around a puddle of water that had collected in the road. "The way he was just standing there, watching me . . ."

"Think he knows something about the ghost?" Ned asked, sounding both eager and unhappy. "Servants see and hear everything, after all. He might know more than he's letting on."

Ofelia cast a sideways look at her husband. "That would not be difficult," she said, a little dryly, "as so far he has let on absolutely nothing at all. And there are no such things as ghosts."

The last was said almost by rote—it was a point that had been repeated half a dozen times in the last two hours of their errand and, she knew, would likely never be settled between them. But this time Ned did not accept the admonition passively.

"Then what has you jumping out of your skin every time you mention Belleford or the Wrights?" he asked, his quiet voice firm enough to surprise her.

A breeze chased its way down the lane, pulling and plucking at their clothes, and Ofelia shivered as it crept down her collar. "Well, I'll not deny that it is a creepy old place," she said, trying to sound carefree, but not sure if she was succeeding. "But Mrs. Adler has decided to find out what she can. Are you saying I should not help her?"

"Sounds like you goaded her into it with your prying, from what you told me," he said, pulling off his jacket and draping it over her shoulders, even as she tried to protest that she was fine. "You do what you like without thinking it through, and Lord knows I love that about you. But perhaps not such a good idea this time?"

"Because there might be a ghost?" Ofelia asked, trying to turn the conversation back to their normal teasing. Neddy had proved wonderfully indulgent, as husbands went, and normally was as game for anything exciting or new as she was. She wasn't sure what to make of this serious turn of mind for him.

"If you insist it's not a ghost, the only other answer is that it's a murderer. Can't say I like you getting mixed up in that any better."

"You could always insist that we leave," Ofelia pointed out. "You are my husband, after all. I should have to obey you."

"Dashed well not going to do *that*," Ned said, and his grumpy countenance made her smile. "Would be shockingly rude to Miss Pierce and Miss Clarke. Besides, Mother always said a wise husband only puts his foot down when it really matters."

"Your mother is a clever woman," Ofelia said, laughing as she threaded her arm through his.

"Doesn't mean I like it, though," Ned grumbled, pulling her close.

Ofelia was still smiling as they came up the hill to Longwood Cottage, just as a smart, sporty curricle was pulling into the drive.

"Look at them," Ned said, his voice dropping as he loosened his grip on her arm to leave a more decorous distance between them. "Quite cozy, don't you think?"

Perched on the high seat, Mrs. Adler was rolling her eyes at something Mr. Spencer had just said, clearly trying not to laugh. Ofelia kept her smile firmly in place, though it took some effort when Ned nudged her. "Must be happy for your friend."

"If she is happy, then I certainly am," Ofelia said, hoping that Ned wouldn't notice it wasn't quite an agreement. Raising her voice, she called out, "Mrs. Adler!"

The pair clearly hadn't realized they were no longer alone; Mr. Spencer leaned back quickly, putting more space between their bodies, while Mrs. Adler handed him the reins she had been holding. "A pleasure to see you both," she said, and Ofelia was surprised to see that her normally cool, impassive friend had high color in her cheeks. "Where are you coming from?"

"Offered to get the post for Miss Clarke," Ned explained, stepping forward to help hand Mrs. Adler down from the curricle. "Said she needed to lie down after she and Lady Carroway visited Belleford this morning."

"One of the letters is for you, Mrs. Adler," Ofelia said, thrusting it forward a little more forcefully than she meant to. "Sent from Portsmouth, so we can all guess the sender, I'm sure."

"Thank you," Mrs. Adler said, taking the letter and smiling down at it, though a little frown drew her brows together a moment later. Glancing up, she hesitated a moment before asking, "Mr. Spencer, will you come in?"

"I thank you, but I am certain you and Lady Carroway will have much to discuss as you compare your observations from the day." Mr. Spencer smiled at all of them equally, and Ofelia softened a little. Just because Neddy had all the hopefulness of a village matchmaker didn't mean Mr. Spencer was turning his thoughts in the same direction—otherwise, wouldn't he jump at the opportunity to stay? "I've no wish to intrude," he continued. "And of course, you will want some time to read your letter. If you respond, I hope you will give the good captain my regards."

Ofelia's scowl returned before she could stop it. Mr. Spencer's tone was perfectly pleasant, but she couldn't help wondering if the suggestion was at all pointed—if he wanted to make sure Captain Hartley knew he was there when the captain was not.

Ofelia held back a sigh. Or perhaps she was getting worked up over nothing. Perhaps the situation was as much in her head as it was in Neddy's. And in any case, there were far more important things to focus on—such as a murderer.

She pulled her attention back to the group in time to bid Mr. Spencer farewell. Once he was gone, she turned to Mrs. Adler. "So you have just come from Belleford as well? Did you learn anything important?"

"A great deal," Mrs. Adler said slowly, staring out across fields as though she wasn't really seeing them. "Will you come inside? I am eager to hear what you learned this morning."

★ ★ ★

Lily shut the door to her room and leaned against it, rubbing the tight spot between her eyes. She and Ofelia—with Ned unable to resist chiming in—had spent the afternoon discussing what they had seen at Belleford, their voices rising with excitement and frustration or sinking into whispers as they remembered where they were.

The butler who saw everything but said nothing. The maid who was clearly hiding something about her encounter with the supposed ghost. Serena Wright's fluttery disinterest in leaving her mother's control—and the hints that her brother's behavior in the village might not always be above reproach.

Then there was that locked door. The manservant, Isaiah, could have unlocked it in the night. But could he have locked it behind him once more? Lily didn't know enough about lock picking to say for certain.

At one point, Ned had interrupted their conversation with the practical but frustrating observation that, even if there had been no ghost, there was nothing to prove for certain that Mrs. Wright had been murdered. "If it wasn't this gray lady, maybe the old woman just died in her sleep, and you'd be stirring up trouble for no reason at all."

"She didn't," Ofelia had said. The certainty in her voice had taken Lily immediately back to that room, the rictus of fear on Mrs. Wright's face, the desperate way her clawed fingers were locked against the pillows and sheets, the awful swelling of her eyes and lips. She had met Ofelia's eyes and nodded in agreement. No one who died peacefully asleep would look like that.

"All the more reason to let it be, then," Ned had suggested, though he did not sound hopeful.

"I cannot," Lily said, thinking of her aunt and Susan, the fear and uncertainty she would feel if she had to leave them with the matter still unresolved. "And if the magistrate is unable to see his way forward . . ."

She had meant to write to Simon Page at Bow Street as soon as possible, but there had been something in Eliza's manner, during those final moments at Belleford, that left her anxious. Her aunt had seen or heard something odd, she was sure. And Lily didn't want to write to Mr. Page until she knew what it was.

But as the afternoon light faded, Eliza still had not returned. After waiting past their usual suppertime—evening meals at Longwood Cottage were early and informal—Susan had finally decided that they should all go ahead and dine. The conversation at supper had been deliberately light and pleasant, touching on everything except the residents of Belleford, and the effort of maintaining a cheerful facade for Susan's sake had left Lily with an aching head.

She had forgotten, in the excitement and frustration of the afternoon, about Jack's letter. But it was waiting on her bed, addressed to her in his friendly, looping script, and just the sight made her smile for the first time in several hours. She kicked off her shoes, curled up on the bed, and began to read.

He was still in Portsmouth, it seemed—a change in orders that was frustrating for the whole crew, as they could neither set sail nor return to their homes and families.

We may be called on to depart at any moment, though I expect we shall be stuck for at least a week more. Were it otherwise, I should likely impose myself on your aunt's hospitality in Hampshire, just to see whether you have indeed kept to your intention of a peaceful sojourn in the country. But as I cannot, I hope you will write and tell me how your days go. Are your aunt and Miss Clarke as cheerful as I remember them from our long-ago meeting? Did they take as instant a liking to Lady Carroway and Sir Edward as you predicted? And what is the village gossip? (Even if I do not know that neighborhood in particular, I know such places, and there is always gossip of one kind or another.)

Lily set the letter aside, her forehead creased in thought once more. Jack, it seemed, knew her better than she knew herself—though even he, she was sure, couldn't have predicted that the shock of unexpected death would greet them so quickly. But he wouldn't have been surprised to know that she refused to sit by while the matter went unsolved.

And perhaps, she thought eagerly, springing up and crossing to the room's miniscule writing desk, he might provide some help. A letter would likely reach him within a day or two if he stayed in Portsmouth as long as he expected.

Jack had a sharp mind for puzzles and problems, and he had stood by her side through more than one confrontation with a murderer. He would have some insight to share, even from a distance, she was sure of it. And even if he wasn't able to help, just the act of writing out what she knew so far might reveal some pattern or idea that she had overlooked.

Usually, she took her time with her correspondence, thinking through each line before she committed it to paper. But this time, the words flowed out of her. She had missed him, she realized as she wrote. She missed his quick wit, his personable charm, his sudden insights that so often prompted her own.

They were a good team. And she very much needed an outside perspective at the moment.

She had just dipped her pen to write his direction on the outside of the letter when there was a gentle knock at the door. "Come in," Lily said absently, not looking up, expecting it to be her maid, Anna, come to help her undress and prepare for bed.

"Am I interrupting, dear?"

Lily started, leaving a blot of ink on the word *Portsmouth*, and turned to find Eliza in the doorway. Her aunt smiled, but it clearly cost her some effort. Lily stood. "What is it?" she asked in a whisper as Eliza stepped inside the room and pulled the door shut behind her.

"Mr. Wright mentioned your plan to send word to your Bow Street gentleman," Eliza said, pacing toward the bed. But instead of sitting, she crossed back again, her footsteps agitated. "Is that what you are about to do?"

"I was waiting to talk to you first," Lily said, hesitating. "But yes, I was going to write to him this evening."

"Good." Eliza nodded. "We haven't a moment to waste. Because you were right, even if Thomas and Selina don't wish to see it. I am certain Mrs. Wright was smothered in her sleep."

CHAPTER 12

Lily stared at her aunt. "What did you discover?" she asked, sinking back down into her chair.

Eliza, apparently unable to stand still, paced around the small room, touching furniture and knickknacks with absentminded agitation. "You must have wondered why I stayed at Belleford instead of departing with you and Mr. Spencer."

"And I hope you will not long keep me in suspense as to the reason?"

"No . . . no, I don't mean to . . . I just am not sure how to say it. I've not your facility or familiarity with . . . I tried to tell Thomas and Selina, but I am not sure they truly understood. And perhaps that was my fault, because how one is supposed to explain . . . But would they have believed me, even if I had shouted it at them?"

"Aunt." Lily stood, crossing the room to take a hairbrush from her aunt's hand and place it back on the dressing table, then lead her to the bed and urge her to sit. Still holding her aunt's hands, Lily met her eyes without flinching. "You saw something when you were preparing Mrs. Wright's body, yes?" When Eliza nodded, Lily gave her hands a brisk squeeze. "Good. Tell me what it was. Unlike Mr. and Miss Wright, you needn't spare my feelings. Just say it bluntly."

"Bruises. On her chest and shoulders." Eliza shuddered, but she did not pull away. "Heavy ones, as though someone had leant their full weight on top of her. And she was such a frail old woman. Forceful in her personality, to be sure, but she had a body like a bird. I'd not be surprised if she had ribs cracked from the pressure."

"So she was smothered, then." Lily couldn't help imagining the terror that the old woman must have felt in her final moments; she had to hold back her own shudder, not wanting to upset her aunt any further. But her mind was already darting ahead, running through what her aunt's discovery could mean. "And that tells us something important about who it could have been."

Eliza's surprise was plain. "You don't mean to say you have a guess as to who it was?"

"Nothing like that—not yet." Lily stood, not really noticing what she was doing, and began her own pacing about the room. Unlike her aunt's distressed movements, though, her steps were firm and measured, as though they were marking out the rhythm of her thoughts falling into place. "But if our murderer had to use his—or her—full weight to subdue Mrs. Wright and gain the upper hand, it must not have been someone very strong, nor someone particularly tall. Strong enough, of course, which I think rules out Mr. Mears, uneasy though he makes me. But it also makes one other person, at least, unlikely."

Eliza was able to follow her niece's train of thought quickly. "The manservant, Isaiah."

"That would be my guess as well," Lily said, nodding. "He's tall, and with shoulders that broad, I imagine quite strong as well."

"Good of you to notice," Eliza said dryly.

Lily, relieved to see her aunt regaining some of her custom-ary calm, gave her a quick smile. "I have eyes," she said, unof-fended. "And if Ofelia was correct, then both of the maids have noticed as well. Which, if any of them had been the one to turn up dead, would lead me to very particular conclusions. But in this case, while we cannot rule Isaiah out completely, his physi-cal stature makes him an unlikely suspect. Especially when taken together with what Mr. Mears said—that if Isaiah had left the rooms belowstairs, he would have known."

"What about Thomas Wright?" Eliza asked. "I'd not call him short."

"No, but nor would I call him particularly tall. And while his coats may be cut to enhance his figure, I would wager there is not much true muscle beneath them."

"He is nearing forty," Eliza pointed out, sounding a little defensive. "You cannot fault a man for growing a bit soft as he leaves his youth behind."

"I never said I faulted him for it," Lily said as she turned and began walking back the way she had come. "And he is handsome and personable enough to make up for any imperfections in his figure. But he is still on the list of suspects, along with the women in the house. Especially as he was the one who, with his mother finally out of the picture, now has full control of his very sizeable fortune."

"Good God, that's true," Eliza said, her expression aghast. "I had forgotten until just now how his father left things, but you are quite right. Though . . . sizeable? Are you sure?"

"What do you mean, 'how his father left things'?"

Eliza looked a little embarrassed. "Something Susan told me last year after a particularly interesting tea she had with Mrs. Wright. You know how she loves to gossip. Susan, I mean," Eliza added, somewhat apologetically.

"And in this instance, I shall be glad of it if she learned something useful." Lily stopped her pacing to sit at the dressing table, her eyes fixed encouragingly on her aunt. "What did Mrs. Wright tell her? Something about the family's money?"

"It seems Mr. Wright had some freedom in how he wrote his will. When he died, control of the family finances actually passed to Mrs. Wright rather than to their son. There was some question . . ." Eliza hesitated, but she was too blunt by nature to dance around what she had to say. "Well, apparently they did not trust that Thomas would be a thoughtful steward of their resources. They hoped that the years after his father's death and before his mother's would be enough for him to learn more restraint. So now that his mother is dead, Mr. Wright has finally come into control of the family's money and property."

"Oh." Lily sat back, unsure what else to say, her mind reeling. She had assumed that Mrs. Wright held only nominal control over the family's fortune and that her son had been content to let her continue managing things.

"But what do you mean, *sizeable*?" Eliza asked. "I assumed— that is, we all did, really, given how things have been for them these past few years—"

"No, they were quite wealthy," Lily said absently, her mind still caught up with Thomas Wright. "Ofelia saw their account books."

His behavior the few times she had interacted with him had been that of a flighty man who lived for entertainment. She had assumed, as a result, that he had been happy to leave the day-to-day practicalities of running an estate and managing the family finances to his mother. But if he had felt she was keeping something that was rightfully his—

"Thank you, dear," Eliza said with a sigh, interrupting Lily's thoughts once more. "I feel much better now that I've shared that with you. Although now I shall have to decide whether or not to say something to Susan."

"Probably best not to," Lily suggested. "Or if you do, find something else to distract her with immediately so she doesn't dwell on it."

"A good idea, that. Perhaps if I set her to planning a dinner tomorrow night . . ." Eliza paused, looking at her niece expectantly.

Lily, her mind still occupied with thoughts of murder, stared at her blankly. "A dinner?"

"We could invite your Mr. Spencer," Eliza suggested, leaning forward just a little.

Lily met her aunt's curious gaze without flinching. "He is not *my* Mr. Spencer,"

"But you like him, do you not?" Eliza pressed.

Lily sighed. "He has become a good friend. But at the moment my mind is occupied with rather different concerns."

"I know your mind well, Lily," Eliza said briskly, sitting back and looking far more her normal, assured self than she had when she first came in the room. "It is perfectly capable of managing multiple concerns at the same time." Her expression softened. "And I do not like thinking of you alone forever."

"I am clearly not alone, as I am at this very moment in your company, and your house is full of my friends," Lily pointed out, trying not to let her embarrassment show. She didn't like discussing things she wasn't sure of, particularly when it came to her own feelings. "Besides, that is rather an unconvincing argument coming from you, dear Aunt. I am fine on my own, just as you are."

Her aunt gave her a puzzled look. "But I am not on my own. I have Susan."

"As I have my friends," Lily said, beginning to feel exasperated.

Eliza's cheeks grew pink. She cleared her throat and seemed about to speak several times before she finally found her voice. "Dear . . . Susan is not just a friend. She is the love of my life."

Lily stared at her aunt, knowing she needed to say something but unable to put any words together.

Eliza cleared her throat again. "I . . . I thought you knew?"

"Well, I . . . no. That is to say, no one ever told me!"

At that, Eliza laughed. "Well, of course no one ever said it outright," she said, shaking her head. Lily felt a hot flush climbing up her neck and cheeks at her aunt's amusement. "But you have a reputation for being an astute observer, Lily. I assumed you'd figured it out years ago." She laughed again. "Why did you think your father objects to me so strongly? And becomes so displeased when you visit his sister?"

"Because you are unmarried!" Lily protested, still trying to wrap her mind around her aunt's revelation. She had always prided herself on her insight. How had she not known? "And independent!"

"Well, he objects to those things too," Eliza said, rising. "As you know from your own experience with his disapproval. But not nearly as much as he objects to my making a life with another woman." Her expression suddenly grew a little anxious. "You'll not behave oddly around Susan now, will you? She looks on you quite as her own niece, you know. We would both be so upset if things between all of us were to change."

"No, of course not," Lily said quickly. She was fairly certain she meant it—but such a revelation, in the middle of everything else occupying her mind, was not what she had expected. She wasn't sure what to think or do. Part of her wanted her aunt to stay so she could find out just how she had missed so many signs that now seemed obvious. The other part wanted Eliza to go so she could be alone with her thoughts.

"Susan is going to be dumbfounded that you did not realize, the poor thing," Eliza said, one hand on the doorknob as she shook her head. "That, at least, should provide her plenty of distraction for tonight. Tomorrow we can see about planning dinner."

"I'm still not certain that is necessary," Lily said, only half paying attention to her own words.

"It is up to you, of course, dear," Eliza said gently. "But whether you seek a friend, a lover, or a husband, no one should go through life alone. And he is a *very* handsome man."

Lily sat, staring at the door without seeing it, long after her aunt had left. Her thoughts jumped around, not certain which revelation to settle on.

Mrs. Wright had been smothered in her sleep.

Eliza and Susan were a couple, and they had been for years.

She was grateful for her aunt's trust, and glad to no longer be in the dark, even if she wasn't sure what she was supposed to do next. Continue on as they had before, as though nothing had changed—but could she do that?

She could, she decided. She owed that to her aunt and Susan both, who had supported her through some of the worst times in her life. They had offered her nothing but love and understanding, providing everything from a respite from her father's moods to a home for the terrible embroidery from her school days. And she loved them in return. She would behave toward them as she had always done.

In time, the newness of the truth would fade, and it would become one more fact of their lives. It wasn't as if anything were truly different, after all. The circumstances of her aunt's life were exactly as they had been half an hour before. All that had changed was her own awareness of them.

At that thought, Lily buried her face in her hands. That locked door made Mrs. Wright's death a near impossible puzzle. Did she really think she could be the one to untangle it? When she had taken so long to realize what was right in front of her nose—when she had not, in fact, realized, until it had been plainly spelled out for her? She was glad no one was there to see her embarrassment.

Perhaps this time it would be best to leave the matter to those it truly concerned. Lord Walter would be arriving within a matter of days and could take charge where the local magistrate would not. And she had promised to write to Bow Street— very well, she would do so. She could lay out the facts of the matter, uncolored by her own suspicions and conclusions. Simon Page was a reasonable man. He would see the urgency and do what he could.

Lily crossed to the writing desk, where her letter to Jack still waited. She stared at it, unsure what to do. Part of her still longed to tell Jack what was going on. The other part thought she should rip up the letter and write one only about the commonplaces of her visit.

She would decide later. For now, she set it aside, then pulled out a fresh sheet and began her missive to Simon Page at his Bow Street offices. The letter didn't take long to write, unembellished as it was with her own thoughts and conjectures. She only laid out the facts as plainly as possible, saying that she was asking for assistance on behalf of Mr. and Miss Wright, who were concerned that the matter would not be properly investigated without outside help.

By the time Anna arrived to help her undress, the letter was folded, sealed, and addressed.

She mentioned it to Anna as she was climbing into bed. "Will you take it downstairs and see that it is ready to go out with the morning post?"

"Of course, Mrs. Adler," Anna said, stopping by the writing table on the way to the door and tucking the letter into her pocket. "Was there anything else you need before I'm done for the night?"

"No, nothing else. Good night, Anna."

And that was that, Lily thought as she snuffed her candle. There was a bright full moon casting a trail of light through the window, and the wind echoed under the eaves just mournfully enough that she pulled the bedspread up a little higher without thinking. She had done what she could, and now she would stay out of the rest of it.

CHAPTER 13

"Mrs. Adler, are you sure you won't walk into the village with me today?" Ofelia asked over breakfast. She clearly expected her friend would jump at the chance to find out more about the residents of Belleford, and had whispered her plan to do just that as she and Lily both served themselves from the sideboard.

But Lily demurred, trying to ignore the surprise on the younger woman's face. "I believe I will stay at the cottage for the day," she replied as she buttered her toast. "You and Sir Edward have both had more time with Susan during this visit than I. I should like to remedy that."

Susan, who sat at one end of the table opposite Eliza, blushed pink with pleasure, looking more like a plump china doll than ever. "Are you sure, Lily?" she asked. "I've no wish to keep you from your friends."

"Of course," Lily said, hoping any uncertainty she felt was not apparent in her voice. She sent a quick glance at her aunt, who was holding a forgotten teacup in one hand as she watched the exchange. "We always spend at least one day of my visits managing some project or other together. I see no reason why this one should be any different."

"What a lovely idea," Eliza said quickly. "Perhaps on your walk you might see if there are any late-blooming flowers to be found. To decorate the parlor for tonight."

Lily caught Ofelia casting frowning glances between the three of them, clearly puzzled by the silent interplay. And when Lily left the table, her friend followed, whispering her idea of finding out what Mr. Wright had been up to while they headed back toward Lily's room. "And we both know you have just as many questions as I do. I don't see why you'll not come with me."

"Because I've no wish to hurt Susan's feelings," Lily said, going to the mirror to settle a hat over her chignon. "If I fail to spend some time with her this visit, she will wonder if something is wrong. And I don't want her to think that. Besides." Lily hesitated, then shrugged. "I think I, at least, might be at the limit of what I can discover. Perhaps it would be best to let someone else handle the matter."

"You cannot mean that," Ofelia said in disbelief, only just keeping her voice low. "Why, I have never yet seen you hesitate to—"

"Sometimes circumstances change," Lily interrupted, feeling her cheeks heat. "And I am no longer as certain as I was that . . . That is to say, I wrote to Bow Street yesterday. I am confident in their ability to handle the matter. And Lord Walter, when he arrives."

"But what about your aunt?" Ofelia demanded. "Just yesterday you were insistent that you could not leave her and Miss Clarke before this killer had been discovered. If we let the trail grow cold before Mr. Page arrives, who knows if the culprit will ever be discovered?"

She was right, and Lily hesitated again. "Something needs to be done, certainly," she said as she went to fetch her coat from the wardrobe. But if she changed her plan to spend the day at the cottage, both her aunt and Susan would suspect it was because she was now uncomfortable around them. She did not want that. "You go. I am sure you will be able to discover what you wish." Giving in to a moment of indulgent self-deprecation, she added, "And you may be better off without me in the way."

"Mrs. Adler, this is nonsense," Ofelia said, firm and even a little exasperated. "You are one of the most self-confident women of my acquaintance. It is one of the reasons we get on so well," she added with a pert smile. "We both have justifiably high opinions of ourselves and of each other. So how on earth have you come to doubt yourself so severely?"

"I . . ." Lily hesitated. It didn't feel right to share what Eliza had told her, even with so good a friend as Ofelia. "I learned something about my aunt—and about Miss Clarke—that surprised me very much. And it was something I ought to have figured out on my own."

"What could you have discovered about them that has upset you so? Is your aunt hiding dead bodies of her own in the garden? Does Miss Clarke travel secretly to London each month to rob the aristocracy of their jewels and heirlooms?"

"Of course not."

"Do they lead double lives as novelists whose work is so gothic and embarrassing that you must disown them immediately?"

"Well, now you are just talking nonsense," Lily said, unable to stop herself from laughing. "Though Miss Clarke would make an excellent novelist if she ever took the idea into her head."

"Then what could it possibly be? They are a perfectly charming couple, just as you promised, and have been the sweetest hosts—"

"What did you just say?" Lily demanded, her mind stumbling over Ofelia's words as though she had missed a step in the dark. "A couple?"

"Oh!" Ofelia's eyes grew wide. "I apologize. I know they prefer that we not say anything. They are very discreet, of course. But so well suited to each other, once you have time to grow accustomed to the idea, do you not think?"

"How . . ." Lily couldn't think how to respond. A part of her felt like she should deny it, to preserve her aunt's and Miss Clarke's privacy. But she couldn't help asking, "How did you know?"

"My maid told me before we arrived."

"How did *she* know?" Lily demanded. "She's never met them before."

"Apparently your maid told her during the journey." Ofelia shrugged. "You needn't worry, Mrs. Adler. I'll not say anything to anyone. I spoke without thinking just now, but that was only because it was you."

Lily, her mind reeling, latched onto the only thing she could make sense of at the moment. And the sense she made of it was outrage. "They had no right to be gossiping about my aunts. How would they feel if someone spread such personal—and potentially injurious—information about them? How would you feel?"

Aunts, she heard herself say with some shock—a word that she had never used to refer to them collectively. But it felt right. And if she was being honest with herself, it had felt right for years. She had only refrained because Susan was *not* her aunt. But she had filled that role in everything but name for so many years—in both Lily's life and Eliza's. The realization made her feel even more ashamed that it had taken her so long to start understanding the reality of their relationship.

"I do not believe it was meant as gossip," Ofelia said gently, though she looked embarrassed. "I see your point, truly, and I'll speak to Sarah about it to make sure she holds her tongue in the future. But I think your Anna wanted to be sure that we would not say anything untoward or unkind during our visit. Two women living alone like this *is* uncommon, after all. We wouldn't have wished to distress or upset them without realizing it."

"And did Sarah say how Anna knew?" Lily could barely wrap her head around the idea that her maid had known—and for how long?—when she had not.

Ofelia laughed, shrugging again. "Because servants know everything? One cannot keep secrets with a maid in the house. Or a manservant. They see just as much. Though personally, I think they are less astute about what it means. But what did you learn about your aunt that could have upset you so?"

"It doesn't matter," Lily said, hoping she wasn't blushing. At least she had the comfort that Ofelia had not guessed on her own—though as she had only known Susan and Eliza for a matter of days, that only counted for so much. But such a conclusion was so unexpected, so out of the ordinary in her life. Could she truly fault herself for not putting those pieces together?

She could, she told herself fiercely. She had known Eliza and Susan for years, spent time in their home, depended on them when she was struggling, shared her life with them in every way she could. That she had been so blind to their own lives was inexcusable.

"Then if it doesn't matter, there is no reason for us not to go see what we can discover," Ofelia said decisively. "I am glad you have come around."

"That is not what I said, nor what I meant," Lily said, unable to keep the frustration out of her voice. "You should ask whatever questions you wish in the village. It will take us some days to get a response from Bow Street, in any case. There is no reason not to gather what information you can in the meantime. Ned, I am sure, can assist you."

"Only reluctantly," Ofelia said, not bothering to hide her disapproval. The elegant arch of her brow was drawn into a scowl, and her tone might have been used on an irrational child. "Mrs. Adler, you are being absurd. I have never known you to start something and then refuse to finish it."

"There is a first time for everything," Lily snapped, tired of being pushed and prodded. "I am perfectly capable of making up my own mind, and I don't need to be told what to do by an impulsive child who hasn't the faintest idea what I am thinking." She was instantly ashamed of her tone. It wasn't Ofelia's fault she was feeling so out of sorts. It wasn't anyone's fault but her own.

Ofelia stepped back, looking as shocked as if she had been slapped. Her expression quickly changed to one of hurt, then just as fast to absolute fury. Lily opened her mouth to apologize, but she wasn't quick enough.

"Very well, then," Ofelia said stiffly. "I apologize so very sincerely, Mrs. Adler, for assuming that you might still care about protecting your aunt's safety, or about the simple fact that a murder has been committed. Clearly, I was overestimating both your love and your integrity."

"Ofelia—"

Lily didn't get any further before she was met with a door slammed in her face. Lily stared at it, unable to believe what had just happened or what either of them had said. It was the first time they had truly quarreled.

Why had she said something so deliberately hurtful?

Why couldn't Ofelia have just let well enough alone and stopped pestering her?

Squeezing her hands into fists, Lily closed her eyes, turned her face up, and screamed—but she kept her lips fully locked, and the sound was reduced to a frustrated rumble in the back of her throat. There was no reason, after all, to upset the rest of the household, no matter how unhappy with herself she was.

Lily paced around the room, finally crossing to the writing desk and shuffling the papers into some semblance of order. She wasn't normally so fidgety. But she didn't feel like herself, and her hands needed to be busy.

That was when she noticed that her letter to Jack, which she had tucked away last night, was nowhere to be found. Anna must have taken it, she realized, at the same time as the letter to Mr. Page. They were both sealed and addressed, after all. There was no reason the maid wouldn't have assumed they should both be mailed. And now Jack would read all her thoughts and suspicions, and likely write back something encouraging, and she would have to explain that she was unsuited to any sort of investigation or deduction and had decided to abandon such fancies.

Lily sank down onto the chair and dropped her head into her hands.

Yet another thing to add to the list of embarrassments.

She owed her friend an apology. But there was no way she would be allowed to deliver one now. They both needed a few hours to calm down and get some distance from their unkind words.

And in the meantime, she had promised Susan a walk.

CHAPTER 14

"Can you believe she would just give up like that?" Ofelia demanded, seizing a handful of leaves from the hedgerow and shredding them to pieces with a furious burst of energy. Tossing them to the ground, she whirled on her husband as though he were next in line for such treatment. "Can you believe she would *say* such a thing? To *me*? How *dare* she?"

"Does seem out of her ordinary way of things," he agreed, looking unconcerned by her ire.

Neddy was dressed somberly in gray, having represented Longwood Cottage at Mrs. Wright's burial that morning so that none of the ladies would have to endure the rigors of public grief. Ofelia strongly suspected that Miss Pierce, at least, would have been more than up to those rigors had there not been a convenient gentleman present to bear her respects to the family. But Neddy, ever polite, had volunteered his services the night before, and Miss Clarke had readily accepted. It had been sparsely attended, he reported, but perfectly proper. Miss Wright had, no surprise, been absent. Mr. Wright had attended, along with the old butler, Mr. Mears. But Mr. Wright had disappeared soon after the funeral was complete, without a word to anyone about where he was going.

Now, Ofelia watched as her husband frowned, running his fingers absently through the red hair that his valet had so carefully arranged that morning, leaving it in complete disarray.

"Mrs. Adler's not the type to throw around hasty words nor to step back from a challenge," he said slowly.

"Exactly!" Ofelia agreed, her eyes snapping with anger. "Which is why—"

"Must have been something particular to throw her off like that. Can't say I'm much surprised, you know, that she would react badly when you kept pushing the matter."

"When I—!" Ofelia glared at him. "You blame me for what happened?"

"Never said so," Neddy replied, taking her hand and giving it a squeeze. "She oughtn't have said that, to be sure. Nothing childish about you. And I like it when you're impulsive," he added with a smile that made her face heat and her mind feel instantly calmer. Maybe when they had been married for more than a few months he wouldn't be able to affect her thoughts so easily, but she rather hoped that wouldn't happen. "But Lord knows how easy it is to say things one will regret when one is already upset. Did she say what was bothering her?"

Ofelia scowled, pulling her hand away from his to tug angrily at another row of leaves and scatter them to the ground. "Something to do with her aunt. That was all she would say."

"Well, there you have it," he said with comfortable assurance that was equal parts irritating and endearing. "Tricky thing, family. Easy to get upset and hard to be rational when they are involved. Mrs. Adler is the type to know when she is in the wrong. No doubt she will apologize when we return."

"I do not care about her apology," Ofelia said quickly, still not ready to let go of her outrage. "And *I* certainly do not owe her one."

But Neddy just shrugged. "As you like, then."

She narrowed her eyes at him. "You are an infuriating man."

"So say my sisters," he agreed cheerfully. "Are we picking up the post again?"

Ofelia hesitated, momentarily distracted. When she had prevailed on her husband to walk with her after Mrs. Adler's baffling refusal, she hadn't told him precisely why she wanted to head into the village. And while she felt as confident of her observations and reasoning as anyone else's—and had, she liked to think, produced more than one helpful insight in the past—she had never yet taken the lead on these sorts of inquiries nor decided for herself where to begin.

She knew there was every chance that the residents of a small village such as this one would look askance at a visitor like her, so obviously different. *"Foreign,"* they would whisper, and they would be right, though not in the way they meant it. The thought made her want to sigh. Neddy—cheerful, friendly, very English Neddy—could get anyone comfortable and talking, but she wasn't sure whether he would agree if she told him outright what she wanted. Neddy, sweet man, was as discomfited by the idea of murder as he was by the thought of ghosts.

"I simply thought a walk would be pleasant," she said at last. "One never knows how many fine days there will be in the autumn, after all."

Neddy gave her a long look, then glanced up at the gloomy sky, where purple and gray clouds hovered low, sent scuttling above the fields by a sharp wind that pulled at their clothes and crept down their collars. "This is a fine day?"

"It is not raining," Ofelia pointed out as the path opened up and the village spread out in front of them.

"Suppose so," Neddy agreed doubtfully. He looked as though he wanted to say something else, but instead simply shrugged and held out his arm to her.

To her surprise, there was no gawking as they entered the village, decorously arm in arm. Ofelia had spent her whole life as the subject of stares and pointed glances that wondered if she belonged, and in a small place such as this, she had expected such looks to be unavoidable. But the villagers they passed looked briefly at them with the normal curiosity that any visitors would prompt, their gazes lingering no longer on her than on Neddy. Perhaps the death of Mrs. Wright had distracted them from all other concerns?

Or perhaps it was the air of money that hung about them. Though there was nothing ostentatious about their appearance, they were well dressed and clearly well-to-do. In most places, money talked louder than anything else.

"You know," Neddy said, his voice low as he nodded politely to a passing local gentleman, "if Mrs. Adler has decided it's best to step aside for this one, p'rhaps you ought to follow her lead? Never liked you getting mixed up in this murder business. Far too dangerous. Not quite proper."

"My love, you married a Black woman from the West Indies." Ofelia patted his arm. "And you have been involved in Mrs. Adler's murders before. You are not nearly as *proper*—" She rolled her eyes at the word, which had been thrown at her with varying degrees of disapproval her whole life—"as you like to think."

"Just the smallest bit involved," Neddy protested. "Offering that boy shelter was— Oh dear," he broke off suddenly, drawing them both to a halt in his surprise. "Doesn't look good, that."

They had just come abreast of the inn, where they discovered Mr. Wright, still in his funeral clothes, talking with an exasperated-looking maid outside. There was a basket of laundry on the ground next to her, but she was more focused on the man currently cozying up to her, his expression drooping with exaggerated sorrow.

"I'm sure you've had a rough day, sir," she was saying as Mr. Wright wrapped an arm around her waist. "And you have my condolences, t'be sure. But that don't mean Mr. Dennings will suddenly be happy to see you inside."

"How could he tell me no on today of all days?" he asked, looking shocked. "I just buried my mother. A man needs a drink after such things."

"Begging your pardon, sir, but it's clear you've already had at least one."

"And I could use another, damn it! He has to know I'm good for it now, at least. No waiting for someone else to pay the bill." He laughed a little wildly, swaying on his feet, and the motion brought his head around just enough to catch sight of Ofelia and Ned.

"Carroway!" he bellowed while the maid flinched away from the loud sound. He dropped his arm from her waist, though, and strode toward them. "Good man, being there this morning. You should know Dennings's inn. Sort of place you might want to visit for some fun if you get bored at the cottage. Come have a drink from me."

"Very kind," Neddy said, looking a little flustered as he glanced at Ofelia. "But my wife—"

"Not to worry," Ofelia said quickly, patting his arm. The maid, seeing that she was at liberty once again, took the opportunity to scoop up the basket of laundry at her feet and make her way around the side of the inn. "Mr. Wright is clearly in need of company on such a difficult day. You go right ahead. I shall go after that young woman."

Neddy narrowed his eyes. "What are you up to?"

"Just going to have a chat." She bowed to Mr. Wright, side-stepping neatly away from them both. "My condolences, sir. Do you think you might be able to return my husband to me in half an hour or so?"

"Don't much like to leave—" Neddy tried to protest, but as soon as she stepped away, Mr. Wright slung an arm about his shoulders and began steering him toward the inn's door.

"You're a fortunate man, upon my honor, to have a wife who is both so beautiful and so understanding of a man's needs," he said as they went inside, Neddy still glancing uncertainly over his shoulder. "In fact—"

Whatever else he might have said was cut off as the door swung closed behind them, and Ofelia was glad she did not hear the conclusion of whatever dubious compliment Mr. Wright was about to pay her. Poor Neddy. Ofelia felt a momentary pang of guilt for abandoning her husband in company he clearly did not wish to be keeping. But as she had said to Mrs. Adler just that morning, servants saw and heard everything. She had every intention of using that to her advantage.

Glancing around to make sure there was no one there to look askance at the presence of a strange, unaccompanied woman in the village, she gave the ribbons of her hat a tug to secure them against the brisk wind and stepped around the corner of the inn where the maid had disappeared.

She hadn't gone far, as Ofelia had suspected. There was an open plot of land behind the building, with a low, humped doorway that seemed to be standing by itself. Ofelia wondered if it might be an old well or icehouse. The open ground was bordered by one of the paths into the village, and the maid was there, busy stringing up a clothesline.

She dropped the line as she caught sight of Ofelia, giving the quick glance that servants were so skilled at using to ascertain a newcomer's rank. Ofelia knew that her dress and manner labeled her a lady of quality, even if she had worn a relatively simple frock that day, and she was unsurprised when the maid bobbed a curtsey.

"Can I help you, miss?"

Ofelia gave the girl, who was probably only a few years older than she was, a sunny smile. "Just looking for a place to sit while I wait. Mr. Wright has commandeered my husband's company for a little while, so they've gone inside to make life difficult for your mister . . . Jennings, I believe it was?"

"Dennings, ma'am. Hopefully not too difficult." The maid smiled as she said it, gesturing at the back wall of the inn before turning to finish tying up the line. "There's a bench there if you like—I won't be but a few minutes—and then you'll have some peace and quiet."

"Does Mr. Wright often make trouble, then?" Ofelia asked conversationally, hovering near the bench without sitting down. "We only just met him a few days ago, and he seemed a lively sort of man. And my husband did not wish to be unkind and refuse to have a drink with him on the day of his mother's funeral."

"Well, he's a fun piece of work, I'll say that for him," the girl said, hefting the basket on her hip. There were lines of worry and stress on her forehead, and her hands were rough and red from a lifetime of work. But she was still young and pretty, and she walked toward the laundry line with a sashaying step that said she knew it. Ofelia drifted over a few steps behind her, trying to be encouraging without being too intrusive. "And I think at this point he's gotten to know every girl in town that's even the littlest bit interested in his kind of fun. His friends too."

It took Ofelia a moment to realize what the maid meant; when she finally understood, her eyes grew wide and she uttered a faint, "Oh."

The barmaid cackled. "Not to worry, ma'am. I seen the way that husband of yours was looking at you. You don't have to worry about him straying. And I'll put the word out that the other girls should keep their distance. Here, can you give a girl a hand?" She gestured at the bag on the ground by Ofelia's feet. "Pass the pins over, if you please, Mrs. Dennings don't mind me having a bit of a chat, but she'll be right cross if she looks out the window and sees I'm not working while I do."

Ofelia, eager to keep the girl talking, not only picked up the bag of clothespins, but she began to follow the barmaid down the line, handing her a pin every time she needed one.

"You're too kind, ma'am," the girl said, and Ofelia was glad she had worn one of her plainer dresses for the excursion. There was every chance the barmaid would have been less forthcoming if she had realized Ofelia's true rank—and she certainly would have balked at allowing her to assist with the washing. "What was I saying now?"

"You were talking about my husband," Ofelia said with a smile. She couldn't help it. Talking about Neddy always made her smile.

"Aye, he's a sweet-looking one, and no mistake. I don't even mind that red hair on him, though it ain't in my usual way." The barmaid laughed, but just as quickly her expression grew grim. "If he's anything like Mr. Wright, though, do him and Mr. Dennings both a favor, and keep him away from here. We don't need any other fellows not paying their debts."

"Oh dear, has Mr. Wright debts?" Ofelia asked, trying not to sound too interested.

She needn't have worried. The maid was clearly happy to have someone to gossip with. "He do now," she said. "Last time his mother came down herself, all high and mighty in that fancy carriage Mr. Wright ordered—and Mrs. Dennings says she heard there was quite the to-do over *that* when time came to pay. Anyway, she swept in here, regal as anything, to settle his bill with Mr. Dennings and say in no uncertain terms—those were her words, mind—*"no uncertain terms"* that she wouldn't be by to pay for her son anymore. If Mr. Dennings had any more bills to argue over, he could argue with Mr. Wright himself."

"Goodness, I imagine Mr. Wright was none too pleased with that."

"Lord no, ma'am. Etta, what works up at Belleford, said there was a horrid to-do over it, shouting and doors slamming like you wouldn't believe from such genteel folks. And not a week later Mr. Wright was back anyway, carrying on at the inn like normal with his friends, drinking and flirting and making a mess of the whole place." The maid shook her head. "They do know how to have a good time, but they don't do it quiet-like, that's for sure."

"I suppose Mr. Wright had remembered to bring his own purse that time?" Ofelia asked, handing over the last clothespin.

"You'd think, wouldn't you?" The barmaid shook her head as she hung up the final sheet, then rubbed her hands briskly together to warm them up after handling the cold, wet linens. "Silly man tried to do just what he'd always done, and then it was Mr. Dennings he was quarreling with instead of his mother. When Mr. Wright and his friends started smashing the crockery, that's when they got thrown in the lockup. Not that it's much of a lockup, mind, just a room behind the magistrate's house. But they were there all night, and none too happy about it, I'm sure." She shook her head. "I hope that don't stop them from coming back, though."

"Really?" Ofelia couldn't keep the astonishment from her voice. "After all that, you'd be glad to have them return?"

The barmaid shrugged. "It makes for an interesting night. And they slip me an extra coin or two, which I can tell you I don't mind at all. Mr. Dennings would be glad to see the last of them, though. But now Mrs. Wright is gone, God rest her, I guess Mr. Wright won't need to worry about getting someone else to pay his bills." She shuddered. "Good thing he was in the lockup that night, or it might have been him the ghost got."

Ofelia's mind had started to wander back to Neddy inside the inn, curious as to what he was discovering. But at the maid's words, her attention returned with a snap. "You mean to say he was locked up the night his mother died?"

"Yes, ma'am. Terrible to think about, it is." She shuddered again. "I could never stay in a place with ghosts, especially not one as kills folk. I hope Etta finds herself a new position soon. I can't think why she's stayed on as long as she has. She's terrified of the gray lady."

"You think it was the ghost that did for poor Mrs. Wright?"

The maid nodded eagerly. "Everyone says so, ma'am. If it weren't the ghost, it would have had to be a person, right? And who'd have wanted to kill a poor old woman like that? Oh, good day, Mr. Samson!"

Ofelia, about to ask more about Mrs. Wright, was distracted as the maid waved toward a figure coming down the path. He was a young man, perhaps just past thirty, tall and slender and dressed in a clergyman's somber black coat. Ofelia remembered, as she heard him greet the maid, that Mrs. Adler had heard gossip about the Wrights not paying their share for repairs to a Mr. Samson's rectory. But that wasn't what made her stare at him, not thinking or caring how rude it would seem. Below his hat, his black hair curled tightly against his head, and his skin was even darker than hers.

He saw her staring and smiled, clearly far less surprised to see her than she was to see him, and one eye dropped in a faint wink before he turned back to the maid. "And how does your sister's new baby get on?"

"Plump as new-risen dough and thriving since her christening. You're kind to ask, sir."

The lack of curiosity from the village residents suddenly made sense. Cities, especially ones like London that were also ports, were likely to have faces of all colors swarming their streets. But in a village like this one, Ofelia had expected her foreign heritage to make her stand out. And it had—but no one had seemed particularly taken aback or suspicious as a result. She had assumed that was due to the ways that obvious money smoothed over every obstacle. But if the local minister was a Black man, clearly there was more to it.

"Well, I'll not dispute that your sister makes a delicious pie, but you be sure she does not put herself to the trouble just yet," he was saying with a laugh when Ofelia finally recalled herself to the conversation. "With four little ones around her now, she has enough to be worrying about without adding my larder to the list."

"I'll tell her, sir, but I can't make any promises," the maid said, picking up the now empty laundry basket and dropping a quick curtsey. "If you'll excuse me, sir, ma'am, I must be getting back to my work."

As she disappeared back around the corner of the building, Mr. Samson turned his full attention to Ofelia. He was not a handsome man—his ears stuck out below the crown of his hat, and there was a hint of gangliness to his figure that would have been more suitable in a boy half his age—but his smile was friendly and engaging as he bowed. "I am going to presume without an introduction, and ask you to excuse my impertinence, to guess that you are Lady Carroway?"

"Word travels quickly, I see," Ofelia said, offering her hand.

"Miss Pierce and Miss Clarke mentioned that their niece was bringing rather distinguished friends on this visit. You are not unaccompanied, I hope?"

"I await Sir Edward Carroway, who is inside the inn. And since I have nothing else to do with my time at the moment, I shall meet your impertinence with my own and ask how a Black man came to be minister in a village such as this? To be quite frank, I'd not have expected you to receive the gift of such an elegant little living."

"It is somewhat of an inherited position. My father held it before me."

Ofelia, who knew the recent history of her country too well to believe that, regarded him skeptically. "No, he did not," she said, unconcerned whether she was being too blunt or rude.

Mr. Samson inclined his head. "Perhaps that simplifies the matter a bit too much. Would you care to stroll around the green while we talk?" He offered his arm, glancing at the sky. "I think we may be able to find a touch more sunlight there."

Ofelia accepted, too full of curiosity to do otherwise. The sunlight was just as fitful on the other side of the building, but at least this way she had more interesting things to occupy her than staring at the laundry. And the local clergyman might be able to tell her a great deal about the Wright family. All she had to do was persuade him to talk—and she was often excellent at persuading unsuspecting people to do what she wanted.

"The previous gentleman who held the living here was also Mr. Samson," he explained as they walked. "He and his wife took me in as a foundling when I was quite young. I believe their original intention was to raise me to be a servant, but they were impressed enough with my intelligence that they decided schooling was the better option. They raised me themselves and even gave me their name. The arrangement provided all of us a good deal of satisfaction, I think, as they had no children of their own. Mrs. Samson died some years ago, and her husband followed soon after. I was flattered to receive the living after him."

Ofelia wanted to ask if they had been kind to him, if they had treated him like their own son or had ever let him forget that they had taken him in as a matter of charity. But even her curiosity had limits, especially with a stranger. Instead, she asked, "Is the living the gift of the Wright family? Or someone else?"

"The Wrights," he answered after only a brief pause. Ofelia wondered what sort of look he was giving her, but she kept her gaze resolutely ahead. "The current Mr. Wright's father was the one who bestowed it on me."

Ofelia thought of Mrs. Wright's refusal to have the rectory repaired and wondered if the dead woman had disapproved of her husband's choice of clergyman. Had she wanted to make things as unpleasant for him as possible, or to persuade her son to give the valuable living to another, more conventional choice? Even a clergyman might have his moments of passion and violence. She hesitated, then asked bluntly, "Are you in danger of it being revoked, then, and given to another, depending on the whims of the younger Mr. Wright?"

"It cannot be," he replied easily as they completed their circle of the green and set off around it a second time. "The terms of the gift state that it is mine until I surrender it or die myself. It is a very comfortable position for a man such as me to be in. Good day, Isaiah."

Ofelia, disappointed that her new theory had been so immediately punctured, had been too busy trying not to frown to notice the Wright's manservant was just outside the inn. He was standing in the shadows, talking urgently with another man who wore a stylish green coat and tall hat. He was much shorter and plumper than the manservant, yet there was an air of menace to him, and he swung his walking stick in lazy circles that, to Ofelia's eye, looked almost like a threat. Isaiah had just handed an envelope to the second man when Mr. Samson spoke; both men, startled by the clergyman's voice, jumped.

Isaiah immediately looked guilty, and his eyes darted to the envelope before he quickly looked away, summoning a pained-looking smile. "Good day, Mr. Samson, my lady. You'll excuse me, I hope, but I must be getting on with Miss Wright's errands." He bowed, polite but clearly flustered, and hurried off.

The man he had been speaking with looked Ofelia and Mr. Samson over with a curled lip, his walking stick still tracing circles through the air. "My lady, is it?" he asked, his voice breathier than Ofelia had expected, and curious rather than menacing.

She lifted her chin. "Yes," she said firmly, offering no other details and hoping the strange man was enough of a gentleman to take the hint. She wanted to know what had just happened between him and Isaiah, but the lazy perusal he was giving her made her skin crawl, and she wanted even more for him to leave as quickly as possible.

He did take the hint, to her relief, and turned to the clergyman. "No greeting for me, Mr. Samson? How shocking."

"I wish you a pleasant day, certainly, Mr. Clive." Mr. Samson very obviously did not make any introduction either, and the greeting was just as obviously a dismissal.

Mr. Clive, rather than seeming offended, laughed. "I suppose I shall wish you both the same, then," he said, tucking the envelope Isaiah had handed him into his pocket. "Must go find my friend Wright, after all. Sir. My lady." He bowed and, still swinging his walking stick, strode off whistling in the opposite direction from where the manservant had gone.

Mr. Samson, after watching him go for a moment, gave a sigh. His shoulders rippled in a movement that was not quite a shrug. "Shall we continue our promenade?"

Ofelia nodded a quick agreement, fully intending to ask about Mr. Clive and what might have been in the envelope Isaiah had given him. But he spoke before she had a chance.

"Isaiah, now, is in a position that is not nearly so comfortable as my own. Poor fellow."

"Because he is a servant?" Ofelia asked, momentarily distracted from her curiosity about Mr. Clive. "Or because that particular position comes with a ghost?" She did not bother to keep the skepticism out of her voice.

"You are not a believer in the supernatural, I take it, Lady Carroway?"

"I am inclined to disbelieve what I cannot see with my own eyes, as I think most rational people are."

Mr. Samson smiled his grave smile. "I am afraid I cannot agree with you on that particular point," he said. Ofelia, recalling that he represented the church and his entire business was faith in things unseen, felt her face heating with embarrassment at her hasty words. But he seemed unoffended, to her relief. "No, I think it is perfectly possible to have a comfortable position as a servant. But you have been to Belleford, have you not?"

There was something in the way he was watching her that felt like a warning, but she couldn't quite put her finger on what it was. She hesitated, then replied, "I have." Ofelia couldn't keep the curiosity out of her voice. "It did seem an odd place."

"In many ways, I think it is much like any old house belonging to an old family. But poor Isaiah has a particular cross to bear, working there."

"Because of the family?" Ofelia guessed. Glancing sideways, wondering how much gossip he would be willing to indulge in, she added with a saucy lift of her eyebrows, "The maids, at least, seemed quite fond of him."

"But the butler, I am sorry to say, is not."

"Mr. Mears?" Ofelia drew to a halt in surprise, remembering the disconcerting way he had stood in the shadows, watching her silently. She shivered. "He seemed a harmless old man, but he . . . was unsettling."

"He is unfailingly polite and proper, as he takes his position at Belleford seriously. But I have come to realize, he particularly dislikes that trait which Isaiah and I share, despite our very different ranks. And which you share as well, Lady Carroway."

Ofelia suddenly understood the warning he was giving her, carefully couched in glances and pointed comments. And she was grateful—it was a warning which, aside from Isaiah, likely no one else in the village was in a position to give.

"There are those, like your estimable hostess Miss Clarke, who may occasionally discomfit one but who always have the best of intentions," the clergyman continued. "But Mr. Mears, I think, is a rather different case. I thought you should be aware, as I understand you have come into more than a little contact with the Belleford family during your time here."

The old butler's silent watchfulness suddenly made sense. And so, she realized, did his insistence that Isaiah sleep where Mr. Mears could keep an eye on him. Which was unfortunate for the poor manservant—but could be useful for her. "Tell me, Mr. Samson. You know your parishioners well, I am sure. How is Mr. Mears's hearing?"

"His hearing?" The clergyman gaped at her in surprise.

"Has it begun to fade with his age? Or is he as sharp as he ever was?"

"As sharp as ever, I am afraid." Mr. Samson shook his head. "He will often approach me after Sunday services to take issue with some point of doctrine from my sermons. All said with perfect politeness, of course. But he does not miss a word." He grimaced, then added with perfect equanimity, "It is of course a great compliment to a clergyman to have a parishioner listen to his words with such attention."

"Of course," Ofelia replied, her mind already elsewhere.

If Mr. Mears had any reason to suspect that Isaiah was responsible for the murder of Mrs. Wright, wouldn't his dislike have led him to proclaim his suspicions immediately? But he had not—had not, in fact, given any indication that he thought otherwise than the rest of the residents of Belleford and blamed the ghost for his employer's untimely end.

Mr. Mears would be a difficult person to live with, she had no doubt, for a man like Isaiah. But to her mind, that was what cleared the manservant of all possible guilt. He could not have committed the murder. He could not have even snuck out to pick the lock for a co-conspirator to do so.

And the barmaid had said that Mr. Wright was locked up the entirety of the night his mother had been killed. They had seen him returning that morning. Which meant that someone else in the house had to be guilty.

Could it have been Miss Wright? Could her expressed contentment with her confined life have been a mere ruse? Or the maid, Etta? But how would she have gotten into the room without the assistance of the manservant to pick the lock? Mr. Mears himself was almost certainly too frail to have the strength necessary to smother a woman, and that other little maid, Alice, had been asleep all night, which Etta herself had confirmed.

She needed to hurry home, to speak with Mrs. Adler and tell her what she had learned and talk over what it might mean.

But no sooner had the thought occurred to her than Ofelia remembered. Mrs. Adler had decided to abandon her investigation, for whatever absurd reason was rattling around in her head, the infuriating woman. She didn't realize how fiercely she was scowling until a voice broke into her thoughts.

"I hope, Lady Carroway, that such a fearsome expression is not directed at me. If it is, I assure you, I shall rush to make amends."

Ofelia, recalled to her circumstances with a start, found that she and Mr. Samson had halted their circuit of the green once more. Mr. Spencer stood in front of them, just finishing bowing a greeting, a friendly smile on his face.

"No, of course not, sir, no amends are necessary," she replied, flustered by his good-humored teasing and resenting that he always managed to make himself so agreeable. "I was simply lost in my thoughts for a moment."

"I hope what I have given you to think on is not too distressing," Mr. Samson said, a note of genuine anxiety in his voice.

Ofelia, realizing he was thinking of his warning about Mr. Mears, hastened to reassure him as well. "Indeed not, sir. I appreciate your insight. It is only that I had expected my husband to rejoin me some time ago," she added, thinking quickly. "And I am hesitant to venture into the inn myself to retrieve him, as I do not know how welcoming it would be to ladies of my position. Gentlemen, of course, are another matter entirely."

"It would not cause anyone to look askance, I am sure," Mr. Spencer put in. "But if it would be of service, Lady Carroway, I should be happy to retrieve Sir Edward for you."

It was a kind offer, and Ofelia wished she could fault him for it. She wished she could fault him for anything. It was infuriating that she could not. "Thank you, sir. He was inveigled upon to join Mr. Wright for a drink some time ago, and I rather dread to see what state the two of them are in. Though it has not been too long, has it?" she asked, turning to Mr. Samson.

"Not quite half an hour, I should say, since I came upon you," he said, pulling out his pocket watch to check the time.

"Then perhaps I shall be able to do both you and Miss Wright a service at the same time." Mr. Spencer sighed, looking grim as he spoke. "No doubt she is long wishing her brother were at home, on such a day as this must be for her. If you will excuse me?" He touched the brim of his hat politely before striding across the green toward the inn.

Ofelia watched him go, lost in her thoughts once more until they were interrupted by a quiet comment from her companion.

"You look as though you would like the earth to open up and swallow him. Has he offended you?" Mr. Samson murmured, and there was an edge to his voice that was almost mocking. "Most women in the neighborhood, I understand, find him handsome and charming. And most men too."

"He is certainly both those things," Ofelia said stiffly. She did not like his tone. But her father always had great respect for men of the church, so she added, with almost unthinking honesty, "But I cannot feel easy around him, as I suspect him of courting my friend."

"How dastardly," the clergyman agreed.

She pulled her arm away from him. "You do not understand, and I do not care to be made fun of." Irritated, she turned her steps toward the inn, stalking across the green with long, aggressive strides.

"Then you have my apologies," Mr. Samson said, falling into step beside her without missing a beat. "But your friend—if indeed we are talking about Miss Pierce's niece, as I suspect we are—has been a widow for some years. You can hardly expect her to remain faithful to her husband when even her own marriage vows no longer require it."

"It has nothing to do with her husband. I am sure he was an excellent man, but I never met him, and I have no particular loyalty to his memory aside from respecting it for her sake."

"Then your loyalty must lie with someone else. Someone still living, I presume, to whom the estimable Mr. Spencer is a threat."

Ofelia scowled, turning to face him. "You are putting words in my mouth. And should a clergyman not refrain from gossip?"

"An observation is not gossip. Are they incorrect words?"

To that she had no reply, so she was relieved to see the door of the inn suddenly swing open and Neddy emerge, Mr. Spencer by his side. Poor Neddy wobbled a little as they came down the steps, and his expression of relief as he spoke to Mr. Spencer made her grimace with guilt. Her husband was not a heavy drinker, and he must have been ready to seize on any excuse to extract himself from Mr. Wright's company.

"If your escort is returning, then I must excuse myself to continue on with my errands," Mr. Samson said, touching his hat politely. "There are many of my flock whom I wish to attend to today. It was a pleasure to meet you, Lady Carroway." He bowed, then did the same in the direction of the gentlemen, who were almost upon them.

Mr. Spencer raised his hand in farewell but did not seem surprised by the minister's abrupt departure. Instead, he bowed, his hand on Ned's shoulder as though to steady him. "Lady Carroway, I am pleased to return your husband to you, fortunately not much worse for wear."

"Hello again, wife." Neddy did not quite slur his words, but there was a fuzzy edge to them, and he bent to place a kiss on her cheek even though they were entirely public. "Who was that?"

"Hello, my love. That was Mr. Samson, the local minister," Ofelia replied, watching the clergyman's loose-limbed, gangly stride carry him away. "How did you find Mr. Wright? Talkative as always?"

"Mopey, poor fellow, though I suppose that isn't surprising," Neddy said. "Kept going on about the ghost, wants to sell Belleford and be done with the whole place but knows his sister would object. I paid," he added, flushing with embarrassment. "Seemed the sort of thing to do, you know. Man's mother was just buried this morning, after all."

"That was kind of you," Ofelia answered a little absently, still watching Mr. Samson. It wasn't until he was all the way across the green that Ofelia remembered she had never asked him about Mr. Clive. "Oh drat!" she exclaimed, wondering if he had kept her distracted on purpose, not wanting to talk about what was clearly an unpleasant connection.

"What is it?" Neddy asked.

"Is something amiss?" Mr. Spencer said just as quickly.

Ofelia hesitated. But he was likely in a position to answer her question, and she had to admit that he had a good deal of respect for Mrs. Adler's investigative inclinations. Presumably, that extended to her as well. And he had been quite helpful a time or two.

"I meant to ask him about someone," she replied, her voice low. "We encountered a man named Clive—a gentleman, I would say, judging by his dress. But there was something not entirely pleasant in his manner. Mr. Samson was so stiff with him. And . . ." She hesitated again, dropping her voice. "I saw Isaiah, the footman from Belleford, handing him an envelope of something. Do you have any idea what it might have been?"

Mr. Spencer's expression had grown serious as she spoke, and now he sighed. "Money, I've no doubt. Mr. Clive is notorious in the neighborhood for facilitating gambling. He is ruthless at cards, and he will take and record bets on just about anything a person might wish to gamble on. He was not born a gentleman, but he has worked his way up into the same set that Mr. Wright spends his nights with because they all owe him money too often to tell him no."

"Not a nice man, then?" Neddy asked.

"No," Mr. Spencer agreed. "Though a clever one, certainly."

"He said he was going to find Mr. Wright, though he did not seem to know his friend was already at the inn. I thought it was to pay his condolences, but now I suspect he had other intentions."

Mr. Spencer's expression grew even more grim. "No doubt he has every intention of using the occasion of Mrs. Wright's death to collect money from her son. Which means I should get him back to Belleford as quickly as I can. If you will excuse me, Lady Carroway, Sir Edward. I look forward to seeing you both this evening." He clapped Neddy on the shoulder, bowed to Ofelia, and strode back to the inn.

Ofelia glanced at the sky, where low, heavy clouds continued to gather. "We ought to head back to Longwood. It looks like it might come on to rain. And you can tell me more about your chat with Mr. Wright."

"Not much to tell, I'm afraid," Neddy said, offering her his arm as they picked their way among the wheel ruts leading out of town. "Kept repeating himself. Raging against the ghost, complaining about Mr. Powell. Didn't mention his mother much except that bit about selling the place. Apparently he has no idea if he even can, legally speaking." Neddy shook his head, disapproving. "Shocking in a man his age to have so little understanding of his own affairs."

"He hasn't your sense of responsibility and obligation, I think," Ofelia said, wrapping both hands more tightly around her husband's arm and smiling up at him.

He gave her a rather narrow-eyed, sideways look in response. "So . . . that Mr. Samuel, was it?"

"Mr. Samson."

"The two of you seemed cozy," Neddy said, and Ofelia was tickled to hear a note of jealousy in his voice. She had once thought it was impossible for placid, easygoing Neddy—raised with every privilege and so full of confidence about himself and his place in the world—to feel jealousy.

She gave his arm a comforting pat. "Being an eternal outsider does rather bond two people right away, even if they have never met before. Especially when they are outsiders for the same reason."

Neddy looked like he wanted to argue the point. But he was an intelligent man, though many people missed that fact because of his absentminded, cheerful manner. And in this case, he was all too aware of the reception that frequently awaited her in both the streets and the drawing rooms of England. He laid a hand over hers and gave it a comforting squeeze. "Then I am glad you found a sympathetic friend to speak with while you were waiting for me."

Ofelia glanced around to make sure no one else was nearby, then stood up on her tiptoes to give him a quick kiss. But they had only been married for a few months, so one kiss turned into several, and there was nothing quick about them. When she drew back at last, her pulse was pounding, and her cheeks were hot. She smiled at her husband. "You are a dear man."

To her surprise, though his cheeks were flushed from drinking and his hair was even more mussed than before, he did not smile back. "It isn't safe, what you are doing," he said quietly, and it took her a moment to realize that he wasn't talking about the kiss. He regarded her unhappily. "Ought to forbid you to, you know. Ought to order our carriage for this very night and insist we depart for Somerset."

Ofelia's pulse sped up again, and this time it was not a pleasant feeling. She could feel a cold prickle of unease across her shoulders that wasn't due to the snaking chill of the wind. It was the first time he had ever made such a statement. "You would not do that, though."

They sized each other up for too many uneasy heartbeats, until the snap of a branch cracking overhead made them both jump, and an entire flock of roosting crows took off with startled cries. Ofelia shivered.

Neddy sighed. "No, I would not," he admitted. "Not yet. But I might if it was the only way to keep you out of danger." He sighed again, then took her hand, looping it through the crook of his elbow once more. "Come, they're probably wondering where we've got to at the cottage."

Ofelia let him pull her along, her mind racing. She had suspected, when she married him, that Neddy's easy nature concealed deep feelings and a stubborn streak that rivaled her own. But she had thought it would take more than a few months of marriage before she would end up provoking either to come to the surface.

If he forced her to leave before she uncovered who was guilty of Mrs. Wright's murder—and especially if it happened before she persuaded Mrs. Adler to rejoin the hunt—then the murderer might go free after all.

If that happened, would the killer, having achieved their appalling objective, be content to settle back into a normal life? Or would someone else be next?

CHAPTER 15

The thunderstorm that had been threatening all day struck in the middle of dinner.

It had been a pleasant evening, if a slightly tense one. Lily was still distracted by her aunt's revelation and her argument with Ofelia. Mr. Spencer, who had been happy to come, was polite and attentive to everyone present, as ready to listen to the stories of others as he was to contribute to the conversation. Sir Edward was doing his best to act like his normal, sociable self, but he kept stealing unhappy glances at his wife, making Lily wish she could ask what had passed between them during their time in the village.

Ofelia herself was in fine form, regaling the group with humorous tales from her childhood growing up in the West Indies and describing with great relish the tribulations of her sea voyage to England. But Lily caught her friend sending more than one surreptitious glance her way, though Ofelia quickly looked elsewhere as soon as she saw Lily looking back.

Lily found herself doing the same thing with Susan, her mind wandering back to the conversation they'd had during their walk. It had taken some time for them to come around to the point, but at last Susan had delicately commented, "I understand you and Eliza had a chat yesterday evening that surprised you."

Lily, normally taciturn and more likely to listen than to speak, had found herself stumbling uncharacteristically over her words. With none of her usual eloquence, she hastened to assure Susan of her continued affection and her gratefulness that she and Eliza had each other. And then she could not seem to help herself as she tried to explain why she was so surprised, how disappointed in herself that she had completely failed to realize something so important. "I, who pride myself on my skills of observation, my insight into the people around me!" But as soon as the words were out of her mouth, she realized she was making the conversation, which had clearly been worrying Susan, all about herself. She had immediately tried to apologize, felt even more uncomfortable, and fallen silent.

"It is not as though we were advertising," Susan pointed out. "We try to be very discreet. People will assume one thing, or surmise another, or they won't think anything of it at all. It's all the same to us, so long as we can continue to live our lives as we wish." She had taken Lily's hand. "But I am glad you know now, dearest. And I am relieved you are not too distressed by the news. Now"—she had given Lily's hand a brisk pat before releasing her—"we ought to discuss our plans for dinner."

That dinner had come together with great speed and a good deal of friendly charm. Lily was still not sure how comfortable she was with her aunt's . . . not quite machinations, as they had been performed with so little pressure as to the outcome. But they were something, and Lily hoped that they weren't as transparent to everyone else as they were to her. But everyone present was comfortable together, the conversation was lively, and Mr. Spencer made himself agreeable to everyone.

Lily had just begun to relax, to think that perhaps the tension was in her own head after all, as they rose from the table and made their way into the sitting room, not bothering with the gentleman staying behind. Ofelia had just taken her seat at the pianoforte when a tremendous clap of thunder shook the cottage. They all jumped, glancing as one toward the windows in time to see a torrent of rain begin to fall.

Mr. Spencer instantly rose and went to see how bad it was, a concerned frown on his face. Eliza went with him while the rest of the group watched with unconcealed anxiety.

"It looks like the sort of storm that will pass quickly," Susan offered from her place by the tea cart. "I am sure you will be able to be home with your children tonight."

Mr. Spencer turned back, smiling politely, though there were still lines of worry at the corners of his eyes. "No doubt, Miss Clarke."

"I do not think I can compete with that noise," Ofelia said, shaking her head as she closed the folder of music she had just begun to page through. "My love, perhaps you would read to us instead? Something deliciously creepy, I think, would be perfect for such a night."

"Not sure that ghost stories are in the best taste this week," Ned said with a glance at his wife that Lily couldn't quite interpret. She wondered again what had happened that afternoon, and she wished she could take her friend aside to ask. "Perhaps our hostesses would enjoy hearing some poetry?"

He made a valiant effort, but the rain and thunder did not abate. When the third crack of lightning in as many minutes flashed through the window, Mr. Spencer rose again and went to look outside. Ned fell silent.

"Can you see the road at all?" Lily asked, setting aside her tea and going to the window with him. The scene outside was briefly illuminated by another flash of lightning, but it was hard to see past the rain.

"I do not think the roads will be passable, even if it does let up," Mr. Spencer said with a sigh. "Not safely, in any case. Miss Pierce, Miss Clarke, I think I must impose upon your hospitality further and ask if you have a bed to spare for the night?"

"Of course," Eliza said, rising immediately. "That is . . ." She glanced at Susan, a sudden frown on her face as she remembered that with three guests already in residence, they did not, in fact, have a bed to spare.

"It will make the most sense for him to stay in the guest room on this floor," Susan said calmly. "If, Lily dear, you do not mind staying in my room tonight?"

"Of course not," Lily agreed immediately. It did make the most sense; Susan's room had an adjoining door to Eliza's, so it would not be proper for Mr. Spencer to stay there himself—Lily hoped she wasn't blushing as she suddenly understood what she ought to have realized about those adjoining rooms years ago. And they couldn't ask Sir Edward and Lady Carroway to give up their room. It only made sense for her to go upstairs and for Mr. Spencer to take her room, strangely intimate though it might feel.

"Then that is settled," Eliza agreed with her usual brisk efficiency. "I shall go find Addie and see about having fresh linens put on the beds. If you will all excuse me?"

"Might be time for all of us to retire," Ned put in as another peal of thunder echoed through the air. "Unless we want to spend the rest of the evening shouting at each other."

Which was how Lily found herself settling her things in Susan's room while around her the rest of the household prepared for the night. Outside, the rain was pelting the cottage, and the occasional crack of thunder still made her jump, but inside felt cozy and safe.

But Lily wasn't sleepy. The nervous energy that had filled her all day, torn as her thoughts were between so many different things, refused to ebb, making her wish that the dinner party she had been dreading had continued far longer. When Ned knocked on her door with a spare nightshirt and a message for Mr. Spencer, she was more than happy to suggest that she carry both down.

At the bottom of the stairs, she would have turned down the narrow corridor that led to the spare bedroom. But a light from the parlor caught her eye, where a lamp had not yet been doused. Curious, she put her head round the doorway and found Mr. Spencer standing still, bathed like a classical statue in the dim light as he looked out the window at the rain.

He turned when she cleared her throat, the worried expression on his face melting into one of pleasure. "Mrs. Adler. Do you need something?"

"I was going to ask the same of you, sir," she said, holding out the folded nightshirt. "From Sir Edward. He had a spare. And he asked me to tell you that his valet is at your disposal, either tonight or in the morning, should you need his services."

"Thoughtful lad," Mr. Spencer said with a smile as he took the nightshirt and laid it on the chair next to him. The description made Lily smile back; Sir Edward might be a man grown and wed, but there was much of the good-hearted boy still in him. Mr. Spencer reached up to rub his jaw, his expression growing rueful. "I will likely ask to borrow his shaving tackle in the morning so I do not arrive home looking quite so piratical."

"It suits you," Lily said, taking a step closer to him without realizing it. "You looked distressed when I came in."

"I do not like to spend the night away from my children without warning," he admitted. "Though they will be able to guess why I could not come home. Still, I do not like them to worry. But enough about me," he added, taking her hand and drawing her toward the settee. Lily was surprised enough by the gesture that she didn't protest, and when he sat, she let herself be pulled down with him until they were sitting only a few feet apart. "Why did you look so pensive at dinner tonight?"

Lily grimaced. "I had hoped no one would notice."

"I might not have had I not been watching you so closely," Mr. Spencer admitted, his eyes fixed on hers with an intensity that made her feel warm all over. "Will you tell me what is on your mind? Or shall I guess?"

"And what would you guess?" Lily asked, feeling a little breathless, though she wasn't sure why.

"I would like to flatter myself with my speculation, but I think I have come to know you too well for that," he said with a rueful smile. "I expect the matter of Mrs. Wright's death, and your search for who is responsible, is weighing on your mind."

Lily didn't argue. "As Mr. Powell said, it seems an unsolvable puzzle, trying to determine not only who could have done it but how they even gained entry to her room."

"And it is a credit to the affection you bear your aunt that you are so determined to see that puzzle solved," he said, giving her hand a squeeze, gentle and comforting. "I have no doubt of your ability to do so."

"Have you not?" she asked, glancing away, feeling embarrassed by his certainty and ashamed of her own lack of confidence. "I do."

"And will you continue in spite of those doubts?" he asked. There was no judgment or pressure in his voice, only curiosity.

"I want to," Lily said, something she had not admitted to herself all day. "I am not used to doubting myself. I do not like it."

At that, he laughed, though kindly. "I know the feeling."

"What do you do when you feel it?"

"I wait for the next right thing to become clear, and then I do that. Sometimes, I think, we most doubt ourselves when we cannot see which path is the best one to take next. But I believe it always presents itself if we are willing to be patient and keep an eye out."

"You make it sound so simple," Lily said with a frustrated laugh, realizing she was echoing his own words from their market day together.

He, in turn, echoed her words back to her. "It is simple. Not easy, not at all easy. But simple." He smiled, leaning his arm against the back of the settee and resting his head on his hand.

It was the most casual she had ever seen him, and without realizing it, she relaxed as well, drawing her feet up under her and settling more comfortably in her seat. "Is there anything else you know of the Wrights that you can tell me?"

"You see?" He gave her another of his warm, intimate smiles. "Your mind will not stop working, even when you doubt yourself. I wish I had more to tell you. Thomas Wright and I, as you have noted, do not move in the same circles, though by rights we ought to, given the smallness of the neighborhood. There is not much difference in our ages, but I've no wish to spend my nights drinking and gambling and pretending to still be a young man with no responsibilities. And . . ." Mr. Spencer hesitated. "I believe he envies me, which precludes any kind of real friendship."

"Because of your family?" Lily asked, surprised. She would not have thought Mr. Wright was the sort of man who wished to settle down.

Mr. Spencer laughed. "Far less noble than that, I am afraid. Because I spend so much time in London. He often asks me about it. I think if the family had more money, he would have set himself up there long ago, no matter how much his mother and sister might dislike it. And Miss Wright would dislike it immensely. She has"—he hesitated, frowning a little—"a fear of leaving her home, I believe. Though I cannot say where exactly it comes from. But she rarely ventures even so far as the village. According to Thomas Wright, he wanted to persuade his mother that they all move somewhere like Lyme Regis for the next summer, but I think it would have come to nothing. They clearly haven't the funds."

"But they have," Lily said, earning a look of genuine surprise. "The family, it seems, has plenty of money. Mrs. Wright simply refused to spend it or to allow her children to do so."

"My word." Mr. Spencer sat up abruptly, looking shocked. "Perhaps Mr. Wright had reason to wish his mother dead after all."

"Or Miss Wright did," Lily suggested quietly.

"How do you mean?"

"If she thought there was a danger of them relocating next summer, and she had such an abhorrence of leaving home . . . Perhaps she thought that the death of their mother would be the best way to keep her brother close to home, at least for the next year. If she was more fond of him than she was of her mother."

"I am afraid I do not know them well enough to say." Mr. Spencer spoke slowly, as though he were turning over his words carefully, and he looked troubled. "But I do have difficulty picturing that timid young woman engaging in anything so brutal as murder."

"As do I. But the possibility is there." Lily shook her head.

"I suppose it is." Mr. Spencer stared at a point beyond Lily's head, clearly thinking it through. "She was with her mother after Mr. Wright left for the night, was she not? Perhaps she did not retire soon after him as she said but remained in the room with her mother long enough to—forgive my bluntness—kill her. Though . . ." He frowned. "The maid came by, did she not, some time later? She would have heard two people in the room."

"Unless what she heard was Miss Wright pretending to be her mother," Lily said, sitting up ramrod straight as the thought suddenly occurred to her. "I never heard Mrs. Wright speak, of course. Were their voices at all similar?"

"They were not dissimilar," Mr. Spencer said, catching some of her eagerness. "And they spent so much of their days together, I imagine Miss Wright could do a fair imitation if she wished."

"Besides which, people hear what they expect," Lily pointed out. "If the maid expected to hear Mrs. Wright, she would be inclined to hear Mrs. Wright, no matter who was actually speaking. Then, after the murder was done, Miss Wright could have left the room and acted her way through the whole scene that we witnessed the next morning." Lily thought it through, then banged her fist against one plump pillow with frustration. "It is that locked door which makes it all so impossible, though."

"Could she not have locked it behind her when she left?"

"It locked from the inside," Lily said, grimacing as she remembered examining the door. "She would have had to lock it behind her as she left, and that could not have happened."

They sat in silence for a moment, each occupied with their own thoughts, before Mr. Spencer shook his head. "What an impressive mind you have, Mrs. Adler." A small smile pulled at the corners of his mouth in spite of the unhappy subject, as he met her eyes. "It is one of the things I most admire about you."

"Well, I knew you could not admire my skill on horse-back," Lily said, trying to lighten the mood at little. She was rewarded with a small chuckle. "I did not mean to fill you head with such grim thoughts before sleep. I would say we should talk of something else, but I had no intention when I came down of occupying your time so thoughtlessly. I am sure you have long been wishing I would say goodnight and leave you in peace."

She started to stand to leave, but he caught her hand. When she did not pull away, he gave a gentle tug, bringing her back so that she was sitting even closer to him than before.

"I could never desire such a thing," he said. His voice was low and serious, but the smile he turned on her was pure, warm flirtation. Lily, flustered by the sudden change, could think of nothing to say in response. "Spending time in your company is always a great pleasure, no matter what we end up discussing."

"Mr. Spencer—"

"Matthew," he interrupted, leaning forward to brush a loose curl back from her eyes. "I wish you would call me Matthew, because I would very much like to call you Lily."

The sound of his voice curling around her name made her shiver. For a moment she forgot all about intrigue and murder, able to think only about the deep blue eyes that were watching her with affection and hope—and something more that she was not quite ready to put a name to. "Matthew," she said, and though it came out as more of a whisper than she intended, she liked the way it felt on her lips. "You are flirting with me."

"I am. Does that fall into the same category as flattery?"

Lily laughed, remembering their second meeting, when she had fended off his compliments by telling him sternly—and a little rudely—that she had no patience for flattery. He had taken it in stride, amused rather than offended by her bluntness and perfectly willing to converse with her as an intellectual equal. "I think they are just different enough," she said. The rest of the household was asleep, or nearly so. And being alone with him made her feel bold in a way that she hadn't felt in many years.

"I am glad to hear it." He smiled. "Lily. I may call you that, may I not?"

"You may. At least," she added, a little challenge entering her voice, "you may when we are alone."

"And given how alone we are," he said, his fingers tracing feathery circles over the back of her hand and up her arm while she shivered, "I would like to do more than just flirt, but I've no wish to shock you."

"I was a married woman once," she replied, uninterested in thinking through the consequences of what she might be starting. "I doubt there is much you could do that could shock me."

"What a challenge to offer a man," he murmured, and Lily felt her heart speed up. But she did not look away or move as he leaned forward.

The first brush of his mouth against hers made her shiver, and the second made her eyes drift closed and her body sway toward his. One of her hands rose without her having to think about it, pressing against his chest, where she could feel that his heart was beating as quickly as her own. His hand slid behind her neck, cupping the back of her head before sliding around to her jaw, his thumb brushing a gentle line back toward her ear as he pulled away.

"That was not too shocking, I hope?" he asked, his voice husky.

Lily opened her eyes, feeling as though she were just catching her breath after a long dash across a field, to find him smiling at her. But it was a hesitant smile, as though he were unsure exactly how she would react.

She did not leave him in suspense long. Thinking of something witty, or even intelligent, to say seemed too difficult. Instead, she simply curled her fingers around the lapel of his coat, pulled him back toward her, and kissed him again.

She felt his murmur of surprise more than she heard it, and it made her smile against his mouth. When they finally broke apart again, both of them were breathing heavily, watching each other from under heavy-lidded eyes.

Suddenly Lily laughed—and then laughed again when he looked at her with endearing befuddlement. "I just remembered where we are," she explained in a breathless whisper, gesturing at the door to the parlor, which was completely open. "The evening ended early, but it is not actually that late. Anyone could have walked in."

"We should probably not continue, then," Matthew replied.

The note of obvious regret in his voice made her feel brave, and she spoke before she had time to second-guess herself. "Not in this room, at least." He couldn't hide his surprise, and that made her smile. "Unless I now have shocked you too much?"

"I am shocked," he said, standing and holding out his hand. She slid her fingers into his and let him pull her to her feet. The motion brought them close together once more, and he bent his head to kiss her again. "Completely shocked, Lily," he murmured, and she felt a shiver chase its way down her spine. She liked the way her name sounded when he said it.

202 ~   Katharine Schellman

"Is that a no?" she asked, her voice a whisper against his mouth that was swallowed by another kiss.

In response, he took her hand once more and led her from the room.

★ ★ ★

The sound of silence woke Ofelia, and she realized that the rain must have stopped. Sliding out of bed, careful not to disturb her husband, she pulled her wrapper around her and padded on cold feet the window.

The sun wasn't up yet, but she thought it might be soon; there was the faintest edge of shivering gold light at the edge of the blackness, illuminating the rippled undersides of the clouds that were starting to break up. She ought to go back to sleep, but she felt too wide awake. Thinking she might get a book from downstairs, she fetched the candle from her bedside, lit it at the banked embers of the fire, and slipped out the door.

The cottage was shrouded in shadows, the sunlight not yet finding its way through the windows, and Ofelia had to feel her way carefully on the unfamiliar stairs. She was so focused on watching her footsteps that she wasn't paying attention to anything else, and she nearly let out a yelp of surprise when she reached the bottom and came face to face with Mrs. Adler.

Luckily, she didn't drop her candle, though she did end up with a spill of hot wax on the back of her hand, and she grimaced as she held in a pained gasp.

"Are you all right?" Mrs. Adler asked in a hushed tone. "I did not mean to startle you."

"Nothing to worry about," Ofelia whispered back. "I could not sleep and thought I might fetch a book from downstairs."

"Of course." Mrs. Adler stepped aside. "Most of them are in the front parlor. Do you need me to show you the way?"

"No, thank you, I—" Ofelia broke off, her eyes narrowing. "What are you doing down here?" In the dim light, she couldn't see whether her friend was blushing, but Mrs. Adler's suddenly embarrassed expression made Ofelia think she might be. "Mrs. Adler, what—" That was when she noticed that her friend still had on the same gown she had been wearing the evening before. "Oh. *Oh.*"

"It is not what you are thinking," Mrs. Adler said quickly, then winced. "Well, no, I imagine it is exactly what you are thinking." She looked agitated, for the second time in as many days—she, who always seemed so assured in all of her decisions. "You'll not say anything, will you? To the others, I mean. Please, not even Sir Edward."

"Of course not," Ofelia said, feeling affronted. However surprised she might be, she wouldn't gossip about her friend. And Mrs. Adler was a woman grown, fully capable of making such decisions for herself—not only grown but widowed several years, as Mr. Samson had pointed out so recently. Ofelia held back an inappropriate giggle at the thought of the clergyman's advice, wondering what he would thinking of seeing it put to such use. "If you are . . . content? With . . . how things are between you and Mr. Spencer?"

This time, she was sure Mrs. Adler was blushing. "For now," she whispered. "I could not say what it means for the future, but . . . oh, it was lovely to feel so free again." Her expression took on a mischievous look that Ofelia had never seen her wear before. "And to have such fun once more."

"Yes, well." Ofelia cleared her throat, surprised at how uncomfortable she felt. Her friend was clearly happy with whatever had

transpired between her and Mr. Spencer. And she could not deny
the appeal the man had, but . . . "What do you think the captain
would say?"

There was enough light creeping into the hall now that she
could see Mrs. Adler's brows draw together in a frown. "I do not
care what the captain would say," she said, lifting her chin defiantly. "He cannot ask me to stay loyal to Mr. Adler forever,
however much we both loved him."

"Oh." Ofelia felt her eyes grow wide. She had always thought
Mrs. Adler exceptionally intelligent—but apparently even the
cleverest of women could have unfortunate blind spots. Either
that or Mrs. Adler was protesting a little too much because she
knew, even if she had not yet admitted it to herself, what the
captain's objection might be. "Oh. No. I am sure he would not
ask you to do that."

"Then it does not concern him, not in the slightest." Mrs.
Adler said, her voice rising before she remembered to drop it to a
whisper once more. "It concerns no one but Matthew and myself."

"Just as you say," Ofelia agreed, a little awkwardly. The two
women stood in silence, still blocking each other from continuing on their way, until Ofelia cleared her throat. "Well, I suppose I should . . ." She gestured in the direction of the front
parlor. "And you will want to . . . You would not want anyone
else to see you wandering the halls at night."

"No, certainly not. I—" Mrs. Adler broke off abruptly, her
eyes growing wide and fixing on a point just beyond Ofelia's
shoulder. "I would not want anyone else to see me wandering
the halls at night . . ."

Ofelia recognized the look on her friend's face. "What is it?
What have you figured out?"

"The maid, Etta. You said she was evasive when you asked why she was out of bed the night she encountered the ghost. Perhaps—"

"Perhaps she was wandering the halls at night for much the same reason you are?" Ofelia broke in, suddenly excited. If Etta had been discovered leaving her room to meet a lover, that could have dangerous implications for her employment. It might even have given her a reason to want Mrs. Wright gone. Or if she had been out of bed the night Mrs. Wright died for her own reasons, she might have seen something that could help them out. "She was very friendly with the manservant, Isaiah."

"Then we need to talk to her today. As soon as we can."

Ofelia couldn't help the surprised lift of her brows. "Does this mean you intend to be involved once more?"

"I . . ." Mrs. Adler hesitated, then nodded firmly. "I do. Everyone has moments where they are not at their most observant, do they not? Particularly when it comes to those who are closest to them."

"Indeed," Ofelia murmured, thinking of the captain once more.

"But we are *not* close to Etta, nor to any of the Wrights. So we ought to find out what we can without letting the trail go cold before we have a response from Bow Street. And I am sorry," she added, her words coming out in a rush, "for what I said before. There is nothing childish about you, and I value your friendship and your insight far too deeply to resent them. I was upset, and I hope you'll forgive me."

"Of course I do," Ofelia whispered. "I apologize, too, for the things I said. We neither of us behaved very well, did we?"

"Should I come with you to the parlor since we are both already awake? And you can tell me what you learned in the village today?"

"I think not." Ofelia shook her head, giving her friend a pointed look. "I imagine you need to get what rest you can before breakfast. I shall fill you in on the details on the way to Belleford."

CHAPTER 16

Matthew Spencer excused himself immediately after breakfast, explaining that he needed to return to his children. His manner toward Lily was not markedly different than it had been before, for which she was grateful. She did not want to deal with any speculative glances or, far worse, pointed comments. The only things that distinguished his farewell to her from the ones he gave to anyone else were the extra seconds he lingered over her hand as he brushed a polite kiss against it and the warm smile as he lifted his eyes.

"I will look forward to our next meeting," he murmured before straightening and turning that charm on her aunts. "Miss Pierce, Miss Clarke, my deepest thanks for your hospitality. Lady Carroway, Sir Edward, a pleasure as always." With polite bows for all, Matthew took his leave.

Lily was only a little sad to see him go. Last night had been enjoyable, to say the least, but it had also been an impulsive decision, and she so rarely made impulsive decisions. She needed to sort out how she was feeling, and she needed to be away from the influence of his many attractions if she wanted to do so with a clear head.

But all that would have to wait until she dealt with the more pressing matter of finding Etta and learning what the maid knew. Confronting Etta would not clear her head exactly. But it was something completely different. And it was far more important than figuring out how she felt about a handsome man with dark eyes and a too potent smile.

She and Ofelia left after breakfast, telling the others only that they were going for a drive. They didn't want to answer questions, and Ofelia said she didn't want to make her husband worry. And they had no intention of making a formal call, so it was unlikely that anyone would find out where they had gone or what they were doing.

They didn't drive up to the front door—the old horse and gig were too recognizable after the number of times Eliza and Susan had visited in the last few days. And they didn't want to be shown in properly and have to explain their errand. Instead, on the way, they agreed to tie up the horse and gig halfway down the Belleford drive, then walk around the property to approach the kitchen door without being seen.

"They've no cook at the moment, after all," Ofelia pointed out as they hiked their way through the overgrown hedgerows and tried not to trip over the gnarled tree roots that were being steadily buried under autumn leaves. "And I think Etta has taken on most of those duties. So we are just as likely to find her in the kitchen as anywhere."

"And less likely to encounter anyone else," Lily agreed, stopping to untangle the hem of her dress from the grabbing branch of a shrub. "They also clearly have no gardener."

"No, indeed." Ofelia glanced around at the wilderness that the Belleford property had quickly become once they strayed from the road. "Though I suppose it could be called pictur-esque, which is stylish these days."

"Not enough ruins for a picturesque view," Lily said with a small smile, too busy catching her breath for a real one. She had not expected the walk to the kitchen to be such a challenge. "Though it does make it easy to picture a ghost on the property."

"Why do you think everyone is so convinced there is one?" Ofelia asked as they set off once more. "Do you think there is any chance it might be real?"

Lily stopped, frowning as she turned to her friend. It was not a question she had expected. "Do you?"

"No. That is, it puzzles me that everyone here seems to believe. Ghost stories are hardly uncommon, especially in old houses. But this goes somewhat beyond that."

"It does," Lily agreed slowly. "It is odd that there is such a strong conviction, even among the people who one would think too rational for such a belief. But half the Belleford residents swear they have seen it in person—and that seems to be enough to convince the village."

"Maybe Etta can shed some light on the matter. After all, she came face to face with it."

"So she claims," Lily said a little grimly. "Perhaps if we con-front her with the truth about her nighttime excursions, she will be more forthcoming about this supposed ghost."

Fortunately, the path back to the manor, though overgrown, was not long, and they were able to slip through the vegetable gardens around back—not barren, although certainly not well tended with only four servants in residence—and find their way to the kitchen door.

Their luck held on the way: they didn't run into anyone, and the kitchen door was open.

For a moment, though, they both hesitated to enter. The door was open to let out a billow of smoke accompanied by the strong smell of burned bread and a female voice cursing loudly.

"Well, that makes one grateful for a trained cook," Ofelia whispered.

Lily nodded, blinking against the smoke stinging her eyes as she tried to decide what the best manner of approach would be. As they stood, just out of sight beyond the doorframe, a second wave of smoke blew out, catching them where they stood and making them both cough.

Luckily, the sound was covered up by shouting from inside the kitchen.

"For God's sake, what have you done now?"

It was Etta's voice, and she sounded more exasperated than anything else. Lily and Ofelia exchanged a glance and stepped closer to the door, each of them trying to peer surreptitiously around the frame to see who was inside.

Alice stood before the smoky oven, looking both unhappy and embarrassed. Etta, who had clearly just come into the kitchen, stood at the foot of the stairs, hands on her hips as she surveyed the scene. She wasn't wearing her uniform; instead, she was dressed in what was likely her best frock, with a pretty but cheap coat, left unbuttoned, and a fashionable, well-trimmed hat on her head.

In spite of her nice clothes, though, she pushed past Alice to grab a towel from the table, using it to cover her hands as she yanked open the oven door. "A right mess you've made of everything," she scolded as she pulled out a blackened loaf of bread. Backing away, she tripped over the wood axe that stood nearby, nearly sending herself toppling to the floor. Cursing as she found her footing again, she slid the bread pan onto the table in the center of the room. "What did you go make such a mess for? It's my half day—I don't want to waste it cleaning up your mistakes."

"Then don't," Alice snapped, the first time Lily had heard her raise her voice. But when Etta turned to her, looking daggers, Alice shrank back, her shoulders hunching. "I was just trying to get a start on dinner. I don't know much about cookery."

"Clearly not. I never met someone so useless in the kitchen," Etta snorted, then sighed. "I'm sure you meant well, but now I'll still have to make the bread when I come back, and we're both going to spend the rest of the day smelling like smoke." She touched her hat and made a face. "And I just bought this."

"I'll run to the inn for the bread—" Alice broke off, staring. "You bought it."

Etta laughed shortly. "The hat? Of course I bought it. The milliner isn't giving them away for free." She preened a little as she fluffed her hair. "Isaiah said it suits me a treat. And it's the prettiest one they've had in the window all month, don't you think?"

"I do," Alice said in a small voice, her face falling. "That's why I was saving up to get it for myself."

It was odd to watch them talking to each other; Lily had thought before they looked similar, had wondered even if they might be related to each other. But the similarities were mostly in their size and coloring; Alice's appearance was more refined. She had a delicate prettiness to her face that Etta lacked, and her way of speaking seemed more gentle than was usual for a housemaid. But Etta, red-cheeked and outgoing, was more engaging. Lily wasn't surprised that, even if they both had a *tendre* for

Isaiah, he seemed to have chosen Etta. Etta might not have been as pretty, but with Alice, one almost didn't notice she was there until she spoke.

"Oh, bad luck," Etta said, grimacing in sympathy. "I had no idea, honest. But don't you need to be sending your wages home to your mother, little mouse?" She laughed. "You never even go out on your half day, so it isn't as though you really need a new hat. But I'll let you borrow it sometime, if I don't need it the same day."

"Do you always get everything just because you want it, Etta?" Alice whispered.

"What was that?" Etta asked, not really listening.

Alice was already turning away. "You can clean up, then, since I'm so useless in the kitchen."

"Alice, don't you dare!" Etta snapped. "You *know* it's my—"

The door shut behind Alice—not slammed, that didn't seem her style, but with a firm and final click that seemed to leave Etta stunned. "My half day, you wretched girl!" she bit off, fuming as she turned back to the ruined loaf of bread. They could hear her muttering a string of curses to herself as she laid off her coat and pulled a large apron over her dress before opening the oven once more to assess the damage.

That sent another wave of smoke out, and Lily and Ofelia both ducked back around the doorway to avoid it. But they weren't fast enough, and Ofelia began coughing fiercely.

The cursing abruptly broke off. "Who's there?" Etta demanded, and a moment later she stood at the door, brandishing a heavy metal ladle in her hand. She lowered it when she saw the two ladies. "Did you lose your way trying to find the front door, then?" she demanded. Her eyes were red and irritated from the smoke, and she clearly was in no mood to be patient.

"No," Lily managed to say, wishing they had made a more dignified entrance. She cleared her throat and straightened, trying to look as serious as possible. "We came to speak with you."

Etta's gaze darted toward Ofelia, and her eyes narrowed. "You was asking an awful lot of questions before, my lady. Can't say I much feel like answering any more. If you'll excuse me, I've got to be cleaning up a mess I didn't make, so I can go enjoy my afternoon." She gave them a curtsey that was almost insulting in its stiffness and turned abruptly back into the kitchen.

Lily and Ofelia exchanged a quick glance before following her.

"I think you will wish to hear what we have to say," Lily said.

"Before we go speak to either of your employers about it," Ofelia added, her tone almost too pleasant for the warning in her words.

Etta's back had been to them; they both saw her stiffen before she slipped her hands under her apron and slid a second burned loaf out of the open oven. "And why would you think that?" she asked as she carried it to the basin, wincing at the heat. Still not looking at them, she scooped a pitcher of water from the bucket that sat nearby and poured it over the ruined loaf, filling the air with a wet, acrid smell.

"Because you lied to me about the night you claim to have seen the ghost," Ofelia said.

Etta whirled around then, her cheeks flushed, though whether with anger or some other emotion it was hard to tell. "I don't *claim* to have seen it—I *did* see it. And that's the honest-to-God truth whether you believe me or not. Do you think I just go running around the halls at night and falling down stairs to please myself?"

"Well, that is a particularly interesting way to phrase it," Lily said. "Because I suspect you would not like it if we went to Miss Wright and told her that you were, in fact, wandering the halls that night in order to meet a lover."

Etta froze, her eyes going wide. "I never," she said. But her voice was hoarse with sudden panic, and her gaze darted between them as if she were a cornered animal.

"And since you lied about the reason you were out of your room that night, who is to say you did not lie about anything else?" Ofelia pressed. "About where you were the night that Mrs. Wright died, for example? The other maid, Alice, she was asleep was she not? She cannot actually say what time you came to bed."

"I wasn't doing anything that night," Etta protested, but her words lacked conviction, and she shifted her weight anxiously as she spoke, looking anywhere but at the two of them.

She was lying, Lily was sure. And though it made her feel bad to do it, she knew that scaring the maid into thinking worse was to come was the best way to get her to confess who she had been meeting and what she might have seen.

"Or perhaps you lied about seeing the ghost at all," Lily said, taking a slow step closer. "Perhaps you *are* the ghost that everyone has been seeing, trying to steal from or scare your employers. Trying to settle a grudge or improve your own position here by chasing the other servants away."

"I didn't—I wouldn't—You can't tell Miss Wright such things. I'll lose my place! You can't do that."

"And we'll not have to if you tell us the truth," Ofelia said. She had stepped around to the maid's other side, and now Etta had to look back and forth between them, her movements growing progressively more agitated.

Abruptly, Lily switched tactics, suddenly starting to feel bad for the girl. "We've no wish to cause you to lose your place, Etta. But you know an officer from Bow Street is coming, do you not? He will find out the truth, and he will not be kind about it. Better to tell us now. We simply want to know what you were really doing that night and what you might have seen."

"Were you meeting the manservant, Isaiah?" Ofelia asked.

Etta laughed at that, though she still looked a little panicked. "Isaiah? And him like a friendly brother to everyone he meets? No, not him. Besides, Mr. Mears would wake up if a mouse was tiptoeing across the floor. Isaiah daren't leave his room until morning chores."

"Then who?" Lily asked gently. That narrowed down the choices significantly, but she wanted to hear it from Etta herself.

Etta sighed. "Thomas. Mr. Wright, I mean, but he likes me to call him Thomas when we . . . well, never mind that," she said quickly, looking embarrassed.

"I suppose that's not much of a surprise," Ofelia said, her mouth twisting in a humorless smile. "From what I hear, he's been all around the town."

"Really?" Lily said before stopping to think.

Ofelia shrugged. "That's what the maid at the inn told me."

Etta laughed shortly. "Aye, that's true enough. I'm just his latest. And I don't expect no more than that," she added with what Lily thought was a bit too much force to be quite convincing.

Etta might tell herself she didn't mean anything to Mr. Wright—who was sinking lower and lower in Lily's opinion every time she learned something more about him—but perhaps she was secretly hoping for more. "How did that come to happen between you two?" Lily asked.

Etta shrugged, picking up the now cold and soggy pan of bread and tipping it into the slop bucket to be tossed out later. "We just got to talking one night," she said, taking the pan to the sink and starting to scrub it. Without turning around, she continued. "He'd been sitting with his mother, like he and Miss Wright usually did, but instead of going out, he went into the library to have a drink. I went to see who was up and if they needed anything, and I found him there, and he started telling me all about how he wanted to get away from here, to go somewhere exciting. But his mother kept tight control of the purse strings and wouldn't ever hear of him leaving. We talked about London and Bath for a bit, and he said something about how there wasn't any more fun to be had in the village. And I told him there was plenty of fun to be had right where he was."

"Why did you want to?" Ofelia asked, genuine curiosity in her voice.

Etta shrugged as she began to give the second pan of bread the same treatment. "Why not? I'm bored here too. And I'd heard from plenty of others that he knew how to make sure a girl had a good time too. So that was that."

"And did anyone else know?"

"No one," Etta said with steely conviction. "We had a way we did things. After I'd check to make sure Mrs. Wright didn't need anything else for the night, I'd go to the old spare room in the east wing, and when he was home for the night, he'd come meet me. It's horrid dusty, but no one ever goes there, and we couldn't risk anyone seeing us. Thomas was already on poor terms with his mother 'cause of his debts. If she knew I was her son's bit of fun, I'd have lost my place for certain, and I couldn't risk that."

"So is that what you were doing the night you saw the ghost?" Ofelia asked.

Etta turned around to face them once more as she wiped her soapy hands on her apron. "I was going back to my room, and I came around the corner and . . ." Etta shivered. "There she was."

"What happened?" Lily asked, curious in spite of her disbelief.

"I don't rightly remember—it all happened so quick, and it's so dark in the halls at night. I think I gasped or yelped or something, I was so surprised, and she was between me and the way back to my room. She turned, and when she saw me, she came after me. Terrifying, she was, all draped in gray and white and with no face at all, just a long veil. I turned and ran, but I heard her coming after me, and when I looked back, that's when I tripped and fell down the stairs. Landed with my arm all twisted up beneath me. But when I looked up at the top of the stairs, she was gone."

Lily listened without interrupting. Unlike a few minutes before, when she had been so evasive and scared, Etta spoke firmly this time, looking between them slowly to meet their eyes. There was no doubt in Lily's mind that the girl was telling the truth—or at least, what she believed was the truth. But Lily still refused to believe that the ghost was real. So what—or who—had Etta run from that night?

And had it reappeared the night Mrs. Wright died?

She exchanged a glance with Ofelia, who was frowning in thought. "Were you meeting Mr. Wright the night his mother was killed?" Lily asked.

"We was supposed to meet, just like usual, but he never came. I fell asleep there and didn't wake up until there was all the hullabaloo, and then I found out Mrs. Wright was killed."

"And did you see or hear anything odd that night?" Lily asked.

Etta shrugged as she pulled off her apron. "That room's so far away from everything else, I wouldn't have been able to hear anything that weren't someone screaming at the top of their lungs. Which is what Miss Wright did, mind, and that woke me."

"So you were alone all night in a room not your own," Lily couldn't help pointing out, her brows lifting skeptically. "And since you didn't see or hear anyone, and no one saw or heard you, you cannot prove that, can you?"

Etta glared at her as she tossed the apron over a chair and retrieved her coat. "Believe what you like, then," she snapped as she pulled it on. "I told you the truth about Mr. Wright and the ghost *and* what I saw that night. Which was nothing. You go tell Miss Wright whatever you want—I don't have time to care. It's my half day, and I'm going out to enjoy myself."

Lily and Ofelia exchanged a glance, and when Ofelia flicked her eyes to the door in a quick question, Lily nodded. They weren't going to get anything more out of Etta just then, and the longer they stayed, the more likely it became that someone else would discover them poking around and asking questions where they weren't supposed to.

"Thank you for your honesty, Etta," she said. "I hope we'll not have to repeat any of this to Miss Wright."

"I don't care if you do," Etta said, her chin raised defiantly. "It's her brother's in charge now, and Thomas ain't going to let that sour nothing of a sister kick me out. He likes me too much for that."

"One final thing," Ofelia asked. "Do you and Mr. Wright still meet at night?"

Etta gave her a disgruntled look. "He's been busy burying his mother. Not really the time for messing about with a maid. We'll get back to it eventually, I'm sure."

Lily had been about to usher her friend out of the kitchen, but that made her pause. There was something inconsistent in how Etta described their affair, but Lily tucked that fact away for the time being, to be mulled over later when they weren't sneaking around someone else's house. "Then we shan't keep you any longer, Etta. Thank you for speaking with us."

"You didn't give me much of a choice," the maid pointed out, crossing her arms.

Lily inclined her head. "True enough. But I thank you, even so. We'll leave you to your work."

★ ★ ★

The wind had picked back up when they got outside, and they needed all their breath for stomping back through the overgrown grounds. It wasn't until they were back on the path, trudging toward where they had left the cart, that either of them finally spoke.

"What did you make of that?" Ofelia asked, panting a little as they climbed out of the ditch next to the road. She was shorter than Lily and having more trouble climbing up the last few feet that they had slid down so easily just an hour before.

"It seemed like she was telling the truth," Lily said, offering a hand to help her friend up. "Even about seeing the ghost. Or at least, she thought it was the truth. But then there was that oddness at the end."

"What do you mean?" Ofelia asked, busy setting her hat and coat to rights after a walk that had been more physically involved than either of them had expected.

"She was adamant at first that she was just Mr. Wright's 'bit of fun.' And she was equally certain that they couldn't be discovered. But then she was so flippant when she said he would never allow his sister to dismiss her, that he liked her too much for that." The horse and gig were still where they had left them tied up; Lily strode over as she spoke, patting the horse's nose to greet him before untying him and climbing up into the gig. "It was odd."

"So that means it was his mother she was afraid of," Ofelia said, clambering up next to her.

"And now Mrs. Wright is gone, is she feeling more secure in relation to Mr. Wright?" Lily added. "And what exactly does she see that as? The way she was speaking at the end there, it sounded like she did indeed see herself as more than just 'a bit of fun.'"

"Do you think she might have done it?" Ofelia asked, her nose scrunching up with the unhappy thought. "To give herself the chance to take advantage of whatever their relationship is now and turn it into something more?"

"Or perhaps Mrs. Wright did discover what they were up to," Lily said slowly. "And Etta, not wanting to lose both her position and whatever potential that relationship might have—or at least that she thinks it has—killed her."

"But how?" Ofelia asked practically as Lily set the horse to a quick walk back down the drive and away from the manor. "There is still that locked door to explain."

"I do not know," Lily admitted. "I thought I would figure it out by now, but . . ." Her speech faltered as they turned onto the main road and back toward the village and Longwood Cottage. "If only we had a good excuse to get back into the manor."

Ofelia nodded, looking equally frustrated, but she perked up suddenly as a new thought occurred to her. "Perhaps when Mr. Page arrives," she said. "He would want to know your thoughts, I am certain. And he would be more than happy to let you look around Belleford."

"Perhaps," Lily agreed, feeling more hopeful. It had taken some time, and no small measure of animosity between them, but she and Mr. Page of Bow Street had come to respect each other, and he had even relied on her insight into the world of London's upper classes more than once in the course of his work. "I hope he comes soon."

"Or perhaps the captain will write back with some insight," Ofelia said, looking cheerful at the thought. "You wrote to him of what happened, did you not?"

"Rather by accident, but yes. He might— Matthew! I mean, Mr. Spencer. What are you doing here?"

He was on horseback, riding toward them and just turned off the road that led to the village. Her surprise made her sound more abrupt than she meant. Worried that he would think she was unhappy to see him—or worse, unhappy about what had passed between them—Lily quickly added, "That is to say, what brings you into town today? I had thought you would wish to be home with your children after being from home all night."

That felt too much like a reminder of what had happened during that night. Lily felt her face heat, thought about saying something else, and decided that silence was the better choice.

"We have just come from Belleford," Ofelia said, her tone deliberately bright and conversational as she gave Lily a look that was an embarrassing mix of sympathy and pity. "We learned something very interesting about Mr. Wright and one of the maids."

Matthew Spencer seemed not to notice how flustered Lily was. His brows were drawn into a pensive frown as he pulled his mount alongside them. At Ofelia's words, he started, looking suddenly even more concerned. "Then I am glad to see you," he said, his voice low and serious as he glanced around to make sure no one was nearby. A little ways away, there were a few people on foot coming and going, but no one was close enough to over-hear them. "I was just on my way to see Mr. Powell, whose home is a short drive in this direction. If you have learned any-thing at Belleford, I think you should come too."

"Why?" Lily asked, exchanging a worried glance with Ofelia. She had rarely seen Matthew so serious and never this unhappy. "What happened?"

"It will be better, I think, if we do not speak here. And I would prefer to share what I learned with you and Mr. Powell at the same time. But . . ." He hesitated, glancing around once more before lowering his voice even more. "I have reason to believe that Mr. Wright profited immediately and tangibly from his mother's death. I think he might have been the one who wanted her dead."

CHAPTER 17

"Explain the whole thing to me," Mr. Powell said, settling behind his desk and leaning his chin on his laced fingers. "Mr. Spencer first, if you please. What did you learn about Mr. Wright? And why were you attempting to learn it?"

To Lily's surprise, Matthew glanced at Ofelia before he spoke. "It was something Lady Carroway said yesterday. She asked me about Mr. Clive, whom she had been unfortunate enough to meet. Of course, the subject of his social activities was impossible to avoid. And as I had recently learned something odd about the finances of the Wright family"—this time he glanced at Lily as he spoke—"it made me curious about where Mr. Wright's debts to him in particular stand."

"And what did you learn?" Mr. Powell asked.

They were in Mr. Powell's library, a comfortable and heavily masculine room that was set in the back of the house, away from the noise of his wife, servants, and six children. After regarding their arrival with unconcealed surprise, Mr. Powell had ordered tea brought for the ladies, then poured drinks for Matthew and himself.

Ofelia, a bundle of nervous energy who was nearly vibrating in her chair, had not touched her teacup since it had been placed in front of her. Lily, on the other hand, was grateful for hers. It gave her something to do with her hands, which wanted to fidget in a way that she was entirely unaccustomed to. There were only chairs enough for the two of them; Matthew Spencer leaned against the dark paneling of the wall. He almost looked relaxed, but Lily could see the tight grip of his fingers around his glass.

"That Mr. Wright has no debts to Mr. Clive." When Mr. Powell set down his glass, regarding Matthew with a look of unconcealed surprise, Matthew nodded. "I know. I was shocked too. That group of young men hardly made a secret of their escapades, and after the scene Mrs. Wright made at the inn, I had assumed that Mr. Wright would have significant gambling debts."

"But he does not?"

"He does not *any longer*," Matthew said, his voice suddenly cautious. "It took some doing to persuade Mr. Clive to divulge the details, but it seems that Mr. Wright's gambling debts were discharged the morning after his mother's death."

"Well, that is a coarse way to behave," Ofelia exclaimed, unable to keep silent any longer. Mr. Powell turned to her, clearly surprised by the interruption, but she didn't seem to notice. "One would think he might wait at least a full day to take advantage of his mother's untimely absence."

"It is in poor taste, certainly," Mr. Powell agreed, taking up his glass and swirling the amber liquid around in it thoughtfully. "But perhaps not surprising given what I know of his character. Which is not one I have been impressed by."

"There is more to it, is there not?" Lily asked quietly. She had been watching Matthew closely and hadn't missed the unhappy look on his face.

"There is," he agreed. "Mr. Wright was not the one who discharged his debts. That was what Mr. Clive was so reluctant to reveal. I could not persuade him to give me a name. But Mrs. Adler, you and Lady Carroway said . . ." He trailed off, shaking his head. "It is speculation at this point, certainly, but perhaps you might have some idea who Mr. Wright's accomplice could have been."

"The maid," Lily said, understanding. "Mr. Powell, Lady Carroway, and I learned something this morning, which, in the regular course of things, would not be very shocking at all. But what Mr. Spencer has just said throws rather a different light on it."

"Please explain," the magistrate said, looking grave.

Lily exchanged a glance with Ofelia, neither of them quite sure where to begin.

"You know about the maid Etta and her story of running from the ghost? When she injured her arm?" Ofelia asked. Mr. Powell nodded. "When I spoke to her before, she was most reluctant to explain why she was out of her bed and her room that night. And Mrs. Adler and I came to suspect, based on her behavior, that she might have been meeting . . . someone."

"A man," Lily clarified, trying to sound neutral about that part of the story and very deliberately not looking toward Matthew. She certainly didn't have any room to judge Etta for her nighttime activities, and she didn't want to encourage either of the gentlemen to make such judgments either. "So we went to speak with her . . ."

Together, with an occasional interruption or correction, she and Ofelia shared everything they had learned from Etta about her affair with Mr. Wright. As they spoke, the magistrate's expression grew more and more grim. Eventually he stood, as though staying still had proved too much in the face of such information, and paced toward the room's fireplace, resting his hands on the mantlepiece for several moments before abruptly turning and striding back toward his desk.

"I've no wish to assign blame without more information," Lily concluded, feeling exhausted from the recitation. "But given what Etta shared—and given what we now know of Mr. Wright's financial circumstances—it seems not improbable that there was some arrangement between the two of them."

"It is damningly suggestive, I agree, madam," Mr. Powell said gravely.

"There is still the difficulty of the locked door," Ofelia pointed out. "We've not yet discovered a way to account for that."

"And Mr. Wright, we know, spent the evening locked up after his behavior in the inn," Lily added. "Under your own auspices, I believe, Mr. Powell."

"That is true." The magistrate paused by his desk, drumming his fingers against the surface in thought. "The maid, by her own admission, was the last person to speak to Mrs. Wright," Mr. Powell said thoughtfully. "After bringing tea and tending to the fire for the evening, she returned around ten o'clock, I believe? To see if Mrs. Wright needed anything before bed. She said they always spoke through the door, but there is no proving that she was telling the truth. Perhaps she had some means of gaining entry to Mrs. Wright's room. Perhaps Mr. Wright did not leave, as he told us, but remained there, and the two of them left together before he departed for his evening's entertainment."

"That does not account for how the door came to be locked again the next morning, when Miss Wright and the manservant arrived." Matthew glanced at Lily as he spoke, and she knew he was remembering their conversation from the night before, when they had been considering Selina Wright's guilt rather than her brother's.

"Well, I am not sure such details matter under the circumstances," Mr. Powell said briskly, standing.

Lily frowned, and she could see the same expression mirrored on Ofelia's face. "With all respect, Mr. Powell, they seem quite important. A person cannot be guilty of a crime they had no way of committing."

"And we shall discover how they committed it," Mr. Powell said, crossing to the bellpull in the corner and giving it a sharp tug. "Whether their intent might have been to rob or to kill, I could not say. But given the result, it does not much matter. I imagine a few days locked up works wonders for loosening the tongues of criminals."

Lily exchanged a quick, wide-eyed glance with her friend; out of the corner of her eye, she saw Matthew lean forward, the carefully neutral expression he had worn throughout the entire discussion beginning to fray with surprise.

"Mr. Powell," he said slowly, glancing at the two women. "I think we were all hoping simply to bring new information to you. We had no intention of causing the arrest of two individuals who may not have—"

"They clearly intended something," Mr. Powell said, no longer looking at the three of them. "You brought the information to me, Spencer, and I am grateful for that. But now my duty is to do what I see as the best course of action. Ah, there you are." The door had just swung open, revealing a neatly attired manservant. "I will need your assistance. There are two criminals who must be locked up, and there is a chance they will not come along quietly."

"Yes, sir," the manservant said, looking excited by the prospect. Lily's stomach began to turn over, uneasy with what they had set in motion. "I'll fetch Robert to come as well, shall I?"

"Likely a good idea," Mr. Powell agreed. "Prepare horses for you and myself. Robert will need to drive the carriage." The manservant bowed and withdrew, and Mr. Powell began to pace around the room once more. "We'll put Mr. Wright in the lockup here, of course," he said, and Lily wasn't sure whether he was still talking to them or merely thinking out loud. "But the maid does present a difficulty. We cannot lock them up together. Perhaps Miss Wright will be able to suggest somewhere on the Belleford property."

"Sir," Lily broke in. He looked at her in some surprise, clearly not expecting the interruption. She didn't let that stop her, though she did try to sound as respectful as possible. "I am sure you know best what to do, of course. But I hope you will keep in mind that the maid, Etta, may not . . . an arrangement such as the one she had with Mr. Wright is by its nature an imbalanced one. He was her employer, after all. Whatever did or did not happen, there is every chance that it was neither her idea nor her choice."

"He might have coerced her, you mean," Mr. Powell said, nodding, and Lily was relieved to see that he did seem to be considering the idea carefully.

"It does happen, sir," Ofelia put in. "She is a woman, and a servant. It is not hard to picture a wealthy, charismatic man like Mr. Wright persuading or forcing her into a course of action that she never would have chosen on her own."

"Well, if she was party to murder, the law is the law. But"— Mr. Powell held up a hand to forestall their protests—"I will take what you have said under advisement. There is no need to be harsh with her right away. She might even be persuaded to turn against Mr. Wright and confess if she knows that she will not be held responsible for anything he forced her to do."

As he finished speaking, there was a knock at the door, and the manservant reappeared. "All is ready, Mr. Powell," he said briskly. Lily watched with no small amount of alarm as he handed over first the magistrate's coat, then a set of pistols.

Ofelia was even less restrained in her reaction; she gasped audibly.

"It is simply a precaution," Mr. Powell said with surprising gentleness as he glanced at her. "One never knows what to expect when apprehending a criminal, and it is wise to be prepared."

"Shall I come with you?" Matthew asked, glancing at Lily. He wanted to be able to report what happened, she realized, feeling a rush of gratitude.

Mr. Powell looked a little surprised. "Are you a good shot?" he asked, glancing quickly at the spot where Matthew's left arm ended above his elbow, then just as quickly looking back at his face, as though hoping no one would notice.

"I am decent enough," Matthew said with a tone of quiet confidence that Lily suspected meant he was strongly understating his own abilities.

Mr. Powell clearly came to the same conclusion. After a moment of thought, he shrugged and handed over one of the pistols. "No harm in having someone else on hand. Though one hopes they will not make too big a scene."

"Miss Wright is likely more inclined to make the scene," Matthew pointed out.

"Too true," Mr. Powell said, blowing out his cheeks and shaking his head. With a shrug, he held out his arm to Ofelia. "Lady Carroway, may I escort you both back to your vehicle?"

And with that, they had to be content. Lily had to watch the road as she guided the horse and gig away from Mr. Powell's house, but Ofelia twisted around in her seat to watch the four men until they were out of sight.

"Did we make a terrible mistake, telling him what we learned?" she asked when she finally turned back.

Lily's grip tightened on the reins, until the horse grew so fidgety that she forced herself to relax. "Let us hope not," she murmured. "For we cannot undo it now."

CHAPTER 18

It was a tense day for the party at Longwood Cottage.

They had arrived home after luncheon, and Lily had claimed a need to rest and retreated instantly upstairs. She hoped to conceal her conflicted feelings as best as possible, not wanting to worry her aunts in particular, and needed time to compose herself.

But Ofelia had told her husband almost as soon as they returned. When Lily came down for tea, Ned—with the best of intentions—had tried to reassure her that she had done the right thing in taking what she knew to the magistrate. After that, there was nothing to do but tell Eliza and Susan everything as well. Soon everyone's tea things were forgotten in the horrified, impassioned discussion of what might have happened, what would become of the suspects, and which of them might really have been behind the dastardly plan.

"But we do not know that it was, in fact, either of them," Lily put in at last. "We still have no idea how anyone could have gained entry to Mrs. Wright's room. And without that information . . ." She shook her head. "If only I could see the room again. I feel certain I would uncover something. But I cannot remember it well enough."

"Whatever Mr. Powell is planning, I hope he'll make no drastic decisions," Ofelia put in, nervously fidgeting with the tassel on an embroidered cushion, as though she had too much energy to keep her hands still. "At least until Mr. Page arrives from Bow Street."

"Good man, Mr. Page," Ned put in, laying a gentle hand atop his wife's and giving her a reassuring smile. "Smart as a whip. He'll know what to do."

"Have you heard any response from him?" Ofelia asked Lily.

"None yet." Lily said, frowning down into her now cold tea, then standing with a sigh and going to pour herself another cup. She would have liked a glass of something a little stronger, but Eliza and Susan did not keep spirits in the house. "I hope that by tomorrow we will have some word."

"Or perhaps he will simply come," Eliza put in, handing Lily the milk pitcher. "It would be swifter for him to ride straight from London, once he gets your letter, than to send a reply, wait for your response, and then come in person."

"Shall we speak of something else?" Susan asked. Her tone was an attempt at lightness, but the trembling of her teacup against her saucer gave away her agitation. She set them down abruptly. "You all may be used to such discussions, but I am afraid I have had my fill of murder and the like."

"Of course, dear," Eliza said immediately. "They have begun plans for the church fete—did you see the notice? I do hope it will not rain as it did last year."

The others followed her lead, talking of mundane matters and attempting to continue on with their evening. Ofelia and Ned took a walk in the garden; Lily read aloud while Susan trimmed a new bonnet, and Eliza went over the household accounts. But the long silences and unhappy faces when they were finally sitting around the supper table made it clear that no one had quite put the matter from their mind.

They were halfway through the meal when there was a knock at the door. Eliza, frowning, rose in her seat. Ned, his mouth just full of a bite of potatoes, scrambled to his feet as well. "Who could that . . ." Before she could finish, their visitor was shown into the dining room. "Mr. Spencer! Were we expecting you?" She glanced at Lily. "Shall I lay another place?"

"That is very kind of you, Miss Pierce, and no, there was no reason you ought to have expected me." He bowed to the company as Addie and John hastened to set another place at the table. "Though I'd not say no to a glass of wine if you have such a thing. I came straight from Belleford, as I assumed Lady Carroway and Mrs. Adler would not enjoy being kept in suspense of what passed today."

"Oh yes, you are too good!" Ofelia exclaimed, looking more enthusiastic about Matthew's presence than Lily had ever yet seen. "Sit down, please, and tell us what happened." She glanced a little nervously at Susan. "That is, Miss Clarke, if you do not object?"

Susan sighed. "Much as I dislike the subject, I will not be able to sleep tonight unless I know what happened. Please, tell us."

"Thomas Wright was apprehended first," Matthew said, taking the place that was set for him between Lily and Eliza. Beneath the table, Lily felt his hand slide into her lap and press briefly against her fingers before withdrawing, a reassuring touch that she had not realized she needed and suddenly found herself grateful for. "He was sitting with his sister and came along easily enough, though poor Miss Wright protested volubly."

"Did he say anything?" Lily asked.

"He insisted on his innocence, of course, and his love for his mother. One would expect no less, regardless of the circumstances." Matthew nodded his thanks for the glass of wine that was set before him and downed a quick gulp. "After he was taken away by Mr. Powell's servants, I thought Miss Wright would succumb to hysterics. Small wonder, after what happened to her mother and then being told her brother might be the one responsible. We had to spend a good deal of time calming her, and that only happened after our repeated assurances that he would be well treated, and no charges were yet being brought against him."

"And the maid, Etta?" Ofelia asked, leaning forward.

"Was she also arrested?" Lily asked. She wanted to look calmer than her friend, but her fingers were locked around her fork and knife so tightly that the knuckles were white. For some reason that she could not quite explain, she was far more nervous about what would happen to Etta than to Mr. Wright.

"We had to wait for her," Matthew explained as a plate of dinner was set before him. "She was out on her half day, and no one was quite certain where she had gone. Mr. Powell was worried at one point that she had gotten wind of what happened and already escaped. But she returned eventually. Miss Wright gave them use of a storage shed at the back of the gardens where she could be detained."

"She did not cause any trouble?" Eliza asked.

"None." Matthew shook his head. "She seemed stunned by the whole matter. The only thing she asked was to be allowed to change her clothes—she was wearing her good dress and hat, I think, since it was her half day—but Mr. Powell would not allow it. She was put under lock and key immediately, with Miss Wright haranguing her at the top of her lungs the whole time."

"So Miss Wright was willing to believe the maid is guilty?" Lily asked, setting down her silverware.

"I must admit, she seemed at least as concerned about the fact that the maid had seduced her brother as she did about her mother's death," Matthew said, shaking his head. "Knowing him, I have trouble believing it was not the other way around. But Miss Wright was fairly screaming, calling her a murdering Jezebel and worse. It was the loudest I have ever heard that woman speak. The entire household was in shock. I had to take the other servants aside and instruct them to make sure Etta would be brought food and whatever else she might need for the night, because I was worried Miss Wright would attempt to starve her into confessing."

"That was very good of you," Lily said, feeling relieved. Not many men of his station would show such concern for a servant, particularly one who stood nearly accused of murder. She smiled warmly at him but looked away quickly when she caught the curious glance Eliza was giving her. She was still not certain how things stood between her and Matthew, and with so much else to think about, the last thing she wanted to do was answer her aunt's eager questions. "Do you know what Mr. Powell is planning?"

"I took the liberty of informing him that you had written to the man at Bow Street," Matthew admitted, taking a bite. "What a delicious table you set, Miss Pierce, Miss Clarke. I hope that you do not object, Mrs. Adler. To be quite honest, he seemed relieved. He is not accustomed to his duties as magistrate requiring him to address anything more serious than poaching or petty thievery. I think he intends to keep them locked up until the Bow Street officer arrives."

Lily let out a relieved breath; across the table, she saw Ofelia do the same. Both of them had been worried that Mr. Powell would be too hasty in assigning guilt. But Mr. Page would be fair in his assessment of what had happened. And as there was reason to suspect that one or the other of Mr. Wright and Etta had been somehow involved in the murder, perhaps it was no bad thing to keep them locked up for a few days, where they could neither escape the county nor consult with each other.

"I thank you for your hospitality on such short notice," Matthew said, pushing back his chair and standing. "But as it is growing late, I should return home to my children. I hope what I was able to report has set your minds somewhat at rest?"

"As well as they can be at rest until such things are resolved," Eliza said briskly. "Thank you, Mr. Spencer. It was good of you to stop by to share your news. Lily, perhaps you can see the gentleman to the door and make sure he has everything he needs?"

Lily half wanted to object to her aunt's obvious manipulation, but it was so politely done that she couldn't. And in any case, she did want a moment alone to speak with Matthew. She murmured her assent and stood.

Susan smiled. "I wish you an easy ride home and a pleasant evening, sir. And do please give my regards to Miss Spencer."

"She will be pleased by the attention," Matthew said, smiling back. "Mrs. Adler, shall we?" He held out his arm, and Lily let him escort her from the room.

After they had given instructions to John to see Matthew's horse saddled once more and brought round, they stood on the step of the cottage together, a spot that was public and therefore proper but, with the closed door standing between them and the others at the dinner table, also quite private.

Matthew cleared his throat. "This was not how I envisioned today going."

"What did you envision?" Lily asked, genuinely curious. While she had no regrets about their night together, she also had no plan or prediction for what would happen next between them. It was a new experience for her; generally, she liked to have things carefully planned out before she made a decision. And she expected Matthew was the same.

He shook his head ruefully. "I had hoped we might have some time together, in some degree of privacy to . . . discuss how we are both feeling."

"And instead we find ourselves swept up in murder once more?"

"Which I think we can both agree takes precedence," he said quickly, though there was a slight question in his voice, and he looked relieved when she nodded in immediate agreement. "But I wanted you to know . . ."

He cleared his throat again and took her hand, looking more hesitant than she had ever seen him. Certainly he had not hesitated at all last night. He was nervous, she realized, being unsure of her feelings. The thought was so endearing that it made her want to kiss him again, though of course she couldn't, not on her aunt's front steps.

"I wanted you to know how highly I regard you. How much I enjoyed the time we've spent together." When Lily's eyebrows shot up in surprise, he immediately realized what she thought he meant and flushed. "I did not mean last night! Though—" His voice dropped, and the low sound sent a shiver down her spine. "I did enjoy that too, very much. And I hope you did as well."

Lily felt her face heating, but she didn't look away. "I think you know that I did."

That made him smile. "I like you very much, Lily, is what I am doing a poor job of saying with any eloquence. And I feel honored by the trust you bestowed on me last night. I want you to know that I have no expectations of what might come next between us—that is, I have *hopes*, certainly. But if they do not align with your own, I also hope we can still remain good friends."

"And you will not tell me what those hopes are?" Lily asked, feeling brave enough to tease him. "Are you afraid they will shock me?"

That made him laugh. "Will you tell me your own thoughts in return for my very awkward honesty?"

"I hope you will not be offended if I tell you I am still figuring out what they are," Lily admitted. "But I also like you very much, Matthew. And once we are through this terrible business, I think I would like to continue spending time together." She took a deep breath and looked him straight in the eye. "In whatever manner you are hoping for."

She would have thought she had thrown kindling on a bonfire, the way his eyes lit up.

What either of them might have said or done next, she did not know. But at that moment, John brought Matthew's horse around from the stable, saddled and ready, and their private moment was gone.

Matthew took a smooth step back, putting a little distance between them, and cleared his throat. "Miss Wright asked me to pass on a message for you."

"Oh?" Lily grimaced, sure that whatever Miss Wright might want of her, it would not be pleasant. "I suppose I owe her a visit after what I set in motion."

"That was the message, yes," Matthew said with a grim smile. "Mr. Powell might have mentioned to her that you were the one who discovered the affair between her brother and the maid. I believe she is hoping for some kind of explanation."

"Thank you for passing on the message." Lily held out her hand, conscious of the manservant's eyes on them as Matthew took it and bowed. "And thank you again for your visit tonight. It set all our minds at ease to know what has passed."

"It was my pleasure." He hesitated, as though deciding whether to say something else, but in the end merely smiled, gave her hand a quick squeeze, and took his leave.

Lily watched him go until he was out of sight, her mind jumping between thoughts of the previous night and thoughts of the Wrights until she was exhausted. When she went back inside, she found the others had left the table and settled in the parlor. Susan and Eliza kept their eyes politely on their occupations, but Ned and Ofelia were watching for her. Ned regarded her with undisguised curiosity that she knew had more to with Matthew than with murder, while Ofelia nibbled her lower lip anxiously, the normally smooth skin of her forehead marred with a deep frown.

Lily spoke to her friend first. "Miss Wright has requested that we visit her tomorrow. She seems to be hoping for some sort of explanation."

"One cannot blame her for that," Eliza said gently, glancing up from her embroidery.

"No," Ofelia agreed, sitting upright. "And that may be to our benefit, Mrs. Adler. You said you wanted to take another look at Mrs. Wright's room, did you not? Perhaps this will be our chance."

"It may," Lily agreed, perking up a little at the thought. She hated feeling as though she were missing something important, and seeing the dead woman's room might jog her thoughts or her memory in just the way she needed. "We shall see in the morning."

★ ★ ★

Their departure the next morning was delayed, however, by an unexpected arrival.

Breakfast was just ending when the housemaid Addie came in with a quick curtsey and wide eyes. "Begging your pardons, Miss Pierce, Miss Clarke, but there's a man here to speak with Mrs. Adler. He says he is from Bow Street in London. I've put him in the front parlor to wait—I hope that was all right."

"At last," Lily said, sighing with relief. "I was beginning to worry that my letter had gone astray." She stood, only to be confronted with four sets of eyes staring at her with varying degrees of eagerness, apprehension, and curiosity. Lily shook her head. "Well, come along then, everyone. I cannot imagine an audience will make much difference to Mr. Page."

But when she came to the parlor door, she halted abruptly, the others crowding behind her. "You are not Mr. Page."

The young man waiting for them shut the book he was perusing with a sharp, nervous snap, tossing it behind him on the couch, as though to hide what he had been doing, as he sprang to his feet. He could not have been more than five-and-twenty years of age, Lily thought, and perhaps less, with sandy hair that stuck out in too many directions and a prominent Adam's apple that bobbed nervously as he bowed to them.

"Mrs. Adler, I presume?" he asked, his voice surprisingly low for such a gangly frame. He winced. "Sorry, ma'am, my apologies, I mean. That's not the right order. I'm George Hurst, of Bow Street, and I've been sent to look into the matter you wrote to Mr. Page about."

"Mr. Hurst." Lily, still stunned and confused, went through the introductions by rote as the others nudged her into the parlor so they could properly see the newcomer. When they were all seated once more, she could not help adding, "Please do not think me ungrateful for your presence, but I had been expecting Mr. Page himself. He and I know each other well, you understand, and I had written specifically asking for his assistance." She wanted to add that Hurst looked far too young to know what he was doing, but managed to keep that thought to herself.

Mr. Hurst nodded, still tripping over his words a little and speaking quickly. "Unfortunately, Mr. Page couldn't be released from his duties, and the magistrate sent me instead. But Mr. Page has told me what he can. I understand there's a local magistrate that I may speak to?"

"Did Mr. Page have any letter for me? Any message?" Lily pressed.

"Just his regards that he sends. But he said . . ." Mr. Hurst hesitated, looking a little embarrassed. "He told me I should listen to what you have to say?" He said it like a question, as though he weren't quite sure whether he had gotten the message right.

Lily resisted the urge to sigh in frustration. She had wanted the insight of a constable she knew and respected, not a young man who was so green that he still spoke as though worried someone would cut him off if he took too long. But there was nothing to be done about it. Mr. Page's superiors had made their decision, and that was all there was to it. She at least appreciated Mr. Page's attempt not only to provide assistance but to make sure she was not cut out of whatever might come to pass.

"The magistrate?' Mr. Hurst asked, looking from one person to another, as though unsure who he should actually be asking for assistance.

"Lady Carroway, do you remember where Mr. Powell's is?" Lily asked.

"I do," Ofelia answered promptly. "Perhaps Sir Edward and I could escort Mr. Hurst there?"

"If you would be so kind, I think that would be best," Lily agreed. She wanted to hear what might be said between the constable and magistrate, but she didn't have the sense that Mr. Powell would welcome a large audience. And she wanted to see Miss Wright sooner rather than later. "I have some calls to make this morning."

"We would be pleased to take you in our carriage, Mr. Hurst," Ofelia offered while Ned offered an agreeable echo. "We will be able to share what we know of the situation on the way there."

The Bow Street constable was torn between staring at Ofelia in surprise and stammering his gratitude, looking overwhelmed at the prospect of being offered a seat in a baronet's carriage. Lily wondered briefly who his parents were and how he had come to work at Bow Street, but she did not have time to dwell on it. Within a few minutes, John was riding for the village inn where the carriage was stabled, and before long the Carroways and Mr. Hurst had set off, the horses moving at a brisk trot.

Lily turned to her aunt, who, along with Susan, was watching her anxiously.

"I am surprised you did not wish to go with them, Lily," Eliza said. Beside her, Susan nodded, looking unhappy.

"Miss Wright is still expecting me to call this morning," Lily said. She did not add that she hoped to spend as little of her time as possible talking to the fluttery, fidgety Miss Wright and fully intended to both speak to Etta and take another look at the bedroom before the constable and magistrate arrived. "Do either of you wish to come with me?"

Susan shook her head, looking horrified, and Eliza slipped a comforting arm around her waist. "Susan will remain here, I think. But I will come with you." She gave her niece a considering look. "I imagine you may need someone to distract Miss Wright when it's time for you to sneak away?"

"I did not—that is, how did you—?"

Eliza smiled. "I'll see the horse is brought around."

CHAPTER 19

They were met at the door to Belleford by the ancient butler, who regarded them with pale, watery eyes and an expressionless face before stepping aside and bowing. "Miss Wright was hoping to see you today, Mrs. Adler. Please, come in, and I will let her know you have arrived."

"A moment, Mr. Mears," Lily said as the door swung closed. He turned to her expectantly, though with the same unreadable expression. "Have there been any more sightings of the ghost in the last nights?"

"Mr. Wright saw the gray lady the night after his mother's death. We all heard her wails two nights ago as well, though I do not believe anyone saw her. Understandably, the household has very little desire to encounter her," he answered gravely. "But last night, we were thankful that she left us in peace."

"You believe in her, then?" Lily pressed. Etta had been locked up last night, she remembered, unable to keep a suspicion from growing in her mind. There had been other nights the ghost did not appear, of course. But Etta—and Mr. Wright—were the two residents of the hall most likely to be wandering the halls at night. They were also the two with the most to say about the ghost's presence, and Mr. Wright made no secret of his wish to leave Belleford. Perhaps . . . "Have you seen her?"

"I do not leave my bed at night," the butler answered, which was not quite an answer to the questions she had asked. He stepped around them, gesturing with one hand for them to follow. "If you will—"

"Wait." Lily paused, unsure how blunt she wanted to be. Very blunt, she decided. "Why do you stay, and under such trying circumstances, when you have no love left for the family?"

Only the slightest flicker of his eyelids betrayed any emotion. Mr. Mears regarded her for a long moment, and at first Lily thought he was not going to answer. But at last, he gave a slight nod of his head.

"My father once held the same position that I am now honored with," he said, his eyes still fixed on her with that disconcerting stare. "Mr. Wright's children have not yet learned to live up to their father's legacy. But until they do, I shall honor his memory by remaining at my post."

"And Mrs. Wright?" Lily asked.

Another flicker of his eyelids, and this time she could see his jaw tighten. "I've no desire to speak ill of the dead, Mrs. Adler. And I do not gossip. But were I to do either of those things, I might tell you that Mrs. Wright didn't prove the helpmate that her spouse deserved. That after his death, she grew miserly, unsociable, and self-satisfied. That she failed to honor his legacy by behaving in ways worthy of the position that the Wrights of Belleford have always held in this neighborhood. I might even say her death was a relief, that it has made me hopeful her children will be forced, now they are at last freed from her shadow and influence, to finally live up to the memory of their father." His voice did not rise during the entire harangue, and the contrast between his soft tone and his bitter, spiteful words so unnerved Lily that she had to fight the urge to shrink back toward the door.

Mr. Mears regarded her gravely. "Is there anything else you wish to ask of me, madam?"

"No," Lily managed to say.

He nodded, still expressionless and polite. "Then if you would be so good as to wait in here, I'll let Miss Wright know you have arrived." He bowed them into the drawing room, then bowed again as he withdrew in search of his employer.

"Do you think Mrs. Wright knew that he despised her so?" Lily asked her aunt, her feet carrying her around the room in her agitation.

Eliza, looking just as rattled, had chosen a spot by the fireplace, which had burned down to nothing but cold ashes, as though no one had remembered to tend it in days. She shivered as she sat. "I do not know," she said, her voice barely above a whisper. "In general, I would say that most women are well aware when a man despises them. But if she had been, I cannot imagine she would have kept him on so long. She was a dignified woman, but not a generous one. And he gives away so little of his feelings, even when he speaks . . ." She shivered again. "Do you think we ought to say something to Miss Wright?"

Lily stared out the window, looking at the shifting shadows on the ground without truly seeing them. "If we think he had something to do with her mother's death, yes. Otherwise, Miss Wright seems to have been particularly attached to her mother and her home. Telling her that a trusted servant—who has likely been here since before she was born—despised her mother and was disappointed in her would do no good." She felt a pang of sympathy for Selina Wright, whose entire world had been shaken to its foundations with her mother's death, then the remains shattered when her brother was arrested.

Eliza nodded, shivering again as she glanced around the room. "Goodness, this is a miserable place to put guests. Do you think he despises us too? One would think it had not been tended to in over a day."

"There is only one maid remaining in the house, with Etta locked up," Lily pointed out, though she could not quell a shiver of her own. "Perhaps she simply cannot keep up with the work." Going to the heavy, dark curtains, she tried to pull them farther open to let a little more light into the room, and was rewarded with a cloud of dust and several sneezes for her trouble. "Since it seems that even between the two of them, they have not been able to tend the house properly in some time."

Eliza looked around, her face drawn with sympathetic unhappiness. "What a miserable place to live."

"It is my family's home."

Lily and Eliza both jumped, startled by the sudden voice, and turned to find Miss Wright standing in the doorway, eyeing them coldly. "It is my family's home," she repeated, "and has been for generations. If you do not like it, you may do me the courtesy of never visiting again."

She spoke, for the first time that Lily had ever heard, with real dignity rather than in her usual timid, hesitating manner. And she made a disturbing, almost spectral figure standing in the doorway—clad this time not in black mourning clothes, but in an old-fashioned, threadbare dress that was covered in white lace. It did not fit her well, hanging from her shoulders and wrists so that she looked like a child dressed up in her mother's clothing. Which is what she was, Lily realized after a moment— she had last seen the dress hanging in Mrs. Wright's wardrobe.

A draught blew in from the hall as a door opened and closed somewhere, sending the thin fabric billowing around Miss Wright's gaunt figure. Lily had to fight the urge to shrink back from the doorway.

But a moment later, Miss Wright glanced around, her face falling as she took in the barren chill of the sitting room. "Though I suppose this room is not very pleasant at the moment," she admitted, her shoulders sagging with exhaustion and a tremulous whine entering her voice. A black shawl trailed from her hands this time, dragging along the floor until she recalled it was there and wrapped it tightly around her shoulders. "Why must everything be so difficult all at once? Mr. Mears!" She turned back toward the hall, glancing left and right before shaking her head. "Gone, of course. Never a servant around when you need one." Still muttering to herself, as though she had forgotten for the moment that she had guests, she crossed the room to the bellpull and gave it a sharp yank while Lily and Eliza watched her, neither of them quite sure what to do.

At last, Miss Wright sank into a chair with a deep sigh, all the dignity and defiance seeming to fade out of her. Her face was pale and ashen, and there were dark shadows of exhaustion under her eyes. "I suppose I should thank you for coming to see me," she said at last. Her tone was ungracious, but Lily could not blame her for that. "You can guess, I am sure, why I wanted to speak with you."

"I imagine you wish to know what I learned of your brother and Etta," Lily replied quietly, taking a seat at last.

"We do not need to say her name," Miss Wright said, her voice sharp and brittle, her eyes narrowing. "I do not believe a word of what Mr. Powell said yesterday. But if it is true, she ought to have known better."

"But your brother's behavior is excused?" Eliza asked in a mild tone.

"I said I do not believe a word of it, so there is nothing to excuse," Miss Wright said, looking agitated once again as she drew her shawl closely around her shoulders. "Why is it so cold? What could Mr. Mears have been thinking, showing guests in here? Mother would never have stood for it," she added, her hands plucking at the sleeves of her mother's dress as she spoke. "She would be disappointed in us, to be sure."

She frowned at the cold fireplace and dirty windows, then reached out to give another sharp tug on the nearby bellpull, still muttering to herself. Lily and Eliza exchanged a troubled glance when Miss Wright wasn't looking. There was something unbalanced in her behavior, as though the news about her brother had been the final blow to whatever reasonableness and self-control was left.

When Miss Wright turned back to them, her fingers were tangled in the fringe of her shawl, alternately twisting and smoothing it as she looked from one of them to the other. "How could such a rumor begin in the first place? And why would Mr. Powell believe such a thing?"

Lily sighed, wondering whether telling Miss Wright what she had learned would actually make anything better. But two people had been arrested, and she felt that she owed the woman some kind of explanation for her role in bringing that about. Steeling herself, she briefly described her conversation with Etta and why the magistrate had reacted the way he had.

"But it cannot be true," Miss Wright insisted, looking more outraged but less sure than she had moments before. "My brother would not do such a thing. Mother would never have approved. He would know better."

"You were there when he was arrested, were you not?" Eliza asked, and Lily could tell that her aunt was starting to run out of patience. For her part, she was beginning to understand the disdain in which the old butler held the Wright children. "Did he make any denials?"

"Why must things keep being so dreadful?" Miss Wright whimpered, all her bravado and anger seeming to fade as she crumpled in on herself, her shoulders hunching up toward her ears as she sank into her chair once more. "Was it not enough that my mother was killed? Must they try so hard to find someone to blame it on? Must they choose my brother?"

"If he had nothing to do with it, I am sure he has nothing to fear," Eliza offered.

"Of course he had nothing to do with it!" Miss Wright said, sitting up abruptly. "He will tell them so, and they will have to take him at his word, will they not? He is a gentleman, after all." She glanced around the room, her gaze landing on the door as she frowned. "Why does no one come?" she pleaded, giving the bellpull another yank. "Why can nothing ever go right?"

"Miss Wright, I do not know if your brother mentioned it to you, but he asked me to write to the magistrate at Bow Street and request their assistance," Lily said slowly. "The officer arrived this morning, and he is currently consulting with Mr. Powell. They'll be here soon, I am sure, but before they arrived, might I look at your mother's room once more? I might be able to persuade them that Mr. Wright could not, in fact, have had anything to do with your mother's death."

"Oh, of course!" Miss Wright said, sitting up abruptly. "Because the door was locked, after all. Only the gray lady could have entered. And my brother . . ." She shook her head. "Well, my brother was otherwise detained for the night."

"That is certainly one way to describe it," Eliza muttered, but fortunately, she said it in such a low voice that only Lily heard.

"Yes, I will have someone show you up—" Miss Wright, broke off, her frown turning more hostile as she stared at the door. "Where is everyone?" she demanded, standing and crossing to yank the door open. "Mr. Mears!" she called. "Mr. Mears!"

There was a long silence, then the sound of quick feet that certainly did not belong to the ancient butler. A moment later, Isaiah appeared at the door, looking a little out of breath. "Beg pardon, Miss Wright. Mr. Mears is downstairs and could not come quickly enough."

"Why was there no fire laid in this room, George?" Miss Wright demanded. "It is frigidly cold. And Mr. Mears showed guests in here!"

"Begging your pardon, Miss Wright," Isaiah said again, looking ill at ease. "But I think with Etta locked up—"

"We have two maids in this house, do we not?" Miss Wright interrupted. "Why did the other one not take care of it? My breakfast was not even sent up this morning—not that I would have had an appetite for anything other than the tea Mr. Mears brought—but still!"

"I don't know, miss," Isaiah said. "I'm sure it was just an oversight, with everything being so topsy-turvy. Shall I find Alice and tell her to come see to it?"

His deep voice was so soothing that Lily could see Miss Wright visibly relax as she sighed. "Yes, please remind her that we *will* need to eat today. Go find her while I show Mrs. Adler and Miss Pierce up to my mother's room. And I would like a fire laid and something done about the dust before the magistrate and the man from Bow Street arrive."

The surprise and curiosity were instantly apparent in Isaiah's face, but he was too good at his job to give any sign other than that. "Of course, Miss Wright. Is there anything else you need of me?"

"No . . ." Miss Wright hesitated, then shook her head. "No. Just find that girl and tell her that no matter what else is happening, Mother would not have stood for such sloppiness in this house, and neither will I. You may follow me," she continued, turning to Lily and Eliza. "We should be quick about it if we want to finish before they arrive."

The upstairs hall was as cold as the downstairs. When Lily craned her neck to peek into a few of the rooms they passed, she could see that no fires had been laid in any of them either. Though a few still had smoldering embers that had been banked the night before, each room was as cold and cheerless as the last.

Mrs. Wright's room, when they came to it, was even worse than the others. The musty smell of death still lingered, and the windows were still shut tight against the wind and rain that had filled the past several days. Though the bed had been stripped of its linens, the rest of the room looked as though it had not been touched. The fireplace had not been cleaned nor the books moved from their places on the tables. The flue must not have been closed properly, because the wind was whispering down the chimney, eerie and mournful.

"Was the key ever found?" Lily asked. She hesitated at the threshold, not wanting to admit how loathe she was to enter the bleak space.

Miss Wright fumbled with the fob of keys clasped at her waist, then held up a single silver key. "Two days ago," she answered. "It was under the bed, after a fashion, tucked up in a little space between the crosspieces. My brother only found it because he dropped his pocket watch and had to look under the bed to retrieve it. By chance he looked up while he was searching, and there it was. But that is irrelevant, of course."

"Is it?" Eliza asked, the first thing she had said in many minutes.

Her face was pale, and she glanced around the room uneasily, but her jaw was set with determination. Looking at her aunt, Lily found her own resolution was bolstered, and she stepped briskly into the room to look around. Eliza followed.

Miss Wright hung back in the doorway, holding her shawl tight around her with white-knuckled hands. "Of course it is," she replied, trembling as she looked around her mother's room and swaying a little on her feet before she caught herself against the doorway with one hand. Lily hoped the woman wasn't going to faint. Her voice was growing agitated once more. "A ghost does not need a key to enter or leave, as we have seen quite clearly."

"Of course," Lily said, trying to placate her. She glanced around the room before bending to examine the lock on the door. "Aunt, would you open the curtains a little further, please? We should have a little more light in here."

Eliza obeyed promptly, though the watery rays of sun that came in barely made a dent in the gloom. Lily had to squint and put her nose nearly against the wood of the door to see what she was looking for.

There were scratches around it on the inside of the door that she had not noticed before. In the dim light, they had been easy to miss the first time she was in the room: the metal was dull, and they were not deep. But they were distinct, as though someone had tried with neither skill nor success to pick the lock.

As she straightened, something on the floor caught her eye. When she bent down, she discovered that several hairpins had fallen into the cracks between the floorboards. That caught at her memory, and she glanced around the room before crossing with quick steps to Mrs. Wright's dressing table.

The objects atop it were strewn about, as though someone had been rifling through the dead woman's things without any care for their order. A box of hairpins was overturned and its contents scattered among the bottles and brushes.

"Miss Wright, was your mother an untidy woman?" Lily asked, glancing over her shoulder.

"Untidy? No indeed. Mother always says that disorder is a sign of poor breeding." Miss Wright did not seem to realize that she had referred to her mother in the present tense, and neither of her guests were inclined to correct her. "That is why the lower orders are so prone to sloth and wastefulness."

The sentiment did not surprise Lily, given what she had learned about the dead woman. She nodded but did not tell Miss Wright—so convinced of the role a ghost had played in her mother's death—what she was thinking as she returned to her examination of the room.

Lily made a slow circuit, stopping at each piece of furniture and opening any drawers or doors it might contain. She wasn't sure what she was looking for, but she hoped if there were anything to discover, it would catch her eye. As she came to the desk, she spotted the ledger that Ofelia had read in the drawer. Her fingers itched to pull it out and examine it herself, but she had a feeling Miss Wright might object to that. Instead, she asked, "Have you and your brother discussed the state of your finances with your mother gone?"

"Oh no," Miss Wright said, sounding shocked. "Mother always says it is unladylike to concern myself with such things, and of course I shall follow her advice."

Lily heard a small sigh from across the room, and she glanced over to see an irritated look on her aunt's face. Eliza never had much patience for anyone who was unwilling to deal with the reality of their life.

Miss Wright, not hearing, continued. "Besides, Thomas—" There was a slight hitch to her voice, as though she had just remembered what was happening with her brother, but she pressed onward. "Thomas is an intelligent man and a kind brother. He will see I am provided for. And I do not mind living a simple life."

"What would you and your brother do if you discovered you had a great deal more money than you expected?" Lily asked, crouching down to examine the long-cold ashes in the fireplace. Some of them were paper, and she frowned as she pulled at a charred corner of a letter. Had Mrs. Wright been burning her correspondence?

"As I told you before, I've no desire to leave Belleford. So I cannot imagine such a discovery would make much difference to me. My life would continue as it always has. Though I would certainly hire a cook and another housemaid. It is highly inconvenient living with such a small staff."

It was the bottom of a letter, Lily realized, the end of a signature barely visible; _live, Esq. was all she could make out. She sat back on her heels. Could it have been the Mr. Clive from the village that Ofelia had encountered? Had he been hoping Mrs. Wright would repay some of her son's debts? If the letter had ended up in the fire, it seemed her refusal to even consider such a thing extended beyond not wishing to recompense Mr. Dennings at the inn.

"And your brother?" Eliza pressed when it seemed that Miss Wright would not answer the second part of the question she had asked. Lily, standing and making her way to the wardrobe where Mrs. Wright's skimpy wardrobe hung—even more meager now that her daughter had begun claiming her dresses—glanced over in time to see the other woman frown.

"I am sure Thomas would be reasonable, even with such tempting circumstances. He has talked of making ridiculous changes, of course, like going to Lyme Regis or even London. But I am sure he would realize that our place is here, at Belleford, as it has been for so many generations." Miss Wright shook her head, as if clearing away the thought. "But there is no need, I am sure, to contemplate such a thing. Our—what is it, Mrs. Adler?"

Lily had been giving the inside of the wardrobe a cursory examination, when an odd shadow caught her eye. For a moment, it looked like a knob of some kind, and her heart sped up, remembering Ofelia's talk of secret passages and hidden rooms. She stepped without hesitation into the wardrobe, barely even needing to push aside the few clothes that hung there in order to examine the spot.

"Did you find something?" Eliza asked at the same moment as Miss Wright, both of them coming eagerly forward.

But the shadow turned out to be nothing extraordinary on closer inspection, merely a knot in the wood rather than a secret knob or lever. "No, nothing, I am afraid," Lily said, feeling a little embarrassed as she turned to step down.

But before she could, Miss Wright, in her agitation and eagerness, bumped into the door. It was well balanced for such a large piece of furniture and swung noiselessly shut, closing Lily in the wardrobe.

She heard twin surprised gasps from the room, and for a moment she felt a surge of panic at the sudden darkness that surrounded her in the small space. But a moment later, her searching hands encountered the door, and before either of the women outside the wardrobe had recovered their wits, she was able to swing it open and stumble out.

"Oh heavens! You are well? You are unhurt?" Miss Wright exclaimed, wringing her hands with a level of distress that seemed completely out of proportion for the simple accident.

Lily looked at her in astonishment. "I am perfectly well, truly," she said. "There is no need to be so upset."

"I know, I know, but everything just feels so dreadful," Miss Wright said, bursting suddenly into tears. She turned toward Eliza, flinging her arms around the older woman as if without thought. "And I do not know what to do."

Lily stared, unsure how to react. But Eliza, to her credit, took the situation in stride, her expression showing nothing but a brisk, competent sympathy. "It is being back in this room, I think," she said, putting her arm around Miss Wright's shoulders and leading her back into the hall while Lily followed behind. "Perhaps you and I can sit in that nice little parlor while my niece attends to whatever else she must do?"

Miss Wright nodded, snuffling a little as she allowed herself to be led to the parlor and settled into the same fainting couch she had occupied the first time they had met her.

This room, too, was cold, and the fire was still banked from the night before. Eliza rang for a servant and then, not bothering to wait for help to arrive, went herself to stir the embers up and add a few small logs of wood from the basket next to the hearth. Within a few moments, small tongues of fire had begun to lick at the dry wood. "What comes next, Lily dear?" she asked as she worked.

Lily contemplated the tiny flames, wondering how long it would take them to chase away the chill. By all reports, Mrs.

Wright had been an unpleasant woman, miserly, selfish, and needy: attached to her children without showing them any real affection, unconcerned about the community around her, condescending and dismissive toward her servants to the point that she didn't even bother to learn their real names. Miss Wright, it seemed, was heading down the same path as her mother.

Would it be any wonder if her son had sought to break free of their influence in his life by whatever means he could? And would it have been at all difficult to draw a maid who was already enamored of him into his scheme?

"Miss Wright, tell me again the order of things the night your mother was killed. You and your brother were sitting with her, correct? And that was usual?"

"Yes." Miss Wright nodded, still sniffing a little, though she seemed to be gaining control of herself once more. "Mother always liked us to keep her company in the evenings. And it was a cozy, pleasant thing, to always be together. I cannot think why Thomas always felt the need to go out afterward."

Out of the corner of her eye, Lily saw Eliza open her mouth as though to say something, then close it again very deliberately, though she could not hide the impatient look on her face.

"Then *that maid* brought the tea in," Miss Wright continued, her displeasure bringing some color back into her cheeks at last. "I ought to have guessed what was happening. She smiled at him too much, poor man. We were there for some time more, long enough that the maid came in and tended to the fire for the night. We finished up our hand of cards, and then it was clear that Mother was growing tired, so we bid her goodnight."

"And who left first, you or your brother?"

"I . . . I cannot recall." Miss Wright frowned. "I think it was at the same time? Or perhaps Thomas departed just before I did? Yes, I remember her locking the door after I left."

Lily nodded, trying not to let her frustration show too clearly. Selina Wright would have seen her brother leave the room, and both of them would have been out in the hall when the door was locked for the night. But someone had clearly tried to unlock it from the inside later that night—someone without a key.

There was a gentle knock, and Isaiah appeared in the doorway, bowing. "Yes, Miss Wright?"

Eliza asked for tea, one cup with a splash of something stronger for Miss Wright, who was feeling faint. Isaiah offered to see to it himself, as the second housemaid, Alice, still could not be found. Perhaps she was unwell, Eliza wondered aloud when Miss Wright seemed about to launch into another tirade—had anyone been to check on her?

Lily attended with only one ear, still lost in her thoughts. Could the person trying to unlock the door with the hairpins have been Mrs. Wright, unable to remember where she had hidden the key for the night? Or her killer? But then how had that person gotten in—and why did Miss Wright and Isaiah not see anyone else there when they opened the door the next morning?

Perhaps there was someone who could be convinced to tell her how it had been managed, if she presented a sympathetic ear.

"I need to go speak with Etta," Lily said at last. "I think it would be best if that happened before the gentleman from Bow Street arrives."

The others fell silent, looking surprised at the interruption, though Lily did not miss the relief on Isaiah's face. He was friendly with both maids, Lily remembered. It couldn't have been easy for him to see Etta under suspicion and locked up.

Miss Wright grimaced at the name, but this time she did not lash out or complain. Instead, she nodded, looking resigned, and fiddled at her ring of keys until she withdrew a small iron one. "The shed where she is locked up is directly behind the kitchen garden," she said, handing the key to Lily. "George, show Mrs. Adler the way. And stay close by while they talk—we'd not want anything untoward to happen."

For a moment, Isaiah looked as though he was going to say something sharp in defense of his fellow servant. But instead, he nodded and bowed once more. "Of course. Mrs. Adler, if you'll follow me?"

"You will stay with Miss Wright?" Lily asked her aunt.

"And if Mr. Hurst arrives, we will entertain him until you return," Eliza said with a small smile that clearly indicated *entertain* meant *stall*. Lily nodded gratefully at her aunt before following Isaiah out the door.

Their footsteps echoed eerily against the high arched ceilings of the empty house. Lily expected the manservant to lead her toward the main staircase, but instead he continued down the hall toward the large bank of windows.

"If you don't object, ma'am, there's a staircase here that will take us down to the kitchens quicker." The door he opened was set back in an alcove and paneled to blend into the wall; when she peered inside, Lily saw a narrow staircase that could have been the twin of the one she had discovered a few days before, though this one went only down from the floor where they were starting. Isaiah smiled a little nervously at her. "It will save you a bit of time, in the coming and going."

"Of course," Lily agreed. "Lead on, if you please."

This one was a little dustier than the one she had been in already; less used, she guessed, by members of the family, and therefore not as clean. It was also brighter, with more windows along the outside wall. "Are there many of these staircases in the house?"

"Just two, other than the main stair and the servants' stair," he said. "Watch your step here—it's a sharp turn. One at each end of the house. Makes it easier to get where you need to go faster in a house this big. I apologize for the dust—with such a small family in residence, they don't get used or cleaned as often as they should. We just pat ourselves off when we need to. It isn't as though anyone important uses them on a general basis, begging your pardon."

"That is quite all right," Lily said, pinching her nose to hold back a sneeze as they came to the bottom of the staircase and he opened the door to the kitchen for her. "May I ask you a question, Isaiah?"

"Of course, ma'am." His words were polite, but the stiffness of his posture and his tone told her that he was understandably wary of what she might wish to know.

"You and Etta are close, are you not?"

"Not like that," he said quickly. "I'm already promised—it's a family arrangement, you see—have been for years."

"No, of course," Lily said. Though she had, not long before, thought exactly that about them, now was clearly not the time to mention such assumptions. "What I meant was, you have worked together for some time, have you not? And you became friends?"

"Oh yes," he said, visibly relaxing. "Etta was easy to be friends with, for me at least. She could rub some folks the wrong way, and she could get a bit high-strung and sniffy when she was in a mood. But we got along just fine."

"And knowing her as you do," Lily continued as she walked toward the door to the outside, hoping that if they were moving as they spoke he would forget to be so guarded, "what do you think of this affair between her and Mr. Wright? And the accusations against them?"

"I was surprised by the arrangement between them," Isaiah admitted. "We all found out when Miss Wright was shouting about it yesterday, and I tell you, every one of us was shocked silent. Not that I was surprised it happened, mind. With Etta being so lively, and Mr. Wright known around the village for being such a charmer . . . well, these things do happen." His voice dropped. "Even if women like Miss Wright want to pretend otherwise," he muttered.

"Then what surprised you about it?" Lily asked, ignoring the last part since she wasn't sure she had been meant to hear it anyway.

"That she kept it a secret. I wouldn't have expected her to be so good at that." Lily glanced over in time to see Isaiah smile before he remembered where that secret had led his friend. His face fell. "I was shocked by the rest of it too. Etta's always game for a joke or a prank—Mr. Mears could get fair exasperated with her—but something like stealing? Or murder?" He shook his head. "I don't know what to think. None of us did."

They were coming up on the cottage, but Lily paused a few feet short, not wanting their conversation to be overheard. "And Mr. Wright?" she asked. "Did the accusations against him shock you as much?"

The wary look crept over Isaiah's face once more. "Of course, ma'am," he said stiffly.

"Isaiah, you can be honest. I'll not tell either him or Miss Wright what you say to me."

"Did you promise that to Etta, too, when she told you about her affair?" he asked pointedly, and Lily felt her face heat with guilt. He regarded her for a long moment, then sighed. "It surprised me about Mr. Wright too. Not that he'd want to rob his mother—he was that strapped for cash all the time, and everyone knew it. And he could cause a fair amount of trouble when he wanted to. But it's one thing to break crockery at an inn when you're surrounded by your friends and another thing entirely to . . ." He trailed off, looking troubled. "Well, you know."

Lily nodded. "Thank you, Isaiah," she said quietly. That fit with what she knew of Mr. Wright's unadmirable character. But she also knew from experience that even the most unlikely people could do terrible things if they had worked hard enough to convince themselves that they were in the right and that everyone else had made them a victim. "Shall we go hear what Etta has to say for herself? I want to make sure she has a fair chance to say her piece."

Isaiah looked relieved. "Yes, ma'am," he agreed. "That's good of you to do."

The shed was an unfortunate, rundown little building, clearly not used much. But the door looked solid and unmovable, and the walls, when Lily pressed a hand against them, were heavy, cold stone. It couldn't have been a pleasant place to spend the night, and Lily felt a pang of guilt. Thank goodness Matthew Spencer had been there to make sure Etta had some comforts.

Lily knocked at the door. When there was no answer, she took a deep breath.

"Etta?" she called gently, not wanting to scare the girl, who had been alone in the storage shed all night and no doubt was deeply anxious about what would happen to her next. "Etta, it is Mrs. Adler. I was hoping to talk to you before the magistrate arrives. He will have the man from Bow Street with him, you see. And I thought you might find it easier to speak to me before you say anything to them."

There was still no response from inside the shed, and Lily sighed, unable to blame the maid for her resentment or fear—or whatever else was keeping her silent.

"Well, whether you want to speak with me or not, Etta, I wish to speak with you. So I am coming in."

Lily slipped the key in the lock. But before she could turn it, something on the ground caught her eye.

There was a puddle slowly growing on the ground, creeping out from under the rough wooden door to pool across the stone step. At first glance it looked like water, but it was too dark. It wasn't until the sharp, animal smell hit Lily's nose that she realized what she was seeing.

Suddenly feeling ill and afraid, she pulled the key out of the door and gave it a push. It was, as she had feared, unlocked already, and it swung open with a heart-stopping screech of unoiled hinges.

The missing maid, Alice, lay sprawled across the floor of the shed, still in her evening uniform. A dinner tray lay overturned next to her, the crockery broken and the food smashed into the ground. Blood was pooling from the wounds on her face, which had been brutally smashed in, and her tidy knot of hair had come undone, its ends trailing in the dark puddle.

Lying on the ground nearby and spattered with blood, as though left behind just to taunt her, was the hat Alice had so admired.

Etta was gone.

CHAPTER 20

Ofelia sat in the corner of Mr. Powell's office, itching to chime in as the magistrate and the Bow Street runner went over the specifics of the Wright matter, but knowing it was better to keep quiet.

Neddy stood behind her, and when he noticed one of her knees jiggling impatiently, he laid a hand on her shoulder as a reminder not to draw attention to herself. She knew he was right: both men seemed to have forgotten their presence, and they might not be so candid if they remembered they had an audience. But it was still hard to stay silent.

Mr. Hurst seemed more sure of himself now that he was dealing with business rather than something resembling social manners, and Ofelia was grateful. It would have been far too painful to watch the interaction between the two men if Mr. Hurst had still been stumbling awkwardly over his words or Mr. Powell had been looking down on him. But the magistrate seemed grateful to be able to turn the whole matter over to someone else, and Mr. Hurst seemed eager to prove himself. Ofelia wondered whether it was the first time the young man had been sent out on a case by himself.

"Well, let's go talk to the fellow and see what he has to say for himself, then," said Mr. Powell, pushing himself up from behind his desk. Mr. Hurst stood as well, agreeing instantly.

"I'll come along too," Neddy said cheerfully, beaming at both men.

They turned together to stare at him, both of them surprised enough that Ofelia knew she had been right: they had forgotten about their audience. Mr. Powell seemed unsure, and Mr. Hurst looked as though he wanted to object but couldn't decide what to say, perhaps because he was loath to argue with a man whose rank was so much higher than his.

If one of them had objected, no doubt the other one would have agreed instantly. But Neddy took advantage of their hesitation to open the door. "Gentlemen? Lady Carroway?"

He was too amiable for them to argue with—something Ofelia had noticed happened with her husband a lot—so they all found themselves trooping out of the house and around to what the locals called the "lockup." The small, rough structure had been added to the back of the magistrate's house, which was not far from the village itself, and it consisted of one room with a single, high slit of a window and a heavy, locked door.

Ofelia squeezed her husband's arm as they walked, smiling gratefully at him. She knew he didn't approve of her involvement, but he had made sure she would be there for the conversation with Mr. Wright. "Thank you," she said under her breath.

"Can't say no to you, somehow," he whispered back. "Leastways, this means I can keep an eye on you."

"I do need a lot of that," she replied in a saucy undertone, looking up at him through her eyelashes. "Thank goodness you are here to do it."

Neddy blushed red, but he looked pleased anyway.

"Mr. Wright?" The magistrate thumped on the wooden door, blowing out his plump cheeks when there was no immediate response. "Mr. Wright!"

"All right, all right, what do you want?" The voice on the other side of the door sounded sleepy and impatient, and somehow rumpled, but not what Ofelia would have expected from a chastened man. "Come to put an end to this nonsense?"

Mr. Powell pulled out the key from his waistcoat. "One of the constables from Bow Street is here to speak with you, and there is a lady present, so mind you watch your tongue and your manners when I open this door."

"Powell, you know me too well for this rigmarole. I have nothing but good manners." When the door swung open, Mr. Wright stood there, blinking in the sunlight, clad in only his linen shirt and trousers. Inside, Ofelia could see his waistcoat and jacket laid over the back of the room's single chair, and behind him, a tousled pallet bed that he had clearly just left. His hair was untidy, his jaw covered in stubble, and there were creases on one cheek where he had been lying down. He squinted against the bright sunlight as the door opened, but still bowed politely when he caught sight of her. "Lady Carroway. Your beautiful face is a ray of sunshine in this miserable hovel. And Sir Edward! I hope you did not leave our last meeting with too much of a headache. To what do I owe the honor?"

"Thomas Wright, I presume?" Mr. Hurst asked, stepping forward. "I am George Hurst, of the Bow Street constables, and I've a few questions for you. I hope you understand the seriousness of the situation, sir. Your life, and that of the maid Etta, may hang in the balance."

"It was my mother that was killed, man," said Mr. Wright impatiently. There were dark circles under his eyes, Ofelia noticed, as if he had barely slept since his mother's death. "Of course I understand the gravity of the situation! And I am the one who asked Mrs. Adler to write to you fellows. Do you think I'd have done that if I were the one who killed her?" He turned to glare at Mr. Powell. "Did you even tell him that the room was locked all night? No one could have gone in or out. How do you explain that?"

"We were hoping you would be willing to enlighten us, now that you've had a night to think on your situation," Mr. Powell said, looking unhappy at the reminder that a good deal of the situation remained inexplicable.

Mr. Wright snorted. "I cannot enlighten you on a matter that I know nothing of. I was locked up in this very room the entire night, as you well know, sir. And I might add, it was the first undisturbed night's sleep that I have had in days. Go talk to our gray lady if you are searching for answers. For my part, I intend to take her warning to heart and leave Belleford as soon as I am able."

"That is quite a change of tune from you, sir," said Mr. Powell, his bushy eyebrows lowering. "Not long ago you were giving tours of your home to those who showed interest in your ghost." He gestured at Ofelia. "Lady Carroway among them, I believe?"

"If one must be trapped in a moldering ruin of a house, in a middle of nowhere village, one must find entertainment where one can," said Mr. Wright, glaring right back at the magistrate. "I've no more love of living in a haunted mansion than any practical fellow. But the gray lady was the most interesting thing to happen here since I was born. Why should I not have made the best of it? How was I to know that her presence would end with my mother's death?"

"The gray lady is the ghost?" Mr. Hurst asked, looking a little harried as he tried to keep up with the quick, sharp exchange. "And that's the prevailing theory, that a ghost is responsible for the murder of Mrs. Wright?"

"No, indeed," Mr. Powell said shortly, his face flushing with embarrassment. "I said from the very first that I did not believe the matter had a supernatural cause. And in fact—"

Mr. Wright snorted, his agitation clear in the way he kept crossing and uncrossing his arms. "That is not what you said to me."

"And in fact," the magistrate continued, raising his voice as his flush deepened, "it might not matter that Mr. Wright was locked up, as there is every evidence he had an accomplice in the matter."

"Listen, man, just because I was—" Mr. Wright broke off, glancing at Ofelia, who was watching the interplay between the three men with fascination. "Begging your pardon, Lady Carroway, I've no wish to offend your delicate ears. But sirs, just because I was involved with a girl does not mean she and I plotted murder together. What possible reason could I have to wish my mother dead?"

"Money, as I understand it," said Mr. Hurst, drawing himself up to his full height, which was, Ofelia had to admit, quite impressive, especially when his gangliness was hidden by stillness. "Which has motivated many a heinous crime. Your mother'd recently refused to be responsible for repaying your debts, hadn't she?"

Mr. Wright grimaced. "She was going to come around eventually," he muttered.

"And then the day after her death, your account with a local—how would you refer to him?" Mr. Hurst asked, turning to Mr. Powell. "Bookmaker?"

"I usually just refer to him as 'that blackguard Clive,'" Mr. Powell said stiffly. "He is a troublesome fellow, to say the least. Though Mr. Wright and his friends seem to enjoy spending time with him."

"Hard to say no to a fellow when you owe him so much money," Mr. Wright admitted, looking for the first time as though he agreed with the magistrate.

"And yet you don't owe him money anymore, do you?" Mr. Hurst pressed. "Your account, as I was saying, was settled the morning after your mother's death. Do you expect me to believe that was a coincidence?"

"If my account was settled, it is news to me," Mr. Wright protested. "I owe the man nearly eight hundred pounds. I doubt he is going to let me off the hook for that."

"So you're saying you didn't repay him?"

"That is exactly what I am saying." Mr. Wright crossed the room, pulling on his waistcoat and shrugging into his jacket as he spoke. "There is one way to settle this. Shall we pay a visit to Mr. Clive?"

"I do not think that is a good idea," Mr. Powell said hesitantly, glancing at the constable.

But Mr. Hurst, to Ofelia's surprise, shrugged. "It would settle it, as Mr. Wright says. Sir Edward, can we make use of your carriage again?"

Neddy glanced down at Ofelia, who nodded, trying not to look too eager. She had no desire to see Mr. Clive again—he had made her distinctly uneasy—but she had no intention of being left behind now.

"Certainly," Neddy agreed. "Mr. Powell, will you be joining us? We could squeeze in five if we must."

"No, I thank you," said Mr. Powell, his tone stiff with disapproval. "I believe it is a mistake to take Mr. Wright anywhere. And I have no desire to speak with Mr. Clive, who I imagine will take great pleasure in being as unhelpful as possible."

"You want to be done with the whole thing, I take it?" Mr. Hurst asked, displaying a moment of shrewdness that Ofelia would not have expected from the young runner. Perhaps he knew what he was about after all.

Mr. Powell nodded. "As you have arrived, Mr. Hurst, I believe I may leave the matter, and Mr. Wright, in your hands. Murder is, I must admit, not quite my forte."

"Suit yourself," said Mr. Wright, running his fingers through his hair in a useless effort to tidy it. He gave the Bow Street constable an assessing glance, smiling a little, as though unimpressed by what he saw. "I am sure young Mr. Hurst will be well able to contain a wily criminal such as myself. I shall likely see you next time Dennings kicks me out of the inn, Powell. Or not." He glanced in the direction of Belleford, and Ofelia thought he might be suppressing a shudder. "Might not be long for this little village." Turning to Neddy, he bowed. "Lead on, Sir Edward."

"A moment. If you'd please hold out your hands." The constable, surprising them all, pulled out a pair of handcuffs, a satisfied edge to his smile as Mr. Wright blanched in shock. "You didn't think I'd let you just traipse around willy-nilly, did you?"

★ ★ ★

It was fortunate that the drive into the village was a quick one. Mr. Hurst was silent the whole way, watching Mr. Wright with an assessing, impassive gaze. Mr. Wright, for his part, seemed determined to show the Bow Street constable that he harbored no guilt or uneasiness, in spite of the way he kept glancing down at the handcuffs on his wrists. He spent the drive making overly flirtatious comments to Ofelia, as though being locked up had left him with a store of bad behavior that he needed to get out.

"Were your husband not here, Lady Carroway, I should be tempted to tell you how ravishing you look today and what a true solace it was to see your face after my imprisonment."

"And had your imprisonment lasted more than a single day, sir, I might be more tempted to take your flattery seriously," Ofelia said severely. "I should think your mind would be on your paramour—who is *still* locked up, as I hope you remember— rather than on a stranger."

"And her husband *is* here," Neddy said, still cheerful but with a sharp edge creeping into his voice. "So I suggest you refrain from saying anything that will tempt me to strike you in the face. I doubt Mr. Hurst wants his primary suspect bloodied at this juncture."

Ofelia was saved having to find out what sort of outrageous thing Mr. Wright might have said in reply by the carriage suddenly drawing to a halt. They were outside the inn, where Mr. Powell had told them the bookmaker Clive could be found most days.

"Ah, here we are then," Mr. Wright said, leaning awkwardly over to glance out the window and losing his balance a little because of his cuffed hands. He sighed and shook his head as he held them out toward Mr. Hurst. "You will do something about these, I presume?"

Neddy hopped out, then turned to hand Ofelia down. The Bow Street runner climbed out next, then gestured to Mr. Wright to join them. "Down you come, sir."

Even in the dim interior of the carriage, Ofelia could see Mr. Wright recoil. "You cannot be serious, man," he hissed, holding up his hands. "I'll not be seen like this! Have you any idea what sort of talk it will prompt?"

Mr. Hurst planted his feet firmly and took a deep breath, as though steeling himself. "You're the one who insisted we come talk to the bookmaker," he said, only a slight quaver in his voice. Ofelia wanted to cheer for him; instead, she exchanged a glance with her husband, who looked downright smug to see Mr. Wright put in his place. "If you've changed your mind, I assume it's because you're afraid of what we might learn."

"Damn it all, that isn't—" Mr. Wright growled, then lurched toward the door, stumbling down the step and nearly landing face-first in the dirt because of his haste. Only Neddy's quick reflexes kept him upright, though Ofelia thought her husband looked a little irritated at himself for his instinctive helpfulness. He dropped Mr. Wright's arm quickly. "Fine then, lead the way. I shall show you I've nothing to hide."

"Lady Carroway," the Bow Street constable said, clearing his throat a little awkwardly. "Would you care to wait in the carriage?"

"Absolutely not," Ofelia replied, polite but firm, and while he was still registering his surprise, she took Neddy's arm and began towing him toward the inn's door. To her relief, Mr. Hurst was too occupied with his suspect to offer more than a brief, "Lady Carroway!" as an objection, and within a few moments all of them were blinking as their eyes adjusted to the dim light of the inn's common room.

"Sir Edward!" The inn's owner, Mr. Dennings, came bustling over, a woman Ofelia assumed to be his wife following in his wake and not bothering to hide her curiosity at all. "A pleasure to see you again, sir, and this must be your lady wife—an honor, madam." He had just begun to bow to Ofelia when he caught sight of the two men standing behind them. His bemused gaze passed over Mr. Hurst and landed on Mr. Wright, at which point his shock seemed to make him forget what he was doing. He stood still, halfway into a bow, his eyes fixed on Mr. Wright's handcuffed wrists, until his wife gave him a forceful jab with her elbow, and he pulled himself upright. "To what do I owe— that is—how can we—what's going on?"

"We need to speak to a Mr. Clive. Is he here?" Mr. Hurst stepped forward, giving Mr. Wright a nudge to do the same, which he obeyed sullenly, his face red with mortification and anger.

"To be sure, I'm here," a voice drawled from the corner. They all glanced over to find Clive, the bookmaker, eyeing their group curiously, his booted feet propped up on the table in front of him and his chair tipped back against a wall. Mrs. Dennings looked aggravated and, walking over, hoisted his heels up and dropped them on the floor. Clive just laughed. "Sorry, Mrs. Dennings, you know how absentminded I am. But I never forget a pretty face." He gave Ofelia a wink, followed by a long perusal of her figure. "My lady, if I remember correctly?"

Neddy tensed. Ofelia's jaw clenched, and she was about to give him a piece of her mind when Mr. Hurst stepped forward. "Mr. Clive, I believe?"

"That's me," the young man agreed, smiling insolently. "And I recognize a London voice when I hear one. What brings you to Hampshire, Londoner?" He glanced at Mr. Wright, his smile growing broader. "And what have you done to my good friend here?"

"You'll find out sooner if you make some room at your table, Clive," Mr. Wright muttered.

"Then I shall," he agreed amiably. "Will her ladyship and the red-faced fellow I presume is her husband be joining us?"

Ofelia gave him a disdainful look, then turned to the inn-keeper. "Mr. Dennings, would you and your lovely wife be so good as to grant us a moment in private? Mr. Hurst is here on official Bow Street business and requires a word with Mr. Clive." She gave Neddy a nudge with her elbow; after a final dark look in Clive's direction, he was quick to produce several shillings, which Mrs. Dennings was just as quick to receive and whisk away under her apron.

"Certainly, Sir Edward, Lady Carroway, whatever you might need. Come along, Mr. Dennings." Glancing at them with undisguised curiosity, she herded her husband toward another room, though Ofelia had the distinct impression that the inn-keeper's wife, at least, would be listening at the door for what-ever gossip she could manage to overhear.

Luckily, there were no other patrons in the common room at the moment. They were left in relative privacy as they all took seats at Mr. Clive's table.

Mr. Hurst leaned forward. "I'll get right to it, then. I under-stand you're the fellow in town most likely to be collecting money from anyone interested in a spot of gambling. Is that correct?"

Clive shrugged, starting to look a little wary. "There is more than one man in the neighborhood who likes to have a bit of fun with his money. I'm happy to provide a way for them to do it."

"And to make a tidy profit when it doesn't go well for them?"

Clive shrugged again. "We don't all have the good luck that my friend Wright here has, to be born a gentleman in a wealthy family. Some of us must make do with the talents God has given us. Mine happen to be for gambling."

"Can't say I feel particularly lucky at the moment," Mr. Wright muttered, and from below the table they all heard the clank of metal.

Clive winced at the sound, and some of his bravado seemed to falter. "What exactly is going on?" he asked.

"As I've learned, your friend Wright here isn't always the luckiest man when it comes to his bets," Mr. Hurst continued. When Clive nodded tersely, he leaned forward. "How much money does Mr. Wright here owe you?"

Ofelia caught the quick, startled look that Clive gave his friend before a bemused smile stole over his features. "How much *does* he owe me?"

Mr. Wright sighed. "You can tell him the truth, Clive. What red-blooded man hasn't got into a spot of trouble gambling, after all?"

"But my friend here owes me nothing at all. His debts were settled some days ago—the morning after his mother's tragic passing, I believe." Clive smiled. "I was most appreciative of the prompt payment, as I have expenses of my own, you understand."

"But . . ." Mr. Wright stared at him, spluttering in disbelief. "But that is not true at all! I owe you near eight hundred pounds, man, and I've yet to settle a single shilling of it." His voice rose as he spoke, and for a moment it seemed his body would rise too. Instead, he gripped the table with his cuffed hands, leaning forward and speaking urgently. "Tell them. Tell them!"

Ofelia didn't believe for a moment that he was a talented enough actor to fake either the surprise or the unmistakable note of panic in his voice. She glanced at Neddy, who was looking apprehensive, and at Mr. Hurst, who was not bothering to hide his skepticism.

"Well, no, you did not," Clive said, raising his eyebrows and looking genuinely confused. "But she said it was to settle your account. And as I didn't see how a housemaid could have come by such a sum unless you had given it to her, I was more than happy to take it."

"The housemaid delivered this payment?" Mr. Hurst asked, leaning forward. Ofelia did the same without thinking and saw that both Neddy and Mr. Wright did too.

"From your big fancy hall," Clive said, a sour note creeping into his voice. "She came knocking on my door bright and early that morning and said I wasn't to spread it around, but she was there to pay off your debt, and I was to confirm it with you in a few days." He gave a mocking half bow in Mr. Hurst's direction. "Of course, I was the soul of discretion until an esteemed officer of Bow Street instructed me to share. And where else would the girl have gotten half your mother's jewelry if you did not give it to her yourself? We all know Mrs. Wright did not willingly part with it."

"But I knew nothing of this," Mr. Wright protested, his ruddy cheeks going pale as he glanced from one face to another, finally turning toward Mr. Hurst with a pleading look. "Nothing, I swear! If she stole my mother's jewels, she did it of her own accord. I never suggested such a thing, and I never encouraged her beyond a mere dalliance. I swear, I never lifted a finger against my mother or encouraged anyone else to."

He was deadly serious, Ofelia thought, more serious than she would have ever thought possible for such a frivolous, self-absorbed man. She was almost tempted to come to his defense, a sensation that surprised her, given how off-putting she found him.

Glancing at Mr. Hurst, Ofelia was surprised to see the considering look on the constable's face. "I think," he said slowly. "It is time for us to go speak with Etta."

CHAPTER 21

The discovery of Alice's body shocked everyone, but it was easy to deduce what had happened. She had been sent the evening before, Isaiah explained, to take Etta a tray of dinner and a blanket for the night. But with everything in disarray, and Miss Wright demanding all their attention and care, no one had noticed that Alice hadn't come back.

"She was always so quiet," Isaiah said once they were back in the kitchen. Lily had made him sit down, and then, unobtrusively and without asking permission, had gone upstairs to the family parlor and poured them each a drink from Mr. Wright's liquor cabinet. Isaiah hadn't argued or asked where it came from, but drank half of it in one gulp and dropped his head into his hands. "She was shy, and she was young—we were always overlooking her—Etta used to laugh that no one ever noticed when Alice walked into a room. And I laughed too, God forgive me. I called her Mouse because she was always scurrying silently from room to room. But now . . ."

When she had first seen Alice's body, Lily had thought she might be sick. The shock had overpowered her nearly as much as it had Isaiah. But she hadn't known Alice well, hadn't lived or worked with her. Once she had turned her back on the grisly sight of the girl's body, Lily had been able to pull herself together and take charge. After closing and locking the door once more, she had herded Isaiah back to the kitchen.

He was shaking as his voice trailed off, and it was unnerving to see such a strong, good-humored man reduced to such a horrified state. Lily poured the contents of her own glass into Isaiah's, resting her hand on his shoulder for a moment before telling him not to leave the kitchen while she went to find her aunt.

Eliza was with Miss Wright, of course, and Mr. Mears was in the room as well. Lily was grateful for that—better to tell them both at once, she reasoned, and let the stoic butler take care of his employer. Eliza looked as though she would be ill, and she asked Lily to repeat herself twice before it seemed she could comprehend what she had been told. Even Mr. Mears registered more emotion than Lily had yet seen on his face at the news of Alice's murder. But that was nothing compared to Miss Wright, who immediately went into hysterics, begging for her brother to be summoned.

"I shall go to Mr. Powell's," Lily said firmly, once she could make herself heard, hoping that Mr. Hurst would still be there. "Perhaps he will allow your brother to come to you."

"It is that girl who did it, that wretched, murdering girl," Miss Wright sobbed, clinging to Eliza. "Oh dear God, we will all be killed—if it is not the ghost, it will be her! Whatever happened, it was her fault, not Thomas's. They will have to see that now, won't they, Mrs. Adler? They will have to!"

When Lily finally removed herself from the room, she stopped only briefly in the kitchen to ask Isaiah to keep an eye on the shed with Alice's body.

He looked visibly shaken by the idea. "Do you mean . . . I've got to go back in there?"

"No, nothing of the sort," Lily said, brisk but gentle. "The door is closed and locked, and I have the key with me. All you need do is sit where you can see the door to make sure no one attempts to open it."

"Do you think Etta will . . ."

"No," Lily said firmly, hoping it was true. "I think she is long gone. She saw her opportunity to escape, and she took it, no matter the cost."

And such a terrible, bloody cost it had been. Lily pushed the image out of her mind; she couldn't afford to take the time to process it just then. Every moment she delayed, Etta was getting farther away.

Ignoring the sick feeling in her stomach, Lily went outside to hitch up the horse and gig once more. But she had taken only a few steps down the front stairs when she was confronted with the Carroways' carriage thundering up the drive.

In short order, Lily found herself crowded by her friends, by Mr. Hurst demanding to know what she was doing there, and to her surprise, a very shaken-looking Thomas Wright. It took her several minutes to cut through the confusion of their demands to see where Etta was being kept and speak with her instantly. But at last she was able to deliver her news: Alice was dead, and Etta gone.

The stunned silence that met her announcement lasted only for a moment before she was bombarded with questions.

The loudest voice among them, and the most bewildered, was Mr. Wright's plaintive, "But what do you mean? What on earth could you mean? Etta would not—Etta *could* not—"

At last, Mr. Hurst, after several timid attempts, found enough volume to overpower the others' questions and demand that Lily take him to the maid's body. Mr. Wright insisted loudly that he

come as well, and the Bow Street runner, after a long, considering moment, relented.

Lily wondered if he wanted to take the measure of Mr.
Wright's reaction, to see whether he had indeed been in league
with Etta or whether she'd acted alone. But she kept her suspicions to herself, only nodding and leading them through the
building.

It was a strange procession. They added Mr. Mears to their
company in the hall, who asked to be allowed to see for himself
what had happened. When they reached the kitchens, Isaiah
jumped up, looking nervous.

"I haven't seen anyone since you left," he said, his voice
shaking. "But I haven't gone any closer than this, I'm not
ashamed to admit. I can't bear to see her like that again."

"That's all right," Mr. Hurst said briskly, clearly better at
taking charge when he didn't have to talk over a group of strangers. "I'll be back to speak with you—what's your name? Isaiah?
I'll need to speak with you and anyone else who was in the
house to find out what happened."

"And just who are you?" Mr. Mears asked, drawing himself
up to his full, frail height and glaring at the constable.

Lily quickly intervened, not wanting any more delays. "Mr.
Hurst is a Bow Street constable, summoned by Mr. Wright himself to look into the matter of Mrs. Wright's death. And now, I
suppose, into Alice's death."

"She cannot be dead," Mr. Wright insisted loudly.

"She is," Lily said gently, pulling the key from her pocket
and leading the way to the shed. "I am sorry to say, but she is."

★　★　★

The Bow Street runner was gone as quickly as he had come.

It hadn't taken long for him to come to the conclusion Lily hoped he would, and his instantaneous action had impressed her. After surveying Alice's body, he had asked only about the hat on the ground, suspicious that someone other than a maid had come into the shed. But once Lily informed him that Etta had been arrested on her half day, while she was in her own clothes, he had nodded briskly and said they would be free to take the body away that night.

A quick interview with each member of the household had given him the information he wanted; Etta's mother lived only a day's ride away, and one of the horses from the stable was missing. Etta, Lily was able to report from that first horrid morning when Mrs. Wright's body had been found, was a decent rider. Mr. Hurst decided immediately that he would go after her.

To Lily's surprise, he was willing to hear Mr. Wright out before departing. Mr. Wright, for his part, seemed a changed man since seeing Alice's body. Gone was his bravado and brashness. His ruddy cheeks were ashen, making his eyes seem even more shadowed and bloodshot. His shoulders slumped, and his hands shook as he protested that he had no idea Etta was even capable of such appalling crimes, much less planned them with her. Lily could hear the note of tormented sincerity in his voice; Mr. Hurst, it seemed, heard it as well.

"Very well," he said, preparing to mount the horse he had commandeered to carry him back to the cottage as swiftly as possible. His own horse and bag waited there still; he planned to leave immediately, he said, in pursuit of their fleeing killer. "You can stay here with your sister, as it's clear she's going to need a lot of looking after. But if you stir an inch—an *inch*—outside this home before I return or another fellow from Bow Street arrives, you'll be arrested again. And if you try to flee, then God help you, because the laws of England certainly won't."

Mr. Wright shook his head emphatically. "I'll not be going anywhere, you may be sure of that. It has become quite clear to me that my judgment is in serious need of realignment. All I wish to do now is make amends for the harm I've set in motion, however unwittingly."

"Then care for your sister," Mr. Hurst said, climbing with little grace into the saddle. But once he was up, he used the height to glare down at Mr. Wright in an impressive manner. "And we will see what happens when I return."

Eliza insisted the rest of them stay until the Wrights were settled, or as settled as they could be. "And we need to send someone to notify Alice's family, poor thing, so they can come collect her body," she added once they were back inside and surrounded by the small remains of the Wrights' household.

"I'll do that," Isaiah volunteered quietly. "Her mother doesn't live too far from here. And I'll stop by to see Mr. Samson first so he can arrange for the undertaker to come collect the . . ." He swallowed. "The body."

"Good man," Eliza said, nodding with approval. "I will send our girl, Addie, with dinner for the rest of you, Mr. Wright, since you will only have Mr. Mears to tend to you tonight."

"Can she stay the night?" Miss Wright asked querulously, calmer now but with an edge to her voice that said her hysterics might resume at any moment. Inside the cuffs of her too big dress, her hands trembled. "Someone must help me prepare for bed and dress in the morning."

Eliza opened and closed her mouth twice before finally finding the words to respond. "No," she said bluntly. "I'll not ask her to do that. Not in a house where there have been two murders."

"And a ghost," Ned added, looking defensive when half of those present turned to stare at him. "What? All of you have been insisting—"

"We ought to be going, then, if everything is settled for the night," Ofelia broke in, putting a quieting hand on his arm. "I think there is not much else we can do here to help."

They departed at the same time as Isaiah, the Carroways going in the carriage, and Lily and Eliza traveling in the gig. Watching Isaiah go tickled something at the back of Lily's mind, and she gazed after him as he disappeared down the drive.

"Lily?" Eliza's gentle voice broke into her thoughts. "Is something wrong? Other than . . . well, everything."

"I do not know," Lily said, frowning. "I think there is something . . . But so much has happened, so quickly, I cannot for the life of me remember what it was." She shook her head. "Let's depart, Aunt. I've no wish to stay in this house a moment longer than we must. And Susan will be wondering what has taken us so long."

"Oh no." Eliza's face fell. "She will be heartbroken when I tell her."

★   ★   ★

Susan had spent the day puttering around her flower beds, preparing them for the winter, and she greeted them with a wave as the two vehicles pulled up before the cottage. Her normally pleasant demeanor was troubled.

"Mr. Hurst has come and gone, and he was in such a rush that he would not tell me a word of what had passed," she said. She went to Eliza and took her hand, but her anxious gaze took in the others as well. "What . . . what has happened? Is it dreadful?"

Eliza glanced at her guests as she made a little shooing motion in their direction. "Take yourselves off to rest before dinner. I am sure you are in need of it," she said gently, threading Susan's arm through her own and turning them both in the direction of the shrubbery so they could speak in private.

Lily didn't join the others for dinner that evening, claiming a headache and a need to continue resting, though she was sure none of them entirely believed her. But instead of lying down, she continued pacing around her room, mentally combing through every detail of her conversation with Isaiah, to try to pinpoint exactly what was niggling at the back of her mind.

When Anna came to check on her after dinner, she found Lily standing in front of the window, reading through a list she had made of every topic she could remember Isaiah mentioning in their short walk from the parlor to the shed. It was not a long list, and Lily was practically pulling at her hair in frustration.

Anna, after asking what on earth her employer was doing and receiving a short, disgruntled explanation, sighed, crossed the room, and pulled the list from Lily's fingers.

"I need that!" Lily protested.

"No, Mrs. Adler, you don't," Anna said firmly. "You need to take your mind off it instead of pacing here in the dark."

Lily glanced around, realizing that the light had faded without her noticing. Night was falling earlier and earlier, and she hadn't yet lit any candles. As soon as Anna pointed out the darkness, the room suddenly felt colder, and Lily had to quell a shiver.

"Don't you always say things come clearer when you stop thinking about them too much? Go down and join the others for tea instead of tormenting yourself up here alone." Anna's face fell, and her voice dropped. "I heard what happened to that poor girl. But you're no good to her, or her memory, just going in circles."

Her maid was right, Lily knew. Sighing, she took herself downstairs to follow Anna's advice. She hadn't changed for the evening, but she knew none of her friends would begrudge her an afternoon dress under the circumstances.

"Lily!" Susan, presiding over the tea as usual, was the first to spot her. "Come sit by me, dearest. How are you feeling?"

"Distracted and distressed," Lily admitted, grimacing. "There is something bothering me about what happened today."

"I think it is bothering all of us," Ofelia pointed out as Susan handed Lily a cup of tea. "You'll not be surprised to hear that we have been talking of nothing else."

"I mean something beyond what is obvious," Lily said, taking a grateful sip. The tea had cooled just enough to drink right away, and she was grateful for its warmth as well as the cheerful light of the fire. "There was something the manservant, Isaiah, said when he was taking me to the shed, where . . ." She trailed off, not wanting to talk of what they had found there. "What I keep coming back to is the servants' stair. But what on earth could that have to do with anything?"

"That is odd," Eliza agreed, her brows drawing together into a puzzled frown. Lily, feeling suddenly sleepy as the distress of the day caught up with her all at once, covered a yawn. "Perhaps it something you saw? If it is anything that can bring justice to poor Alice . . ."

"But why kill her?" Ned asked, looking at his wife, who nodded. Lily's eyes wanted badly to close, and she had to fight to keep them on Ned as he continued. "That is what I want to know. If all that other maid, Etta, needed to do was get away—which was clearly what she wanted—why be so brutal? Why not simply knock her out and run?"

"Was there some kind of grudge between them?" Susan asked hesitantly.

Lily's heavy eyelids suddenly snapped open, a sudden realization shaking her out of her sleepiness. "I think Alice might have seen something she was not supposed to," she said, setting her teacup down. "Because I am fairly certain she was the ghost."

"What?" The question came from four voices at once.

"Alice lied about Selina Wright using that small staircase." Lily said, still fitting the pieces together as she spoke. "She had said it was kept clean for Miss Wright's use. But Isaiah told me only the servants used those stairs. And she was so quiet and overlooked . . . perhaps it seemed a fun prank to tease and taunt everyone. It would have been easy for her to do."

"The stairs would help her get from place to place easily," Ofelia said, her excitement making some of the tea slosh over the edge of her cup and into the saucer. She muttered what sounded like a sharp curse under her breath. Ned, looking unsurprised by either the spill or the curse, handed her a napkin.

"Precisely." Lily nodded, standing without realizing it and beginning to pace around the room. "There were plenty of clothes for her to choose from in that old storage room, after all. And she was so surprised to see me there."

"You mean that if there were people other than her using the stair, she wouldn't have been surprised?" Eliza asked, setting down her own cup of tea and leaning forward.

"Not surprised to that degree, at least. And . . . she didn't take the candles with her," Lily said, realizing it only as she spoke. "She said she was there to fetch candles, but she did not take any with her when she left."

"So you think perhaps she saw something she was not supposed to," Eliza said, looking ill at the thought. "If she was wandering the halls as the ghost, she might have seen Etta with Mr. Wright."

"Worse than that," Ofelia said. Her eyes were fixed on her teacup, and when she lifted them, the excitement was gone from her expression. "She might have seen precisely how Mrs. Wright was killed, and by whom, and how they got into the room."

"Because that is still the remaining question, is it not?" Lily said, pacing from the fireplace to the windows and back again. "How did Etta get in there? How did she do it?"

"If Alice had the answer, she was a threat that had to be removed," Eliza said, nodding.

"And then Etta escaped." Lily frowned. "No, that cannot be quite right. Etta wouldn't have planned to return. Everyone would know she was guilty of two murders. So she would not have needed to worry about the details of how she did it being exposed. So the question remains: Why kill Alice?"

Ofelia gasped. "Perhaps she was protecting her lover," she said, half rising from her seat. "What if Mr. Wright's shock and horror today was just a performance? If Alice saw that they were both party to Mrs. Wright's murder—and how they did it—he would still be in danger. Perhaps Etta killed again to protect him."

"Dear God." One of Lily's hands rose to cover her mouth before clenching into a fist, which she thumped against the mantlepiece. "I want to talk to Mr. Clive again. I do not for a moment believe that he told Mr. Hurst everything he knew about Mr. Wright's debts and Etta paying them off. First thing in the morning, we must seek him out and see what he can reveal."

"But how to convince him?" Ofelia said, looking queasy. "You've not met him, Mrs. Adler. He is not the sort of man to do anyone a favor. There will have to be something in it for him."

"Pay him," Ned said suddenly. When they all turned to look at him with matching surprised expressions, he shrugged. "Fellow clearly wants money, and plenty of it. Wants to set himself up as a gentleman. I'd not go so far as offering to introduce him around—not even at the Newmarket races. Standards, and all that. And he's an unpleasant sort. But paying him for the information you want?" He shrugged again. "Easy enough to do."

"He's right," Eliza said, and Susan nodded, though she looked unhappy at the prospect. "Mr. Clive is known to have aspirations. Aspirations take money, and he is decidedly unscrupulous about where that comes from. He'll not balk at taking payment for information."

"But Mr. Hurst is gone," Susan pointed out. "What do you propose they do without him?"

"We still have a magistrate," Eliza said, picking up her tea once more and looking calmer now that a course of action had been decided. "He placed Mr. Wright under arrest once; he can do it again if what Mr. Clive says proves his guilt."

"Don't like to think what that might do to Miss Wright," Ned muttered, looking unhappy rather than sympathetic at the prospect. "Prone to hysterics as it is without her brother being taken up for murder a second time."

"No help for that," Ofelia said, shrugging. "If there is reason to think him guilty once more . . . Better we find out now than wait out of care for her delicate feelings. Who knows what might happen if we delay?"

"First thing tomorrow," Lily said, nodding in agreement. "We shall see what else Mr. Clive might reveal and where that leaves us."

Ofelia turned to her husband, asking without a trace of embarrassment, "Neddy, what have you got around in the way of ready money?"

He sighed. "All right, but if I am to foot the bill, I insist on coming with you."

CHAPTER 22

In the end, Ned did not accompany them to meet with Mr. Clive.

"What if we are right, and Mr. Wright did have something to do with his mother's death?" Lily argued as they stood in the drive before the cottage. Ned, standing in front of his carriage with his arms crossed, looked deeply uneasy with the confrontation but equally unwilling to budge. "You cannot expect me to send my aunt or Miss Clarke to keep an eye on him."

"What could either of them do, if he thought we suspected him?" Ofelia added. She and Lily had discussed the matter between them before retiring the night before, and they had come to the same conclusion: until they knew what Clive might share, someone had to be at Belleford. "What if he grew violent? You are certainly the most capable of dealing with him."

"But how would he know anything is amiss?" Ned asked. Behind him, the coachman stoically pretended not to hear what was going on, and the horses tossed their heads and stamped impatiently. "As far as he is concerned, Mr. Hurst has released him, and he got away free."

"Not quite," Lily said, shaking her head. There was a sharp breeze rising, hurrying the light scattering of clouds across the sky and ushering in an ominous billow of stormy gray. She hoped the rain would hold off long enough for them to make it to and from the village. She hoped no one would be stranded at Belleford, which seemed less safe now than ever. "Mr. Hurst made it clear that Mr. Wright wasn't to go anywhere, as he was not completely clear of suspicion. If he becomes fearful or impulsive, there is no telling what he might do."

"You are quite sure he is guilty, then?" Ned asked, beginning to look uneasy.

"I am quite sure we do not know," Lily said firmly. "Which means we must act with caution."

"Miss Pierce has offered to go to Belleford, under the pretext of delivering foodstuffs," Ofelia said, taking her husband's arm and looking at him hopefully. "They are down to only two servants, after all, and both without any cooking ability. But you must agree that she oughtn't go alone."

"I shall be easier in my mind if you are accompanying her," Lily agreed. "Please, Ned?"

She so rarely called him Ned that her use of his name seemed to make more of an impression than all her persuasive words. He relented at last, reaching out to take her hand. "Of course, ma'am. Of course I will look after your aunt." He turned a stern eye on his wife. "But *I* shall be easier if you keep a servant with you at all times."

Which was how Lily and Ofelia found themselves, a short carriage ride later, approaching the inn while accompanied by the coachman, who seemed determined to prove his worth as a bodyguard by glowering at anyone who came within his eyeline and staying no more than two paces behind them at all times.

The inn was open, with one or two visitors who were passing through the village down in the common room to break their fast. But Clive was nowhere to be found. That was not too surprising, given the hour, though Lily had harbored a faint hope that he would be the sort who lingered there at all hours of the day, waiting for his customers. Ofelia, too, looked discouraged.

"I suppose we ought to ask the innkeeper where he lives," she said hesitantly. "And just hope that we do not set too many tongues wagging with curiosity."

"We can tell them Sir Edward had a small commission for us. They will assume he was gambling, like any young man," Lily suggested.

Ofelia looked affronted at the idea but didn't protest beyond a mutter; there was no better option at hand. They had just begun to cross the room in search of Mr. Dennings when a familiar figure, emerging from the kitchen, hailed them.

"Lady Carroway! Mrs. Adler! Can we be of assistance?"

It was Isaiah, just taking a heavy basket from the hands of the inn's maid, who regarded Ofelia with surprise as she heard her addressed by her title and dropped a curtsey that had an air of panic to it.

"How are you, Isaiah?" Lily asked while Ofelia gave the maid a reassuring smile.

"Well, thank you, ma'am. As well as can be expected, that is." He hefted the basket. "Collecting our cold meats and pies for the day from Mrs. Dennings's excellent kitchen," he added. "Since we've no cook at all, not even . . ." He trailed off, clearing his throat. "Well."

A sharp voice called from inside the kitchen, and the maid glanced over her shoulder, dropped one more embarrassed curtsey, and disappeared in response to the summons. Isaiah hesitated, then asked, "Begging your pardon if it's presuming, but is there aught I can help you with? You looked as though you were in search of someone."

The way he gestured toward the kitchen made it clear he meant Mr. or Mrs. Dennings. But Ofelia stepped forward instantly.

"Isaiah, do I remember you had dealings with that fellow Clive, the bookmaker?"

He balked, looking embarrassed. "I don't know who's been telling you things, my lady—"

"I saw you give him an envelope, and Mr. Samson told me about him," she interrupted him. "I've no wish to lecture you about the morality of gambling. I ask because we need to find him."

"Find Mr. Clive?" Isaiah looked, if anything, even more worried by that prospect. "Begging your pardon, but what could the two of you need Mr. Clive for?"

"We have a question or two that only he can answer." Lily dropped her voice. "About Etta."

The pained look on Isaiah's face almost made her wish she hadn't said anything so explicit. But a moment later, he seemed to rally himself and nodded. "If it'll help justice be done, I'll be glad to take you to him." He glanced at the coachman, who was still hovering only a few paces behind them. "And you stay close by them, man. Clive isn't a rough sort of fellow, but he's not the kind of man ladies ought to be associating with, as a general rule."

"Well, hopefully after this, we shall never need to again," Ofelia muttered, scowling. "Lead on, if you please."

Clive, it turned out, lived close by; his parents had owned a small house in town, which he inherited after their deaths. "But everyone suspects he means to set himself up with a country property, likely far from here, as soon as he can afford it," Isaiah said as they walked. He shook his head. "If he weren't such an unpleasant sort, I might admire him. He certainly runs rings around everyone in town."

"Including Mr. Wright and his friends?" Ofelia asked.

Isaiah glanced at her uneasily. "It'd be worth my job to agree with such a thing, my lady."

Ofelia smiled at him, in spite of the seriousness of the situation. "That is a yes, I believe."

They had only gone across the green when they were hailed by an enthusiastic, "Lady Carroway! Begging your pardon, Lady Carroway!" A plump young woman, her brown hair flying out of its pins, hurried down the street. Something white fluttered in her hand.

The young woman stopped in front of them, her pale cheeks flushed from exertion as she dropped a curtsey. "I beg your ladyship's pardon for shouting and running like that, but I know you picked up the letters for Miss Clarke a few days past, and we forgot to give her this one when she was by yesterday, on account of her name not being on it, nor Miss Pierce's. And since it looks like it's coming on to rain, I thought I'd hurry and catch you, in case she's not able to take her walk today as usual." With another curtsey, she presented the fluttering letter to Ofelia, who took it with a bemused smile.

"Of course, I should be happy to take it back to Longwood Cottage. You are good to be so conscientious in your duties," she said, and the young postmistress beamed at the praise before dropping a third curtsey and backing away as though she were in the presence of the queen and didn't dare turn around, offering both apologies and thanks in overwhelming profusion until she had backed up enough to turn and scamper away.

"How diligent," Lily remarked dryly.

"I thought she seemed very excitable when I first met her," Ofelia murmured, turning the letter over to look at the direction. "I do enjoy being proved right. It is addressed to you, Mrs. Adler. That must have been the source of the confusion." She gave Lily a pointed look as she handed it over. "It looks as though it is from the captain."

Jack. Lily's heart sped up, remembering that she had last written him about her suspicions regarding the Wrights. If he had written back so quickly, it had to be because he had some thought to impart, some insight that she had missed. She had always had the benefit of his help when confronted with such cases before; she hadn't realized until that moment just how much she had missed it. Not caring that they were still standing in the middle of the village, not remembering that they were on their way to confront Clive, she tore open the seal.

But her face fell as she scanned the letter's contents.

"What does he say?" Ofelia asked eagerly. "Does he have some idea to share?"

"No," Lily said, feeling deflated. "He wrote it before I sent my last letter. He says they were about to leave Portsmouth at last but were delayed by an accident among the men of the crew. One fellow nearly lost his life, and he may have lost the vision in one eye. It sounds horrid, even without the details." Recalling the task at hand, she folded the letter back up and tucked it in her reticule. "I shall read the rest later. For now, Isaiah, will you lead on?"

"Yes, Mrs. Adler. It's not far now."

But they had gone only one more street over when they were stopped once again, this time to exchange bows with a tall, somber-looking man in the dark garb of a clergyman. It seemed everyone in town knew her friend, Lily thought as he, too, hailed Ofelia politely and inquired after her husband.

He was accompanied by a plainly dressed older woman with wispy gray hair pinned under a hat of brown felt. She held a handkerchief to her eyes, which were red with crying. As Ofelia was introducing Mr. Samson to Lily, the older woman latched onto Isaiah, clinging to his arm and talking to him in an urgent, hoarse whisper. For his part, he seemed to be patting her hand and responding with feeling.

"I am taking Alice's mother to see her body," the clergyman explained in a low voice.

Alice's mother. Lily felt a sudden rush of sympathy that made her fall silent. She was the one who had discovered the body, after all. She knew what Alice's mother was going to see, and she could only begin to imagine how heartbreaking the sight would be for a parent.

But Ofelia stepped forward, her hands outstretched to clasp the other woman's. She was the sort of girl who always knew what to say to set other people at ease, a trait Lily had long regarded with equal parts admiration and envy. And this time was no different. "I only had the opportunity to meet Alice a handful of times, but she seemed like a truly sweet girl," Ofelia said. "So diligent and intelligent. Such a pillar of the household. Would you not agree, Isaiah?"

"Indeed, Lady Carroway," the manservant said, nodding rapidly. "I don't know how we'll go on without her, but I count myself lucky to have known her as long as I did."

"You're good to say so, both of you," Alice's mother said, wiping her eyes with the back of her hand until Mr. Samson offered his own handkerchief, which she took gratefully.

As Ofelia continued to offer condolences, Lily pulled Mr. Samson a little aside. "Alice mentioned that she needed to work,

I assume to support her mother," she whispered, not bothering to dance around the matter. They could both plainly see the ragged cuffs on the grieving mother's sleeves. "Will the parish assist with the cost of Alice's funeral?"

"Aye, we will," he said, smiling gratefully at the question. "We wouldn't leave poor Elsbeth to pay for such things herself."

"If you need additional funds, I can supply them," Lily said, more vehemently than she intended. But she couldn't shake the image of Alice's bashed and bloody face, which seemed to lurk just behind her eyelids. "She deserves a proper headstone."

"You are good to offer, Mrs. Adler," the clergyman said. "And if we have need of further resources, I'm sure I will take you up on it. But for now, we'll not detain you any longer. Shall we continue?" he asked, raising his voice as he turned to the others. He laid a gentle hand on the woman's arm. "It will not grow easier for being put off."

She swallowed, nodding through a fresh wave of tears. "I know," she whispered, taking his arm. "You can lead on, sir."

Lily watched them go, a lump in her throat, until an impatient noise from Ofelia recalled her once more to the task at hand. "We mustn't delay any longer, Mrs. Adler," she said, glancing at Isaiah. "I'd not want Clive to evade us today. And Isaiah will need to return to his duties soon."

"And if we take too long, Sir Edward will send a search party after us," Lily added, with a return of her usual dry humor. Ofelia rolled her eyes but nodded. "Which way, Isaiah?"

"It's just that house there, ma'am," he said, gesturing to a small residence tucked between two larger buildings. "I'll hang back, if you wish, but I'll still be close by if you need assistance." He glanced at the coachman. "He ought to stay with me too.

Clive is more likely to be loose-tongued with ladies, I think, especially if he wants to seem impressive. But he won't be chatty in front of servants. Wants to maintain the dignity of his station, I suppose. Whatever that station may be these days," he added with a derisive snort.

Ofelia nodded her agreement, and the coachman, looking put out, remained with Isaiah while the two ladies went and knocked on the door. Lily was grateful for the early hour, which meant that there were few villagers about to see them visiting the home of a man whose reputation was far from pristine.

Ofelia had to knock twice, and it took several minutes, but at last they heard the sound of footsteps on the other side of the door. It was unceremoniously yanked open, and Clive, with disheveled hair and no cravat, stuck his head out. "What do you—" He fell silent abruptly as he saw who his visitors were, and he stared at them, clearly stunned and embarrassed. But a moment later, he recovered what seemed to be his typical swagger, and he gave them a sardonic smile. "To what do I owe the honor of being visited by two ladies of quality at such an unusual hour?" he asked, though he gave his hair a quick pat and pulled the two halves of his collar closer together, trying to surreptitiously make himself more presentable. "I've nothing beyond tea to offer, but please, do come in." He raised his eyebrows. "If tea isn't to your liking, I'm sure I could find some other way of entertaining you."

"No, thank you," Lily said, laying a quelling hand on Ofelia's arm when her friend bristled. The fellow's behavior was atrocious, to be sure, but it seemed to be something of an act. Lily suspected that unlike Mr. Wright, his unsavory reputation might not be entirely deserved. "We will talk right here, if you please."

Clive glanced behind them to where the two servants waited, just out of earshot, and shrugged. "By all means, ladies, by all means. What can I do for you? I had not expected either of you to be interested in gambling, but I am happy to facilitate anyone's vices. Especially when I suspect the person has plenty of money to spend."

"Must you be so odious?" Ofelia burst out, though to Lily's relief she kept her voice to a low hiss.

Clive shrugged again. "It seems I must. I would have thought you'd be sufficiently warned about me by now that it wouldn't surprise you." He bared his teeth in something resembling a smile. "Mr. Samson is no admirer of mine, and I saw your ladyship speaking with him. So, if not gambling, what other service might I provide for you?"

Lily ignored the suggestive arch of his brows. "We want to know what you didn't tell the Bow Street runner."

It was clearly not what he was expecting her to say. If his mouth had fallen just slightly more ajar, he would have been gaping at her. But a moment later, he collected himself. "What makes you think I didn't tell him everything I knew?"

"Did you?" Ofelia asked bluntly, her accusing glare enough to make him take a step back in spite of her small stature.

Clive gave them a considering look. "Come inside."

"I think not," Lily said firmly.

"You may prefer to discuss this where anyone might hear, but I do not." Clive stepped back, inviting them in with a sweep of his arm. "Come inside or take yourselves off. It's no concern of mine which you choose."

Lily and Ofelia exchanged a cautious look. But their options were limited; Clive had the information they needed, and they had no means of forcing him to reveal it. At last, Lily sighed and stepped into the hall. Ofelia delayed only long enough to call over her shoulder, "Wait here, we shall only be a moment," before she followed.

"They'll not be pleased about that," Lily murmured as her eyes adjusted to the light.

"Nor will Neddy," Ofelia agreed, sounding unhappy. "But there is no help for it."

"No, there isn't," Clive agreed cheerfully. "This way, if you please."

The dim hallway opened into an equally dim sitting room, though that was merely because the curtains were still partly drawn. Clive didn't open them further, but he did gesture them toward the settee, in front of which a respectable tea tray was laid out. Crossing to the sideboard, he fetched two more cups and set them down before pulling a coat from the back of a chair and shrugging it on. He still had no cravat, but he looked far more respectable. And as Lily glanced around the room, she realized it looked quite respectable too. Shelves of books lined one wall, the furniture was old-fashioned, but not shabby, and over the fireplace was a portrait of a man and woman, both red-cheeked, gray-haired, and smiling. The fireplace was bare, though, and the room chilled. Lily tried not to shiver.

"My parents," Clive said, noticing her staring. "They'd have approved of my knowing two such distinguished ladies. Though I would have to neglect telling them the nature of our acquaintance so as not to shock them."

"They would not approve of your livelihood, then?" Ofelia asked shrewdly as he poured a cup of tea for each of them. It was fragrant and still steaming, and Lily suspected that he had brewed it himself, as there was no sign of a servant in the small house.

"Not in the slightest," he agreed, smiling as he draped himself over a chair. "They had no real desire to rise in the world. I have. And that requires money, which I make how I might." He eyed them both. "Does my crassness in discussing such things shock you?"

"Well, we came here to discuss murder," Lily said dryly. "So no, it does not."

"I know nothing of murder, unfortunately," he said, still smiling. It was an unnerving smile, one that she suspected he had cultivated to make those across a card table uncomfortable. It was certainly working on her; she wished he would look elsewhere, though she met his eyes and did not show it. "My business is cards, wagers, and the like."

"And recently Mr. Wright's debts," Lily said. Beside her, Ofelia took a careful sip of the tea, watching Clive through narrowed eyes but content for the moment to let her friend take the lead in the conversation.

"Though as I have already said, those debts were discharged. I really have nothing more to add on the matter." Clive yawned, looking bored. "So if that is all—"

He broke off as Ofelia pulled half a guinea from her reticule and laid it on the table. Her eyes were wide and innocent as she raised her gaze to meet his. "You were saying?" she asked as she slowly added a second.

He contemplated the gold coins, then cleared his throat. "Those debts were discharged by the maid, who I assumed was there on Wright's behalf. It would have been easy for him to get her to do it, you know. He always has a bit of muslin on the side, and he could twist them around his finger with a little skillful bedroom play," he added with another smile, clearly hoping that one or the other of them would balk at the statement. When neither of them flinched, he shrugged. "She paid in gems, not coins, two pretty sets of jewelry that were more than enough to cover what he owed. And she bid me keep quiet about it, as I said before."

Lily exchanged a look with Ofelia. "Do you remember either of the Wrights saying there were jewels missing from their mother's room?" she murmured.

Ofelia frowned. "I do not recall. But they were so focused on that damned ghost, I'd not be surprised if they failed to even look at her jewelry. Or perhaps Mr. Wright made sure his sister did not."

Clive had followed the exchange with beady, interested eyes. "You think the maid offed the old lady and stole the gems, then?" he asked, clearly unperturbed by the idea. "Or was it Wright who did it and sent her to pay me so he wouldn't be caught? Damned clever trick to pull. Wouldn't have thought he had the brains for it." He tapped the side of his head. "Not what I'd have called a strategist, at least not when it comes to cards. But maybe murder is different."

"We did not say he had anything to do with it," Ofelia said quickly, glaring at the man. "And I'll thank you not to repeat your speculations to anyone else."

Clive shrugged. "You didn't say you were paying me to keep silent."

Ofelia drew in a sharp breath, then let it out slowly and added five more shillings to the pile of coins on the table. "How did she act when she came to pay you?"

He stared pointedly at the pile until she added five more shillings, then he shrugged again. "Timid, maybe? Or *shifty* might be the better word. Said she'd be needed back at the house soon, so she didn't have long to stay. But we didn't need long, in any case. I like to keep my business efficient." He swallowed the rest of his tea in one gulp and stood, stretching before reaching out to sweep the coins off the table with one practiced motion. "Speaking of which, ladies, it is time for me to begin my day. So if there is nothing else . . ."

Lily's heart sank. There hadn't been anything there, after all. Nothing that they hadn't already known. She rose slowly, barely noticing as Clive led them to the front door and opened it with a sweeping, mocking bow.

Ofelia looked even more distressed. "Are you sure there is nothing else you can tell us?" she asked, pausing on the threshold and turning back, a final half guinea glimmering between her gloved fingers.

"Anything else that Etta said or anything strange she did?" Lily added. "Nothing you remember?"

Clive had been about to close the door, but he paused long enough to frown at them. "Etta? I know that girl—always on the lookout for a bit of fun—and I never said it was her as came to see me."

Lily felt as though her heart stopped for a full five seconds. "But you said—"

"The housemaid, yes." Clive reached out to pluck the half guinea from Ofelia's fingers while she stared at him. "What was her name? Can't for the life of me remember." He snapped his fingers. "Alice! That was it. The pretty one who was so quiet. It was Alice who came to see me, not Etta."

CHAPTER 23

Lily stared at the door as it closed in their faces, a sick feeling spreading from the pit of her stomach. Overhead, thunder rumbled—still far away, but a glance at the sky showed her the storm clouds rolling closer. They were running out of time before the storm hit.

Suddenly frantic, Lily pulled the letter from Jack out of her reticule, nearly tearing the paper in her haste, and scanned it once more.

"But . . ." Ofelia shook her head, half in confusion, half in denial. "Why would Alice pay off Mr. Wright's debts?"

Lily pushed the letter at her. "There," she said, tapping the important passage.

Ofelia looked at Lily in a moment of blank confusion before snatching the letter from her hands. "Dear God," she breathed as she read.

Lily knew what she was seeing, as if the words had been imprinted in her mind.

. . . If I'd not seen the accident happen myself, I shouldn't have known it was poor Rogers when I got there. The crate struck his face as it fell, and he was such a mess of gore that we could

barely recognize him. Fortunately, the main injury was to his forehead and one eye, so the doctor says he will live, though likely his vision will never recover. I am accustomed to such things happening at sea, especially after the war, but this has shaken me far more than I would have expected. All I want is to keep my men safe, but to fail at that when we are merely at port, in peaceful times . . .

Lily spun around. Isaiah and the coachman were hurrying toward them, both men looking relieved to see them emerge from the house no worse for their time inside it. "Isaiah!" she called. "Where would Mr. Samson have been taking Alice's mother?"

His confusion was evident, but he answered promptly enough, to her relief. "Likely the old icehouse behind the inn. They don't use it for ice anymore, but it's underground and stays cold."

There was no time to waste. Lily didn't wait for the others or stop to explain. She took off back the way they had come, not caring that she was running in public or wondering what people might think. Close behind her she heard Ofelia's labored breathing, but her friend asked no questions and offered no protests as they dashed through the village. Lily knew she must have come to the same conclusion, or half a conclusion. The sick feeling began to grow.

Luckily, it had not been far between the inn and Clive's house. When Lily paused, catching her breath, Ofelia led the way around the back, toward a small, low structure that looked like a roofed door to a building that did not exist. Lily followed as Ofelia yanked the door open, and a wave of cold, musty air hit them. There was light below, from candles or lamps, enough for them to see the stairs leading down.

Ofelia clattered down, with Lily following close behind. A small, cold space opened before them, as much an earthen cave as it was a room, with two dimly glowing lamps set in brackets on the walls. It was empty except for the table in the center of it, where a white sheet covered the shape of a still figure. The chill set Lily shivering, and the flickering light cast eerie shadows on the walls, but she barely noticed. She gasped in relief: Mr. Samson was still there, clasping both of Alice's mother's hands in his in what was clearly a moment of prayer.

"Lady Carroway, Mrs. Adler, what—"

"Is it Alice?" Lily demanded, too impatient with fear to explain.

"What? What do you mean?" the maid's mother asked, confusion breaking through her sorrow as she stared at them.

"It is your daughter?" Lily panted, gulping in huge breaths of air and trying to ignore the sharp pain in her side from the run. "I am sorry, but did you check to be sure? Look again."

"Mrs. Adler, not to be indelicate, but you have seen the condition of the poor girl's body," Mr. Samson said sternly. "To ask her mother to continue looking at such a—"

"She must," Ofelia broke in, her voice rising. "She must look right away!"

"Her face . . ." The woman's voice quavered, setting off a fresh wave of tears.

"Then do not look at her face," Lily said, trying to find a way to sound gentle in spite of her urgency. "She must have had some kind of mark or scar that you, as her mother, would know about. Somewhere on her body?"

Alice's mother nodded slowly, clearly confused. "There was . . . she has a scar on her thigh. A burn, from when she was a child. That's the sort of thing you mean?"

"Yes, exactly that," Lily agreed, striding to the table where the still figure lay. She avoided the side where the girl's face, or what was left of it, lay shrouded, not wanting to upset the poor woman anymore—and truthfully, not wanting to see it again herself. Twice had been more than enough.

"Mrs. Adler!" The clergyman's shocked protest cut through the still, cold air as he started toward her. "You cannot disrobe the girl. It would be unchristian."

"It is necessary," Ofelia said, lifting her chin and stepping forward to block his path. "To avoid a terrible error, it is necessary. Mrs. Adler will proceed."

Mr. Samson looked at her with disdain. "Lady Carroway, whatever rank you may hold in the world, the authority of the church, not to mention the demands of common decency—"

Lily didn't listen any further. She yanked the sheet aside to the dead girl's waist, then pulled up the skirt of her uniform and the petticoat underneath. "Which leg was it?" she asked.

Alice's mother inched forward, looking scared but determined. "Her left one, on the inside."

Lily eased the legs apart, and they both gaped, Lily in mounting horror, the woman in mounting confusion. "But . . . but there's no scar on either leg at all. Where did it go?"

"It was never there," Lily said, closing her eyes as if she could deny the evidence in front of her. "Because that is not your daughter."

"Not my Alice?" The woman's voice rose, frantic with hope and confusion. "Then my girl is alive! Where is she?"

Lily didn't answer as she dropped the sheet back over the body. She turned to Mr. Samson, relieved to see horrified comprehension on his face. "You'll stay with her?"

"Of course," he said quickly, looking ill. "I do not . . . Can you fetch the magistrate?"

He meant to come see the body, Lily was sure, but she had no intention of wasting that sort of time. They could not afford any more delays. But instead of taking the time to tell him that, she just nodded. "We will."

"We will go at once," Ofelia said, already turning back toward the stairs. Lily wished she could stop to explain to Alice's mother what had happened, to prepare her for what was to come. But there was not time, and she wasn't sure she could find the right words even if there had been. Better the clergyman stay; it was his calling to give comfort in the face of tragedy. She hurried after her friend.

"It was the clothes," Ofelia moaned as they rushed up the stairs. "She must have switched them to throw us off."

"Etta was arrested on her half day, so she was not in uniform," Lily agreed. "And we all knew it. And they looked so much alike, if you could not see their faces. They were both so small in stature—" She broke off as a sudden thought occurred to her. "They were both so small," she repeated slowly. But before she had time to say anything else, Ofelia had pushed the door to the outside open once more, and a gust of cold wind chased the thought away.

They emerged, blinking, into less sunlight than Lily had expected. The wind had picked up too, sharp and nearly as cold as the air had been in the old icehouse. The two servants still waited for them there, both watching the door uneasily.

"But why?" Ofelia continued. "Why would she have done it?"

Lily felt suddenly breathless, a feeling that was both realization and regret hitting her in the solar plexus. "Isaiah," she said urgently, grabbing his arm without realizing it. "Did Alice know that you were betrothed?"

"Does it matter?" he asked. "She's dead now."

"It does, very much. You said Etta knew. Did Alice?"

"Of course she did." Isaiah shrugged as Lily dropped her hand, horror joining the sick feeling in the pit of her stomach. "Wasn't as though I made a secret of it. I'm going to work at Belleford for two more years, to save up a little more before I go home and we wed. At least, that was my plan. Don't rightways know if I'll stay now." He shuddered. "Too many bad memories here."

"So there is no chance that Alice was sweet on you?" Lily pressed. "She would not have been trying to impress you or win you over or anything like that?"

"No more'n she would have tried to impress anyone else, poor mite. She was an awkward thing, always ending up overlooked and unappreciated." He gave a sad smile. "I tried to be her friend to make up for it, you see."

"But . . . but I saw you two together!" Ofelia protested, a frown gathering between her brows like the storm overhead. "She gave you a muffler she had made herself and said something about wanting it to be just perfect. You even had some sort of little pet name for her!"

"Mouse?" Isaiah smiled. "Aye, I called her that from time to time. On account of her being so timid and quiet; she could creep into a room with no one even noticing she was there. And yes, Lady Carroway, she did give me a muffler. But that was just practice. She said she needed to make sure the next one was just right."

Lily felt cold all over. She had to ask the question, though she was sure she already knew the answer. "And who was the next one to be for?"

"Well, she never rightly said, but it weren't hard to guess that it was intended for Mr. Wright. She thought he was a magnificent gentleman, she did. Not always the sharpest girl around, poor Alice, but full of feelings. Anyone could see Mr. Wright was the sort who found his fun wherever he could and never stayed for long. She was better off without him." Isaiah shook his head, letting out a surprised huff of air as though just realizing something. "No wonder she looked even more shocked than poor Mears when Miss Wright started screaming at Etta that day. She must have been so upset to find out Mr. Wright had been carrying on with Etta. What a horrid thought to have on your mind when you die."

"Yes," Lily agreed, exchanging a horrified look with Ofelia. "But I do not think it was Alice who experienced such a terrible thing."

"What do you mean, ma'am?"

"I mean, Isaiah, that we just looked at the body with Alice's mother, and the poor maid left for dead was not, in fact, her daughter."

"But then . . ." Isaiah halted, a sick, disbelieving expression on his face. "You mean . . . Etta?" Lily nodded, wishing there were a gentler way of delivering such horrible news. They had been friends, after all. He shook his head, as though trying to deny it. "Dear God, no. How . . ."

"If only Mr. Hurst had not left so quickly," Ofelia wailed.

"But he did, so we must do what we can without him. We have to warn them right away." Lily gripped the manservant's arm. "Do you have a horse?"

"Aye."

"Then I need you to fetch Mr. Powell and bring him to Belleford instantly. You're to come with him too. We will need all the help we can get."

"But, Mrs. Adler, what do you mean? What's going on?" Isaiah begged, looking desperate to deny everything he had just learned.

"What is going on is that we have to stop a revenge tragedy from being enacted," Ofelia said. "Let us hope we are not too late."

CHAPTER 24

The coachman had caught their urgency, and he set a blistering pace as they thundered toward Belleford.

"Neddy is there," Ofelia whispered in a pained voice, just once, the only thing she said during the whole drive.

Lily nodded. "My aunt too."

They didn't speak again, each one trying not to think of the worst thing they might find when they arrived. Ofelia leaned against the window, her eyes straining forward, as though she could will the coach to get there faster. Lily looked fixedly straight ahead.

"I'd have thought she'd want to get as far away as possible," Alice had said that day in the storeroom, when she had been so surprised to see someone else in her secret domain. *"I know I would."*

"The next one has got to be just perfect."

"Do you always get everything just because you want it, Etta?"

"No one ever talks to me, ma'am."

"No one even notices if I come into a room or leave it."

Thunder rumbled in counterpoint to the clatter of the carriage wheels as they pulled to a stop in front of the manor. The door was shut, but that was not surprising—the kitchen door, Lily suspected, was unlocked, and what better way to enter the building unseen? No one in the family would venture down there, and there were only two servants in the house, neither of whom concerned themselves much with cooking.

Lily and Ofelia tumbled out of the carriage, almost falling over each other in their haste.

"What should I do, my lady?" the coachman cried out from his perch, his face wreathed in confused anxiety. "What are you going to do?"

Ofelia paused to look back at him. "I am going to find Sir Edward," she said. Her voice was shockingly calm, but Lily could see the tension trembling through her body. "Tie up the horses quickly, then come with us."

She didn't wait for a response before turning to dash up the steps, her hat tumbling from her head and her gown whipped around her legs by the wind.

Lily followed. For a moment, she was afraid the front door was locked as Ofelia struggled with the heavy handle. But it hadn't taken the coachman long to lash the reins around a hitching post. He lent his weight, and when they all pulled together, the door swung ponderously open.

The stood for a moment in the silent front hall, catching their breath and getting their bearings.

Ofelia swallowed. "Where do you think—"

Her whisper was cut off by a scream. Lily recognized the sound of Miss Wright's voice. Lily gave Ofelia only one quick, panicked glance before running toward the back of the house. The other two followed, their footsteps echoing against the cold ceilings.

The sound had come from the parlor where Selina Wright often sat. She was not sitting there now. Instead, she lay across the threshold of the opposite room, the one that her mother's body had been laid out in what seemed like ages ago. Her hair was tumbled over her face and her arms stretched out awkwardly, her dress tangled around her legs. Scattered across the ground near her lay the shattered remains of a porcelain vase. The ancient butler, Mr. Mears, knelt next to her, shaking her shoulder.

He started back when he heard them coming, terror on his face. He relaxed only a little when he saw who it was. "She was here . . . How can she be here? She was dead! And poor Selina . . . little Selina . . . What do we do?"

Ofelia drew back. "Is she . . . ?"

Lily swallowed. But there wasn't time to hesitate. She knelt next to the butler and searched for the pulse in Selina Wright's neck.

"Alive," she said, letting out a hoarse, relieved breath. When she pushed the hair away from Miss Wright's face, she could see an ugly purple bruise spreading across her temple. A thin trickle of blood had left a sticky trail to the edge of her lips. But she was breathing. "She must have heard something in here and got bashed over the head for her trouble."

Ofelia shuddered. "That seems to be this girl's favorite way of handling her problems."

"We are lucky she did not have time to do more." Lily stood, wiping her hands against her skirts. "I think we have to leave her here."

Ofelia turned to the coachman. "You stay here. Do what you can to revive her. And make sure Mr. Mears is well."

"But shouldn't I—" He shook his head. "Shouldn't you—"

"I am going to find my husband," Ofelia snapped. She turned to Lily. "Which way?"

It was growing darker outside, the gathering clouds blocking the sunlight and plunging the manor into gloom. Lily pointed into the room, toward the shadowy corner where the edge of the door was just visible. "That way." There was a single candle left burning on a table by the door, one of the crude tallow ones from the kitchen. Lily took a deep breath and picked it up. She swung the door open. "Follow me."

Ofelia drew back, just for a moment. Then she squared her shoulders, picked up the poker from the fireplace, and nodded. "Lead on."

The staircase was even dimmer than Lily had remembered, with almost no light coming through the narrow windows. The candle sent their shadows racing ahead of them, looming around the curve of the passage. But their steps were nearly silent. When they reached the second floor, the door was ajar.

Lily inched it open a little more. There was no one in sight in the upper hall, but she could hear voices, low and urgent. Motioning to Ofelia to follow, she set off down the hall. The voices were coming from Mrs. Wright's room, she realized, the cold feeling of dread spreading through her body.

As they drew closer, Lily blew out her candle and set it on a hall table, not wanting to attract too much attention until she knew what sort of situation they were walking into. Ofelia was shaking visibly next to her, her fingers clenched around the handle of the poker, but her jaw was set with determination. They inched forward until suddenly the voices ahead of them rose in volume.

"Get away from him!" That was Alice's voice, shaking with emotion. "I don't want to hurt you two, but I will, I will, if you don't get out of my way!"

"But why do you wish to hurt Mr. Wright then?" That was Eliza, soothing and practical at the same time. Lily's heart clenched in her chest.

"Because he hurt me." They could hear Alice sobbing now, but they could also hear the undercurrent of seething rage. "I thought he would choose me—maybe even love me!"

The door to Mrs. Wright's room stood ajar, and Lily and Ofelia could see the whole of the horrible tableau as they came around the corner. Mr. Wright stood by the far wall, shrinking fearfully back toward the fireplace, but at the same time holding tight to Eliza's arm to stop her from moving any closer to Alice.

The maid stood in the center of the room, brandishing the wood axe from the kitchen. And between her and the other two stood Ned Carroway, his hands held forward, palms out, as though trying to calm a wild animal. But when he caught sight of Ofelia in the doorway, he gasped, losing his composure as he cried, "What are you doing here?"

Alice didn't turn around, simply tightened her grip on the axe, her eyes still fixed on Thomas Wright. "I suppose that's Mrs. Adler behind me, come poking into other people's business again? Don't come in, thank you, or I'll let you guess what I might do."

"I shall stay right here, then," Lily said, trying to sound as calm and in control as she could, and unable to tell whether or not she was succeeding. "But does Mr. Wright know why you are so angry with him?"

"I've no clue!" His answer was immediate and frantic. "I thought she was dead—I thought Etta killed her! And I was so terribly upset, Alice, you've no idea—"

"Liar!" she screamed, taking a step forward, while Mr. Wright pushed Eliza behind him, ignoring her protests. Thunder rumbled, closer now. "I did everything for you—I tried to set you free, just like you wanted, from this stupid house and your stupid family. But you only cared for Etta, didn't you? I thought you cared for me. You told me I was pretty!"

"I did? I mean, you are! But I'd no intention of—if I said that, I swear I never meant anything by it—"

"Of course you didn't." Alice took another step forward. "I thought I meant something to you. I was doing *everything* for you. And instead you were carrying on with Etta. Everyone always liked Etta better, everyone *noticed* Etta—they cared whether she was in the room or not. Well, no one can like her better now. I've taken care of that because she's dead." Her voice grew calm, an eerie counterpoint to the thunder that crashed outside. They all jumped, except for Alice. "And you will be too."

Lily could see Ned gulp, but he stood his ground, now only a few scant feet from the furious girl brandishing an axe. "Afraid I shan't let you near him," he said stoically. He planted his feet and planted his chin, while his hands clenched and unclenched as though wishing for a weapon of his own.

"Very well." Alice's sounded regretful but determined. She lifted the axe higher, prepared to swing it. A sudden flash of lightning lit up the room. For a moment her shadow loomed over all of them. "Then I shall deal with you first."

"Get away from him!" Ofelia screamed, brandishing the poker as she dashed forward.

"Ofelia, no!" Ned's agonized cry cut through the air.

Ofelia collided with Alice as the next peal of thunder rolled through the room. The maid turned from her deadly task, but not in time. Ofelia hit her from the side, axe and poker both useless as they stumbled, off balance. They crashed into the spindly chair that sat in front of the desk, snapping its wooden back. Ned threw himself forward, grabbing his wife around the waist and trying to pull her away. The movement gave Alice room to swing her weapon. And Ofelia and Ned were the closest people to her.

Shrieking, she heaved it over her shoulder, preparing to cut down anyone that stood between her and Thomas Wright. But Lily was still behind her. Without thinking, she flung herself forward, reaching up to grab at the handle of the axe with both hands. She felt a sharp pain in one temple as she did so, but she managed to get a grip. Alice screamed again, this time in fury and frustration, trying to shake Lily off. But Lily clung on, dragging backward with her full weight.

Alice was small and slight, in spite of her rage. She was pulled off balance, and her fingers lost their purchase on the axe handle. Lily stumbled backward, her own momentum carrying her backward without Alice's weight to keep her upright. The axe flew above her head, but she managed to keep hold of it even as it crashed into a window. Another streak of lightning dashed across the sky, and a gust of cold air blew in.

Above the sound of shattering glass, Lily heard a voice yell, "Get away from her!" She saw Thomas Wright grab both Ned and Ofelia, pulling them away from Alice as the sudden report of a pistol echoed through the crowded room.

Alice screamed and crumpled to the ground, a crimson stain blooming across her right shoulder. Then there was silence, broken by another crash of thunder and the sudden rush of rain.

Lily, breathing heavily, let the axe drop to the ground. The rain was blowing in the ruined window, but she barely felt the cold or wet. Mr. Powell, the magistrate, stood in the doorway, a smoking pistol in his hand. His normally ruddy face was pale with shock as he took in the wreckage of the room. Isaiah stood behind him, and he was the first to move.

He went to Alice first, who lay in a sobbing pile, clutching at her shoulder. "Let me see it," he said gently, easing her into a seated position. Alice snarled at him, trying to pull away, but he was nearly twice her size. Firmly, he pulled her closer again, examining the wound on her arm. "Grazed the arm," he said. Alice moaned but didn't try to move away again. Isaiah pulled off his own neckcloth. Eliza, taking a deep breath, joined him and offered her handkerchief. Together they began to bandage the wound. "Took out a chunk of flesh, but it didn't hit the bone. If no infection sets in, it'll scar but likely nothing else."

Lily could see a muscle twitching in his temple, but his voice remained calm, almost devoid of emotion. He had lived and worked side by side with Alice for years. And to see her so transformed . . . Lily wondered what it was costing him to maintain that stoic front and wished she hadn't told him to come with the magistrate.

"Good shot, Powell," Thomas Wright said, panting.

The magistrate grimaced. "Thought I was shooting to kill," he said. "Not much good with a pistol, I'm afraid."

"Glad you didn't hit one of us, then," Lily heard Ned mutter, but he said it in such a low voice that the magistrate didn't seem to notice.

Mr. Powell thrust the weapon into his waistband before going to join Isaiah on the floor. He followed the manservant's example and pulled off his cravat. "Could use yours as well," he said shortly, glancing at Mr. Wright.

He obliged, and in a few minutes Alice's arm was tightly bandaged, and both hands were bound behind her back. She winced a little, and whimpered in pain, but she didn't try to fight them or pull away. Instead, she kept her eyes fixed on Thomas Wright, an unnerving stare that made him step quickly back from her once he had handed over his cravat.

Mr. Powell cleared his throat as he stood. "So, girl, care to explain how it is you are not dead after all?"

Alice gave him a brief, scornful look but said nothing.

"She is wearing Etta's clothes," Lily said, stepping gingerly around the shattered glass that covered the floor where she had ended up, and pushing her wet hair out of her eyes. The wind was driving rain into the room, but it wasn't strong enough to reach beyond the few feet closest to the window.

The axe she left lying on the ground where it had fallen. Looking at it made her feel ill, and she tried not to imagine what Alice would have done with it if they had not arrived in time.

"Lily, your head!" Eliza exclaimed, starting forward.

Bemused, Lily reached up to touch her temple where she had felt that glancing shock of pain, staring at her fingers when they came away bloody. As if from very far away, she felt her head throbbing. "I think the axe hit me when I grabbed it," she said, not really caring.

Eliza ordered Ned to hand over his cravat and handkerchief as well. He let go of his wife long enough to do so, though he pulled her close to him again once he'd given them to Eliza. Lily couldn't tell which of them was comforting the other. Eliza fussed over Lily's wound until it was bandaged to her satisfaction.

"It's not deep at all, just a graze. But head wounds bleed so. We shall have to clean it properly when we get home," Eliza muttered, her hands shaking as she worked.

Lily laid her free hand on her aunt's arm. "I am well, I promise," she said gently. "We all are."

"That girl is not," Mr. Powell said sternly, pointing at Alice. "And I mean to know why and what happened. You were saying, Mrs. Adler?"

Lily tried to step forward but was surprised to realize she was swaying on her feet. She felt Eliza's arm slip around her waist and gave her aunt a brief, grateful smile.

But her expression grew grim once more as she turned to the magistrate.

"Etta was getting back from her half day when you arrested her. So she was wearing her own clothes. Alice swapped them, leaving Etta in her own uniform with her face too injured to be properly identified. Since Etta was the one who was arrested, and the one who was having an affair with Mr. Wright, we all assumed she was the one who had fled." She glanced at Alice. "Does that sound about right?"

Alice gave her a black look. But the only thing she said was, "All of you are getting wet."

"She is not wrong," Eliza said, firm and practical as always. "It would be absurd after all this if every one of us caught a chill. And my niece needs to sit down. We ought to move to another room and put something over that window."

"My sister," Thomas Wright said, suddenly starting forward. "I've no idea where—"

"She is downstairs," Lily said as Ned, unable to help being a gentleman, assisted Alice in climbing awkwardly to her feet. "She took a blow to the head when she surprised Alice, but we left Mr. Mears and your coachman tending to her. Lady Carroway, perhaps you and Sir Edward could go check on them?"

It took some time, and no small amount of confusion, but at last a blanket was tacked over the open window and they were all ushered into the family parlor, where, Lily noted grimly, their involvement in the whole strange business had begun. She found herself wishing that Mr. Spencer were there, as he had been at the beginning.

Selina Wright, still pale and dazed, was seated on the same fainting couch, her brother nearby. Alice was in a chair by the fireplace, Mr. Powell hovering over her. The others were seated around the room while Mr. Mears and the coachman, both looking shaken but not as badly as the rest of the party, distributed brandy and sherry to ward off the chill. Isaiah had found time to fetch a stack of towels; when he handed one to Lily, she made herself meet his eyes.

"I am so sorry," she murmured. "I know they were both your friends."

He nodded stiffly. "Just a few hours ago I thought Alice dead and Etta a killer. Now . . . I suppose it's no worse. But it's a lot of shocks, so close together." He clenched his jaw and turned away, and Lily didn't press him further.

When they were all settled, the coachman left to tend to the horses that were still outside in the rain. Mr. Mears stepped back to join Isaiah, who had withdrawn uncomfortably against the wall. But to Lily's surprise, Thomas Wright gestured them forward.

"Join us, if you please. We have all lived together for many years. You deserve to know what has happened as much as Selina or I do."

Mr. Powell gulped down his brandy, then cleared his throat. "So, what you were saying, Mrs. Adler, is that we made an unfortunate assumption?"

"We made quite a few assumptions we ought not to have," Ofelia said, her voice shaking, her hands curled around the glass of sherry. She was sitting far closer to her husband than either of them would have permitted in public under normal circumstances, so close she was practically in his lap. But no one in the room seemed to begrudge them that.

Lily nodded in agreement, then winced as the motion made her head ache. "We assumed the maid who paid off Mr. Wright's debt was Etta, for one. It seems we all fell into the trap of noticing her instead of Alice." She gave the bound girl a cold look. "I imagine that has grated on you for years."

Alice glared at her but said nothing.

"Wait, you mean Alice paid off Clive? For me?" Thomas Wright looked between Lily and Ofelia, frowning and confusion. "How? And why?"

"If you've not figured out the *why* yet, Mr. Wright, you've not been paying attention," Lily said sternly.

"No, I mean . . . I understand that she thought . . ." Mr. Wright cleared his throat. "But why that specifically?"

"Just as she said," Lily explained, pushing a lock of wet hair out of her eyes and wincing again. "She meant to free you of your family and the house. You have often said how you would like to go to London or Bath, anywhere but here, have you not?" He nodded, shamefaced. "She went through quite the charade to attempt to chase your family away from Belleford so you could. Posing as the ghost—that was very cleverly done, Alice," she added, turning to the maid.

"*She* was the ghost?" Miss Wright burst out, unable to help herself, while Mr. Wright's jaw fell open in surprise.

"She was," Lily said. "Only you used that old staircase, Alice, which let you move from place to place easily. The house is so dark at night, no one could see you clearly, and you could disappear with no one being the wiser."

Ofelia took up the narrative. "The only snag in your plan came when Etta surprised you one night. You were worried she would be close enough to recognize you. So you chased her. Did you mean for her to injure herself?"

"I didn't mind," Alice muttered, the first thing she had said in over half an hour.

Lily shook her head, unsurprised. "And she made a plan to pay off your debts, Mr. Wright, when your mother would not. She planned to steal some of your mother's jewelry one night and take it to pay Mr. Clive the next morning. Things went awry, though, when she could not find the key to leave." Lily turned to Alice once more. "Mrs. Wright, I assume, woke up to find you searching around her bed? Or perhaps her person?"

"Why should I tell you?" Alice asked defiantly, lifting her chin, though she winced when the movement pulled at her injured and bound arm.

"But how was she in the room in the first place?" Eliza asked, her glass of brandy forgotten on the table before her. "The door was locked. How could she have gotten in?"

"That part I do not know," Ofelia admitted, her mouth twisting with frustration.

"By entering when it was unlocked," Lily said. "Is that not so Alice?" When the girl didn't answer, Lily turned to the magistrate. "Do you remember what Mr. and Miss Wright said about sitting with their mother that evening? Once they were done with their tea, what happened?"

The magistrate frowned, turning his glass of brandy absently between his fingers. "They said good night to their mother—no!" His face lit up. "Etta came and tended to the fire. But how does that help Alice?"

"They told us a maid tended the fire." Lily turned to Miss Wright. "Was it Etta?"

The two siblings exchanged a puzzled look. "I . . . I do not entirely recall. Did she not?" Miss Wright asked.

"No," Mr. Wright said, snapping his fingers. "I am certain I would have noticed specifically if it had been Etta." When his sister shot him a look of disapproval, he shrugged. "Well, I would have. But as I do not remember"—he turned back to Lily—"it must have been Alice, mustn't it?"

"But I feel certain I recall someone saying it was Etta!" Ofelia protested.

"Many times," Lily agreed. "We all said it. I did as well. But not because we knew it to have been her."

"Neither Mr. nor Miss Wright ever said so, and they were the ones who were there that evening," Ofelia said, her shoulders slumping. "We assumed—and we kept assuming. Once again."

Lily turned back to the Wrights. "Neither of you were paying much attention to Alice at that point, were you? You were likely engrossed with your mother. In any case, the three of you ceased to notice her almost the moment she was in the room. Which you were counting on, of course," she added, turning back to Alice, whose face was slowly turning crimson with anger as Lily's calm narrative progressed. "Since your plan was that you would never leave the room."

"But she was not— We would have— Dash it all, we would have seen her if she were still in the room!" Mr. Wright protested.

"Of course we would have," Miss Wright agreed, giving Lily a displeased glance. "Are you saying she turned invisible? Is that more likely than the ghost doing such a terrible thing?"

"She did not," Lily agreed calmly. "One thing that Alice and Etta both had in common was their small size. And even someone of *my* height could fit in your mother's wardrobe easily. Perhaps you recall, Miss Wright? Your mother kept few enough gowns that there was plenty of room for someone of Alice's stature to sit and wait until the house grew quiet for the night. And since both maids knew your mother always dressed for bed before she took her tea with you, Alice could be confident Mrs. Wright would have no reason to open the wardrobe while she was hiding there."

"So she would have spent the whole night in the room," Ofelia said slowly. She thought it over for a moment. "Of course! Etta told us that Alice was asleep in order to cover her own absence. But when Etta spent the whole night waiting for Mr. Wright, who was in the lockup, that meant there was no one to say that Alice had, in fact, been in her room sleeping all night, as she claimed."

"And you were able to open the wardrobe door from the inside," Eliza murmured. "So Alice could have easily done the same."

"Precisely." Lily turned to Mr. Powell. "Alice was able to slip out and accomplish her robbery easily. She would know where everything was, of course. But Mrs. Wright hid the key in a new spot each night, and I would guess Alice had trouble finding it to let herself out. That was when Mrs. Wright woke. And Alice silenced her before she could raise the alarm. After that, her only option was to hide again until someone opened the door in the morning, then slip out and return to her room in the confusion."

"And then she paid off Clive that morning," Mr. Powell said nodding. "And made a few more appearances as the ghost for good measure, just to increase suspicion that Mrs. Wright's death was due to supernatural causes." He raised his eyebrows at Mr. Wright. "And all this just for you? I'd not have expected you to inspire such devotion, Wright."

"Nor I, sir," he said, his voice shaking, his normal flirtatious bravado gone. Lily wondered if it were perhaps gone for good.

"And the other maid, Etta?" Mr. Powell cleared his throat, his face falling. "I suppose I am partly responsible for her death, then. It's a heavy thing to bear. But if I'd not arrested her, and if Miss Wright here had not shouted the news of her affair to the heavens, perhaps . . ."

Lily exchanged a look with Ofelia but didn't say anything. She felt too culpable herself. And judging by the anguished look on her friend's face, she was not alone in the feeling.

Mr. Powell glanced at Alice. "But we know now where the final guilt rests. Who was it wrote that line about a woman scorned?"

"Congreve. *The Mourning Bride*," Alice bit off. Her angry flush was gone, her face now pale with fear, and her whole body was shaking. But she still looked at them malevolently. "He was right, you know."

Mr. Powell regarded her in surprise. "You know Congreve, then?"

"I know lots of things," Alice cried in anguish, her rage crumpling into pain. "I read, I watch . . . No one notices me, but I notice so much!" She turned a pleading look on Mr. Wright. "If you had just talked to me, we could have . . . we might have had so much to share." Her voice dropped to a hoarse whisper. "The ghost, the jewels—I did it all for you. I didn't plan to kill anyone. But even that was for you."

"She killed our mother," Miss Wright breathed, raising her handkerchief to cover a sob. "Our poor mother. Our dear, sweet mother."

"Well, she was not that sweet," Mr. Wright said, clearing his throat. Lily was surprised to see tears in his eyes. "But she did not deserve to die like that. No more did Etta. And these good people." He gestured at Ofelia and Ned; Ned put a protective arm around his wife and pulled her even closer. "What you would have done to them does not even bear imagining." Mr. Wright turned a cold gaze on Alice. "Hanging is too good for you."

She crumpled before their eyes, hers fixed uncomprehendingly on Thomas Wright, as though she had not believed until that moment that he wouldn't understand and forgive her. Her shoulders slumped, and her whole body seemed to shrink in on itself while she cried.

"I think we have learned all we need to," Eliza said, setting down her glass and standing. "Mr. Powell, this young woman ought to be removed from the house."

"Yes, of course." The magistrate stood, looking overwhelmed by the day's revelations but still determined to do his duty. "And we ought to get Dr. Mills to look at that arm of hers. Mr. Wright, perhaps your manservant could assist me?"

Mr. Mears cleared his throat. "Begging your pardon, sirs, but Isaiah's had shock after shock these past few days. He knew these girls better than any of the rest of us. He ought to have a cup of strong, sweet tea and some quiet to recover. Hopefully not in this house." When Isaiah turned to regard him in disbelief, the old butler shrugged uncomfortably. "It's what I would want, were I in your shoes."

"Thank you, sir," Isaiah said quietly, looking a little bewildered by the sudden bout of understanding from the normally hostile Mr. Mears.

"I will assist you, Mr. Powell," Ned said, standing. "Mr. Wright ought to stay here and tend to his sister. And my coachman will take the ladies back to Longwood Cottage. They also have had a shock."

"We all have," Ofelia said, threading her fingers through her husband's for a brief moment before releasing him.

Alice didn't speak as she was helped to her feet, her hands still bound behind her back. But at the doorway she held back long enough to turn, her pleading eyes fixed on Mr. Wright.

"I did it all for you," she repeated in anguish.

"You were going to kill him too," Ofelia pointed out, ignoring Ned's attempts to hush her.

Alice turned to give her a black look, and her fury seemed to give her strength once more. Her back straightened, and she contemplated each of them in turn, her eyes red from crying, her gaze cold and unnerving. She finally settled on Mr. Wright, but this time he didn't shrink back.

He met her eyes. "Hanging is too good for you," he repeated, and Lily was not the only one who flinched at the ice in his voice.

Alice lifted her chin. "Then you deserved to die too."

Mr. Wright put an arm around his sister and turned to the magistrate. "Mr. Powell, if you would, please remove her from our home."

CHAPTER 25

Alice awaits the next session of the assizes now, though a fever seems to have set in as a result of the wound in her arm. There is no saying what will happen or whether she will recover enough to stand trial eventually. I believe the Wrights are hoping she will not, if only to spare them the indignity of a trial.

Mr. Hurst returned from the home of Etta's parents, and after learning what had passed in his absence, promptly called for his horse once more, saying he had to ride back instantly to explain the new facts of the situation to them. I like him the better for his willingness to do so, no matter that it did not reflect well on him to have been so mistaken. (It did not reflect well on any of us, of course, but he is the one who had to admit so publicly.) I think he has great potential in his profession, and I hope you are able to impart to him a little more of your—

"Lily!"

Eliza's call interrupted Lily's letter to Simon Page of Bow Street; after requesting his help—what seemed like months ago rather than a matter of days—she felt she owed him as immediate and full an explanation as she could manage. Mr. Hurst would, no doubt, carry his own report back to Bow Street. But

Lily considered Mr. Page a particular friend in spite of the differences in their lives. She felt sure he would want to hear her report of what had passed.

But there were voices downstairs—she had taken over the upstairs guest room once Ofelia and Ned departed, Ofelia with some reluctance, Ned with obvious relief. Two of the voices were male, and Lily was curious to know who might have called. Tucking her letter away to finish later, she wrapped her shawl more warmly around her shoulders and went to see who it was.

As she approached the parlor, the two male voices rose in heated but, she was relieved to hear, good-natured debate. She found herself smiling, recognizing them now that she was closer, and tapped lightly on the doorframe to announce her presence.

Lord Walter, the husband of her friend Serena, started, looking guilty at being caught arguing in the middle of someone else's drawing room. And Matthew Spencer smiled, his face lighting up with genuine pleasure at seeing her once more. Both men stood quickly and bowed. Eliza, looking amused, rose more slowly to her feet, while Susan stayed in her seat by the fire, busy with her embroidery but still watching both men with undisguised curiosity.

"Lord Walter." Lily held out her hands, smiling warmly. The gap in their ages had made her shy with him when he and Serena had first married. But the handsome older gentleman, with silver wings in his hair and a solid devotion to his family, had won her over with his kindly smile and gentle manner. (Though Lily hoped he would never find out she had once suspected him of murder—or rather, had hoped very much that he was *not* guilty.) "What a pleasure to see you. We did not expect you until tomorrow at least."

"And I did not expect to have the beginnings of a Parliamentary debate in the middle of my drawing room," Eliza said. "How nice to have entertaining surprises again, at long last."

"What was the subject this time?" Lily asked, glad for the distraction from the letter that awaited her upstairs.

Matthew looked pleased by her interest. "A reform bill concerning soldiers returning from the war," he explained. "Many of them come home with serious wounds that prevent them from finding new trades, or indeed working at all. And when they are released on only half or quarter pay—or worse, none at all—they have no way to support their family. Many turn to drink, which leads to either crime or poverty."

"But you did not have enough support from the very beginning," Lord Walter said pleasantly. "No one wants to take money away from the army to pay a common laborer not to labor. Not enough *good* support, at least. If you reformers had been able to get someone on your side—someone like General Waring, perhaps—more members would have listened."

"Someone like General Waring can have very little understanding of why such a bill is important," Matthew countered calmly. "Like you, sir, he has never been short of income, so he has as little sympathy for the plight of working men as you do." He lifted the stump of his arm pointedly. "If the general had returned with an injury like mine, he still would have had a home and food and the ability to support his dependents. If a man who knew no trade but soldiering returned with such an injury, what would you expect him to do with the remainder of his life?"

"Well, the ladies do not want to hear us hash it all out here," Lord Walter said. "Mrs. Adler, your friends have told me about the dreadful events of your visit. I am glad you all have emerged unscathed." He glanced at the bandage that still went around Lily's temple, though she and Anna had tried to arrange her hair to disguise it as much as possible. "Or mostly unscathed."

"Dear me, yes," Susan said, shuddering. "I think I will have nightmares for weeks, imagining the whole thing. But being there would have been far worse."

Matthew let the subject change with good grace; in fact, Lily even thought he looked amused. When she gave him a puzzled glance, he leaned over to whisper, "If he had a good point of his own, he would have made it instead of changing the subject. I shall gain his support yet, never fear." His confidence made her want to laugh—and how good it felt to want to do so again—but she held it in. Still, she was grateful for his presence and for the smile he sent her way when no one was looking.

"Though I wish, Mrs. Adler, that you had less of a nose for trouble," Lord Walter was saying gravely when Lily recalled herself to the conversation. "Lady Walter will not be surprised at all, I am sure, when we tell her of it. And I wish I had arrived even earlier, now, that I might have been of some assistance to you."

"If you had, I would have insisted on it," Lily said, attempting lightness, though she was not sure she succeeded. She still did not like to think too much of what had happened—she would have dreams for a long time of Alice brandishing that axe at her friends. And the tightly bandaged wound on her head still throbbed when she least expected it, an unwelcome reminder when she wanted to be thinking of other things. "But you are more than welcome, sir, whenever you arrive."

"Shall we have the pleasure of your company until the morning?" Susan asked. "It would be a long day of travel for you indeed, to turn around and immediately head back to Surrey."

"Unfortunately, dear ma'am, I must decline your hospitality," Lord Walter said with a bow. "Lady Walter's doctor believes her confinement may come to an end more swiftly than the last time, and I do not like to be away from her overly long."

"Then I must make haste," Lily said. "My things are nearly packed; I've only a few last-minute additions to make. And I will need to let my maid know that we are leaving quickly."

"I would be happy to do so for you," Susan said, rising. "I must go in search of our Addie and ask her to take another basket over to Belleford." She shook her head. "They are talking of leaving, did you know? Miss Wright suggested it. It seems a ghost and a death were one thing, but being attacked in their own home has proved too much, even for her. Terrible, terrible . . . If you will excuse me? Lord Walter, a pleasure to meet you. Mr. Spencer, I am sure we will see each other again soon."

The gentlemen rose once again to make their bows as Susan left, and Lord Walter remained standing. "I left my carriage in the village and came on foot. If you will excuse me as well, Miss Pierce, Mrs. Adler, I will head back to let my coachman and grooms know we depart imminently. I expect we shall return for you in . . ." He consulted his pocket watch. "Would an hour be sufficient, Mrs. Adler?"

"More than, I am sure," she replied, rising to take his hands. "You are good to come all this way for me."

He smiled. "Lady Walter has said she cannot do without you for long, and I am more than grateful that you are willing to bear her company. I only regret that I have missed seeing Sir Edward and Lady Carroway."

"The dear boy could not wait to get his wife away and safe at home," Eliza put in quietly. "I certainly cannot blame him for that."

"No indeed." Lord Walter looked very serious for a moment.

Lily felt a pang of sympathy for poor Ned, so looking forward to his rest in the country, and instead caught up very much against his will in a murder investigation. She hoped their time in Somerset would prove perfectly mundane.

"Well, I am sorry you will be deprived of your all your guests in so short a time, Miss Pierce. And I thank you for the offer of your hospitality," the viscount continued, inclining his head politely. "Perhaps another time? Mrs. Adler, I will see you soon."

"I shall be happy to walk you out, sir," Eliza said, rising. "Lily, before I forget, there is a letter for you on the table there. Susan just returned from fetching the post."

After a few more quick pleasantries, they were gone, and Lily was left alone with Matthew, who was eyeing the door with a bemused smile. "That felt deliberate," he said. "From both your aunt and Miss Clarke. They do not . . . That is to say, you did not . . ."

"Tell them?" Lily asked, feeling the heat rise in her cheeks and trying to chase it away with a deep breath. She and Matthew had not been alone for any stretch of time since the night they had spent together, and she was not sure how to behave. "No. But my aunt is perceptive enough that she might have guessed."

"It must be a family trait," he said, stepping closer, "since you are far and away the most perceptive woman of my acquaintance."

Lily's eyes crinkled up with amusement. "That is one compliment I shall accept. Any man can praise a woman for her appearance. It takes somewhat more discernment—and a good deal more respect—for him to praise her mind."

"I cannot think anyone who knows you could feel anything but respect for your mind, Lily," he murmured, stepping closer still and reaching out to brush a curl behind her ear. His fingers hovered briefly over her bandaged temple, but he did not fuss nor berate her for the risks she had taken. Lily was grateful for it. "If your aunt does know, it seems, at least, that she does not disapprove."

"Not yet, at least," Lily replied, trying not to seem too flustered in spite of the way her heart had sped up. Trying to regain her composure, she moved away, heading toward the table her aunt had indicated, in search of her letter. She recognized the handwriting at once as Jack's, and to her surprise, she felt her blush growing. For some reason, her mind kept darting back to Ofelia's surprise that early, early morning in the corridor, and her whispered question, "What would the captain think?" But she pushed it out of her mind, slipping the letter into her pocket as she turned back. "But whether she approves or disapproves, she does not make my choices for me."

She found Matthew watching her, looking a little hesitant. "No, you are certainly a woman who decides such things for herself. Which means I must ask, has your mind changed since last we spoke?"

She could hardly blame him for the question. After all, she had practically run across the room to get away from him. "Not at all." Admitting the truth was difficult, but Lily wanted to be honest. She took a deep breath. "You leave me flustered, sir. It is not a sensation to which I am accustomed.'

"I can imagine not," he murmured, smiling as he came toward her. This time she did not back away, and he stopped just before her. "May I tell you a secret in return?" When she raised her brows in invitation, he dropped his voice. "I am glad to hear it because I feel the same around you, and I've no idea what to do about that."

Lily felt a smile spreading across her face. "You do not act like it."

"Pure ego, I am afraid," he said, taking another step closer. She felt his fingers reach out and twine through hers, but she did not look away from the deep, hypnotic blue of his eyes. "I am working very hard to impress you."

"Would it make you feel better to know you are succeeding?"

"Very much. It would also make me feel better to kiss you once more before we must go our separate ways." When he saw her dart a quick glance at the open door, he smiled ruefully. "Beginning an affair at your aunt's house, and when you were days away from departing once more, was perhaps not the best plan I have ever had." His voice dropped, becoming cajoling. "But that just means I need something to tide me over until we meet again in London."

"Then I suppose I do as well," Lily murmured. She didn't hesitate any longer. Instead of telling him he might kiss her, she raised herself up on her toes and kissed him herself. She felt his breath catch, and his fingers tightened around hers, as though he wanted to lift his arm and had to stop himself.

"That will have to do, I suppose," Matthew said, prudently pulling back after only a few moments. His voice was husky. "Unless we want to risk being caught by some enterprising servant. Or worse, Miss Clarke."

Lily laughed. "Our secret might never be safe again if she discovered us." She reached up to brush her hand against the stubble on his cheek; he turned his head and caught her fingertips with his lips, pressing small, nibbling kisses against them. "You are a bad influence, sir."

"I wish I could be a worse one," he said ruefully. "Alas. You must prepare to depart, and I must return home." His expression grew serious. "I wish I had been there with you at the end. I thought my heart would stop when I heard what had happened."

"You needn't worry about me," Lily said, trying to sound lighthearted but shivering a little at the reminder. "I am well able to take care of myself."

"It is impossible not to worry when we care about someone," he said, and she felt a wave of warmth sweep up her spine at his words. A moment later he smiled. "You're not likely to find any dead bodies in Surrey, are you?"

"Good God, I hope not," Lily said sincerely, and he laughed at the quickness of her response. The old, tall clock in the corner chimed the quarter hour suddenly, making them both jump. "I think that, unfortunately, is our reminder to actually say our goodbyes. I've no wish to keep Lord Walter waiting."

"Of course not." He glanced at the door once more, than pulled her close for another quick kiss. "Take care of yourself, Lily. Write to me if you wish. You can be certain I will write to you." He bowed and made as if to leave, but in the doorway turned and smiled. "Who knows? I may even be unable to keep away from Surrey in the coming weeks."

When he left, Lily found herself staring after him, two fingers pressed against her lips, until she recalled herself with a shake of her head. Lord Walter would expect her to be ready when he returned. She would read her letter, and then she would hurry upstairs to finish her packing and change for travel.

Quickly, she broke open the seal on Jack's letter. His writing was even more of a hasty scrawl than usual, as if he had begun before he quite knew what he was going to say but could not help himself. She smiled, comforted by imagining his look of surprise and by the way she could almost feel the mix of amusement and worry in the way his pen hurried across the page.

Lily,

Not that I am shocked. If you recall, I predicted you would find trouble when we said our farewells. And you know I love being proved right almost as much as you do.

But in this case I must demand: What—what what—have you gotten yourself mixed up in?

How I wish I were there to bear you company and talk things through as you pace around the room . . .

Lily read through the rest of the letter, then glanced at the clock. She had time to respond, if she hurried.

AUTHOR'S NOTE

Longtime readers will know that Ofelia's character is inspired partly by Miss Lambe, a mixed-race heiress from the West Indies who appears in Jane Austen's unfinished novel *Sanditon*. As Ofelia notes in the text, seeing a variety of races and faces would have been common in cities like London. England was a hub of trade and colonization, and this meant people from all over moved through its ports. It was less common, though not improbable, to encounter residents of different races in smaller towns and villages. To learn more about people of color living in England in the nineteenth century, I recommend *Black London: Life Before Emancipation* by Gretchen Holbrook Gerzina and *Representing Mixed Race in Jamaica and England From the Abolition Era to the Present* by Sara Salih.

If you've noticed a slightly different flavor to Lily's third adventure, that isn't by accident. The Gothic romance was a staple of nineteenth-century reading, made popular by works such as Ann Radcliffe's *The Mysteries of Udolpho* and satirized perfectly by Jane Austen in *Northanger Abbey*.

Other popular Gothic works from the late eighteenth and early nineteenth centuries that shaped the genre include *The Castle of Otranto* by Horace Walpole, *The Old English Baron* by

Clara Reeve, *Zofloya* by Charlotte Dacre, *The Giaour* by Lord Byron, and *The Wanderer* by Frances Burney. If you know the work of the Brontë sisters or Charles Dickens, you know the Victorians loved them too—as do many modern readers and writers.

ACKNOWLEDGMENTS

This book was one of those projects where life tried its best to get in the way of the writing. Somehow everything got done—but it wouldn't have happened without the help of a lot of people. I owe them a great big thank-you.

To my agent, Whitney Ross, and my editor, Faith Black Ross, who aren't related but make an amazing pair. Thank you for loving these stories and characters as much as I do.

To the team at Crooked Lane Books, especially Madeline Rathle, Rebecca Nelson, and Melissa Rechter. These books would not make it from my computer to readers' shelves without them. And especially to every copyeditor out there—I'm sorry I always write *towards* instead of *toward*.

To Nicole Lecht, who designs such beautiful covers for me, and Henrietta Meire, whose voice brings these characters to life.

To Maggie Kane and Barbara Poelle at Irene Goodman Literary Agency, who stepped in during a hectic summer.

To Johanie Martinez-Cools, an insightful reader and generous editor who helped me give Ofelia the POV she deserved.

To Gemma and Bryan, who keep letting me borrow their home office, even when they're trying to put their kids to sleep upstairs. To my parents, siblings, and in-laws, who brag about me every chance they get and know the value of putting in a request at the library. To the friends who gave Lily such a touching celebration last summer, especially Becky, who planned the whole thing.

To the daycare teachers who love and care for my children while I write. You are the glue holding my work (and my sanity) together.

To Brian, always, who is a partner in everything. I could probably do this without you, but it would be a lot harder and a lot less fun.

To you, if you are reading this, thank you from the bottom of my heart. Sharing Lily's adventures with you is the best part of writing them down.

And finally, to my daughter Hazel, who waited to make her debut until the draft of this book was finished and in my editor's hands. Thanks for giving me the chance to make my deadline, sweet pea.